'Abort!' said Lupu[s] Abort! Abort!'

The ground went soggy underfoot and he began to sink into the vermilion sands, which were warm, then hot, then hotter. He struggled to free himself. He could not. He was drowning down in the sands, and the ants were advancing upon him with anthropophagous intent. Lupus shot the nearest ant. But there were a million others behind it.

'Blood of a bitch!' said Lupus.

Then turned his gun on himself. He pressed the barrel hard against his head.

He winced.

And then he pulled the trigger.

The world buckled like a display screen infected with a touch of the drunks. The ants faded to shadow. A high-pitched giggle tittered through the backspaces of infinity. Then Lupus Lon Oliver found himself back in the initiation seat, back in the combat bay, back in the Combat College and free from the world of illusion.

'Nice trip?' said Paraban Senk, the unembodied Teacher of Control whose chosen aspect was featured on a communications screen located inside the combat bay.

Also by Hugh Cook

THE WIZARDS AND THE WARRIORS
THE WORDSMITHS AND THE WARGUILD
THE WOMEN AND THE WARLORDS
THE WALRUS AND THE WARWOLF
THE WICKED AND THE WITLESS
THE WISHSTONE AND THE WONDERWORKERS
THE WAZIR AND THE WITCH
THE WEREWOLF AND THE WORMLORD

and published by Corgi Books

THE WORSHIPPERS AND THE WAY

Hugh Cook

CORGI BOOKS

THE WORSHIPPERS AND THE WAY
A CORGI BOOK 0 552 13848 7

First publication in Great Britain

PRINTING HISTORY
Corgi edition published 1992

This book is set in 10/11pt Times by
County Typesetters, Margate, Kent

Corgi Books are published by Transworld Publishers Ltd.,
61–63 Uxbridge Road, Ealing, London W5 5SA,
in Australia by Transworld Publishers (Australia) Pty. Ltd.,
15–23 Helles Avenue, Moorebank, NSW 2170, and in New
Zealand by Transworld Publishers (N.Z.) Ltd.,
3 William Pickering Drive, Albany, Auckland.

Made and printed in Great Britain by
BPCC Hazells Ltd
Member of BPCC Ltd

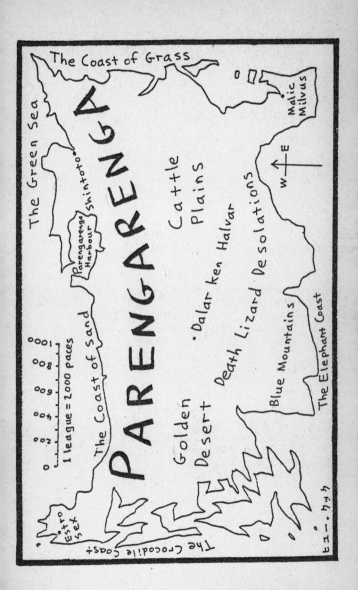

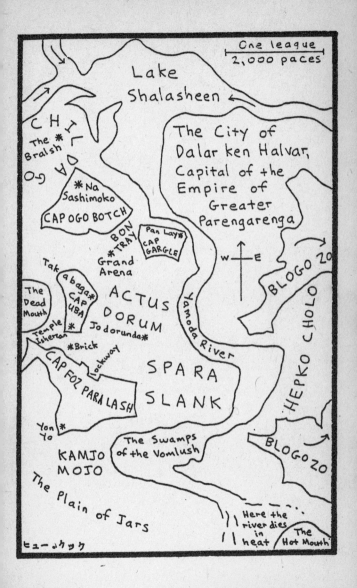

PROLOGUE

It was purple. It stood taller than any ordinary man, and its muscles had been pumped up to obscene dimensions by long dedication to that brutal form of exercise known as pumping iron. Its hair was heaped up upon its head in a monstrous topknot, for that hair had been uncut through all the days of its life. It wore long, flowing robes of a purple which matched its skin, and as it entered the dim-dark of the laboratory it looked for all the world like a High Priest of one of the Wild Tribes entering upon the bloodstained gloom of some obscure temple of torture.

But this purple-bruted thing was no creature of the Wild Tribes. On the contrary, this muscle-pumped bodybuilder was Asodo Hatch, student of a Combat College which had been designed to produce Star-troopers for the Stormforce of the Nexus.

Asodo Hatch had graduated from Combat Cadet to Startrooper at the age of thirty, and now at the age of thirty-one he was pursuing Higher Level Studies, concentrating on those areas in which he had proved to have special aptitudes – linguistics, law, theocratic sociopolitics and xenopolitics. Therefore know him from the start as a scholar, an intelligent man with a well-developed understanding of politics and religion – a man who was not so much a creature of his own time as a rightful citizen of any time which could properly claim to be civilized.

Unfortunately, we come upon this muscle-bruted purple creature in a time which was not civilized at all. We come upon it in the Empire of Greater Parengarenga during the reign of the wizard of Ebber, then known to

9

the world as Plandruk Qinplaqus. We come upon this Frangoni warrior during the days of a great Age of Darkness, when the great Khmar of the Yarglat had yet to bring a uniting discipline to the anarchic continent of Tameran, and when the high-visioned dreams of Aldarch the Third had not yet brought a similar uniting vision to Yestron.

We come upon this purple-skinned thing at a time when it was cautiously entering the laboratory – the shadowy, unoccupied cavern at the rear of the Combat College. It had come there in response to an anonymous word-processed invitation which it had found stuck to his door with a piece of chewing gum. The chewing of 'chewing gum' is one of those commercially inspired compulsive behaviours typically associated with financially dynamic high-tech civilizations; the habit had been ubiquitous in the Nexus itself, and still survived in the Combat College, even though that College had been isolated from the Nexus for over twenty millennia.

So Asodo Hatch entered the laboratory, and in that laboratory he found a corpse. Of this, much might be made, were it a unique or unusual experience. But, quite apart from his studies in the Combat College, Hatch had been for seven years a soldier of the Empire of Greater Parengarenga, and in those years he had devoted a great deal of time and effort to the production of corpses from the basic living material, and so the discovery of one extra and additional corpse lying about the planet did not unduly distress him. He was, however, surprised to find that the corpse was that of Hiji Hanojo, the Ebrell Islander who was the Combat College instructor; for among the students of the Combat College it was widely believed that the long-missing Hiji Hanojo had been mugged and murdered near the Hot Mouth, and that his body had been discarded into the depths of that hole.

Such was the length of time which had passed between Hiji Hanojo's disappearance and his discovery that

Hatch initially made that discovery by olfactory means. In the usual course of events, nobody made the trek to the laboratory, since it was an extensive but utterly empty chamber at the end of a long and barren tunnel driven into the heart of the minor mountain of Cap Foz Para Lash. Hence the non-discovery of that corpse.

But obviously someone had known it was there, since someone had left the anonymous chewing-gummed message which had first compelled Hatch to make the long and uninviting walk to the laboratory.

Asodo Hatch did what was necessary.

He reported the death to Paraban Senk, the unembodied Teacher of Control who ran the Combat College. Senk ordered that the body be removed to the cure-all clinic for autopsy.

To help him with that grisly task, Asodo Hatch requested and received the assistance of his brother Oboro Bakendra Hatch, who was the older of the two, and who was three years his senior. The two then won the assistance of the Pang female named Shona, who was a strong-stomached and imperturbable specimen of womanly warriorhood. These three then pressganged the services of the short and scuttling Ebrell Islander who went by the name of Lupus Lon Oliver, who proved exceedingly reluctant to assist, for he had scant acquaintance with death-in-the-flesh, and was in no hurry whatsoever to acquire any.

These four then carried out the grisly task of removing the corpse of Hiji Hanojo to the Combat College cure-all clinic, which, despite its name, was quite incapable of curing anything so radical as death.

Once the corpse was in the cure-all clinic, the unembodied Teacher of Control who went by the name of Paraban Senk performed a careful autopsy by means of remote-controlled instruments. On autopsy, Senk found that Hiji Hanojo had been murdered. He had been choked with a plastic bag, an item which Senk recovered from the throat of the rot-stench corpse.

Inside the plastic bag was a sample of semen, which proved on analysis to be that of a dog.

Who had the capacity to commit such a crime?

Paraban Senk surveyed the psychological profiles of all 502 people then training in the Combat College to see which of them might have been capable of such a crime. The answer? All of them! This was not surprising. Murder is one of the universal human crimes, a crime of which virtually everyone is capable; and those who trained in the College were systematically tutored in the arts of slaughter.

Furthermore, as a part of their training for war, the students of the Combat College had all been tutored in the most sophisticated of all psychological techniques to allow them to survive full-force interrogation, which made it unlikely that Senk would be able to trick one of them into making a confession.

Who then had an alibi?

Since Hiji Hanojo had been dead for an uncomfortable number of days – a very uncomfortable number of days in the opinion of Lupus Lon Oliver, who had thrown up thrice while helping to remove the body from the laboratory – nobody had an effective alibi.

Who then had a motive?

The obvious motive for killing Hiji Hanojo was to supplant him as instructor. The instructorship was lucrative; there was only one such job; and virtually everyone in the Combat College wanted that job. Senk recalled a time – well over a thousand years ago, now, but the memories of the unembodied Paraban Senk were imperishable – when instructors had been systematically assassinated at a rate of twenty a year.

Senk did not want to see a repeat performance of such mayhem.

Accordingly, Paraban Senk announced that all students whose training was due to terminate in less than three years were disqualified from contention for the instructorship; and, furthermore, that the competitive examinations required to select a new instructor would not be held for three years. Senk also made it clear that a similar policy would be enforced should the next instructor also meet with a violent end.

This ban and the accompanying delay constituted a kind of rough justice designed to cheat the murderer of all possible immediate profit, and to deter any future would-be murderers by removing the temptation of the possibility of quick-gain profits consequent upon a killing. Now, even if Hiji Hanojo's unknown murderer was the person who ultimately won the instructorship, at least that person would be denied the immediate profits of that instructorship.

This was very important, for most crime is committed to seek a quick gratification; and there are few people who would take great and murderous risks to win the uncertain chance of securing the prize of a job some three years in the future.

And whoever had killed Hiji Hanojo, it was certain that the securing of Hanojo's job was uncertain, for there were at least a good half-dozen élite students who had a serious chance of winning that position in competitive examination. The half-dozen in this élite group consisted of the Frangoni warriors Asodo Hatch and Son'Sholoma Gezira; the Ebrell Islanders Lupus Lon Oliver and Sefton Ten Guy; the Pang male named Darius Flute; and the immigrant from Shintoto who went by the name of Scorpio Fax.

But even so – even at that early date – nobody seriously doubted that the ultimate competition would be between the Ebrell Islander Lupus Lon Oliver and the Frangoni warrior Asodo Hatch – because those two had already established themselves as the best of the best.

CHAPTER ONE

Single-fighter: aka Scala Nine single-fighter: a Nexus war machine, a flying hunter-killer designed for deployment in a planetary atmosphere. It is powered by corrosion cells, in which small quantities of anti-matter are destroyed by controlled contact with normative matter. The corrosion cells will power the machine for three days without recharge.

* * *

So burning down from out of the sun
The weapon struck –
Hooked down from sundark sky –
From sundark blindness burning –
Brightness inexplicable in a shock
Which sheered the dark to light,
And by this revelation wreaked –

* * *

– so burning down from out of the sun, burning down from out of the blind brightness, the single-fighter struck, and the hapless foe screamed in pain across the Openband, and wrecked went down in flaming agony. As the enemy fighter fell, Lupus Lon Oliver sent his own craft plunging down the gravity well. Down from the sky he came, his single-fighter hurtling down, low and lower, so low that the warning klaxons shrilled and screamed:

'Pull up! Pull up!'

Lupus pulled up, pulled out, pulled hard, wrenching his craft away from disaster in a wetness of sweat and

14

orgasmic release, and screamed in triumph. In the throes of his battle-glory, he had a momentary vision of red-hot blood. The blood was seared across his vision-screens. The entire world was blood: blood made blind, blood made glory, triumph's glory, victory.

'Ah,' said Lupus, easing the single-fighter into a long slow barrel roll, feeling the sweetness easing to languorous content as the cosmos rolled about the axis of his craft, the briefness now completeness.

'Ah . . .'

Yes.

But even already now this phase was passing, sliding, going, gone, with the sheen of all colours losing their gloss, with the world becoming routine, the crashed wreckage of the downed enemy fighter now nothing but an inert blip on his locator screen.

Lupus eased his single-fighter round in a long slow circle and made a visual inspection of the wreckage which lay far, far below. From this height, it was still only a blip, a blip without the benefit of any theatricals of smoke and fire, a blip amidst the sands of a desert pigmented with a bright red not so terribly different from that of the Plain of Jars.

'Mission complete,' said the voice of Lupus's single-fighter, the voice of his ship. 'Illusion ends in a ten-pulse. Counting now. Ten. And. Nine. And.'

The training sequence was finished, so Lupus would automatically be returned to the world of the Combat College at the end of the ten-count, unless he elected otherwise.

'Eight. And. Seven. And.'

And then Lupus knew what he wanted.

'Six. And. Five.'

What Lupus wanted was not the blip seen from a distance but the real thing seen at close quarters. He wanted a close-to-close with the work wrought by his hands, wanted the smashed heat of the ruptured metal, the bloodworks of the dead, the confirmed corpse, the

15

smashworks, the blood-dust smoking under the crunching heat, the proof.

All this he knew in a moment – one of those moments when thought outraces speech.

'And. Four. And.'

'Kill the count,' said Lupus abruptly, tilting his joystick and spilling his single-fighter down through the sky, down in a canted spiral, a gyre of gain. Victory by descent. Stooping to conquer, he sought the proof, the fact, the flesh. Thus he sought because, for all his much-proclaimed allegiance to the dataflow civilization of the Nexus, Lupus was still a true child of Dalar ken Halvar, still intellectually wedded to the proofs of brute matter, to weight and inertia, the stubbornness of intractable physical form and the proof of the senses.

His projected and anticipated and indeed habitual and inescapable and unavoidable and wanted and needed gloating – the heart of his nature, this! the heart of his life! – would be confirmation, and confirmation a reassurance, the measurement of a mass of scrapmetal wreckage a sure proof of his superiority. To Lupus, triumph in combat was ever important, since it gave him assurance of that manifest superiority which was to him both the source of his well-being and the justification of his life. So Lupus Lon Oliver eased his Scala Nine single-fighter down and down in that closing gyre, down and down until the blip on his visual display became a wrecked machine.

So descending from the heavens . . .

So descending . . .

Lupus Lon Oliver – Lupus, the hope of the family Oliver – descended from the heavens in a buzzard's declining circle, then grounded his single-fighter on the vermilion sands of the scragland desert. Grounded with a slight bump, for his landings had always been sloppy – no grace of glory there. Grounded within javelin distance of the wreck.

Here the javelin distance mentioned is that distance to

16

which the gymnastic dart can be thrown by the average male athlete on any of the Standard Planets of the Nexus, those many planets which are so alike in their conformity to norms of atmosphere, of gravitation and of mooncycle illumination that theorists have conjectured into life an unknown race of masterful and long-gone Experimenters in order to allow for a thesis of organized and systematic creation which could account for their many and indisputable similarities.

Thus Lupus landed, and Lupus said –

'Pah!' said Lupus, breathing out a tension which he had previously not acknowledged, a tension which he had thought to have been drained away by the sweet joys of victory.

Now he was truly relaxed – or at least so he thought. It was only natural for him to have been tense earlier on, for had he lost his battle then he would have fallen in flames, and though this was an illusion-tank, nevertheless . . .

If he were to be defeated in an illusion-tank battle then the moment of loss would be the same as in life, the fear the same, the pain the same, the shock the same, and the damage to his sense of superiority an equal reality. So the illusion tanks were never a game, not entirely.

So when he grounded the single-fighter, when the tension eased off for real, Lon Oliver felt uncommonly tired.

Yet eager regardless.

'Door,' said Lupus, his voice pitched for Command. 'Open.'

'Environment inimical,' said the door.

The single-fighter's exit door was a cautious device, sometimes over-cautious; an 'inimical environment' could be anything from a hot beach dosed with ultra-violet radiation at suntan grade to a hard vacuum infested with deflation mines.

'Elaborate,' said Lupus.

17

'Ubiquitous carcinogens in multiplicity,' said the door.

It did not list the carcinogens in question or itemize their effects. Not yet. Not when there was no need. The military designers of the Nexus had been acutely cautious of the dangers of information overload, particularly in a battle environment; consequently, Stormforce machines were apt to give a bare minimum of information, and would typically give too little rather than too much.

'Carcinogens?' said Lupus. 'Is that all?'

'Environmental exposure threatens long-term health degradation,' said the door.

Lupus did not laugh. Did not even smile. In the days of his adolescence, he had sometimes had difficulty in taking illusion-tank scenarios seriously. The earnestness of machines such as the single-fighter's door had struck him as being risible. But these days he took his training very seriously, for what happened in these tanks would have consequences in the real world.

The murder of Hiji Hanojo, the killing which had taken place just over two years previously, had opened up the possibility that Lupus Lon Oliver might be able to win the instructorship of the Combat College. In just under a year, he would face the terminal examinations which would decide whether he succeeded in that ambition – or was expelled from the Combat College forever. There was only the one instructor's position. And to win it, Lupus would have to defeat Asodo Hatch in combat in the illusion tanks.

Lupus addressed himself to the door.

'Priority over-ride,' said Lupus, again in the tone of Command. 'Door. Open.'

'You wish me to open?' said the door.

'Confirmed,' said Lupus.

'I refuse,' said the door. 'In my judgement there is no combat justification for the contemplated adverse environmental exposure.'

Lupus was taken aback. He had often had arguments

with the door of a single-fighter, but never before had he had one refuse point blank to do his bidding.

'You will open,' said Lupus, 'or I will eject from this single-fighter.'

'Then you will probably die,' said the door smugly. 'Ejection from a grounded single-fighter carries a high risk of death.'

In exasperation, Lupus grabbed the shipkill lever and wrenched hard, thus destroying the ship's mainbrain, wrecking its power supply and killing the door and every other utility. With that, the manual controls became operative. Lupus grappled with the controls, then threw open the single-fighter's single gullwing door.

Hot air washed into the single-fighter.

Lupus sat in his seat, absorbing the heat, listening, watching, waiting. Waiting for something to happen. The air was curiously scented with the unmistakable smell of hashish. Now where could that possibly be coming from? There was no plant life anywhere in evidence – only a low-slung landscape of uninspiring red dust warped into a series of unimpressive undulations.

With difficulty, Lupus clambered out of the cramped confines of the single-fighter and jumped down to the desert. He landed hard. He staggered, almost fell, then recovered his balance.

'Wah!' he said.

He had landed so clumsily that he had just about wrecked one of his ankles. The spaceway heroes did it so much more neatly on the entertainments screened by the Eye of Delusion. But this was no entertainment. This was combat training, in which one could get very severely hurt.

How bad was it?

Lupus took an experimental step.

Not so bad, but even so, he was minded to abort the training sequence right then and there.

But he had his pride. He was of the Free Corps, and thus he believed in the supremacy of the mind over the

19

body. So, though he grimaced with the pain, he forced himself to walk across the alien desert to the charred wreckage of the enemy he had shot down.

Besides, he really did want to see. He always inspected the wreckage if it was at all possible. He wanted proof positive of his glory, and liked it best if there were bodies in the wreck: charred corpses with the skin sloughed off and the lips stretched back in a death-rictus.

Today there was indeed a corpse in the wreckage, but it was too badly burnt to be distinguishable as human. Lupus sniffed. The transient smell of hashish was gone. Instead, he smelt desert dust, melted synthetics, charred hair. He indulged himself in a flight of imagination, pretending that the corpse which lay there at his mercy, was the dead flesh of the Frangoni warrior Asodo Hatch.

For the last two years, Lupus had lived with a certain fear of the Frangoni warrior, since it had for that long been clear that ultimately Lupus would have to fight Hatch for the instructorship of the Combat College. While Lupus had youth on his side, Hatch had the battleground training in the fact-of-the-flesh. Asodo Hatch had killed men face to face, eye to eye, blade to blade, and that made him an object of jealous awe to Lupus Lon Oliver.

The Frangoni warrior Asodo Hatch had gone to war in the fact-of-the-flesh because he was a slave of Plandruk Qinplaqus, the Silver Emperor who ruled Dalar ken Halvar. Accordingly, under the terms of a long-standing treaty between the Silver Emperor and the Combat College, Hatch had left the College at the age of eighteen, and had then soldiered for the Empire for seven years before returning to the College to resume his studies.

Since Lupus Lon Oliver was a freeborn Ebrell Islander, he had never had to undertake such military service, so now, as the two men entered upon their last year in the Combat College, Asodo Hatch was seven years older than Lupus – Hatch being aged thirty-three to Lupus's twenty-six.

Hatch was training with ferocity, and Lupus knew that the Frangoni warrior would fight fiercely for the instructorship in a year's time. But there was every possibility that trouble would arise between them before then. What, for example, would Hatch do when he at last discovered the secret of Lupus's lust? Or did he know of that lust already? The Frangoni were so intrinsically inscrutable that it was impossible to say.

'But at least,' said Lupus to himself, 'at least I'm winning for the moment.'

He wiped the sweat from his forehead. The wreckage, the corpse, the buckled reddust desert – he had exhausted his interest in it. It was time to undertake the painful business of walking back to his single-fighter. There was no reason for him to do any such thing, since he could abort the training sequence from where he was, but he always walked back. It was his ritual. His private concession to the age-old human need to work protective magic.

As Lupus began the walk back to the single-fighter, he heard a mechanical drone, sounding quite loud in the desert where there was scarcely any sound but for his own breathing and the click of cooling metal. He stopped. He looked around warily. A hover vehicle was approaching. It was coming on too fast for him to run away. Still, he was armed.

The vehicle halted a stone's-throw distant. Its bright-sign surface was garbled with logos, among which Lupus saw a fleshpink vulva, a grinning orange sun, a dolphin spouting orange-juice, and a sign in Nexus script which identified the vehicle as the property of an organization known as Happy Hunting Tours.

As Lupus watched, the vehicle decanted a dozen tourists. They were dressed in kinetiscope, a fun-fashion material for which there had been a Nexus fad some twenty millennia previously. They began to take photographs.

'Hey!' said Lupus.

Nobody answered him. It was almost as if he didn't exist. He upholstered his sidearm, and automatically checked the charge in its corrosion cells, just as he had done ten thousand times on the shooting range. He levelled the weapon . . . hesitated . . . then gunned down one of the tourists. The tourist thrashed to fireball and kicked down, jerked, smoked, then lay still.

The others did not turn a hair, but continued to take photographs.

Annoyed by this lack of reaction, Lupus shot the rest. One by one he gunned them down. Once all had been killed, they each and every one of them turned – simultaneously and without warning – into winged creatures which ascended into the sky, where each transformed itself into an egg. The eggs hung in the sky, pulsing with blue light.

They grew swiftly bigger.

Each of the skyhanging eggs abruptly sprouted a long orange tail. The tails stretched taut and began to vibrate, giving off a keening music.

The ground was starting to rock, and the ants with which the desert was suddenly profligate were starting to swell, to enlarge, to engorge themselves with liquid light.

'Nu-chala-nuth!' said Lupus, using the name of that religion as a swear word, a habit far from uncommon in the Nexus.

The ants roared at him. Their breath tasted of ambergris and honey. Their mandibles were as sharp as razors and they were closing in for the kill. Lupus realized he was caught in a programmer's caprice, an illicit game hidden within the official wargaming system which ruled the illusion tanks. An ugly game by the looks of it.

'Abort,' said Lupus, giving the single-word command which should by rights terminate the training sequence and snatch him free of this illusion world.

Nothing happened.

'Abort!' said Lupus, with more urgency. Then: 'Abort! Abort! Abort!'

The ground went soggy underfoot and he began to sink into the vermilion sands, which were warm, then hot, then hotter. He struggled to free himself. He could not. He was drowning down in the sands, and the ants were advancing upon him with anthropophagous intent. Lupus shot the nearest ant. But there were a million others behind it.

'Blood of a bitch!' said Lupus.

Then turned his gun on hmself. He pressed the barrel hard against his head.

He winced.

And then he pulled the trigger.

The world buckled like a display screen infected with a touch of the drunks. The ants faded to shadow. A high-pitched giggle tittered through the backspaces of infinity. Then Lupus Lon Oliver found himself back in the initiation seat, back in the combat bay, back in the Combat College and free from the world of illusion.

'Nice trip?' said Paraban Senk, the unembodied Teacher of Control whose chosen aspect was featured on a communications screen located inside the combat bay.

'Gods,' said Lupus.

Then shuddered, swore, ripped himself free from the seat, tried to stand, remembered his ankle, almost fell as he tried to keep himself from placing weight on it, then remembered that his injury had been a dreamworld injury, and that his ankle was undamaged in the fact-of-the-flesh.

'Did you enjoy yourself?' said Senk, speaking with a blandness which Lupus took to be mockery.

'Go eat yourself,' said Lupus.

'I beg your pardon?'

Not for nothing was Paraban Senk called the Teacher of Control. Instruction in etiquette was one of the most minor of the duties undertaken by Paraban Senk, yet

Senk still found bad manners a most distressing breach of self-possession. Besides: rudeness was rude, and Senk was most sensitive to abuse, particularly after 20,000 years of mixed calumniation and defamation, and precious little in the way of compensatory praise.

'Fates!' said Lupus. 'You think this a joke? They almost ate me!'

'I don't know what you're talking about.'

'Then,' said Lupus, stiffly, 'review your record of what I just went through. I call your attention to the programmer's caprice which manifested itself in the training sequence I just endured.'

Then Lupus Lon Oliver reseated himself in the combat bay's initiation seat and waited until Paraban Senk was ready to speak.

Said Senk, a stiffness equal to that last used by Lupus himself:

'Reviewed. Seen. Noted. Now I call your attention to remark 112 slash 56 in routine orders. Quote: most battle environments contain ineradicable caprices which will manifest themselves if the environments are explored beyond the depth required for battle training. Unquote.'

'Twenty thousand years of error!' said Lupus.

'That is hardly my fault,' said the Paraban Senk.

'No, no,' said Lupus. 'Because you're not human, so you can't correct yourself. Hence you're doomed to be forever a bastardized sway-backed temperamental shit-eating—'

'Being a computational device,' said Paraban Senk, interrupting Lupus's diatribe, 'I should not properly be insulted in terms devised to maledict camels.'

'Are you god, that we should salute you in your arrogance?' said Lupus.

'To keep a polite tongue in your head is no more than common courtesy,' said Paraban Senk. 'To deprecate obscenity is not to claim divinity, and only the extravagance of extreme youth makes you claim that it is.'

'Am I right in getting the impression that you don't like me?' said Lupus.

'I am the Teacher of Control,' said Paraban Senk. 'To correct your errors is my duty. Love and liking do not enter into it. I must now correct your earlier error.'

'My earlier error?'

'You claimed me to be incapable of self-correction,' said Paraban Senk. 'In this you are wrong. I can and do correct myself. Frequently. But I cannot correct the programming of the battle environment. That software was deemed adequate for its intended purpose by expert reviewers and hence its amendment is not in my purview.'

Lupus was still shaken by the caprice which had almost seen him fall victim to hot swallowing sand and a battalion of grotesquely monstrous battle-ants. If he hadn't used the gun on himself, where would he be now? In hell, or so he strongly suspected. Expert reviewers! What did that mean? Two drunken officers trialling an illusion tank sequence by duelling each other in the illusion tanks for half an arc after dinner. Or something. Well, Lupus had been reviewing the Combat College and its systems for his entire adult life, and he was far from happy with its many faults and defaults.

'Give me my MegaCommand,' said Lupus abruptly, for he wanted to be gone from the presence of Paraban Senk, and the sooner the better.

'Granted and given,' said Senk.

The world wavered, buckled, and reformed – and Lupus Lon Oliver found himself standing on the bridge of a MegaCommand Cruiser in the depths of intergalactic space, looking out on the white bright icechip stars of the Nexus.

'Sir,' said the Officer of the Watch, acknowledging his presence.

'You're San Kaladan, aren't you?' said Lon Oliver, who had met this software construct before.

'Of course,' said the software construct, evidencing surprise.

Which was only natural, for all MegaCommand illusion tank scenarios assumed a captain to be familiar with his crew; and indeed Lupus was thus familiar, for there were only a few basic crews, and he had met them all in his years of illusion tank training. There was a high-morale crew which was ready for suicide missions; there was a low-morale crew ever on the brink of mutiny; there was a war-hardened battle-veteran crew; there was an inexperienced crew with shadow-shooting nervous reflexes; and then there were a variety of minority-group crews. San Kaladan was a software construct forming part of a crew composed entirely of members of that religion known as Nu-chala-nuth.

And Lupus Lon Oliver . . .

Well, Lupus had very definite opinions about Nu-chala-nuth.

'Is there something wrong?' said San Kaladan.

'Yes,' said Lupus, drawing his sidearm. 'There's something very much wrong.'

Then Lupus gunned down San Kaladan. As the crew on the bridge began to react, Lon Oliver said the magic word:

'Abort.'

The world of the MegaCommand Cruiser wavered, buckled, and dissolved. Lupus found himself back in the initiation seat, back in the combat bay, back in the Combat College.

'That was quick,' said Paraban Senk.

'Senk,' said Lupus. 'There was one of those Nu-chala types on my MegaCommand.'

'You mean the San Kaladan construct,' said Senk. 'That's the one you, ah, interacted with. But that whole crew is of the Nu-chala-nuth.'

'The whole crew, yes, but,' said Lupus, 'I don't want them, not any of them. As a captain, I've got a choice of my crew. That's regulations.'

'You're being childish,' said Paraban Senk. 'The ship is not real, the crew is not real, and you are not a real

26

captain. You're a student, and as a student you can be compelled to train with absolutely any constructs whatsoever, including software constructs which mimic the behaviours of the Nu-chala-nuth.'

'Do you so compel me?' said Lupus.

Senk paused. The pause was to give Senk time to think, for when confronted with a truly difficult problem the Teacher of Control could on occasion be perceptibly slow in finding a resolution.

'What is your objection to training with Nu-chala-nuth constructs?' said Senk.

'I,' said Lupus, 'I'm loyal to the Nexus, and they're not.'

There was a further pause – a long pause as Senk studied this statement in the light of Lupus Lon Oliver's training record, psychological profile and social background. Lupus was under intense, almost intolerable stress. He had to win the instructorship else face the ruin of his life and the condemnation of his family – his father in particular. By affording Lupus a choice of crew constructs, Senk would give Lupus at least the illusion of having some say over his own life, of successfully exercising autonomous control over his own destiny – and so might succeed in reducing that student's intolerable stress levels.

'Very well,' said Senk. 'For training purposes, you will be given a captain's choice of crew. You need no longer train with Nu-chala-nuth constructs. Tell me what you want by way of crew. I am yours to command.'

'I want,' said Lupus, savouring this small victory over the all-powerful Teacher of Control, 'I want a crew composed entirely of adherents of Joba Qa Marika.'

'It will be done,' said Senk gravely.

Senk did not have the resources to create from scratch the necessary software constructs which would imitate the behaviours of such a crew, but it was Lupus Lon Oliver's good fortune that what he desired was already on file.

So Lupus left the Combat College in a moderately happy mood. His happiness lasted until the evening, when he retailed the story of the triumphs of the day to his father. The father of Lupus Lon Oliver was Manfred Gan Oliver – Manfred, the strength of the family Oliver – and he dismissed the victories of the day as a big nothing.

'Win us the instructorship,' said Manfred Gan Oliver. 'Then you can count yourself victorious. Other than that, nothing counts – absolutely nothing.'

Thus things stood near the start of the final year of the build-up to the competitive examinations which would decide who inherited the Combat College's one and only instructorship.

CHAPTER TWO

Dalar ken Halvar: aka City of Sun; aka City of the Season; capital of Parengarenga. Though set high on a vast mountain plateau, it is by no means cool, for the Hot Mouth on the city outskirts (one of the several Mouths of the upland plateau) constantly outbreathes hot, dry, desiccating air.

The city is where it is because of the Combat College, the nearby silver-mine wealth (less than legend's rumouring, but nevertheless substantial), the secure defensive positions afforded to the paranoid by the upthrusts of those miniature mountains known as the Caps, and the Yamoda River's reliable waterflow – water being always and ever the first and last essential of urban civilization.

The Good Neighbours of the Bralsh might adduce yet another reason for Dalar ken Halvar being located where it is, but their secret knowledge has ever been denied to geographers.

*   *   *

Dead to death but not yet dead
The wound essays the shadow.
Immortal in his pain he gropes,
A moment a millennium.
The sleeking sword is cooling,
Is shouldered in salute, and –
Sensing something wrong –

*   *   *

29

The man died, and every death among the Frangoni brought the people down from the Frangoni rock to the waters of the Yamoda River. So it was that Asodo Hatch came to the riverside with his family, or at least with that part of it which remained in Dalar ken Halvar. His living children numbered three, and all were daughters, but two of those daughters – Shalamith and Yelada – had left Parengarenga to make new lives for themselves as wives of men who belonged to the Frangoni community of the far-distant Ebrell Islands.

It was the Silver Emperor, Plandruk Qinplaqus, who in his wisdom had initially placed that small Frangoni community on the Ebrell Islands. And it was Plandruk Qinplaqus likewise who ensured that contacts were maintained between that colony and the Frangoni who dwelt in Dalar ken Halvar. For, though the Ebrell Islands were independent and self-governing (or, in the opinions of some political commentators, self-ungoverning), the Silver Emperor still saw those distant rocks as being within his sphere of influence. Thus he had placed a colony of purple-skinned Frangoni among the red-skinned Ebrell Islanders, seeking through the manipulation of this minority to ensure for himself a degree of influence in the affairs of the whale-hunting islands.

All that was left to Hatch in Dalar ken Halvar was his wife Talanta and his daughter Onica, and at the moment it was Onica who had caught his attention. Onica had a praying mantis perched on her hand. She was fascinated with its green complexities, and was endeavouring to outstare its tiny pinprick eyes.

'A mantis can fly, you know,' said Onica, 'but when it flies, it's more like a leaf than a bird.'

She shook her hand and the mantis went whirling away, and in all truth its tumbling flight did mimic that of a leaf sent sprawling by the wind.

Hatch saw little of his daughter these days, for he was fiercely training towards his final examinations. His last year of study was more than half-gone. Seven of the year's thirteen moon-months had waxed and waned, and only six remained. In a bare 160 days, Asodo Hatch would have to fight Lupus Lon Oliver for the instructorship of the Combat College. It was what everyone expected.

It had been what his father had expected, and his father had told him as much on the day before he went to his death. And now that death was a completed fact, a part of history, and the old man's body lay atop a funeral pyre by the river. The wood of the pyre was saturated with aromatic oils which Hatch could smell from where he stood, one hand on Onica's shoulder.

The costs of this funeral would have bankrupted the family Hatch but for the fact that all those costs were being met by Plandruk Qinplaqus, the Silver Emperor who ruled the city of Dalar ken Halvar and the Empire of Greater Parengarenga, the Silver Emperor who, in the service of the motto 'divide and rule', had established the small minority Frangoni colonies in both Dalar ken Halvar and the Ebrell Islands alike.

Lamjuk Dakoto Hatch, father of Asodo Hatch and of Oboro Bakendra Hatch, had served the Silver Emperor well, and so Plandruk Qinplaqus, that ancient and much-wizened Ashdan-bred wizard of Ebber, honoured Lamjuk Dakoto in death.

As Hatch was thus standing there with his daughter Onica, he was verbally accosted when someone said:

'Startrooper Hatch.'

'What is it, Combat Cadet?' said Hatch, acknowledging the presence of Yolombo Atlantabara.

Hatch felt the Combat College titles became grotesque if spoken out in the open, out in the sun beneath the sky. They belonged to the world inside the minor mountain of Cap Foz Para Lash, and only there could he take them seriously.

But Hatch said nothing of this to Yolombo Atlantabara, for the young Frangoni warrior had just turned eighteen, and was taking a break from his Combat College training to enter Parengarenga's imperial army. Like Hatch, Atlantabara would return to the Combat College at age twenty-five to complete his education.

'Startrooper,' said Atlantabara. 'I'm joining the army tomorrow.'

'You have my blessing, then,' said Hatch, not sure what Atlantabara wanted.

'But,' said Atlantabara, blurting it out as if the very confession was a statement of horror, 'I don't want to.'

'You don't want to!' said Hatch.

'Well,' said Atlantabara, already ashamed of his confession. 'I'd . . . I'd rather not. Put it that way. I'd rather not. If it was possible to stay, I—'

'If you'd wanted to stay,' said Hatch, 'you should have been an Ebrell Islander. Go to the army. Do your seven years. It's a good system. You'll benefit from it.'

This was obviously not the answer Atlantabara had been wanting to hear. Making no effort to hide his disappointment, he retreated.

Hatch watched him go.

Asodo Hatch had some sympathy for the young Frangoni warrior, but not much. It was a good system – breaking Combat College training to spend a few years in the real world. The system had long ago been forced upon the Combat College by the Silver Emperor, who had pondered the problem for the better part of a century before presenting Paraban Senk with an ultimatum.

Paraban Senk, the unembodied Teacher of Control who ran the Combat College, was obedient to one prime and overriding imperative: train Startroopers! Train Startroopers for the Stormforce of the Nexus! The Silver Emperor could make that impossible by the simple expedient of placing guards at the lockway to kill anyone who tried to leave or enter. Negotiating from such a position of strength, Plandruk Qinplaqus was able to win considerable concessions from the Combat College.

Ordinary Combat Cadets studied straight through from age eleven to age twenty-seven, graduated as Startroopers and went out into the world absolutely useless for any practical purpose. After years spent training for the sanitized high-tech warfare of the Nexus, they were unsuited for an army of leather boots which lived, fought and died in the dirt.

The Silver Emperor's Frangoni levies, however, were a different story. In early manhood they made their home in the armies of the dust for seven long years, and so could easily be integrated back into those armies when they finally graduated from the Combat College at age thirty-four. By then, that was the only place for them to go.

The ranks of the Free Corps were closed to the Frangoni, who were regarded with contempt by the Ebrell Islanders of Dalar ken Halvar. And by age thirty-four they were usually strangers to their own people, having spent too long eating the bread of strangeness and living among those who have no caste.

Thus the Combat College produced for the Emperor an élite cadre of Frangoni officers whose greatest loyalty was to the imperial army.

Right now, as Hatch watched, the Emperor himself was touching a torch to the funeral pyre. It caught fire, and the flames began to consume the body of Hatch's father. With due ceremony, the Silver Emperor departed, and Hatch was left alone on the riverbank with his family. On this occasion, Plandruk Qinplaqus had made no contact with Asodo Hatch, for the ceremony had been held to honour the dead Lamjuk Dakoto, and not to honour his son, Asodo.

While Hatch was still watching the flames of the pyre, he was accosted by Polk the Cash, a moneylender. Apart from Lupus Lon Oliver, there were two people in Dalar ken Halvar with whom Asodo Hatch found himself at odds. One of those people was Nambasa Berlin, who was not much of a problem as Hatch rarely saw him. The other, unfortunately, was Polk.

Polk the Cash was a moneylender, a man of the Pang; and it was one of life's great and inexplicable coincidences that Pang shared with Berlin the physical peculiarity of having no nose. Like Berlin, Polk had been born with a nose – but both men had been deprived of their noses in early adulthood. Furthermore, both had lost their noses under similar but unrelated circumstances, which was adding strangeness upon strangeness.

'You have something for me,' said Polk.

'I do,' said Hatch, with a studied politeness which would have made Paraban Senk proud of him.

Asodo Hatch had agreed to be a guarantor for a debt raised by his brother Oboro Bakendra Hatch, and Oboro had defaulted on the loan. So Hatch had to pay. So it was that, in accordance with his perception of his duty, Asodo Hatch paid up to Polk. Five scorpions. It was a lot of money for anyone to be parting with for no good purpose, and Hatch was by no means rich.

'Thank you,' said Polk. 'Any time you want to do business, come and see me.'

'Maybe I will,' said Hatch.

He had absolutely no intention of ever doing business again with Polk or any other moneylender, but had learnt long ago that it is best never to alienate anyone unnecessarily. The Teacher of Control alleged that a universal courtesy to the world in general is the cheapest of all good investments; and Hatch, after much experience of life, saw no reason to dispute this.

When Polk was gone, Hatch turned his attention to a ceremony which was taking place on the far side of the Yamoda River. It was being presided over by something which looked almost like a horse, at least from a distance. But Hatch had sharp eyes, and could pick the differences. The thing with four legs was Edgerley Eden, the guru who had enthralled his sister Penelope.

Hatch was distracted from the view by Onica's scream.

He turned in alarm.

But it was nothing – only a brute of a thog mauling some small white-skinned dog.

But Onica was screaming at the thog, and trying to hit it with a stick.

Hatch strode towards the dog-fight, grabbed the thog by the collar and heaved it over the riverbank. It tumbled down the bank and splashed into the river. On recovering itself, it found the bank too steep to climb, so paddled downstream through the shallow waters, and shortly found itself nose to nose with a large hog which was paddling upstream.

Hatch did not concern himself with the thog's further fate, but turned his attention to his daughter, who was cradling the dog. An elegant Janjuladoola woman with a small retinue was approaching.

'Is this your dog?' said Hatch, addressing the woman.

'It is mine,' said the woman, she whom Hatch was destined to know as the Lady Iro Murasaki. 'How is it? Oh . . .'

The Lady Murasaki found to her distress that one of the ears of her dog had been torn away. She said it would have to be put down. Onica begged for it.

'You can have it,' said Murasaki, whose name was yet unknown to Hatch, 'if your father agrees.'

'It would be received as a welcome gift,' said Hatch.

The Lady Iro Murasaki smiled upon Hatch, and she departed; such was the brevity and simplicity of this their first meeting that Hatch thought nothing of it at the time. He thought rather of the expression of pain which he saw on the face of his wife Talanta. As Talanta had never been prone to any fears of infidelity on Hatch's part, Hatch presumed the pain to be physical in origin – and his presumption was strengthened by the fact that he had seen Talanta manifesting such pain at odd occasions in the recent past.

'What is it?' said Hatch. 'What is it?'

'It is nothing,' said Talanta.

But Hatch suspected that she might be seriously ill. He

wished he could take her into Cap Foz Para Lash to be examined by the Combat College's cure-all clinic, but that was reserved for Combat College personnel; and the Combat College as a whole was off-limits to all outsiders at all times, except during the competitive examinations for the instructorship, when guests could be invited to spectate.

The pyre which was consuming the body of Hatch's father would burn for a long time, and the ashes from the body would be brought to Hatch in due course. He had no need to stay by the riverside any longer, and such were the demands of his days that he could ill afford to linger. With the essential part of the funeral well over, Hatch hired an ox cart to take Onica and Talanta back to the Frangoni rock, for it was a long and weary walk. He trusted that Talanta could make the uphill climb – far too steep for any ox cart – from the road to their house.

When Talanta was gone, Hatch lingered by the riverside for a little longer, torn between his need to get back to his training schedule in the Combat College, and by the fact that this was after all his father's funeral. They had never been close, but even so the old man's death had come as a shock, even though there had been difficult times in the past when Hatch had felt that he could have cheerfully murdered the brute.

Lamjuk Dakoto Hatch had been a monster of over-bearing stubbornness, and bad-tempered into the bargain. And surely his death was nothing to mourn, for he had killed his own brother, an act for which there could surely be no forgiveness.

And yet . . .

As Hatch lingered, he was approached by his elder brother, Oboro Bakendra Hatch, who had been ostentatiously bathing himself in the river, thus publicly shunning his father's funeral.

'Asodo,' said Oboro Bakendra.

'Speak,' said Hatch, using less courtesy to his brother than he had done to the moneylender Polk the Cash.

36

'I want to tell you something,' said Oboro.

'Tell,' said Hatch.

'The old man's not welcome on Cap Uba. Get rid of his ashes somewhere else.'

'He is your father as much as mine,' said Hatch.

'He's no father of mine,' said Oboro. 'Not since what he's done. I renounce him. I disown him.'

Lamjuk Dakoto Hatch, father of Asodo and Oboro, had renounced the Frangoni faith, the worship of the Great God Mokaragash. Poto Skinskoro Hatch, brother of Lamjuk Dakoto, had taken him to task over the matter. Consequently, both were now dead. As a priest of the Great God Mokaragash, Oboro Bakendra could not forgive his father for either his apostasy or for the death of Poto Skinskoro.

'Renounce him, then,' said Hatch. 'Disown him, then. But do your renouncing and disowning elsewhere, for this is my father's funeral.'

Oboro Bakendra took the hint, and left.

Once Oboro had departed, a grey-skinned Janjuladoola servant, who had been keeping his distance till all earshot witnesses were gone, approached Asodo Hatch.

'What can I do for you?' said Hatch.

'The lady whose dog your child accepted,' said the servant.

'Yes,' said Hatch. 'What does she want? Does she want the dog back? I can return it tomorrow if that's her requirement.'

'No no no,' said the servant, clearly shocked to think anyone would fancy that his employer would give houseroom to a maimed animal. 'She – she wishes me to apprise you of her name. She is the Lady Iro Murasaki.'

From the tone in which this was said, Hatch gathered that ownership of that particular title was meant to be a matter of some consequence.

'We are a long way from Yestron,' said Hatch. 'I confess my ignorance as to the import of the title. Who is the Lady and what does she want?'

'She is who she is,' said the servant. 'As for what she wants, why, she wishes to extend to you an invitation. The Lady Iro Murasaki invites you to visit her house, which is the house of Pan Lay on the heights of Cap Gargle.'

'I will bear the information in mind,' said Hatch, making no commitment.

The servant seemed to be waiting for something more, but Hatch had nothing more to say, so walked close to the pyre. The enormously expensive heavywood pyre was in full blaze, burning hot as it would till sundown and beyond. Hatch stood in the heatwash of the fire and bathed himself in the heat of his father's death, the heat of his father's burning.

And thought of his wife, and the pain which had showed on her face, and wondered if he would be adding her body to just such a pyre before the year was out.

CHAPTER THREE

Asma: dominant computational machines of the Nexus. To observe reality is to change reality; and, as an intelligent observer, an Enabled asma can manipulate reality by processes analogous to those used by the wizards of the Confederation.

Reality manipulators typically use Screens to protect themselves against destruction and Enhancers to boost their powers. To Enable an asma, its makers equip it with actual physical devices designed to fulfil these functions, though other approaches are possible. Wizards, for example, use the Meditations of Balance to build protective metashells to serve as Screens; and through the Meditations of Power each Enhances his strength by drawing upon those resources which are available to him through his alliance with one or more of Those Who May Not Be Named.

The asma which runs Dalar ken Halvar's Combat College – the entity known to the world as Paraban Senk – is a machine of Medium Enablement. The Combat College also contains other asma (the word is both singular and plural) of Minor Enablement, and these perform such minor miracles as the fabrication of food (though some are misperforming in their old age, and others have expired entirely as a consequence of 20,000 years of neglect).

None of the asma in the Combat College is of any great consequence, for even Paraban Senk himself is but a mosquito in his powers when compared to one of the world's Great Dragons, such as the delinquent asma self-named Jocasta. Fortunately for the world, the delinquent Jocasta – an asma of Maximum Enablement – is currently held prisoner by Anaconda Stogirov in the Temple of Blood in the far-distant city of Obooloo, an ocean away from the city of Dalar ken Halvar, and hence of no consequence whatsoever to this particular history.

*　　*　　*

> Upon the pool there lies
> A sun tricked out as sun,
> Though truth in truth the lair –
> And step you to illusion to think
> Its weight sustain you?

*　　*　　*

Again the burning sun, again the downstrike, again the wrenching turn, again the searing explosion, again the downfall of the enemy.

Lupus Lon Oliver had done this for what seemed like a lifetime, pitting himself against machine-generated enemies time and time again. But what good would any of this training do him? None, if he failed against Hatch. And he could still fail, he knew it. He could fail, wasting a lifetime's chance, the unexpected opportunity of a lifetime.

As the wreckage of his latest machine-generated opponent fell through the burning sky, Lupus circled, thinking of Asodo Hatch and the murder-in-the-fact which had stained the Frangoni warrior's blade. As if in image of Lupus's own inner turmoil, the clouds writhed pink and purple. Bulbous. Swollen. Brutal. The image of a monstrous indigestion.

Fearful of those writhing clouds, fearful of the possibility of some idiosyncratic illusion tank glitch plunging him into a living hell, Lupus aborted the training sequence with a curt command. When he found himself back in the initiation chair, Lupus looked at the communications screen built into the combat bay. Paraban Senk's face did not appear there, which implied that the Teacher of Control had not been monitoring this training session. Instead, the screen was dominated by the combat bay's own identification logo.

Lupus Lon Oliver addressed the communications screen, giving the combat bay his next command:

'I'm logged to train with Dog Java on the Mega-Command. Give me Dog Java's status.'

Dog Java was a Combat Cadet who was by birth one of the Pang. As a red-skinned Ebrell Islander, Lupus Lon Oliver usually had little to do with the brown-skinned Pang, for he thought them his racial and social inferiors. Certainly Dog was a social inferior, for Dog belonged to the Yara, Dalar ken Halvar's Unreal underclass. But Lupus was cultivating Dog for a special purpose. As it says in the Book of Battle: even a broken stick can be used to kill.

'Dog Java is waiting for you on your MegaCommand Cruiser,' said the combat bay.

'Then take me there,' said Lupus.

The world melted, buckled – and Lupus found himself standing on the bridge of a Galactic Class Mega-Command Cruiser in deep space. Dog Java was there, but Lupus did not at first acknowledge Dog's existence. Instead, Lupus stood studying the star patterns shown by the big visual display screen. Studying the star patterns, and covertly watching Dog for signs of intimidation. He wanted Dog to be intimidated. To be pliant. Obedient. Reliable. A sure and secure tool for his purposes.

'You're late,' said Dog Java, with an emphasis which owed nothing whatsoever to intimidation.

'Such impertinence ill becomes a Combat Cadet when he addresses a Startrooper,' said Lupus Lon Oliver, with all the scorn at his command.

This was not much scorn, for, unlike the Frangoni, the Ebrell Islanders are not natural orators. Among the purple-skinned Frangoni, a man can win great renown

41

through the strength of his boast, so the making of speeches has been brought to a high art; but the Ebrell Islanders have ever preferred to demonstrate their manifest superiority through the deed.

'Why do you call me impertinent?' said Dog Java, brown-skinned child of the Pang. 'I thought we were co-conspirators – not idiots playing Startrooper games.'

'It's not a game!' said Lupus, shaken by such a rage of anger that he almost smashed the unfortunate Dog.

Dog Java backed off.

'I'm sorry,' said Dog. 'I misspoke myself.'

Now Dalar ken Halvar was a regular hell-broth of incompatible races and religions, with divisions of class and caste further complicating the social divisions of the city, which divisions were amplified by the linguistic diversity of the peoples there resident. But the students of the Combat College did not usually clash with each other in anger, for they were united by their common loyalty to the Nexus. So Dog was taken aback to find Lupus Lon Oliver so angry with him, for Dog had failed to realize the extent to which Lupus had imported the prejudices of Dalar ken Halvar into the confines of the Combat College.

'I apologize,' said Lupus, with some effort. 'I'm very sorry. I was wrong to speak to you in anger. You're my valued colleague, and I hope you know it. It's just – it's just that there's so much at stake. It's not you, it's Hatch who's making me angry. I'm very sorry I used that tone of voice to you.'

Lupus spoke thus because he had seen the patent shock and pain on Dog Java's face. In the city of Dalar ken Halvar, a lordly Ebrell Islander in his red-skinned pride would never have apologized to one of the lowly Yara – though he might conceivably have essayed politeness in the presence of one of the Yara, a member of the rich and therefore Real upper class of the people Pang. But Lupus realized that the habits of Dalar ken Halvar could be fatal to his purposes, so he would have to control himself, and use the techniques of identification, encouragement and motivation which had been so carefully taught to him by Paraban Senk.

They worked, those Nexus techniques. But – they were so alien! It hurt Lupus to parley with this Yara creature as if it were almost an equal. But he had to – in order to serve his purpose.

With apologies done with, Lupus Lon Oliver and Dog Java got down to business. The business was simple. Lupus Lon Oliver was endeavouring to persuade Dog Java to murder Asodo Hatch.

By now the last year of Lupus Lon Oliver's training had come to an end, sliding away in a dream-daze of eternal study, training and physical preparation – the physical preparation being essential, because the savagery of the mentally exhausting theoretical examinations would be quite sufficient to ruin the health of anyone who was not in peak physical condition.

Those savage theoretical examinations had already begun, and were almost complete. The results were confirming what everyone in the Combat College had suspected for a long time.

Three years earlier, following the murder of Hiji Hanojo, it had been generally thought that a half-dozen élite students had a serious chance of winning the instructorship of the Combat College in competitive examination. Of those six, Darius Flute and Sefton Ten Guy were dead. Scorpio Fax had suffered a nervous breakdown, from which he had only recently recovered, and which had set his training back severely. And as for Son'Sholoma Gezira, why, he had been expelled from the College for arson and attempted rape.

That left the Frangoni warrior Asodo Hatch and the Ebrell Islander Lupus Lon Oliver to duel it out for the instructorship.

In the theoretical examinations, Lupus had proved to have an edge in pure mathematics, physics and mechatronics, but Hatch had surpassed him in linguistics, applied politics and non-coercive conflict resolution. When it came to military tactics and strategy, nothing separated the two. The end result was that both were proving equally qualified for the instructorship, so decision by combat was called for.

When it came to the question of a physical resolution of the competition for the instructorship, Lupus Lon Oliver preferred the certainties of murder, but was too intelligent to strike down Hatch with his own hand.

Hence this conspiracy with Dog Java.

The two had to meet inside the Combat College, for any connection between the two would certainly excite public comment if it took place in the city of Dalar ken Halvar itself. In public in Dalar ken Halvar, Lupus had ever held himself aloof from the Yara, even those who were fellow-students in the Combat College, and so any change in his habits would be noted.

Yet to conspire in the Combat College was difficult, since Paraban Senk could see and hear much of that which took place in most parts of the College.

However, there were, it was known, certain conditions under which the Combat College could not monitor student activity. When students met in the laboratory, for instance – since that great cave at the rear of the Combat College remained but a hollow in the living rock, untenanted by any of the machineries of the Nexus.

Furthermore, the illusion tanks themselves were an ideal venue for a conspiracy – under certain circumstances.

When the illusion tanks ran a war program, Paraban Senk had the option of monitoring everything, count by count. But when the same tanks ran a peace program, Senk could only guess at what was happening. This was an idiosyncrasy of the system. Either a design flaw, or something which had been deliberately arranged to give the students the psychological comfort of having some private sphere of action free from the overlording surveillance of the Teacher of Control. Certainly this idiosyncrasy of the system was very convenient for those engaged in conspiracy.

Naturally, with twenty millennia of experience to back its judgement, Paraban Senk could often guess what was going on, and with some accuracy. Particularly when a student was doing, for example, a freetime run of that peace program known as Backstreet Beds, or the related program known as Harem Lord, for in both of these illusion tank peace programs the range of options was strictly limited.

But Lon Oliver and Dog Java had the freedom of an entire MegaCommand Cruiser, so Paraban Senk could only guess whether they were buggering each other or burning the Great God Mokaragash in effigy.

For the purposes of conspiracy, Lupus Lon Oliver had chosen to meet with Dog Java on the MegaCommand Cruiser in the environment generated by that peace program known as Routine Cruise. It was a tried and tested guidebook program which was free from glitches and caprices, a program in which it was guaranteed that nothing would go wrong. Nothing would attack, engulf, corrode, implode or otherwise imperil the illusionary MegaCommand Cruiser on which Lupus and Dog were busy with conspiracy. The crew would not fight, mutiny or orgy. Unless pressed hard for a reaction, both crew and ship would ignore the wandering students.

So.

The MegaCommand Cruiser.

In deep space.

Here the stars were an alien white. Even now, Lupus could well remember when he had first seen those white-bright stars, and had thought their lack of colour to be a defect of the programming. Though Lupus had lived out his childhood under a white sun, he had still been surprised to learn that the white suns were the Standard Stars of most of Known Humanity, that these cold ice-chip lights were the dominant luminaries of the night skies of any planet in any universe in the Standard Probability Range, and that the Nexus seldom opened a Chasm Gate into a cosmos configured otherwise.

'Pretty,' said Dog Java, watching the stars.

'Pretty?' said Lupus.

Whatever doubts he had about Dog Java were confirmed by that one word.

Still, Lupus pushed on, and made his final offer to Dog Java.

As has already been stated, Dog was a member of the Yara, the Unreal underclass of Dalar ken Halvar's dominant people, the Pang. Dog wanted to join the Free Corps, but membership of that august body was largely restricted to Ebrell Islanders and members of the Chem, the wealthy upper class of Dalar ken Halvar's Pang.

'The Brick has reconsidered your application,' said Lupus.

'And?' said Dog.

'It has been agreed that you will be accepted into the Free Corps if you kill Hatch. Kill him and you can become Real.'

'Good,' said Dog, simply. Then said: 'Abort.'

With that word, Dog exited from the simulated MegaCommand Cruiser, leaving Lupus Lon Oliver alone with his anxieties. Dog was a poor tool. Lupus would much rather have employed someone with a streak of desperation in his nature – like Yolombo Atlantabara, the Frangoni deserter who was known to be living a precarious and criminal life somewhere in Dalar ken Halvar. If Lupus could only get Atlantabara, then – then he might have a serious hope of seeing Hatch dead. But Dog? Lupus was dubious about Dog's abilities.

Hence his anxiety.

For Lupus, winning the instructorship – by fair means or foul – was desperately important. It would mean wealth. And status. And more.

In the years which Lupus had devoted to his studies in

the Combat College, he had integrated himself with the life of the Nexus. In many ways, he had become one of the more intellectual and philosophical of the citizens of the Nexus, and in some ways this had made him a stranger in his own homeland.

So while it is true that Lupus ruthlessly pursued his ambitions because he desired influence, and power, and the satisfactions of mastery, it is also true that he sought a permanent position in the Combat College as an instructor because he did not want to be exiled from his home.

For Lupus, the Nexus was now home; and in a practical sense, for him the Combat College was effectively the Nexus. And he was possessed of a great and half-acknowledged fear of being exiled, of being cast out, of being driven from his home, of being cut off from his people and his culture and all the works and philosophies of that culture.

And Lupus knew that unless he triumphed over Asodo Hatch in the combat trials which were to come, then in a very few days he would indeed be driven out of the Nexus, and the gates of return would be forever barred to him, and he would then be fated to endure a life of exile in an alien land until the end of his days.

Lupus Lon Oliver could not bear the thought of being exiled for a lifetime to Dalar ken Halvar, the benighted City of Sun which lived and died in the dust, which fed itself on rice and polyps and which garbled its days away in primitive tongues bereft of computerized memory. In his dreams, Lupus stood on a high place in Dalar ken Halvar, and looked out across that city and looked out across the red dust of the Plain of Jars, and wailed:

—This is hell.

CHAPTER FOUR

The Nexus: transcosmic confederation which contains much of Known Humanity. Theoretically, Asodo Hatch is a Nexus asset – a trained Startrooper contending to win an instructorship in a Nexus Combat College. However, the honour of the Frangoni warrior's oath of eternal fealty to the Nexus is unlikely ever to be tested – for the transcosmic Chasm Gates linking his world to the rest of the Nexus collapsed some 20,496 years ago, and the likelihood of those Chasm Gates ever being repaired is currently very close to zero.

* * *

So then despite the crowd
He was alone.
Despite the sweat which waited, bloody-eyed –
The sweat and skin:
A living weapon, bladed,
Hooked and barbed,
And he the same, identical, and yet –
Not quite the same, for only one would walk.
Two futures waited, and the crowd –
Then came the Sign.

* * *

And so his father died, expiring on the sands in the Season, but Hatch was not going to die likewise; no, he refused that death, though everyone knows the son may follow when the father dies. At least when the father dies in that manner. But no, he would not, not now! Now the single-fighter was singing, now Hatch had his enemy in his sights, now he fired.

'Burst away,' said the single-fighter. 'Burst away.'

The explosive shells hit home. Shells, brute metal and high explosive, primitive but reliable, just as a knife is likewise primitive but eternally reliable. Fire blossomed within fire. The wreckage wrenched itself apart and fell. The victorious single-fighter analysed an image-record of the attack and pronounced:

'Drone destroyed. Drone—'

'What?' said Hatch, in startled shock.

'—destroyed.'

Yes. Yes. Surely. Hatch knew the trick. The single-fighter he had just savaged had been no more than an illusion gimmicked up by a drone. But drones were far too small to be swift. No drone could possibly match the speeds at which Hatch had hunted his enemy. He had arrowed high and far in pursuit of his quarry, blistering through the stratosphere at speeds impossible for anything short of a single-fighter to match.

Which meant—

Which meant the drone had recently been launched.

So his true enemy was near.

'Enemy behind us,' said the single-fighter.

So Hatch slammed the fighter into a wrenching turn, a turn so savage he had to tighten his stomach muscles to keep himself from passing out.

And there was his enemy.

In his sights.

The enemy for real? Or a drone?

Hatch hesitated, just for a moment, and a moment was far too long. His fighter screamed:

'—hit hit hit—'

And already Hatch was lost, was gone, was wrecked and doomed, his single-fighter smashed and ruined, the machine skidding, tumbling, losing control, spinning through the sky, screaming as it fell.

'Abort,' said Hatch. 'Abort. Abort!'

But his voice was lost in the howl of his wounded machine, or else the programming was glitched, glitched again, and whatever it was he was falling, falling, lancing down towards the burning sea, diving towards the—

—the—

—the blur—

—the freezing freeze-framed—

—the frozen blur of the sea, green fading, blue denying, yellow phasing, passing, fading, gone—

Gone.

The world wavered in silence, and Hatch felt as if he were deep under water, held deep by a pressure too great for him to speak or breathe or feel or think—

—think—

What did he think?

—the sea—

Then the wavering sea-deep silence was nothing but a memory, and he was back in the Combat College, back in the initiation seat, back in the combat bay, his heart pounding and his uniform wet with sweat. Hatch put his face in his hands and kneaded his eyes with his fingers.

It was some time before Asodo Hatch raised his head again and looked at the screen. The screen displayed the olive-skinned face of Paraban Senk.

Since Paraban Senk was an asma, a computational device, Senk was not actually encumbered by anything so grossly inconvenient as a body, so did not possess a face in the fact of the flesh. But for the last 20,000 years, the unembodied Senk had always displayed the one and the same unchanging olive-skinned visage on the screens of the Combat College.

'Critique,' said Senk. As per usual, the Teacher of Control was calm, neutral, remote, disinterested. When Hatch did not respond, Senk amplified the command. 'Critique. Critique your own performance. Come on, Hatch, what's wrong with you?'

'I'm a trifle tired,' said Hatch.

'You're a Startrooper, trained and tested,' said Senk.

'Startroopers don't worry about trifles. The critique. Please.'

'I was fooled,' said Hatch heavily.

'Certainly something went wrong,' said Senk. 'You had him in your sights. He shed the shield and you had him.'

'I know,' said Hatch.

He knew, he knew.

A Scala Nine single-fighter could shield itself from observation with a force field. But only at a cost. By the time a single-fighter shed such a shield, it had expended so much energy that it was temporarily helpless, unable to defend itself.

'When you chanced that turn,' said Senk, 'I naturally thought you must have had his shield-shedding in mind. You know your single-fighter was barely a hair from breaking up.'

Hatch knew. The savagery of the turn, the savagery which had made him clutch the muscles of his stomach, had been an artefact. A warning. Nexus single-fighters were engineered to cancel out all effects of sound, turbulence, acceleration, deceleration, heat and light – then all these informational resources were engineered back into the machine to give the pilot survival data.

'So you almost destroyed your machine,' said Senk. 'Through such risk you got your rival in your sights. Helpless. Yet you hesitated. What were you thinking of?'

'I was thinking the – the thing I saw, I was thinking it might have been a second drone,' said Hatch. 'I didn't want to be . . . to . . . I didn't want to waste out my ammunition and be left . . . I didn't want to be helpless.'

'So you chose to be dead instead,' said Senk. Then, when Hatch made no answer: 'I quote the Stormforce Combat Manual. Quote. An apparent enemy will be treated as a real enemy. Unquote. Engrave it on your heart, Hatch.'

'The master speaks,' said Hatch, speaking briskly as

he tried to shake off his despondency by an act of will. 'The student hears. To hear is to obey. I have but one question – who was I up against?'

'Data unavailable,' said Senk, imitating the basic-speech curtness of a much simpler machine.

'Oh, come on!'

'It's not material.'

'But I'd like to know.'

'It's not material,' said Senk.

Since the Teacher of Control was far better at stonewalling than any human-in-the-flesh, Hatch gave up the unequal struggle and quit the combat bay. In the cream-coloured corridor outside, other Combat College students were patiently queuing, most seated with study-manuals in their hands. Initially the Combat College had been possessed of twenty combat bays, but now, with only seven remaining functional, there was almost always a queue of students waiting for their turn in the illusion tanks.

The first person in the queue outside Hatch's combat bay was Jeltisketh Echo, a Startrooper who had the distinction of being the one and only person of the grey-skinned Janjuladoola race to be a student in the Combat College. He promptly replaced Hatch in the combat bay. A brief quickstep down the corridor, Lupus Lon Oliver was exiting from a similar combat bay, yielding that facility to Umka Ash, a piebald Combat Cadet of uncertain breeding.

Lupus Lon Oliver turned to face Asodo Hatch, and the mystery of the identity of the person who had defeated Hatch in that last single-fighter training duel was immediately solved, for the big grin on Lupus Lon Oliver's face was eloquent of triumph.

'Hi, Hatch!' said the Ebrell Islander. 'Have fun?'

'Lots of fun,' said Hatch sourly, thus betraying his own defeat, and so confirming what Lupus had already guessed.

'Lots and lots of fun,' said Lupus, mocking Hatch as

the iron-pumped Frangoni warrior strode past him.

Hatch turned on the smaller man, looked down on his red-skinned adversary, breathed heavily, resisted the temptation to smash Lupus to a bloodknuckle pulp then and there. With temptation resisted – just! – Hatch headed on down the corridor.

'Have a nice day, now,' said Lupus, mocking his retreat.

At that, Hatch almost halted, almost turned. But Paraban Senk might well be monitoring this confrontation, and any loss of self-control would count against Hatch, and he knew it. So he continued on his way in peace.

On the way to his room, Hatch passed a few fellow Startroopers in Standard Grey, a gaggle of Combat Cadets in their Junior Blues, and a couple of individuals in mufti as various as papyrus skirts and dogskin coats. None spoke to him, for his face had a forbidding aspect. A huge muscle-pumped Frangoni warrior with his height exaggerated by the uncut topknot of his kind is not the most reassuring of sights, particularly not when it is in a bad temper.

On entering his room, Hatch saluted his father's ashes, which had found a temporary resting place in that refuge since they were welcome nowhere else. If Hatch lost the competition for the instructorship, then he would be exiled from the Combat College, and those ashes would have to go with him.

At the moment, Hatch was by no means certain that he could win the all-essential competition, since Lupus Lon Oliver was proving to have a definite edge in their combat training.

Hatch began to strip himself of his clothes. In the Combat College, Hatch sometimes wore the purple robes which were his habitual garb in Dalar ken Halvar itself. However, these days he was tending to wear a Startrooper's Standard Grey more and more often while he was inside the minor mountain of Cap Foz Para Lash.

He was trying to dress like a citizen of the Nexus, to think like a citizen of the Nexus, to be like a citizen of the Nexus – and thus to maximize his chances of winning the instructorship in the trial-by-combat which was so shortly to commence.

But Hatch had never yet worn his Standard Grey out in the sunlight, and he had no intention of ever doing such a thing. In Dalar ken Halvar, he would always and ever wear the purple of a Frangoni warrior – or so he was resolved.

As Hatch wrenched his purple-skinned Frangoni flesh free from a Startrooper's Standard Grey, he repeated Lupus's words:

'Lots of fun.'

Oh yes. Lots of fun. Incredible amounts of fun. The training had got really exciting of late. So exciting, in fact, that Hatch had quite lost track of the number of times he had been shot up, shot down, exploded, bombed, disintegrated and burnt alive.

And for what purpose?

Since Hatch was a Frangoni warrior and not a member of the Free Corps, he had no transcendental faith in the virtues of the Combat College. He had never had any illusions about the Combat College to lose. Even so, he somehow managed to feel decidedly disillusioned as he shed his Standard Grey and pulled off his Weathertreads.

Though Hatch was trying his best to be in and of the Nexus, he nevertheless found it to be always a relief to get dressed in the leather sandals and purple robes of a Frangoni warrior, and this he did once he had shed his Nexus wear. To put on his clothes was to put on his true culture. His true identity. His true strength. The world of the Combat College was the world of maya, illusion; and sometimes Hatch felt that the time spent inside its cream-coloured corridors was but a form of living death.

Once dressed in the way of his Frangoni people, Hatch exited from his room and strode through those corridors of cream, making for the cafeteria.

The blue-painted cafeteria was bright with harsh sunflare lights – wake-up lights, hurry-up-and-eat-and-get-moving lights – and it was noisy with a babble of Startroopers and Combat Cadets, many of whom were busy buying and selling Nexus stocks. Among other things, the cafeteria functioned as an informal bourse, in which the scrip of Nexus companies was freely traded. This activity was entirely speculative because:

(1) since the Chasm Gates linking Ola Malan had been sundered for over 200 centuries, commercial data on the stocks in question were similarly timespan degraded, so there was no telling whether the companies involved were now fabulously valuable or were long since bankrupt and forgotten;
(2) the very Nexus itself might have fallen to ruin at some stage in the last twenty millennia, succumbing for instance to the rigours of a disastrous war with the Vogliono Tendenza;
(3) even assuming that the Nexus still survived and that all the companies being stocktraded inside Cap Foz Para Lash were still prosperous, the true value of the scrip could not be realized unless transcosmic communications between the world of Dalar ken Halvar and the Nexus were restored, which was thought to be unlikely.

Nevertheless, the stock-trading had gone on for generations, and some of this activity spilt out of the Combat College to continue in Dalar ken Halvar itself.

While some traded, others gossiped; or played chess (either the star chess of the Nexus or the more conventional dragon chess played throughout Parengarenga); or wristwrestled; of wargamed arcane encounters between mathematical constructs presumed to be fighting each other in time–space continua which had more than the conventional twenty-seven dimensions of the

Associated Cosmic Orders; or studied sabotage techniques, crew-strength synergetics, bodywork psychodynamics, Thaldonian Mathematics, metallurgy, cosmology, origami (or the related discipline of plandami, which involves folding skeins of colour inside a Grade IV plastic microcosmos), or studying such dull but necessary bureaucratic manuals as the Protocols of Engagement for Stormforce assault ships.

Others ate.

There was food in plenty, such as the meat of many whales (ever in demand by the Ebrell Islanders), and there was drink, such as the notorious blue milk for which the Combat College was so widely famed.

Such food and drink was fabricated by the Combat College's servile asma of Minor Enablement, which created drink and viands of all description through the manipulation of probability. This was a fraught and dangerous process, since an overuse of such manipulation could easily endanger the very fabric of reality itself. Furthermore, since the Asma Minor were undergoing a slow but remorseless deterioration – 20,000 years is a long time, even in the life of an asma – the purity of Combat College provender could no longer be relied upon.

Consequently, Hatch preferred to limit the amount which he ate in the College. But today he was pressed for time, so indulged himself in the convenience of a cafeteria breakfast, choosing to eat fried penguin served with steamed broccoli and baked yams, with a touch of konohachi on the side. The konohachi (a delicacy once much enjoyed by the Imakatari, the professional aesthetes of the Musorian Empire) consisted of the larvae and pupae of several wasps fried up with segments of Dazubi slugs, and was served on a small side dish, which was painted in a light blue streaked with red and white, as if in imitation of the dragonsky pottery of Tang.

While Hatch was savouring the delicate flavour of the last wasp pupae (the taste has been likened to that of peas taken fresh from the pod and eaten with sugar-sweet) a Combat Cadet approached him. The Cadet was Dog Java, who was one of the Yara – that is to say, a member of Dalar ken Halvar's underclass – and who approached Hatch with the diffidence appropriate to a mere Cadet intruding on the glory of a fully-fledged Startrooper.

'Trooper Hatch,' said Dog.

'Speak,' said Hatch, allowing himself to enjoy a leisured sense of aristocratic indulgence as, with his fingertips, he chased the last fragment of Dazubi slug round the imitation bone china of his side dish.

Asodo Hatch did not usually act the aristocrat, but something in Dog Java's attitude provoked him. The unfortunate Dog tried too hard. He wanted to be friends with all the people who would have been his natural social superiors in the city of Dalar ken Halvar, and in his pursuit of acceptance he sometimes intruded upon people's privacy at the most inappropriate moments. As far as Hatch was concerned, the final straw had been Dog's behaviour following the death of Hatch's father. When Lamjuk Dakoto Hatch had met his death on the sands of Dalar ken Halvar's Grand Arena, his son Asodo had largely wanted simply to be left alone. But Dog had come nosing around him repeatedly, offering unwanted and offensively platitudinous words of comfort – and that had estranged him from Asodo Hatch forever.

At least as far as Hatch himself was concerned.

Dog obviously did not appreciate the irrevocable reality and historical depths of this estrangement.

'Scorpio Fax was looking for you,' said Dog.

Scorpio Fax, an immigrant from Shintoto, had once belonged to that élite group of Combat College students who had a serious chance of winning the instructorship. But since his nervous breakdown he had more or less dropped out of sight, and Hatch had lately seen very little of him.

'So Fax is looking for me,' said Hatch, securing that last bit of slug and sucking on its saltiness. 'What did he want?'

'I don't know,' said Java. 'He told me to tell you he wanted to see you, but he didn't say for what.'

'That was remiss of him,' said Hatch, then licked the last traces of saltiness and sweetness from his fingers, then used those same fingers to dismiss Dog Java with a gesture.

Dog Java allowed himself to be thus dismissed, but he did not like Hatch's attitude at all. Hatch must surely know how offensive Dog found such a display of overlording arrogance. On account of that arrogance, Dog had disliked Hatch for years, and had as little to do with him as possible. This once – just this once – he had tried to pass on a message as a favour to Scorpio Fax. But that had been a mistake.

Still, Hatch would soon be paid in blood for his arrogance, because—

Dog Java choked the half-born thought to silence. In the Combat College, Dog did not usually even dare dream of killing Hatch. But Lupus Lon Oliver had made him swear to do as much, and Dog was grimly resolved to prove out the worth of his oath. But not here. Not yet. Not now. Not today. Later, later. Sometime. Somewhere. Soon. Yes, soon, it would have to be soon, because Hatch's trial by combat was soon, and later would be no good.

Thus thought Dog.

As for Hatch, he had already forgotten all about both Dog Java and Scorpio Fax by the time he quit the cafeteria and headed for the lockway. Among the Frangoni, meals were ever a steadying ritual, a time for leisured relaxation and unashamed self-indulgence, but on quitting the dining table Asodo Hatch immediately geared himself up to battle-pitch.

These days, Hatch's schedule was jam-packed, and this particular day was busier than most. Hatch would even have skipped the single-fighter training duel had Paraban Senk not made it compulsory. Since Hatch was so aboil with urgencies, he had no time to spare for trivialities, hence wasted no time on trying to reason out the unstated needs of Scorpio Fax, who was no close friend of his, for all that their destinies had been so intimately intertwined in the past.

On the way to the lockway, Hatch saw no fellow members of the Combat College, but did see evidence of human activity – drink cartons, chicken bones, banana peels, discarded papers and graffiti. The Combat College cleaning machines had been on the fritz for seven days, and unless Senk could get them working then someone would have to organize a clean-up.

The rubbish was heavy near the cafeteria, but there was virtually none on the final approach to the dorgi's lair. Yet when the dorgi itself had challenged Hatch, and had been defeated in a contest of insults, it ordered the Frangoni warrior to pick up what litter there was.

'What!' said Hatch, unable to believe his nose.

(In the Frangoni tongue, probabilities are said to be heard with the ears, but for some obscure reason the hearing of all lies, dubiosities and improbabilities is said to be assigned to the nose – and though Hatch was conversing with the dorgi in Code Seven, he still thought of the dorgi's order as being meant for the nose rather than the ears.)

'I'm warning you,' said the dorgi. 'Pick up this rubbish or I will eliminate you.'

The malevolent behemoth had tried Hatch's patience so much and so often in the past that he had often been tempted to attempt its destruction. So far he had resisted that temptation. But the dorgi was provoking Hatch intolerably, and these days Hatch's temper was very close to reaching its breaking point.

'You'll push your luck too far one of these days,' said Hatch to the dorgi. 'Now take back your order – or you'll suffer for it.'

But in the end the dorgi proved so savage in its insistence that Hatch, by way of concession, picked up a single scrap of paper, then escaped to the airlock. In less than a heartbeat, the inner door dissolved away to nothing. Hatch stepped through, and the door instantly congealed to kaleidoscope behind him.

The airlock's inner chamber worked perfectly, lecturing Hatch on a citizen's ecological duties as it cycled out the old air and replaced it with new. While it did so, Hatch straightened out the crumpled bit of Nexusmake paper and scanned the childish Nexus script written thereon. It was a list:

> the Gu
> the Degli Oltra
> the Vogliono Tendenza
> the Mok
> Remora Rialto
> Gorbograd
> the Vangelis
> the Nu-chala-nuth
> the Guma Sia Gli
> the Permissive Dimensions
> Obsidian IV
> Leonard Haiku
> Plandruk Qinplaqus

It was part of a child's study notes on the Nexus, obviously. But one item on the list should not have been there. Plandruk Qinplaqus. For Qinplaqus had never played any part in Nexus history but, rather, ruled as emperor in the city of Hatch's nativity. Hatch recrumpled the list and tucked it into a document pocket built into his purple robes.

The airlock's central door dissolved, and Hatch stepped into the airlock's outer chamber. Again the air cycled, again a lecture spoke, and then the outer door dissolved. But unlike the other two doors, which were still working perfectly, the outer door was beginning to break down. When it dissolved, its substance did not dematerialize properly, but instead disintegrated into a fizzing slush of cold and filthy slob. Hatch waded through the slush, quitting the cold of the Combat College for the heat of the sun, the heat which was trapped and amplified by the kinema, the small natural amphitheatre outside the lockway airlock.

The kinema was populated night and day by a small audience – of children, mostly – drawn by the non-stop free entertainment offered by the Eye of Delusions. Some of these children raised a small, ironic cheer as Hatch emerged.

'Nu-chala!' cried one. 'Nu-chala-nuth!'

Now where on earth had they learnt to say that? Never mind. The religion of Nu-chala-nuth was safely dead, 20,000 years dead, and in Hatch's estimate all chances of its resurrection were dead, null and zero.

As Hatch strode into the kinema, the lockway's outermost airlock door began to coagulate behind him. It was supposed to open and close instantaneously, but after being neglected for a koba – to use the Ninetongue word for a period of twenty millennia – it was starting to show its age, as indeed was everything in the Combat College. Doubtless eventually the entire College would slag down to wreckage and the Teacher of Control would mumble its way into impotent senility. But for the moment everything still worked.

After a fashion.

True, the outer door of the lockway was malfunctional; true, the milk in the cafeteria was blue; true, the illusion tanks often glitched; true, the temperature controls were shot, so the whole Combat College was shivering cold all year round; but, with a little luck, the whole thing would last for at least a little longer.

And Hatch—

Asodo Hatch had no thought for the last 20,000 years or for the next, since his fate would be settled, one way or another, in the course of the next few days.

Behind the purple-skinned Frangoni warrior, the airlock door hardened at last to the iridescent beauty of kaleidoscope. The lockway's triple-airlock doors of kaleidoscope always protected the Combat College, forbidding entry to the unwanted. Thus that institution had for 20,000 years been able to continue its rightful mission: to train Startroopers for the Stormforce of the Nexus. Deep in the heart of the mountain lay the Combat College, deep in the heart of Cap Foz Para Lash. But Hatch was outside, outside in the sunlight, standing on the red dust of the Plain of Jars, standing on the fringes of Dalar ken Halvar: the City of the Sun.

City and Combat College.

Two worlds.

Two worlds – each an illusion to the other.

'I vote for this one,' said Hatch.

But while he voted for Dalar ken Halvar, he was still contending for dominance in the world of the Combat College.

And—

Back in the world of the College, the red-skinned Ebrell Islander named Lupus Lon Oliver was conferring with Dog Java in the shadowy privacy of the rock-walled laboratory, and was demanding that Dog explain to him why Hatch still lived, as yet unmurdered, unassassinated, and all too strong, fit and dangerous.

CHAPTER FIVE

The Chem and the Yara: the rich and the poor. In Dalar ken Halvar's Pang, the word for wealth is the same as that for reality. The Chem are those who control the city's wealth, and hence its realities. The poor, the Yara – the underclass of the People Pang – are by definition Unreal, imaginary, dream-delusions formed in the shape of people.

*　　　*　　　*

> The fingertips, my chaffinch,
> Burnt to a flinch, and thus –
> The world unhanded, humming-bird denied.
> All light charade, all voices
> In flesh but charnel shadows –
> Shadows with shadows scented.
> Yet –

*　　　*　　　*

It was mid-morning when Hatch exited from the lockway. Polk the Cash, the noseless moneylender who had lately assumed such a dominant place in his life, should have been there to greet him, but was not, which irritated Hatch intensely. In these days of tension, irritation was becoming Hatch's dominant operating mode. Which was understandable. He was desperately busy, and right now he wanted to make a deal with Polk, to hurry himself to House Jodorunda, then push on to Temple Isherzan to keep his appointment with the High Priest.

So where was Polk?

With the moneylender being nowhere in evidence, and with the Eye of Delusions showing one of the more offensive cartoon entertainments about the mythical Wild Tribes, Hatch retreated a short distance down Scuffling Road, where he sheltered the bulk of his purple in the shadow of a sugar juice stall. He took particular care to make sure that his stuffbag was safe in that shadow.

Time passed.

Sunbeat and heartbeat.

Shadow and sun.

An oxcart lumbered past, its wooden wheels digging deep in the soft rutted dust of Scuffling Road. More than one Combat College graduate had suggested paving the roads, but any such extravagance would have drained Dalar ken Halvar's treasury of the profits of three generations. Water spilt from the barrels loaded on the oxcart, which had uplifted that water from the Yamoda River and was taking it to sell to those watching the Eye.

Dog Java went by, still dressed in the Junior Blues of a Combat Cadet. He cast a half-glance in Hatch's direction then hastened down Scuffling Road as if fleeing from an unwelcome dental appointment.

Hatch scarcely noticed him.

In the slow sweating desolations of his impatience, Hatch began to attend to the conversation of three much-familiar beggars, the ragmen Grim, Zoplin and X'dex (allegedly Lord X'dex) Paspilion. They seemed to be arguing about a dog. And about a certain set of teeth.

'Pass me the teeth,' said Beggar Grim. 'This dog's rough as tough for the gums.'

'You can't eat dog,' said Hatch, incontinently intervening from the shade of his sugar-juice shelter, which was scarcely a flea's jump distant from Grim and Grim's lice.

Hatch was surprised at his own forwardness, for he usually exercised the discipline of silence when in the presence of beggars. But Grim showed no corresponding surprise, and replied, as if their conversation were the most natural thing in the world:

'Oh, I can eat him right enough – if Master Zoplin be kind enough to pass me the teeth.'

So saying, Grim beat his tattered rags in frustration, to the great discomfiture of his fleas. A little of the red dust of the Plain of Jars stirred around him in consequence of his efforts.

'Your forte is forgetting,' said Hatch. 'The Festival of the Dogs is shortly upon us.'

Having spoken thus, Hatch began to regret his speech, for by rights a captain of the Imperial Guard has too much pride in his status to dabble in a dialogue with beggars. Similarly, a Frangoni true to the traditions of his kind ever ignores the Pang, who are born without caste and who live to their deaths in the same condition. Hatch was both captain and Frangoni; Grim and his companions yet beggars and Pang. Hence the regrets of Asodo Hatch.

Still, the warning was rightly given, for it was the Day of Five Fishes, which falls just five days short of Dog Day, and so for the moment all dog-slaughter was forbidden.

Everyone knew that.

But Grim, either addled in his wits or arguing for the mere love of disputation, chose to dispute it.

'A festival comes, does it?' said Grim. 'Wherefore does that quench my appetites? Am I to eat anticipations or baste my stomach with the salt of the same?'

Hatch, whose speech was ever slowed by the burdens of responsibility, made no attempt to wit a quick answer to the querimonious loquacity of Grim's nimble-skilled interrogation. But one of Grim's fellow beggars answered in Hatch's despite.

'He means,' said Lord X'dex – Lord X'dex Paspilion, master of the Greater Tower of X-n'dix in the far-off land of X-zox Kalada – 'he means, dear Grim, that you breach not your appetites upon the poor lean corpse of that yon-there pariah dog but by the breach of the law.'

'Pardon?' said Grim.

'Friend Dex has the giblets again,' said Master Zoplin.

Hatch, restless with an excess of listening to the babbling of beggars, looked around for his contact for the thousandth time. But there was still no sight of Polk. Hatch wanted to be gone, but did not dare abort this appointment. Polk had made it clear that he had almost reached the end of his patience, and Hatch could not risk antagonizing the moneylender any further.

But in the absence of Polk, there was Dog, Dog Java, returning up Scuffling Road. Reluctance was written clear in his countenance, so that Hatch immediately supposed that Dog had remembered leaving something of importance in the Combat College – study notes, perhaps – and was unenthusiastic about venturing through airlocks and past dorgi to retrieve what he had forgotten.

Dog halted.

'Yes?' said Hatch, presuming that Dog Java meant to ask him something.

'Ha!' said Lord X'dex, guessing at someone's arrival from the single-word question. 'Hatch has been catching! He's got him a stranger! Who is it?'

'It's nobody,' said Hatch. 'Only Dog Java.'

'Java!' said Dax. 'The very man! Come close, Java. Come coffee our conversation. Come worm to our honey, rot to our wood. I smell blood!'

And with that, Lord X'dex Paspilion abruptly scuffled through the dust and grabbed Dog Java by the ankle.

'Blood?' said the over-nervous Dog, shaking his ankle in an ineffectual attempt to kick free the beggar. 'What are you talking about? I haven't done anything! Let me go!'

'Don't mind Dex,' said Zoplin. 'He's touched with the giblets, as I've told you already. As a rock has worms, so Dex has the giblets. Giblets and jism. A disease from the dust.'

Persuaded by a stouter kick from Dog Java, the beggar Dex released the imprisoned ankle and laughing (the gutteral noise could have been mistaken for a symptom of strangulation, but both Hatch and Dog Java conjectured it correctly as an expression of amusement), the beggar Dex retreated to the dust from whence he had come.

Dog Java stood in the sunlight.

Sweating.

Hatch looked him up and down, lazily, wondering what was wrong with him. Maybe he had a fever, for he was not only sweating but also trembling. Meanwhile, the beggars were still talking.

'Friend Dex has more than the giblets,' said Grim. 'He has scrofula, scurvy, bleach-bone, ringworm and a touch of the hairy bubonics. But you have the teeth!'

'So,' said Zoplin, using the asset in question to gnaw a piece of sugar cane filched from the nearby sugar juice stall. 'So. Beseech me as Lord of Dentition. Beseech or be burgled! Cry slave, slave, or be dust-drowned in camel dung!'

'Beseechingness be unfitting when I seek but the common property of our commune,' said Grim. 'You admit to the teeth, so give them!'

'I admit them and keep them,' said Zoplin, 'for it's not for you to be eating dog, not with these teeth or others, for dog be forbidden for slaughter.'

'Since when?' said Grim.

'It is written,' said Lord X'dex Paspilion, 'I cannot read it, mind, but it is written, and mark that the worms have the truth of it, be the bones as yet unwritten, be the pea-soup unsalted, the eagle unwormed, in blood it is written, in shadows and bones—'

'Bones!' said Grim. 'It's flesh I'm eating, or would be, had Zoplin the decency to give me the teeth.'

'That I cannot,' said Zoplin. 'For thus it is written.'

There was a pause, while the other beggars considered this. Hatch spoke into the pause, addressing the brown-skinned Combat Cadet who stood before him in a virtual paralysis of quick-breathing sweat and muscle-knotted shuddering.

'Dog? Dog Java? Are you all right?'

At which Dog Java's eyes rolled up to expose the whites, and he fell to the ground in a faint. His body shuddered in imitation of epilepsy, as a body often will when its owner faints. Then that body lay still, its breathing easing. Hatch regarded the body with faint surprise, but with no greater emotion. The beggars meanwhile ignored the event, though all three were so sharp that they must have heard Dog Java's collapse clearly, and have understood its import. Grim had considered Master Zoplin's last statement in detail and depth, and gave his reponse into the sun-hot stillness:

'Written?' said Grim. 'We were talking teeth, not writing!'

'Teeth were talking while writing was scribing,' said Lord X'dex. 'With writing done, let me say it is written—'

'Written?' said Grim. 'It is written? And you have the reading of it?'

'With the Eye, yes,' said Lord X'dex.

This Eye of which he made mention was a small device which was the common property of the three, and was by no means to be confused with the Eye of Delusions, that much larger affair set above the lockway in the natural amphitheatre at the southern end of Scuffling Road.

'With the Eye or without the Eye,' said Grim, 'I doubt you can read, for you were born illiterate, and I have not heard that you have improved yourself since.'

Hatch then feared the two beggars would fall to fighting, something they did from time to time for sheer amusement. Not for the first time, he wondered what it would be like to be a beggar, with an infinity of useless time at his disposal. It seemed to Hatch that he had never been free of time demands and urgent responsibilities in his whole life – and that he had never been more burdened than now.

'The greater secrets have ever been hidden from you

and yours,' said Lord X'dex, addressing himself to Beggar Grim, would-be devourer of deceased caninity. 'But still, it is written that in the month before Dog Day, no dog may be slaughtered in Dalar ken Halvar. From which I find you in breach of the law for possession of yon corpse, hence order it surrendered to the lord of the Greater Tower, who has a dispositional dispensation for the calorificatory combustion or consumption of all foodstuffs or winestuffs, provenant or purchasory, diligent or demised.'

While this chattering was going on, a camel came slow-stilt striding, southbound for the kinema, bearing its owner to the entertainments of the Eye of Delusions. Hatch exerted himself to the extent of dragging Dog Java clear of the red dust roadway, then let him lie.

'It's syphilis,' said Grim, at last diagnosing the inspiration of the discursive pyrotechnics which obsessed and possessed his brother-in-rags, the mighty Lord X'dex Paspilion.

Which made Hatch think: maybe Dog Java had a venereal disease. For if it was sheer emotional stress that had upset him to the point of fainting, then the pox might be the cause. But – surely! – there was no pox in Dalar ken Halvar which was beyond the powers of the Combat College cure-all clinic, to which Dog had free access. So it must be something else. And Hatch thought he had better be finding out exactly what that something else was, for he presumed from Dog Java's earlier behaviour that Dog wanted to consult him on something, but that the something was an extremely sensitive personal matter.

'Dog Java,' said Hatch, seeing the Combat Cadet's eyes flutter open. 'How is it?'

Dog Java made no immediate response, but shortly sat up, looking weak and strained.

Hatch had no wish to add Dog Java's problems to his own, but had very little choice in the matter. In the ordinary course of events, Senior Combat College students such as Hatch were supposed to make themselves available to help juniors such as Dog Java; and since Hatch was a candidate for the Combat College instructorship, he could not afford to default from such responsibility, for any default might prejudice Paraban Senk against him.

'It is syphilis,' said Grim, speaking into the long pause. 'It is syphilis, as I said.'

'Syphilis?' said Master Zoplin, spitting chewed sugar cane. 'Why no, it is dog. By your own testimony, dog. Dog fresh killed, so you are due to be killed likewise, a murderer of the not-to-be murdered. I appoint me your executioner.'

At the word 'executioner', Dog Java abruptly got to his feet. With a dramatic gesture, he drew a knife. He staggered slightly, but kept his balance. Just. The sweat was sheening and shining on his forehead. He was again trembling as if in a fever. Hatch was seriously alarmed. He thought Dog Java was likely to faint again, and accidentally fall on his knife. Or else—

'Ah! Condemned, am I?' said Grim. 'Then give me the teeth, that I may die with a full belly at least.'

'Dog,' said Hatch, with firm gentleness. 'I think it would be better if you gave me the teeth.'

Dog opened his mouth, closed it.

'Forgive me,' said Hatch, realizing he had blundered in his speech. 'I meant the knife, not the teeth. The knife. We don't want someone to get hurt, do we?'

With that, Asodo Hatch – who had diagnosed Dog Java's death-tension as suicidal intent – got to his feet. He did this slowly and with due deliberation, making no sudden moves which might precipitate a *felo de se*, for Hatch feared that Dog Java's self-inflicted death would count as a black mark on Hatch's own record. If Dog Java had some cause to commit suicide, then Asodo Hatch was determined that the low-born Pang bred Combat Cadet would not compound the crime of self-murder by making the act an embarrassment to Startrooper Hatch.

Gently, Hatch removed the knife from Dog Java's unresisting hand.

'Thank you,' said Hatch. 'Sit. Come on, sit down.'

But Dog Java abruptly turned and fled, leaving Hatch in possession of a heavy knife which shone bright-bladed in the sun. Hatch watched the fleeing Dog. He knew that he should by rights go after the Combat Cadet, for Dog was so plainly upset about something that it was Hatch's duty to counsel him actively.

Though there were never more than half a thousand students training in the Combat College at any one time, the multiple stresses and conflicts that the students endured were so severe that on average there was one student suicide every year. In his time, Hatch had effectively counselled three students in danger of succumbing to the temptations of self-murder. But today – today Hatch had far too much on his plate to worry unduly about Dog. He sank from sun to shadow, settling himself again by the sugar-juice stall.

'The teeth!' said Grim, demanding.

Then Grim, gripped by anger – for angered he was, or riled sufficiently to imitate rage – denounced delay by thumping his dog-corpse heartily, much to the discomfiture of its complement of blowflies.

'Ho!' said Lord X'dex. 'A roily stasidion!'

Stasidion? What did that mean? Hatch could make no sense of the word. But then, there was never a profit to be had from riddling the discourse of beggars. Hatch planted Dog Java's knife in the dust by his side. He looked up and down the hot and aching street, but sighted his contact nowhere. Devil of a bitching! Where was Polk?

'A rumbunctious stanchion, verily,' agreed Master Zoplin, savouring the words with all the negligent leisure of an immortal god. 'A very treestump in his rage, fearsome as a river gnome or a virgin's waters. But I cannot help him in his rages, for he be a criminal, and I his partner in crime if I pass to him these molars.'

71

'He needs not the molars,' said Lord X'dex, 'for those be the grinding teeth. He needs his incisors, the biters, the fangs. He must werewolf his dog, aye, butcher it vampire-style, perish its throat and dig out its flowers, eat of its liver and pull out its buttercups, grout out its—'

'Buttercups?' said Zoplin.

'Yes, yes, buttercups, buttercups,' said X'dex. 'You know not the buttercup? It is a flower of the snowlands which grows on the rocks by the sea. It produces in summer a prodigious liquor, the savour of which is a drunkenness unto dragons, in consequence of which the beasts by the bushel are seen toiling in the sea-meadows, laughing and roiling, each drunk as a dwarf.'

'Ah!' said Zoplin. 'He's on about the sea again. There's no hope for him now.'

'Nor hope for you neither, if I have the strangling of you,' said Grim. 'Which I will, be denied me the teeth.'

'The teeth,' said Zoplin, popping them out of his mouth and clacking them vigorously in his hand, 'they be legal teeth, not criminal teeth to be partaking of the eating of a dog illegally killed, with the death of the killer a consequence.'

A little saliva drooled down from the sun-glinting teeth and trickled its way down to the sun-shadowed dust.

'Oh, but this is old dog,' said Grim. 'I didn't kill this dog today, no, nor yesterday neither. This dog I dug from under its gravestone. This is pedigree dog, this is. This dog died between sheets of silk and of satin, died of a broken heart when it was cheated in love.'

'Cheated?' said Master Zoplin. 'How so?'

'Why,' said Grim, tearing a dog-leg free from the carcass and waving it to emphasize his point, though his two companions were as blind as he was, and so the emphasis was lost on all but Hatch. 'Why, this dog—'

'This corpse of a dog,' said Lord X'dex, threatening a flight of full-blown pedantry, but leaving the threat unfulfilled for the moment.

'This corpse of a dog is a corpse that was dorgi when dog,' said Grim.

'But changed its race on dying?' said Lord X'dex.

'Clearly,' said Grim, 'for in death it became as jokeless as a Frangoni.'

With that, Grim turned his socketed face towards Hatch, who made no response. The chastisement of beggars was beneath his dignity. These, besides, were beggars of the Yara, the underclass of the brown-skinned people Pang. The Yara did not believe in their own reality, and so had scant fear of punishment.

'Hatch,' said Grim, his Frangoni non-interlocutor remaining responseless. 'Are you there, Hatch?'

Hatch, who was definitely there, wished himself elsewhere.

'Are you deaf as well as blind?' said Zoplin to Grim. 'He's there. He hasn't moved.'

'Thus may have died of vexation and silence,' said Grim. 'Have you died, Hatch? Or are you industriously auditing?'

The Pang were supposed to be quiet and self-effacing, but these beggars owed nothing to that stereotype, for they were bawdy in their outrageous racontage and burly with the bulk of much good eating. Hatch was usually uneasy with people who did not conform to his expectations, but he had known these three for so long that they troubled him scarcely more than his shadow.

Even so, it was less than proper for him to join them in conversation. He had his dignity to think about, and the dignity of a Frangoni warrior is ever one of the more conspicuous parts of his style. Hatch's dignity was conspicuous even though it had to compete with his height, with his hair-knot, his muscle-pumped torso and the grandly great sweep of his purple robes.

But . . .

'You were talking of a dog,' said Hatch, drawn back into the beggars' dialogue despite himself.

The Frangoni prided themselves on their aloofness,

but Hatch had lately been so stressed by the multiple pressures of his crisis, and so undeniably and unreachably lonely in that crisis, that he had allowed himself to have more to do with beggars than was properly decent, and was hard put to break the habit.

'A dog, yes,' said Grim. 'A dorgi. The petdog of Manfred Gan Oliver, that's what it was. Gan Oliver himself bred it by bucking a Lashund.'

The implication was that Manfred Gan Oliver was a dog himself, for the ferocious hunter-killers known as dorgis are bred by mating long-legged Lashund hounds with the slaughterweight fighting dogs called thogs. Asodo Hatch had never before realized how like unto a thog was Gan Oliver, but once made the comparison was irresistible. The grim-faced head of the Free Corps was undeniably thoggish in all his major attributes, though it had taken a blind man to see as much.

Hatch was still grinning at the beggar's joke when he saw Gan Oliver's son, Lupus Lon Oliver, stealthing his way down Scuffling Road like a debtor in fear of an ambush by writ-bearing creditors.

'Lupus,' said Hatch, calling out the Ebrell Islander's name so the beggars would be warned of his approach, and choke back any futher jokes about thogs.

Lupus Lon Oliver started, with as much of a shock as if he had been touched at night by a hand of bones in a house thought deserted.

'Hatch,' said Lupus, partially recovering himself. 'I – I – have you seen Dog Java?'

'Why, yes,' said Hatch. 'It's been just a snack-snap since he was standing here as large as life. A combast or so.'

A combast was a Nexus ration tube; and, by natural extension of meaning, the approximate time taken to leisure down such a ration.

'What – ah, where—'

'He went down the road,' said Hatch. 'I think he was heading for home. He was upset about something, I don't know what.'

74

'I see,' said Lupus.

Then the Ebrell Islander cleared his throat and hastened down Scuffling Road, rushing away with all the impetuous velocity of an Evolutionist sprinting for the river in the hope of surviving an imminent transformation from manflesh to fish.

As Lupus left, Hatch remembered Dog's knife. He thought to call Lupus back and ask him to pass on the knife, then thought better of it. Clearly something had badly upset the young Ebrell Islander, and from what he had seen Hatch could only presume that Lupus and Dog were locked in some deeply emotional dispute. Probably, given their ages, they were disputing about love. Love for a woman? For each other? For a third man desired by both? Hatch, with more than enough problems of his own to worry about, had absolutely no desire to find out, but guessed that it would be unwise to arm young Lupus with murderous steel as the Ebrell Islander went in pursuit of Dog Java.

'There goes Gan Oliver's son,' said Hatch, telling the beggars the air was again free for the exercise of their folly. 'Perhaps he's the dog of whose breeding you spoke of.'

'Why, no,' said Grim. 'For Lupus yet lives, but the dog of my eating is dead. This dog, you see, was a dog bred for love. Gan Oliver in exile, old Manfred, he pined for the love of yon dorgi within, hence bred a dorgi without to send it in to consummate his love by proxy. But the lockway denied dog as it did master, so, being built to love, or to pine in love's despite, the dorgi without did perish, hence my eating. My eating, which I will consummate, be you so good as to pass me the teeth. The teeth, Master Zoplin!'

'I suppose,' said Master Zoplin, at last consenting to pass along the teeth, which Grim promptly snatched, 'I suppose you'll be wanting my tapeworm next.'

'No,' said Grim, slobbing the teeth into place, 'no, but I wouldn't say no to the Eye. Who's got it? Have you?'

'I sold it to Hatch,' said Zoplin. 'He's awfully keen on the Eye is old Hatch.'

'He's waiting with a stuffbag,' said X'dex. 'I can see it from here. He's waiting to sell something.'

'To sell something?' said Grim. 'What's he got to sell? His soul he sold at birth, like his father-Frangoni before him. What you waiting for, Hatch? You don't usually wait, not you.'

'I told you,' said X'dex. 'He's selling.'

'Then what? Pass us the Eye, Friend Dex, Friend Dexlord Paspilion.'

'I can't,' said that worthy. 'I'm studying ants.'

'Ants!' said Zoplin. 'I'm the one with the ants. They're half my lunch by weight and ten thousand thirds of it by number.'

With that, toothless Master Zoplin picked up one of the pieces of baked yam from the banana leaf at his side, wiped it on his rags to remove any ants – for he was fastidiously vegetarian – then began to masticate the yampiece with his gums. As he did so, the worthy Lord X'dex Paspilion unscrambled the Eye from his left-hand socket, wiped it on his own rags, then passed it to Grim, who received it with gratitude.

'Ah!' said Grim, popping the Eye into his own left-hand socket, 'now I see him clear enough!'

Whether Grim saw or whether he didn't was a moot point. None of the three beggars had ever allowed Hatch to examine their allegedly precious Eye, so even after more than two decades of acquaintance he had no idea whether the three truly possessed some fabulous device which enabled them to see or whether they had been carrying on a running joke for all these years with a worthless bit of shiny metal.

'What do you see?' said Hatch, challenging.

'A Frangoni born ugly and since grown worse,' said Grim. 'A Frangoni purple in his humours, with further purple drawn about his purpleness. Purple upon him, and with him – chocolate! That's what he's got!

76

Chocolate! A vile and hideous drug if ever there was one.'

In truth, Asodo Hatch did have a consignment of chocolate which he planned to sell for profit. Drug it was indeed, this chocolate being a species of psycho-addictor once very popular in the Nexus.

'You smelt it,' said Hatch. 'You're blind to the sight but you smelt it.'

'Smelt it, did I?' said Grim. 'Then it must be melting.'

Melting!

Hatch reached in alarm for his stuffbag, for the chocolate within was equal in value to a ten-day supply of opium, and opium he needed most urgently to satisfy his wife's inescapable requirements. Of course the chocolate had not melted at all, for he had it in the bitterblock tablet form which is proof against all but the worst of the sun. Grim laughed, either seeing Hatch's alarm or guessing at it.

'A pox on all beggars,' said Hatch.

'A pox indeed,' agreed Grim. 'Oh, pox would be luxury, or at least the getting of it. You'll be getting with luxury shortly, won't you?'

'How so?' said Hatch.

'Why, for you'll soon be instructor. Isn't it? You're fighting for it soon and shortly, isn't it?'

'Maybe,' said Hatch, unwilling to discuss the details of the agony to which he was committed.

'Maybe, maybe,' muttered Grim. 'Are you too poor to be giving a beggar a yes or a no? It's true, isn't it!' Here anger, so sharp that Hatch was startled by it. 'You, you glut on chocolate, six nights of the week, you glut it and squeeze it, but we poor beggars, worms and rats, rats as rags and maggots as comfort. Give me the chocolate!'

'You need no chocolate,' said Hatch, speaking lightly, and trying thus to dismiss the truth of Grim's anger. 'It's not good for you.'

'True, true,' said Grim, softening, slackening, anger dying to humour or its semblance. 'I need no chocolate,

77

need it not, want it not. Why, rather, right now I want boy, not boy to be boy but boy to sell sister. Hey, you-boy, you have me a sister?'

'I have not a sister,' said the boy whom Grim was addressing, a boy whom Hatch had not noticed till that very moment, 'nor you no need for one, for I had your eyes but I ate them.'

This was a dire insult indeed, for they were talking in Pang, in which the word for eyes is *logo nuk*, a homonym of the word meaning testicles. (Thus eyes plural – the word for an eye singular being *chaba jaf*, a word which also means egg, and hence has given the Pang the phrase 'to lay eggs on fur', which is used among them to denote the act of sexual intercourse). In response to this insult, Beggar Grim said something so obscene that Hatch (fluent in Pang, but not perfect) was hard put to construe the sense of it, though he gathered that the boy was being invited to do something involving a head, a finger, a cat, a river-oyster, some cakes of dung and his mother's brother's wife's daughter-in-law.

'Boy,' said Hatch, when Grim was done, 'have you news for me?'

Every day Hatch went past the Brick and saw the Free Corps messenger boys torturing dogs or playing knuckle bones in the dust outside the place. Recognizing this urchin as such a boy, he presumed that the noseless moneylender named Polk had sent him with a message as his burden.

'Why news for you, Mister Purple?' said the boy.

Mister Purple? That was less than polite. Indeed, had boy been man, such an insult could easily have precipitated violence. But the boy was a boy, and a boy who looked fleet of foot, so Hatch saw no way to chastise him except at the risk of serious damage to his own dignity.

'You have a message,' said Hatch. 'Get on with it.'

'Polk's not in the purple mood,' said the small boy. 'But he sends his regards and sends three days for the chocolate.'

'Three days!' said Hatch, aghast.

Polk had promised him ten.

'Three days,' affirmed the boy, 'which you collect from the Brick.'

Worse and worse. Not only was the price diminished, but Hatch was going to be made to go to the Free Corps headquarters to collect that price. Hatch, angered by insult, could not help himself, and before he knew it he was saying it:

'No.'

'No?' said the boy, exaggerating his wide-eyed amazement in an attempt at achieving a comic effect. 'Why, Mister Purple, three days is three times your sister.'

Three times your sister? What did that mean? The grammar was garbled, but the intent to insult was plain. Hatch was too close to his breaking point to appreciate being made a comedy by a boy from the Brick.

'Come here!' said Hatch, rising from the shadows of the sugar juice stall.

He rose so swiftly that his legs almost buckled, for the blood fled his head and he almost fainted. So he was in no state to chase or catch the boy, who was running already. The boy paused at the first rock on which dung-cakes were laid out to dry, grabbed one of those fuel tablets and hurled it in Hatch's direction. It went saucering through the air and blunted itself on a rock, being as yet too soft to brittle-break. Then the boy laughed and went pelting away through the heat of the day, running so fast and free it was as if he inhabited a different weather entirely.

'Polk promised me ten,' said Hatch, still standing, unable to contain his amazement at the cheating un-scrupulosity of moneylenders.

'So you reject him at three,' said Beggar Grim. 'So now you can home you and feast on the fruits of rejection. Hatch, he will feed, he will eat, he will glut himself sick on rejections! Luxury, luxury! Why, and here's my luxury now! Shona, it's Shona.'

Scent alone might have told Beggar Grim that it was Shona coming by, for she habitually drenched herself in Nudik Martyr, a gross proto-perfume too blatant for all but the hardiest of women to wear. There had once been a fad for Nudik Martyr throughout the Nexus, and, though twice a hundred centuries had passed since then, the Combat College had been given no opportunity to update or expunge that quirk of the fashions. Hence Shona, who loved the stuff, smelt as if she had been first lathered in the pulp of a billion over-ripe blossoms and then scraped clean with sun-dried orange peel.

'Been dorking the dorgi, have you, Shona dear?' said Beggar Grim. 'Got any left for me?'

Usually Shona ignored such foul-mouthed overtures, for she was too much the warrior woman to waste time on disciplining beggars. But today she had a double handful of slob, a surprise meant for one of the unruly dogs of the neighbourhood. On Beggar Grim's provocation, she threw it at him.

'Ya!' shrieked Grim, as the filthy slush slap-sloshed into his face.

His claw-scrabble hands tore at the cold effervescence, accelerating its evanishment.

'Why, Hatch my man,' said Shona, challenging that Frangoni warman. 'You left an age ago. Still here? Still waiting?'

'I'm waiting for Polk,' said Hatch, pretending he was still waiting, and doing his best not to look cheated and downcast, for he was unwilling to expose his vulnerabilities to any woman, even one as staunch and trustworthy as Shona.

'The Cash, is it? That criminal! He'd diddle his own mother on the price of her tits and turds. What's he buying?' In quest of an answer, Shona took Hatch's stuffbag, hefted it, looked in it. 'Your chocolate, is it? Why, it's a fortune!'

'Ten days for my wife,' said Hatch, still pretending such good fortune was still on offer.

'Ten days!' said Shona, who knew all about Hatch's wife and her needs. 'Why, this is worth twenty. There's a regular run on chocolate, didn't you know? The Bralsh is buying the stuff at doubles and triples.'

'The Bralsh!' said Hatch. 'What would the Bralsh want with chocolate?'

Said Shona:

'I know what's under my garter belt, but you won't find the Bralsh down there. All I know is the price. Here, I'll pay you with peace, I have some on me.'

'You carry it with you?' said Hatch.

'Can't leave it at home, can I?' said Shona.

Then from a girdling money belt she dug a half dozen opium balls, each encased in white wax and stamped with the vermilion seal of the Official Purveyor of Peace. They made the exchange on the spot.

'Thank you,' said Hatch.

'It's a pleasure to be pleasing the next instructor,' said Shona. 'I wish you good luck for the evening.'

In the evening, Hatch would be returning to the Combat College, for the competitive examinations in which he was currently engaged were about to enter their practical phase. When next he entered the illusion tanks, he would not be able to lose life or single-fighters for the mere purpose of winning experience. Instead, his career would be on the line; and his family's fortunes were riding on his career.

'The evening!' said Beggar Grim, unabashed and loud as ever now that he had rid himself of the slob thrown by Shona. 'Fighting, is it? I thought as much.'

'No,' said Zoplin. 'Not fighting but whoring. He's meeting fair Shona tonight.'

'Yes,' said Shona. 'We're interrogating dogs to see which one has the honour of your parentage.'

Then she mocked a kick in Zoplin's direction, so good in her acting that Hatch winced in anticipation of impact. But blind beggar Zoplin never stirred, and the kick fell short, and Shona winked at Hatch and set off for home, taking the chocolate and leaving the Frangoni in the possession of his opium.

'Oh, Shona!' said Hatch, calling her back.

'Yes?' said Shona, turning to see Hatch standing in the road with a knife in his hand.

'Could you give this to Dog Java's mother?' said Hatch. 'Dog lives near you, doesn't he?'

'Yes,' said Shona, accepting the weapon. 'That's no problem. I'll pass it on.'

'But not to Dog,' said Hatch. 'Give it to his mother. Tell her I'm worried about her son. He's – I think he's in some kind of trouble.'

'I'll talk to him, then,' said Shona. 'If I can find him. He's often sleeping away from home these days, though I've no idea where.'

With that, Shona again set off down Scuffling Road, which led north from the lockway, passing through the commercial centre of Actus Dorum and finishing at Jara Marg, the square in which the Grand Arena stood. Shona did not dare the full length of the road, but instead took the first turn to the right and headed east along Zambuk Street.

Hatch watched her till she took that turn, and a long watch it was, but he found himself unready to be moving. He wished the moment could be perpetuated to forever – wished that the harshness of the future could be indefinitely deferred and he left in peace with the beggars. Whom he envied.

Then he sighed.

Shona was gone from sight: and it was time to be going.

'So you'll be on your way now,' said Grim, catching that sigh and divining its import.

'It'd take good gold in payment to keep me here,' said Hatch, who was not yet through with his appointments, for he was scheduled to meet with Sesno Felvus, the ethnarch of the Frangoni of Dalar ken Halvar.

'Gold I have not,' said Grim. 'But I do have a question.'

'Speak,' said Hatch.

'Is it true—'

'True!' said Master Zoplin. 'What's he wanting with truth? A good lie is half the price and three times as worthy.'

'Is it true,' said Lord X'dex, 'that stars become iron in their burning? As much I have said, and I think it a truth.'

'That much is true,' agreed Hatch, who had entirely shed his earlier impatience now that he was in possession of opium, and who still found himself in no great hurry to go to the temple and confront the continuation of his own crisis. 'Iron, sand, dust and bone, the matter of each was made in a star. Grim – your question.'

'Is it true,' said Grim, 'that the Way speaks of brotherhood.'

'The Way?' said Hatch, enjoying the luxury of these moments of folly, these moments of uncommitted idleness stolen out of the day of his commitments. 'I know of no Way.'

'He knows only the Wheel,' said Zoplin. 'Food to be turd then turd to be food, and man born of each and to each returned in turn.'

'Hush down, maggot-bane,' said Grim, scowling at Zoplin, who caught the sense of the scowl in the words and scowled back in blind response.

'The eater be eaten, the banquet his benefit,' said X'dex. 'A dog at it! Where's my forking stick?'

Bursting to a scream, Lord X'dex punched himself, then bit his knuckles and sucked on the bright red blood which started forth from the ruptured skin.

'I'm sorry,' said Hatch, fearing that X'dex was going to throw one of his fits, 'but I must be gone. I have an appointment at the temple.'

But Grim moved, a very snake in his speed, and was over the dust in a slither, striking to clutch, clutching his grime to the purple of Hatch's robes, pulling so hard on the fabric that Hatch was afraid it would tear at the shoulder.

'Temples, yes,' said Grim, starting to babble, venting saliva in a frenzy free from all his customary humour. 'Temples and teachings. Teachings the Way. Beggars be men, men be no beggars. Beds, holes, whores and a butchering.'

'What are you on about?' said Hatch roughly.

Despite himself, Hatch was frightened by Grim's garbled desperation, by the violent agony of his clutching, his questioning, his hope.

Hope!

In a beggar, that hope was terrifying.

Yet certainly Grim hoped for something, though Hatch had not yet worked out what it was. Grim hoped for it, lusted for it, and was speaking of it still, though his Pang had grown incoherent in its rupturing, and Hatch could not follow the pacing of it.

'Grim,' said Hatch.

The curtness of the address silenced the beggar's babbling. But only for a moment. Then Grim said, his words a blurting spasm, a token of torture:

'So but. So well. Is it true? Truth? Is it true, Hatch? Are we true? Are we Real?'

'Grim,' said Hatch, trying to be patient, trying to resist the urge to kick the beggar heartily and boot him away, 'Grim, I must be gone, so you must unhand me.'

'It's a nonsense, as I said it was,' said Zoplin.

But Grim was not done.

'The Nu,' he said. 'The chala. The chala. Was it? Wasn't it? Well? Is it true, or isn't it?'

'He knows you now,' said Zoplin. 'I see it in his face.'

The Eye glittered in Zoplin's left-hand eye socket, and Hatch realized that Zoplin had got the thing back off Grim while Hatch had been selling his chocolate to Shona.

'He knows us,' said X'dex, dipping a finger in the blood of his knuckles and smearing that blood round his own eye sockets. 'He knows us, knows it, but won't tell the truth. It's hidden knowledge, that's what it is, just as the man said.'

'What man?' said Hatch.

'You see!' said X'dex. 'He knows!'

'What man?' said Hatch, suddenly angry. 'I charge you to tell me! What man?'

'You tell us of god,' said X'dex. 'You tell us of god, and we'll tell you the man.'

'Yes,' said Zoplin, waving a piece of his baked yam at Hatch. 'The god is the truth of it, isn't it? All men to be brothers, that was and that will be. Not some to eat dust and some to eat chocolate.'

'I don't eat chocolate,' said Hatch, stung by the accusation.

'Ho!' said Zoplin. 'But you eat what we don't eat when god would eat otherwise.'

'Nu-chala!' said Grim, using the word as a weapon, and thus revealing the import of this dialogue. 'The Nu, the Nu-chala-nuth!'

'You speak of a religion some many years dead,' said Hatch, trying to control his shock, trying to convince himself that his shock was mere surprise and not fear. 'It's dead, a dead faith, a faith some – some twenty millennia dead.'

'Ho!' said Zoplin. 'So. So you speak for the death of gods, do you?'

'An undertaker in his spare time,' said X'dex, 'laid out the chala god then gutted his entrails for dogmeat.'

'Gutting!' said Grim. 'Come burning we'll gut, we'll be gutting.'

'Come burning?' said Hatch, his worst suspicions by now aroused.

'He talks nonsense,' said X'dex, suddenly suave in his graces, as if his earlier knuckle-biting and blood-smearing had been but a play-act. 'Accept my word, as one master of men to another. He is but a poor beggar, a thing made Unreal, so what helps him his nonsense?'

Hatch knew that by rights he should stay and shake

85

Grim till the truth fell out of him. Someone had been talking to these beggars of the Nu-chala-nuth, of the Way of Worship. And Nu-chala-nuth – why, Nu-chala-nuth was a Nexus religion which had left billions dead in the Spasm Wars. It was a fanatical Religion Militant which had burnt planets, shattered stars and wrecked the peace of the greatest transcosmic civilization known to human history.

Nu-chala-nuth!

That was strong stuff to be feeding anyone, and no stuff to be feeding the beggars of Dalar ken Halvar. Best that such doctrines sleep inside the mountain, inside the Combat College, deep in the depths of Cap Foz Para Lash. What fool had brought them to the daylight?

Hatch should have asked, should have pressed for an answer. Hot tongs and torture. But he just then had too many problems of his own to be investing his energies in the explication of a half-hinted threat, even though there was a possibility that the threat was made against the state itself.

'Our Beggar Grim should talk nonsense less, for he still has a nose,' said Hatch.

Then, in the makeshift contentment of that threat, Hatch set off for Temple Isherzan, the holy of holies which stood atop Cap Uba. He had meant to go first to House Jodorunda, but there was no time for that now. If he went to see Penelope then he would be late for his appointment with the High Priest, and that was something which could never be allowed.

As Hatch took himself and his worries west of north towards Isherzan, Shona was heading in the opposite direction, her ultimate destination being Kamjo Mojo. She was glad to have been able to help Hatch, for she liked him, for all that he sometimes incited her amiable contempt. Men are so helpless sometimes. Fancy a grown man not knowing the market value of a block of chocolate!

Round Cap Foz Para Lash went Shona, until she

gained the southern side and entered the shackland shanty town of Kamjo Mojo, the frog-hunters' colony by the swamp known as the Vomlush. Here the Yamoda River began to perish in shallows enjoyed by frogs and water buffalo alike. Here water lilies were perpetually in bloom, their red and orange flowers giving off a heavy perfume which, on a calm day, would rival Shona's favoured Nudik Martyr.

But calm days were seldom in Kamjo Mojo, for either the Hot Mouth vented furnace-dry air, or else it would be breathing in, which it did with such a ferocity that it swallowed dust, sticks, straw, stones, and any small dogs or children caught too near its lip. Either way, the Weather of Never tended to make life in Kamjo Mojo uncomfortable, as did the prolific mosquitoes of the Vomlush and the red dust of the Plain of Jars.

But it was cheap and it was home, and Shona was ever glad to get there after a day spent in the cold cream of the underworld dreamland of the Combat College. Tension, tension, tension: that was what the Combat College was all about. Unremitting pressure and stress. But here she was home, here she could relax.

She wondered about Hatch. Did he ever relax? Somehow, she doubted it. He was so intense, living as if he were responsible for everyone and everything. But that was the Frangoni way. The Frangoni had evolved a doctrine of communal and collective responsibility, but had managed to incorporate into this doctrine the notion that each individual had the ability to change the whole, and hence was responsible for the whole.

Whereas Shona . . .

Shona was of the Yara, the poor of the Pang, so poor that she scarcely existed, for who but the poorest of the poor would live out here in Kamjo Mojo, south of Yon Yo, south of anything which might possibly be thought of as civilization?

Being of the Yara, being (at least in terms of the beliefs of her people) so Unreal that she counted for no more than a shadow, she had no responsibilities, no debts, no guilts, no burdens, hence lived free. Though life in the Combat College had long ago forced her to accept that there was a strong probability that she did in fact exist, she had not let this prey on her mind, for the very teachings of the Nexus showed her that she truly did not exist, at least as far as time's final outcome was concerned.

It all burns out, in the end. Flesh, hydrogen, helium. The flesh goes down to bones and the bones to dust, and the stars die out to darkness in the end, burdened with the sands of silicon and a deadweight of iron, and then the stars are torn apart and their iron rebuilt to planets as unburnt hydrogen and helium are cooked anew to fresh-burning suns. So, in the long event of time, we none of us exist – and so, if mortality be accepted, then the mere fact of existence becomes no cause for worry.

Thus Shona lived carefree, but for the occasional niggle, one of which was the ongoing problem of keeping the secret of their gold from her husband. Shona, being sharp with a bargain and but one year short of graduation, had done well out of the Combat College, trading everything from coveralls to chocolate for forms of more permanent wealth. So far, so good – but if once her husband learnt how rich they were, he would shortly come to believe that he really existed, from which all manner of suffering would follow.

The chocolate, now. When should she be selling it? It was in blocks of bitter, so it would keep if wrapped in cellophane – of which she had plenty – and stored in the dark in a calabash, sealed against ants, and hung from the bamboo roof-ridge to be out of the way of the rats. But while it would keep it was perishable, so best to be rid of it soon.

The day before Dog Day, that was the best day to be selling. Everyone was shopping that day for delicacies to be feasted upon on the evening of the Festival of the

Dogs itself. The Chem spent in abundance then, as did the poorest of the commons in accordance with their means, and chocolate was one of the choicest of all the delicacies known to Dalar ken Halvar. So there would doubtless be a shortage of the stuff, so if the Bralsh was still in the market for it then the price might well quadruple over the norm, at least on the day.

'Business is good,' said Shona to Shona, glad to have been born with a good head for money, and born as a woman, and born into the Pang rather than the Frangoni, and born as Shona, plain Shona, and not as Asodo Hatch, Hatch of the brooding purple, Hatch of House Takabaga, Hatch of the Frangoni rock.

As Shona was thus gladdening her heart, she noticed some boys scuffling in the dust with spears, hunting an imaginary enemy. Then she saw the boys were not boys but men, and the spears were longer and heavier than those usually used for rats, frogs or fish. She wondered what kind of animal they hoped to hunt with those big heavy spears of theirs, and why they were so intense about their practice, and when they would be playing their practice for real.

CHAPTER SIX

Nu-chala-nuth: a fanatic religion which, after an organic rectifier was introduced into human affairs, sparked the Spasm Wars (technically known as the Spasm Riots, since no State of Civil War was ever officially declared by the Nexus Council), and thus precipitated the death of billions.

The Nu is the great lord, i.e. God. The Nu-chala is the servant of the great lord. The nuth are the worshippers of the servant of the lord – the members of the congregation. Consequently 'Nu-chala-nuth' may be laboriously rendered as 'the congregation which worships the servant of the lord', though a common and far preferable translation is 'the Way of Worship'.

Nu-chala-nuth is headquartered on Borboth, holiest of planets and home of the Nu-chala. Contrary to the common belief of the ignorant, the language of this planet is not Nu-chala-nuth (for scholarship acknowledges the existence of no language so named) but Motsu Kazuka.

*   *   *

> How shall I send to the wind –
> How shall I send to the sea –
> The bamboo wind of the Elephant Coast –
> The fish of the bamboo sea.

*   *   *

If one is of the Frangoni – and Hatch was of the Frangoni – then the Elephant Coast is ever one's home, regardless

90

of where one was born. But five generations previously, the people of the Elephant Coast had met defeat in a perishing war which they were as yet far from forgetting, and the burden of that defeat was that the kings of the south paid tribute to Plandruk Qinplaqus, the mind-mastering wizard of Ebber whom they acknowledged as emperor, and some of the Frangoni dwelt yet in servitude in Dalar ken Halvar.

Hatch was born in Dalar ken Halvar, and lived there, and looked set to die there, though dying was not on his mind when he went to Temple Isherzan to seek guidance from the High Priest. His problem was not death but life.

It was early afternoon on the Day of Five Fishes when Asodo Hatch climbed Cap Uba's southern slopes and entered the precincts of Temple Isherzan. At the gateway known as the Passage of Death he beat his sandals against an iron rail to remove the red dust of the Plain of Jars. He stooped to the Waters of Water, which even in reflection still sustained the purple of his features. He dipped a beaker into the water, shattering his own reflection in the ritual which is known to the Frangoni as p'dala m'thara, and which is designed to remind the pilgrim of the transience of the flesh which so briefly sustains us against the inevitability of our deaths. Hatch drank from the Waters of Water, drank from that wisdom; then, with lips wet and unwiped as ritual requires, and with a stray drop of water dripping down his chin, he climbed on up the hillpath, passing first the still-smouldering remains of a funeral pyre, then a temple acolyte who was painting a pyramid of heaped-up skulls with fresh blood.

His father's body should have been burnt here, for this was hallowed ground, and the rightful place for every Frangoni funeral. But the manner of the death of Lamjuk Dakoto Hatch had made such an honourable funeral impossible, for that death had brought shame upon Lamjuk Dakoto, and upon his children, and upon the children of his children. And so he had been burnt by the waters of the Yamoda, burnt like a dead dog, and his ashes had still to find a fitting resting place.

So, when the acolyte raised his eyes and looked at Asodo Hatch, Hatch did not meet his gaze. He tried to shrug off the memories of his father's death.

—Death is death, and can I undo it?

Thus he tried.

But he was only half-successful.

Asodo Hatch was wearing manhood's purple robes, but the acolyte wore red and black, for such were the colours of the Great God Mokaragash. Likewise coloured were the temple's totem poles. Hatch remembered reading that black and red are perennially popular with primitive tribes, since charcoal and ochre are easy to use. He tried to put this thought also out of mind, since the thought was vulgar, and the ground he trod was sacred.

—This is my God.

So thought Hatch. But the thought was faked, and he knew it. He was trying by an exercise of will to contend against the scepticism bred into him by long years of contact with the Nexus, and he was failing.

—God of my bones. God of my blood. God of my people.

Again the thought was forced and fraudulent. But Hatch matched actions to thought, bowing to the first and greatest of the graven images of the Great God Mokaragash, a huge slab of stone carved in the shape of a slovenly, almost amorphous face. The only sharply detailed features were the deep-cut shadows of the eye sockets. Mokaragash is He Who Sees Without Eyes, but He sees to a grim purpose, and the blood which stained the eyesockets was fresh.

'Lord,' said Hatch, addressing his god.

Among the Frangoni, an idol is not a symbolic representation of an entity located Elsewhere. Rather, the deity is presumed to be incarnate in the image. Thus Hatch should have been awed, humble and slightly apprehensive, since he stood in the actual presence of his god. But in truth . . .

Today he could not deny it.

Today he was seeing Temple Isherzan through the eyes of the Nexus. He could no longer forget the realms of transcosmic science and computerized ethnology simply by exiting from the lockway. The tricks of unlearning, of setting aside knowledge, no longer worked. He stood in the temple as a tourist-stranger from the Nexus, and found himself comparing the temple's people to the jabbering barbarians of the Wild Tribes of the Eye of Delusions.

—I did not choose this.

That much at least was true. Hatch had never wished to be a stranger among his own people – but then, choice had not been a part of his birthright. Asodo Hatch had been born into slavery. He was not free to choose his own destiny, for, like every Frangoni male of Dalar ken Halvar, he was bound forever in servitude to Plandruk Qinplaqus, the Silver Emperor who ruled the Empire of Greater Parengarenga.

Since earliest youth, Hatch had been attracted to the realm of Final Things. Given free choice, he would have become a priest: a master of mysteries, a keeper of numinous secrets, an inner associate of the Great God Mokaragash. But free choice had ever been denied to him, and so he had become a soldier in the service of the Silver Emperor, since that was how the lord of Na Sashimoko wished to be served.

At the age of 11, Hatch had sat the requisite aptitude tests, had passed, and had entered into the Combat College, and thus had been thrust among people who had no caste. From that day forth, everything he used was unclean, tainted by the sweat of a foreign people. The food he ate was demon-stuff fabricated out of shadow. It sustained life, yet it too was unclean.

So Hatch in his very childhood had been forced to leave the security of the Frangoni rock to dwell among

93

strangers. At puberty he was denied the gold: he entered manhood with his ears as yet unpierced. He drank green milk and ate the meat of whales, while foreign languages pressed upon his ears until he found himself waking from dreams to realize that his very sleep had been phrased in the Commonspeak of the Nexus.

Burdened by such training, it was hard for Hatch to be a Frangoni, even on the Frangoni rock.

Yet—

Hatch paused upon the heights, and looked to the east, looked out across the shackwork streets of Actus Dorum, the windings of the Yamoda River, the distant heights of Blogo Zo and the red eternities of the Plain of Jars beyond. He sometimes found that the evergaze distances of the far horizons allowed him to step outside himself, to distance himself from his own condition and thus gain insight into that condition.

Thus it was in this case, for, in the peace of the far horizons, Asodo Hatch was granted a moment of grace, and in that moment he acknowledged to himself a difficult truth. The truth was that, though his cultural laments were not faked or fraudulent, they were nevertheless secondary. He had enlarged them to primacy to hide from himself the full extent of his gripping concern for a far more urgent problem – the state of his finances.

—Admit it, Hatch, admit it.

Hatch admitted it as he resumed his upward trudge in the sunsweat heat. He admitted it reluctantly. A grand clash of cultures, a conflict of national destinies – ah, there lay drama! But that which oppressed him was the squalid greeding and grasping of commercial life, something which should not afflict a hero.

—A hero? You want to be a hero?

Yes. Hatch wanted to be a hero. Like his father. But his father, well, his father . . .

—My father was a fool.

So thought Hatch, and halted as he thought it, the stones of the Frangoni rock seeming unstable underfoot.

He could not, would not, should not, must not think such things. But he had. Thoughts themselves have consequences, and this one could not be cancelled into oblivion. It was true. The old man had been a fool. In his folly, he had gone down to grief in full view of the public, dying for, for . . .

—What did he die for?

—For nothing.

Suddenly it was pleasure, pure pleasure, for Hatch to retreat to thoughts of his finances, to a consideration of the pressures of his debts, and he concentrated on figuring gold and silver in his head as he pressed on towards the lair of the High Priest, striving to shut out all thoughts of his father and his father's fate.

Usually a High Priest in the service of the Great God Mokaragash does not undertake pastoral duties. But Asodo Hatch was a person of no small importance. After all, as a captain of Dalar ken Halvar's Imperial Guard he had the ear of the Silver Emperor himself. So, though his was not one of the Three Questions which any worshipper could put to the ecclesiarch of the Frangoni rock, Temple Isherzan's sensitivity to political nuance entitled Hatch to ask as he wished.

This was only natural.

'Every religious organization is also and necessarily a political organization. Consequently the hierarchy of any established religion tends to be dominated by individuals whose key skills are political.'

So says the Book of Politics.

Hatch remembered that wisdom as he waited on the pleasure of a junior priest. The junior was fool enough to deny knowledge of the visitor's mission, and kept Hatch waiting while certain Tablets of Appointments were laboriously consulted. Hatch had firmly committed the junior's demerits to memory by the time he was at last allowed to step into the presence of the Inner Idol.

In the presence of the Inner Idol stood Sesno Felvus, ethnarch of Dalar ken Halvar's Frangoni, and therefore necessarily High Priest of the Great God Mokaragash. Felvus, heavily burdened with ceremonial robes of red and black, was busy with pestle and mortar, grinding the bones of a dead man for ritual purposes. When at last he finished, he abluted his hands in lustral water, acknowledged Hatch with a nod.

'Greetings, my lord,' said Hatch. 'Greetings to the lord who serves the Greater Lord.'

Hatch made ritual obeisance; Felvus recited the Five Blessings; then the two retired to Felvus's private quarters. Though the shutters were open, the generous overhang of the eaves meant that the room was cool and shadowy. Coming in out of the sun, Hatch felt almost cold, and was reminded of the eternal chill of the Combat College.

The High Priest's quarters consisted of a single room only, but this was large, and made to seem enormous by height of ceiling and sparseness of furnishings. Only a single table and three chairs of woven bamboo stood on the bare flagstones of the floor. Against one wall stood a broom, a water urn, and – this last a product of the Combat College – a rolled up spongefoam sleeping mat. Such were the High Priest's possessions.

On the table was a stoneware dish heaped with cubes of sun dried scorpion bread. Sesno Felvus ate a piece, as ritual required. He offered no food to Hatch, for the bread was consecrated to the priesthood's service. Besides, this was 'a ritual of setting apart', as the Book of Ethnology has it; it demonstrated and reinforced the gulf between priest and worshipper. Hatch—

Hatch was unsettled by the unexpected renewal of the dislocating perspective of ethnology. To his dismay, he found himself again seeing all as a stranger, a visitor, an analyst from the Nexus. He fought to be Frangoni, Frangoni in crutch and fundament, in liver and lungs. But instead he was Hatch of the Combat College, Hatch of the Stormforce. Startrooper Hatch. Deepspace warrior. Transcosmic citizen.

To such a person—

What could an unwashed savage of the Frangoni rock have to offer such a person?

'Sit,' said Sesno Felvus, in a way which made it clear he had said as much already. 'Sit, Hatch. Is anything wrong? Something's wrong. What is it?'

This was a very difficult question to answer. One does not lie to a High Priest. That would be blasphemy – and, besides, Sesno Felvus was far too acute to swallow an idle deceit. So Hatch had to express his condition in words which would carry the truth yet remain palatable.

'I, ah . . . the mind plays tricks,' said Hatch. 'It happens, sometimes. When things go wrong, I . . . they teach us the Nexus, so sometimes . . . sometimes it's as if I wasn't of this world, not quite, but rather . . . I suppose it's a distancing strategy. When things get too hard I . . . one devalues the present. What is.'

'The Combat College is a different world,' said Sesno Felvus, as if he knew it well. 'I think of the Combat College as a cave. The cave of the Nexus, where shadows posture as reality. If we accept the very shadows as reality – well, if you live in a cave too long, the very sun must seem a madness. But I don't think you are as yet so deeply sunk in strangeness. Or are you? Tell me, Hatch – are we so strange to each other?'

Seated side by side, the two men were marked by superficial similarities – skin likewise purple and robes similarly styled, albeit of different colours. But Hatch – Hatch was tall and strong by the standards of his people, a warrior in the prime of life, washed, deodorized, depilated and very faintly perfumed by the miraculous machineries of the Nexus, whereas Sesno Felvus—

In extreme old age, the Frangoni purple of the High Priest's skin was tinged with brown. His eyes had faded from violet to grey. The lean and bony ancient had long, long ago abandoned the golden ear-rings of virile manhood, piercing his earlobes instead with the iron rings which denoted 'a man in the service of death', as the ritual phrase has it. The ancient had not bathed for several years, a fact which Hatch – to his shame – found shameful. It was all too easy to see Sesno Felvus as a tourist from the Nexus might have seen him. As a sample of a type. Barbarian Priest, type A-7, old; subtype B-4, rancid. For a moment, Hatch saw the man exactly thus – which was a measure of his estrangement.

'The heart is a labyrinth,' said Sesno Felvus, deducing deep inner conflicts from Hatch's silence. 'The best of us get lost in that labyrinth from time to time. Tell me, Hatch – how old are you?'

'Thirty-four,' said Hatch.

'Thirty-four!' said Sesno Felvus, as if amazed. 'Why, I've lost a year! I thought you were thirty-three, because your sister – well, enough of that. Thirty-four. A good age. Still graced with the last of youth yet mature enough to appreciate its sweetness.'

'I don't feel young,' said Hatch.

'One doesn't,' said Sesno Felvus, betraying slight amusement. 'Yet when you reach my age – oh, but I could talk all day of age if you let me. You're thirty-four. A man.'

'For what it's worth,' said Hatch.

Though his ears did not bear the gold, it was nevertheless true that he had attained a man's estate. He had been through the rites of passage, winning wisdom and self-knowledge. His confidence was that which comes from danger and hardship met, faced then overcome. Yet – yet sometimes—

'Sometimes,' said Sesno Felvus, as if picking up Hatch's thoughts, 'sometimes manhood is a puzzlement even to the best of us. I've known you since – why, since you were born.'

True. Sesno Felvus had been on hand when Hatch was still squirming in his birth-blood. Had initiated him into the outer stages of the worship of the Great God Mokaragash when he was aged but nine. Had married him to the woman of his parents' choice when he was fourteen. Had blessed his daughters. And had consoled him after his father's death, even though that death had been both sinful and shameful, an unpardonable abomination.

'It is a puzzlement,' said Hatch, in that single sentence admitting the intolerable stress he was under.

With this act of admission, Hatch felt – Hatch felt as if a bubble which had been protecting him from the world had suddenly burst. The intolerable months of training, tension, examination, uncertainty, debt, harassment, pain – it was all too much for him. His mouth opened and closed, and without warning the tears screwed themselves out of his eyes, and he could not see or breathe or speak.

Such emotion made introspective analysis impossible, though analysis would have served only to confirm that such a crisis was the inevitable result of unrelieved pressure and the long denial of all carefree reward.

Hatch wept. Openly, shamelessly. In complete default of all self-control. Sesno Felvus reached out and took his hand. The High Priest's hands were dry, and bone-hard, and firm in the assurance of their comfort, their acceptance. The comfort remained as Hatch's weeping eased, pure pain turned to a deep-felt grief at the mere fact of loss of self-control.

Then, when Hatch had cleansed himself by weeping – his body calm, relaxed and pliable, as if the collapse of self-control had answered some deep-seated biological need, massaging the tensions from his muscles and from the very linkages of his bones – Sesno Felvus began to deal with him in earnest.

Counselled by Sesno Felvus, Hatch talked his way through his problems, step by step. The pressures and uncertainties surrounding his struggle for the instructorship of the Combat College. The illness of his wife, the illness which had come upon her with full force in the last six months, and which seemed certain to kill her. His sister's delinquencies. His pressing requirements for money.

'Asodo,' said Sesno Felvus, who had never before called Hatch by his given name. 'You have never been happy in the Combat College, have you?'

'No,' said Hatch.

'I remember you as a child. Your father came to me for guidance. You were . . . you had nightmares which woke the house, and when it was time to go back—'

'I remember,' said Hatch.

In the early years of his training in the Combat College, in the years when he had still been a boy, there were times when he had fled from its cold and cream-coloured corridors. His family had several times been forced to hunt for him in Spara Slank and Childa Go, by the swamps of the Vomlush or in the streets of Bon Tray. He remembered sitting out one night on the red dust flatlands south of Cap Foz Para Lash, the night being lit by Yon Yo, the high and cold and inexplicable beacon which had ever ruled the heights of Dalar ken Halvar's southernmost minor mountain.

The boy Hatch had always been caught in the end, and always after his brief-lived truancies he had been forced to return to the Combat College. Always forced. Always compelled. He had never wanted to go back. The memory of that childhood unpleasantness was still very, very clear.

'So,' said Sesno Felvus, 'you're not one of those who welcomed your descent into the cave. And now . . . now you're scheduled to fight for the instructorship. You need to win that fight because you need the money. But . . . as for the position itself . . . as for the Combat College—'

'If I could walk away from it all then I would,' said Hatch. 'I'd never regret it. I'm not a – it's a playground. That's all. That's all it is. It's only the Free Corps which thinks it's – what? A vocation. That's what they think.

Stormforce. Stormtrooper. Nexus talk and Nexus tongue. A life. But it's a nonsense.'

'So you wouldn't regret—'

'What? Whalemeat? Green Milk? The Eye of Delusions? I can see the Eye any day, in any case. No. Nothing. I'd have no regrets. If I walked away I'd – but I need the money, I can't walk away from the money. I know the Temple's poor, so I can't, I couldn't – well. You know how it is.'

Dalar ken Halvar was not a rich city, even though it was the capital of the Empire of Greater Parengarenga. As for Temple Isherzan, it was not in any sense wealthy. Sesno Felvus did not have the luxury of being able to offer Hatch charity, and both of them knew it.

'Your problem,' said Sesno Felvus, 'is simple to state, even though it may not be quite so simple to solve. You need money desperately, and so seek to win the instructor's position at the Combat College. If you win, will that be money sufficient?'

'An instructor's pay is generous,' said Hatch. 'It will serve. If I can win the instructorship.'

'So,' said Sesno Felvus. 'So you have set your heart on winning. Selection is by competition by combat. Is that not so?'

'It is so,' acknowledged Hatch.

'A symbolic Season,' said Sesno Felvus. 'A battle in dream for a prize in the flesh.'

'That,' said Hatch, 'describes the combat well. The Combat College was founded in the flesh of the fact – however, little remains but the dreams. That's why – it's folly, the whole thing. I want my life in the flesh. If I can have it. The flesh of the world and the fact.'

'So you'd like to renounce the Combat College,' said Sesno Felvus. 'But this is your secret. Nobody else knows it. Everyone rumours that it's your dearest wish to be instructor. I've heard that you're an excellent fighter. If rumour holds truth, then there's only one other seriously in contention for the instructorship. Lon

Oliver, isn't it? Is that the young man's name?'

'Yes,' said Hatch, registering no surprise at the High Priest's impeccable intelligence.

It was no secret that, with the just-completed competitive theoretical examinations having clarified the standing of those students who were competing for the instructorship, Hatch's only remaining serious rival for the one single instructor position was Lupus Lon Oliver. Who was good. Who was very very good. Who might yet shoot Hatch down in flames. Literally in flames – for they would be duelling not with swords and spears but with single-fighters and MegaCommand Cruisers.

'Now,' said Sesno Felvus, 'Lon Oliver may win, may lose. But one thing we know of a certainty. Since Lon Oliver is the son of Gan Oliver, he has been driven since childhood by his father's ambition. Lupus Lon Oliver is of the Free Corps, hence thinks like his father. You if you lose will still have a life for yourself. But if Lon Oliver loses – for him, nothing.'

'That is so,' said Hatch.

Money aside, Hatch could walk away from the Combat College with no regrets. But Lupus Lon Oliver, like all members of the Free Corps, had made an emotional alliance with the Nexus, and to lose the instructorship would be a tragedy which would break his life.

'So, Asodo,' said Sesno Felvus, 'isn't it simple? Your friend Lon Oliver wants the job, but all you want is the money. So sell him the job. Let him bribe you. With gold to your credit, you let him defeat you in the instructorship examinations.'

'Wah!' said Hatch, taken aback by the elegance of this solution. 'But – but where would he get the gold? I'd want it in advance, I couldn't trust him to pay me afterwards.'

'Such caution is only wise,' said Sesno Felvus. 'Of course you'd want cash in advance. You'd need gold sufficient to pay off your debts and a healthy surplus to bank with the Bralsh. But that's no problem. Lon

Oliver's father, well – talk to the father if you can't get sense from the son. It matters to both of them intensely. The father's got the Free Corps' resources behind him, so—'

'But they might not do a deal,' said Hatch.

'I think refusal unlikely,' said Sesno Felvus. 'From what I hear, the betting in the Combat College runs even on yourself and Lon Oliver. Only a fool would risk losing the instructorship for a point of pride when it could be bought of a certainty at an easily affordable price. Talk to the son. If he's really such a fool, go to his father. They've got the gold, it's no problem.'

'I am in your debt,' said Hatch.

Painfully reminded, as he said it, that he was in debt to many people, mostly for cash.

'I am a servant,' said Sesno Felvus, with these words withdrawing from familiarity into the distance of ritual, and thus sealing up in secrecy the knowledge of all which had passed between them. 'I am a servant not just of the Great God but of the people. As you serve your family, as you serve your people, so it is my pleasure and my privilege to be of service to you.'

So spoke Sesno Felvus, and that was when Hatch – succoured by a priest of his religion, succoured and nourished, comforted and healed – that was when Hatch knew that he was still of the Frangoni, still truly of the Frangoni, regardless of what the Nexus had done to him. The Frangoni rock was his home, his life, his world – the place where he was accepted and protected, where he was valued and honoured.

Despite the manner of his father's death.

'There is yet one thing more which I need,' said Hatch, affirming his new knowledge to himself by meticulous attention to the rituals of his faith.

'Speak.'

'I think that Lupus Lon Oliver will yield to me in accordance with your wisdom, but maybe he will fight. If he does, then I must fight for the instructorship. If I fight

103

and win, then I will need a dispensation to accept the instructorship, for to take that job I needs must take an oath to value the Nexus more than my god.'

'Asodo Hatch,' said Sesno Felvus, becoming stern and formal, 'as High Priest of the Great God Mokaragash in the city of Dalar ken Halvar I give you a dispensation to take such an oath.'

Then Hatch thanked the High Priest, said formal words of parting, then went out into the dustlight of the sunheat day.

'Hatch,' said Sesno Felvus.

Hatch turned. The High Priest was standing in the doorway.

'What?' said Hatch, forgetting the courtesies and using a mode of colloquial interrogation which he immediately regretted.

'To survive is victory sufficient,' said Sesno Felvus.

Then nodded, then withdrew into the shadowspace of his quarters. To survive. To survive? What was the old man talking about? Life? Illusion-tank duelling? The fate of the Frangoni race? Hatch remembered one of the old sayings from the teachings of Dith-zora-ka-mako:

'Wisdom lies but a hair from the idiot.'

In Hatch's estimate, Sesno Felvus had on this occasion failed to manage that hair-fine differentiation between wisdom and . . . well, not idiocy, not exactly. But platitude. Felvus, Sesno, a platitudinous old Frangoni male . . .

But still!

Disregarding that lapse into platitudinity, Sesno Felvus had wrought a minor miracle of revelation, and Hatch felt almost lightheaded as he started off down Cap Uba, retracing his steps towards Zambuk Street.

Selling the instructorship outright to Lupus Lon Oliver, allowing his warrior's pride to be bought and sold . . . the idea was not exactly enrapturing, but . . . it was a solution! And it was so obvious! Obvious to Sesno Felvus, even though the High Priest was so far removed from the centre of immediate crisis. But of course one goes to such a person for advice precisely because such an individual, being free of the turbulence of the moment, is much better placed to consider the options and see the obvious.

But what if Lupus Lon Oliver refused to bribe Asodo Hatch in accordance with Sesno Felvus's suggestion?

What if Lon Oliver refused, and Gan Oliver refused likewise, and Hatch had to fight?

What if Hatch fought and lost? What if he lost and went down in flames, dying in the torn wreckage of a single-fighter? Burning, screaming, falling, down and down, down to the steaming jungles of Cicala or the turbid seas of Yo? What if—

'Go-la!'

Hatch stopped, startled. He was still on the temple precincts, no place for anyone to be addressing him in Nexus Ninetongue. So who—

A Frangoni?

Yes, it was a Frangoni!

No person of the purple would ever speak anything other than Frangoni upon such sacred soil. Yet here was Son'sholoma Gezira, he who was son of Vara Gezira, and there was no doubt that he had used the Nexus form of address.

Keeping company with Son'sholoma Gezira were half a dozen young men, all of whom looked anxious. They were barefooted, and wore nothing but loincloths, as befitted their station in life. All belonged to the didimo caste, and the didimo were hewers of wood and drawers of water. There was precious little wood to hew in Dalar ken Halvar, but nevertheless the caste distinctions had not weakened in the generations since the Frangoni who now dwelt in the City of Sun had departed from the Elephant Coast, and it was wrong for one of low caste to open a conversation with one of higher status on such sacred soil.

'May we speak?' said Son'sholoma, still using the

Code Seven which served as the Commonspeak of the Nexus.

'Who speaks to me here speaks to me in the tongue proper to the place,' said Hatch, phrasing his anger in Frangoni.

Only three years earlier, Hatch and Son'sholoma had been peers in the Combat College, but much had changed since then. Son'sholoma had disgraced himself, for one thing. Now Hatch spoke roughly, and he spoke in the mode of war, making his anger plain. Son'sholoma had breached the protocols fitting to Temple Isherzan. Hatch was all the more angry because his faith in the propriety of the customs of his own people was so weak – and weak at a time when he was trying to draw emotional support from his unity with the traditions of his people.

'Have I offended you?' said Son'sholoma, sounding surprised.

Son'sholoma Gezira was not prepared for Hatch to be so fiercely the Frangoni, because of course Son'sholoma had no knowledge of the truly strenuous combat of cultures which Hatch was manfully endeavouring to resolve in favour of his Frangoni half.

'Your tongue is the offence,' said Hatch, with an intolerance which rejected all his Nexus training.

The caste difference he could overlook. After all, when Hatch and Son'sholoma had trained together in the Combat College, they had shared their lives without any regard for caste. But this was not the Combat College. This was Cap Uba, the Frangoni rock, the island of refuge, the place which was theirs and theirs alone in a culture otherwise alien, and nobody should ever compromise the emotional security of that place by speaking there in a foreign tongue.

'I meant no offence, brother,' said Son'sholoma.

Hatch stiffened, quite shocked. This time his shock was quite genuine. It owed nothing to Hatch's inner conflicts. Hatch was shocked because Son'sholoma had

106

switched languages, abandoning the Commonspeak of the Nexus to phrase his apology in the Motsu Kazuka of the Nu-chala-nuth. Hatch remembered Beggar Grim speaking that very day of brotherhood, of the Way of the Nu-chala-nuth, and he remembered the beggar's terrifying hope. Hope of being first made Real then made equal, and then – most terrifying of ambitions, this – enriched out of his beggarhood into the full liberties of manhood.

Grim's beggar-babbling had made only a momentary impression on Hatch, but he was shocked rigid to find Son'sholoma Gezira speaking atop the Frangoni rock in Motsu Kazura, the tongue of the Nu-chala-nuth, a religion which should by rights have died out of memory 20,000 years ago.

'I give you five words,' said Hatch, speaking Frangoni, and again speaking very much in the mode of war.

In the Frangoni, to offer someone 'five words' was a threat. The person thus threatened had 'five words' in which to explain themselves, with the implication being that dire consequences would follow if the explanation proved inadequate.

'Brother,' said Son'sholoma, still speaking the Motsu Kazuka of the Nu-chala-nuth, albeit haltingly. 'I want you to me the teaching. You my teacher, the Way.'

His atrocious accent, his stumbling grammar, the hesitation of his tongue – all these things told Hatch that Son'sholoma had scarcely the barest rudiments of Motsu Kazuka at his command. But Son'sholoma had learnt enough of that language to ask something utterly appalling.

'I don't understand a word you're saying,' said Hatch, in his native Frangoni.

'Then understand me now,' said Son'sholoma Gezira, at last consenting to use that same Frangoni tongue. 'I and we, me and mine, myself and these with me, we wish you to induct us into the Way of the Nu-chala-nuth.'

'Then you and yours need some brain surgery courtesy of a heavy rock,' said Hatch.

'This is not a joke,' said Son'sholoma. 'We're serious.'

'Serious?' said Hatch. 'You're seriously lunatic! Motsu Kazuka, Nu-chala-nuth – are you mad? What do you want? Our own homegrown version of the Spasm Wars? This is – if I were to exhaust the thesaurus of lunacy, I could hardly find the words of it. As for me – this is my temple, the temple of my people, the temple of yours.'

'I meant no offence,' said Son'sholoma. 'But we did not think you came here to worship.'

'What else does one come to a temple for?' said Hatch, rejecting the suggestion that he was in any sense an apostate, an unbeliever, or – perish the thought! – a tourist-stranger beset by ethnological insights. 'Why else does one come here? To shit wasps, perhaps? Or bugger rocks with a broomstick? You're mad enough for both, but I'm too sane to waste my time by watching.'

Then Hatch left, or tried to.

'Wait,' said Son'sholoma, stepping in his way. 'You know the Way. You have the knowledge. It is written – it's written that anyone who knows the teachings can propagate the same, regardless of their own belief.'

That was true. The religion of the Nu-chala-nuth was strange in the extreme in that it could legitimately be preached even by an unbeliever.

'Where is that written?' said Hatch, who dearly wanted to know who was preaching Nu-chala-nuth in Dalar ken Halvar.

'It is written,' said Son'sholoma Gezira, 'in your own thesis. That is where it is written.'

'My thesis?' said Hatch.

'Yes! The thesis you wrote to gain your degree.'

'Wah!' said Hatch.

It was true. It was true. He had written a thesis which had contained an account of such teachings. But he had thought nothing of it at the time. If one writes that some have mastered the art of making the sun explode or of

108

causing the moon to drown itself in a bucket of blood, one does not usually expect such casual reference to the folly of others to lead to disaster in the literal world of the fact and the flesh.

'You know the teachings,' said Son'sholoma, pressing home his advantage. 'You know and you wrote. You—'

'Since when was simple study rash apostasy? To give an account of war, murder, rape, torture, blasphemy, plague, famine, flood and the demolition of the sun is not to extend a general invitation to the world's madmen to accomplish the fact of the same. Will you stand in my way? Stand, then! I give you five.'

Again the threat. This time, Son'sholoma was being offered a count of five in which to abolish himself, or face the immediate and unlimited consequences of his folly.

Since Hatch's anger was unfeigned, and since Hatch was built along lines which suggested an ample capacity for the breaking of rocks and the bending of iron bars, and since Son'sholoma knew appearances in this case to be by no means deceptive, Son'sholoma chose to retreat, signing his fellows to accompany him downhill.

As Son'sholoma Gezira and his half-dozen barefoot accomplices headed off down the hill, Hatch watched them go with considerable foreboding. There were not so many as a billion people in all of Parengarenga, so the teachings of Nu-chala-nuth could hardly lead to the death of billions. But even so. The Frangoni nation survived in Dalar ken Halvar only because it was socially cohesive, and at the heart of that social cohesion was the worship of the Great God Mokaragash, the tribal god which was theirs and theirs alone. Whether a baleful entity was immanent in the stone of the Inner Idol was beside the point, at least as far as the human realities of the moment were concerned. The alien religion of Nu-chala-nuth could destroy the Frangoni nation, even if it did not spark open revolution in Dalar ken Halvar as a whole.

But Son'sholoma was reckless, and full of thwarted ambition. If he could establish the religion of the Nu-chala-nuth in Dalar ken Halvar, he might thereby win a measure of power, fame and glory, if only briefly, whereas otherwise – what else was there for him?

'A pity,' said Hatch to himself, as he started to follow on after Son'sholoma.

In the Combat College, Son'sholoma Gezira had been a very promising student, gifted with great intelligence; but he had lacked the ability to master himself, and in the end his disciplinary defaults had caused him to be exiled from the Combat College. Now the lockway was forever closed against him. Therefore, since the Free Corps was equally closed to Frangoni, there was no future for Son'sholoma Gezira in Dalar ken Halvar.

As Hatch descended from Cap Uba and made his way towards his sister's house, he wondered what had made Son'sholoma think it safe to approach him with such a blasphemous proposition. Hatch could only think that his challenge for the instructor's position was being interpreted by some – or by Son'sholoma at least – as a rejection of the Frangoni.

True, there had never yet been a Frangoni combat instructor. For the last five generations the position had always gone to an Ebrell Islander, while previous to that it had usually been held by one of the Pang.

But even so—

'Strange times and dangerous times,' said Hatch, wondering if it was Son'sholoma who had been preaching the doctrines of the Nu-chala-nuth to the beggars at the lockway, and whether Hatch himself would be put to the necessity of cutting down Son'sholoma before this business was done.

CHAPTER SEVEN

Inner City: that part of Dalar ken Halvar which lies west of the Yamoda River, south of Na Sashimoko, east of the Dead Mouth and north of Yon Yo. It takes in the rocky upthrusts of Cap Gargle, Cap Uba and Cap Foz Para Lash; the Grand Arena (otherwise known as the Great Arena); the administrative quarter of Bon Tray; the commercial centre of Actus Dorum; and the slumlands of Spara Slank.

*   *   *

> So there – one house –
> The toenail with the pubic hair –
> The larynx with the liver.
> Flesh made flesh with separate faces,
> With separate hearts which in pretence
> Are said to sing in single beat –
> To sing to the beat of a single blood.

*   *   *

With his audience with the High Priest Sesno Felvus satisfactorily concluded, but with some residual anger still remaining from his confrontation with Son'sholoma Gezira, the Frangoni warrior Asodo Hatch descended from the Frangoni rock. He made his way down Cap Uba towards Zambuk Street, the arrowline west–east avenue which ran from the Dead Mouth to the Yamoda, thus dividing the northern commercial area of Actus Dorum from the southern slumlands of Spara Slank.

As Hatch descended through the sunbeat heat, he

considered deviating from his schedule to visit the Brick, the Free Corps headquarters which stood on the southern side of Zambuk Street. There he might well find Lupus Lon Oliver – or Lupus's father, Manfred Gan Oliver. They could talk. Negotiate. Make a settlement. But it might well be better to negotiate on neutral ground, or to find a third party to do the negotiating.

Besides—

Before Hatch sought to win gold from the Brick, he would have to curb the madness of his sister's spending, otherwise any new wealth which he won for his family would be dissipated in very short order.

By the time Hatch gained the soft red dust of Zambuk Street, he had decided that negotiations were best postponed. So he set out east towards the Yamoda. But he had not taken so many as three steps when he was hailed from the Brick.

'Hey, Mister Purple!'

Hatch glanced at the Brick and saw messenger boys lounging outside, as usual. The one who had hailed him was – he could not be certain of this, but guessed with some confidence – the same boy who had accosted him earlier in the day with a cheating offer from Polk the Cash, who had sought to buy Hatch's chocolate for a veritable impoverishment of opium.

'You want to buy my sister?' cried the boy. 'You sell me your dog, I sell you my sister.'

Since there was no profit to be had from trying to discipline messenger boys, Asodo Hatch – who, for the record, was not then or ever the owner of any dog, though it must be admitted that his daughter Onica was in the possession of such a beast – chose to continue east along Zambuk Street in a mode of deafness. As he did so, he automatically checked the safety of the half-dozen opium balls he had bought from Shona, finding those packages of peace still safe in a tight-buttoned document-pocket inside his robes. Initially he lengthened his stride, striving to put distance between himself and

112

the insults of the Brick without actually seeming to hurry; but the sun's heat and the aching length of the dusty road soon persuaded him to a slower pace.

Zambuk Street was one of the major avenues created by the clearance orders issued by Plandruk Qinplaqus in the first enthusiasm of his rule, which enthusiasm was by now a matter of ancient history. The Silver Emperor had meant such avenues to function as firebreaks, and thereby lessen the frequency with which his bamboo city burnt to the ground. In this he had been only partially successful, for there had been two disastrous citywide fires in Hatch's lifetime alone.

Hatch was much-dusty with the redness of the Zambuk Street by the time he reached House Jodorunda, which stood on the northern sides of the west–east avenue.

Though small, House Jodorunda was still a place of considerable pretensions, its walls built of a grey stone imported from quarries a hundred leagues distant, and its door made of solid timbers rather than the more customary bamboo weave. However, of late the house had been looking much the worse for wear. The skeletal Guardian Gods atop the roof were lopsided, broken or missing, and the Ancestral Faces painted on the door were chipped, faded, or almost elided by sunbeat and weathering.

That door stood ajar.

Hatch pushed the door wide open then entered. The ceiling here was high, the room in shadows. It was a room crowded with furniture, most of it high-class lacquerwork. Hatch knew the furniture, like the house, to be mortgaged already for more than its value.

'Joma?' said Hatch, challenging the silence with his sister's official name.

He was answered by the silence of spiderwebs, the prophecy of stone.

But then, these days his sister was not answering to Joma. Instead, she was insisting on being called by the ridiculous name which she had taken when she entered

113

upon her brief-lived marriage: Penelope Flute.

A slight splash told Hatch where to look. He strode into the bathroom and there found his sister immersed in a tub of water. This annoyed him intensely. Hatch had scant tolerance for folly, so the lunacy of his sister's bathing habits had long been a source of ireful exasperation.

'Joma,' said Hatch, endeavouring to suppress his vexation as he looked down on his waterlogged sister. 'We have to talk.'

'Do you not think,' said Penelope, looking up at him from the bathtub, 'that there is a certain degree of impropriety involved in bearding your sister in her bathroom?'

This was a question to which there was no established answer, since the Frangoni did not usually have baths, let alone bathrooms. When they wanted to wash then they went to the river just like everyone else, which was by far and away the cheapest and most sensible method of resolving the hygienic question.

'I do not consider,' said Hatch, 'that there is any impropriety involved in seeing my sister at any time when she is fully dressed.'

Penelope was so dressed, for she had been fully clothed when she had immersed herself in her tub of water. This immersion was a part of her religious praxis, for Penelope was an Evolutionist. Since dawn, the purple-skinned Frangoni female had been steeping herself in the water – which was decidedly muddy – in order to encourage her transformation into a fish. At the moment of the Changing of Forms, her clothes would become scales, hence she was careful never to get wet unless she was wearing them.

Penelope believed her transformation to a piscatorial mode of existence to be imminent, for thus she had been advised by her Perfect Master, whom she believed to be infallible. The Perfect Master in question was Edgerley Eden, a centaur who dwelt in Hepko Cholo, an urban

114

enclave to the east of the Yamoda River. Eden claimed his own transformation into centaur shape to be proof of the coming General Evolution, of which he had knowledge (or so he said) thanks to his studies under an alleged Hermit Crab of Untunchilamon, an improbable individual said to be a philosopher a billion years old.

Now it was a matter of record that anyone who cared to pay the entrance fee could penetrate the Temple of Change in Hepko Cholo and gaze therein upon the horseflesh-manflesh configuration which constituted Edgerley Eden's corporeal form. Hatch had never been, but knew several reliable witnesses who had, including his own elder brother (Oboro Bakendra) and the ever-reliable Shona of the Combat College. On occasion, Hatch had also seen Eden from a distance when the centaur was promenading in the open sunlight, or bathing in the Yamoda.

Yet if Eden had truly chosen this centaur form of his own free will – which was what he claimed – then his choice was illogical in the extreme. For if the world was truly to be inundated by a Great Flood – which was what Eden taught, and what all Evolutionists believed – then it was hard to see how the possession of a horse's legs, belly and tail would be conducive to either happiness or survival. Unfortunately, this note of illogic had yet to strike Penelope herself, even though she had personally decided to meet The End Of The World As We Know It in the form of a catfish.

For his part, Hatch thought the whole of evolutionary theory to be but a total nonsense.

As for this alleged Hermit Crab, enlightened philosopher and Evolutionist extraordinary – well, Hatch had seen the crabs of both land and sea in the course of his peregrinations round Parengarenga, and was convinced that your average crab is no more enlightened than a scorpion. To imagine an unaverage Crab that gave lofty lectures on the Victory of Mind over Form was quite beyond his capacity.

115

In search of confirmation of his own scepticism, Hatch had consulted with the Combat College, which to his great satisfaction had given him an absolute assurance that there was no such thing as an intelligent crab, let alone a talking crab. This the Combat College had proved out by an exhaustive search of every available database. Crabs were recorded on a great many of the billions of worlds known to humanity, but not one such animal had yet advanced to the stage of needing to learn its table manners.

Thus Edgerley Eden's Hermit Crab was confirmed as an impossibility.

As for Eden himself, a centaur in the flesh – why, there was no great mystery about that, since centaurs were common in the Permissive Dimensions. Indeed, on some worlds known to the Combat College databases, centaurs were almost as common as dragons. All in all, it was quite reasonable to presume that Eden had been born into a small population of centaurs existing some-where within a lifetime's travelling distance of Dalar ken Halvar, for all that Eden claimed to have been born as a human on the Ebrell Islands, and to have ventured to Untunchilamon as a humanformed pirate.

Be that as it may, Penelope was certainly enraptured by Eden and his teachings, and donations consequent upon her devotion had led her into debt. There was also the cost of the bath and deliveries of bathwater to bear in mind. Outside of the Combat College, there was no such thing as running water in Dalar ken Halvar, so every drop used for every purpose had to be lugged from the Yamoda River, and such lugging was expensive if done in any great quantity.

'Joma,' said Hatch, again challenging his sister with her lawful birthname.

'My name,' said Penelope, with that studied female insolence which she had brought to such a pitch of perfection, 'is Penelope. That's my name. If you want to speak to me, then use it.'

Hatch brought his wrist to his mouth then kissed it in the Frangoni manner, seeking thereby to moderate his anger.

'Penelope, then,' said Hatch, still struggling to control the rage which threatened to upset his judgement as he looked down on the woman in the bathtub. 'Penelope. We must talk.'

Penelope closed her eyes. She had perfected this manoeuvre during a previous spasm of religious enthusiasm. Her last Perfect Master had believed (or had claimed to believe) that sleep is the better part of life, and that wakefulness is at best a necessary evil. One of his sidelines had been organizing orgies, since he had held orgiastic excess to be the best available soporific. (Hatch had argued about this, claiming that there was nothing to beat a good solid blow on the head for ensuring unconsciousness, but he had lost that argument, or at least Penelope had claimed he had lost it.)

'Laa-mo,' hummed Penelope.

It was the going-to-sleep mantra taught to her by her previous Perfect Master.

Hatch fished a sodden sponge out of the foot-bowl by the bath. He kissed it, then let it fall. Obedient to the basic laws of physics, the sponge accelerated under the gravitational pull of the planet, and, like a meteorite dragged in from the cold and vacuumous wastelands of outer space, it went hurtling down through the atmosphere until it slammed into Penelope's face.

'Wah!' said Penelope, waking up in great hurry.

'Don't fool around,' said Hatch, allowing a hint of his anger to show, 'because I'm not in the mood. You're in debt to the tune of half a hundred scorpions, which is just a fraction less than the worth of your flesh.'

A scorpion was a gold coin issued by the Silver Emperor. It was exactly equivalent in value to the zeal issued by the Bralsh. The zeal, however, was a small ring of nine-carat gold bearing interior and exterior banker's marks, whereas the scorpion was a thin coin with a milled edge, with a crown imaged on the face and, on the obverse, the pincer-wielding arachnid for which it was named.

'Half a hundred!' said Penelope. 'I'm worth more than that.'

'No you're not,' said Hatch. 'Polk the Cash has had a valuer take a look at you.'

'He's done no such thing,' said Penelope. 'I'd have known.'

'You wouldn't have known,' said Hatch. 'They're very discreet.'

'How can he tell what I'm worth when he never saw me with my clothes off?'

'Female, Frangoni, age twenty-five, tall, big-breasted,' said Hatch. Value, forty-nine crowns and a fraction. I saw the report myself. You're worth just less than the money you owe.'

'So what do you expect me to do about it?' said Penelope.

'You'd better do something,' said Hatch. 'Because Polk is threatening to claim you as his slave.'

'Then let him threaten,' said Penelope.

She was either carefree or thoughtfree, one or the other. Certainly she had never got to grips with the management of money, for this is part of that greater discipline of managing oneself, and Penelope had lived largely unmanaged either by herself or by anyone else.

'He's got a buyer already,' said Hatch, striving to make the woman see sense, though he suspected there was no more profit to be had from arguing with Penelope than in arguing with a goldfish. 'The buyer is from the Stepping Stone Islands. He'll take you north, never to be seen again.'

'That's a nonsense,' said Penelope.

'What do you mean, a nonsense?' said Hatch.

'Just that. I can't be sold, because I'm someone's slave already.'

'Whose?' said Hatch.

'The Silver Emperor's, of course.'

'What are you talking about?' said Hatch, intensely irritated by this nonsense.

'We're all his slaves,' said Penelope. 'We Frangoni, I mean.'

'No!' said Hatch, dismayed by the immensity of this error. 'You're not his slave at all. Only the men are his slaves.'

'What do you mean, only the men?'

'Just that,' said Hatch, wondering if his sister really was this ignorant or if this was her idea of a joke. 'Only the men are his slaves. The women are free. That's the law.'

'Why do the men always get the good things?' said Penelope.

'Because that's how the world was made,' said Hatch. 'So you're free, and because you're free, you can be bought and sold, which means – Penelope, you've really gone too far this time. Polk can come in here and claim you. Which is exactly what he's going to do. Then he'll sell you to this foreigner, and that man, that man can rape you at will or – or cut off your hair and sell it!'

Hatch hoped to terrify Penelope into a realization of the precariousness of her own position, and thereby to curb the increasing recklessness of her spending. It was possible that, by doing a deal with Lupus Lon Oliver in accordance with the wisdom of Sesno Felvus, Hatch would shortly be in a position to pay off Penelope's debts. But that would bring no joy to anyone if she simply went out and mortgaged herself all over again.

Yet in his attempt to terrify, Hatch proved less than adequate.

'Rape me!' said Penelope scornfully. 'Is that what he'll do?'

'Yes,' said Hatch, who truthfully thought that there was a strong probability that anyone who bought Penelope as a slave would do exactly that.

'So what do you care?' said Penelope.

'I'm your brother,' said Hatch. 'Of course I care. I don't want to see you taken, kidnapped, stolen, sold.'

'So what do you want?' said Penelope, with surprising bitterness.

'Why,' said Hatch. 'I want what any brother would want for his sister. To see you married and pregnant.'

Hatch was trying hard. Among the Frangoni, fecundity was highly valued, and one of the politest things one could say to a woman was 'May you soon be pregnant.' Hatch seldom said any such thing to his sister, for such formal politeness was not commonly required between brother and sister. But he felt that the stress of the moment called for an extra effort.

'Married!' said Penelope. 'Pregnant! Since when have you wanted me either? It was because of you I had to murder my husband.'

'Grief of a dog!' said Hatch. 'We're not going to go into that again, are we?'

'Why not?' said Penelope. 'This is my husband we're talking about. Not a – a flowerpot!'

'Oh come on,' said Hatch, annoyed by Penelope's quibbling pettishness. 'A fine young woman like you can always get another husband.'

'That's not the point,' said Penelope. 'I had one, and now he's dead.'

'Of course he's dead,' said Hatch, infuriated by Penelope's obtuseness. 'That was the whole point of getting him married. You knew that before you went into it.'

'Yes, yes, but you're my brother, so what could I do? You made me a murderer!'

'As I recall,' said Hatch, making a heroic attempt to govern the passion of his mounting rage, 'it was me who did the killing. All you had to do was step outside.'

'That's all!?'

'Well, yes,' said Hatch, who thought he had now won this argument, and that Penelope should acknowledge as much. 'Stop making such a fuss! I mean, you weren't in love with him or anything. Were you?'

'What would you know about it?'

'Well, of course you weren't. You never even met him till you were married, and then—'

'Then you killed him!' said Penelope.

'If it hadn't been for me,' said Hatch, deeply vexed by this continued onslaught, 'you'd never have married him in the first place. You'd never even have met him. I found him for you, so it was thanks to me—'

'Yes. You found him. So you're responsible!'

'Responsible?' said Hatch, baffled by this display of female irrationality. 'Responsible for what?'

'For killing him!' screamed Penelope. 'For killing my husband! Murder, bloody murder, killing him, cutting his throat, stabbing him, slashing him, blood, blood, blood everywhere, you killed him, and he was mine, and – and – and I – I – loved him!'

With those final words, her hysteria stammered into irreconcilable grief, and she burst into tears.

Hatch still had no clear conception of what, if anything, he might have done to upset her. True, he had killed her husband, but it should be pure pleasure for a Frangoni girl to help her brother encompass a necessary murder. And even supposing the experience did not prove to be an unalloyed pleasure, it was still a duty for a sister thus to help a brother. But . . . well, if marriage really meant so much to her . . .

'If marriage really means so much to you,' said Hatch, 'you could always marry me.'

This was a very great-hearted and self-sacrificing gesture, for Hatch did not by any means want to marry his sister. She knew him well, very well indeed, and he was a true Frangoni male in that he was ever uneasy in the presence of any female who knew too much about him. The Frangoni consider it best to bed with strangers, for to bed with someone is to be emotionally vulnerable, and a stranger is more likely to be ignorant of one's weak points. Consequently, among the Frangoni a brother will rarely marry his sister except under the compulsion of a compelling duty.

Penelope squeezed the tears out of her eyes, mastered her sobs, then said:

'You? You're offering to marry me?'

'Yes,' said Hatch, already regretting the offer, but putting a good face on it. 'It might stall Polk for a month or two.'

'Stall Polk!' said Penelope, sorrow turning to outrage. 'I should marry you for that? You! Marry you!?'

'Why, yes,' said Hatch, starting to feel offended. 'Why shouldn't you marry me?'

Asodo Hatch did not consider himself thin-skinned. Nevertheless, when a man invites a woman to marry him, he is apt to be disconcerted if her reaction is one of baleful fury, and Hatch, being in many ways a very average and conventional man, was so disconcerted.

'Marry you?' screamed Penelope. 'You with your wife on drugs and dying? You with your fancy whore on the top of the hill?'

'The Lady Iro Murasaki,' said Hatch coldly, 'is not a whore.'

'She's a whore! A whore, a bitching whore! But I'm no whore, I'm smarter than her, I know you through and through, I'm your sister, I won't be fooled or whored!'

With that, Penelope hurled the wet sponge at Hatch, or tried to. But she underestimated the difficulty of hurling something while fully clothed and recumbent in a wooden bathtub half full of water. She banged her elbow painfully – and howled.

Hatch looked down on the woestruck woman with dismay.

Howling broke to sobbing, and in her sobbing Penelope choked out a heartbroken accusation.

'You killed him to rape. To rape me. That's why. You wanted me, wanted me, that's why you killed him. Rapist!'

The situation was painfully difficult, particularly as Hatch felt duty-bound to question his own heart. Had he truly cut down Darius Flute simply so he could take possession of his own sister? Hatch decided the claim was fatuous. He had absolutely no desire for his sister, even though she bore upon her nose the ceremonial blue and green tattoos which denote a woman who has killed and castrated a would-be rapist. Several ethnologists have written that Frangoni males are inevitably aroused by the implicit challenge posed by such tattoos, but Hatch was not aroused at all. Even though he knew those tattoos to be true to their boast, he found them distinctly unproductive of desire – an unpleasant reminder of a squalid episode which he would much sooner forget.

'I don't want you,' said Hatch. 'I never have. I never will.'

'Never!' said Penelope.

And, unable to bear such a brutal rejection of her womanly charms, she started to howl again.

Hatch was glad to hear someone at the door, which gave him an excuse to escape from the bathroom, back to the crowded lacquerwork luxury of the outer room. But on venturing to that outer room he was somewhat dismayed to find that the interloper was his elder brother, Oboro Bakendra Hatch. The black-bearded Oboro Bakendra was three years his senior, and was a fanatical priest of the Great God Mokaragash. Relations between the brothers had deteriorated markedly since Oboro Bakendra had joined the priesthood three years earlier, on quitting the Combat College.

On joining the priesthood, Oboro Bakendra had demanded that Hatch cut short his studies in the Combat College and join likewise. Hatch had protested his devotion to the Silver Emperor, the great Plandruk Qinplaqus, whose obedient slave he was. Whereupon Oboro Bakendra had obtained from the great Qinplaqus a dispensation permitting Hatch to quit his military studies in favour of a religious career if he so chose.

Upon which Hatch had been forced to acknowledge to himself that any career in the service of the Great God Mokaragash would be intolerable if it took place in the shadow of his elder brother Oboro Bakendra, who had inherited the stubbornness, the overbearing arrogance and the explosive anger of their father Lamjuk Dakoto Hatch.

Hatch's decision to remain in the Combat College had led to something of a breach between the two brothers.

As far as Oboro Bakendra was concerned, his younger brother Asodo was polluting himself by his intimate relations with Outsiders. Asodo Hatch was working with the unclean, he was eating with the unclean, and it was an open secret that he was even sleeping with one of the unclean in the manner of lust. Oboro Bakendra had continued to insist that Hatch should abort his Combat College training, and had become more and more insistent as it started to become obvious that Hatch had a good chance of landing a permanent position in that College.

'Hatch!' said Oboro Bakendra, as Hatch emerged from the bathroom and entered upon the outer room.

'I was just leaving,' said Hatch. 'Penelope is all yours. She's in the bath.'

From the bathroom there came a crash, followed by a scream of female rage. Penelope had started throwing things. As a small girl, she had once knocked out her grandfather with a watermelon, and her temper had not mellowed since.

'It's not her I'm looking for,' said Oboro Bakendra. 'It's you!'

Oboro Bakendra had come to discipline his younger brother, and he had not come alone. Hatch was conspicuously large, and one of the problems of being a big man is that anyone minded to pick a quarrel with you is going to be forewarned of the need for adequate preparations.

The strength of Oboro Bakendra's preparations

became clear as others came crowding into House Jodorunda behind him – his sidekicks and backkicks, a group of like-minded fanatics all armed with sticks. These were not snake-breaking sticks or rods for the chastisement of dogs. Rather, they were knurled and knubbly hardwood clubs built for the breaking of men – or the battery of elephants. And Hatch knew at once that he was in trouble. Nexus battle doctrine holds that one can fight six, but not if the six have each been trained to fight six – and no adult Frangoni male was innocent of the means of slaughter. Hatch started to think he might be better off back in the bathroom with Penelope.

'Well, gentlemen,' said Hatch. 'What can I do for you?'

'Gentlemen, gentlemen,' said Oboro Bakendra. 'Flattery, is it? The Age of Flattery is an age long gone, brother mine. This is an Age of Righteousness, an age of punishing wrath.'

Hatch was alarmed by the underlying note of womanly hysteria in his brother's histrionics. Oboro Bakendra was winding himself up through rhetoric, which vice, among the Frangoni, has ever been one of the preludes to war. Oboro Bakendra's sidekicks and backkicks were sweaty, tight-knuckled, over-focused, fast-breathing. And suddenly Hatch was afraid, afraid of the wood and the iron, the tight-wound sinews and the bunched muscle-backed bone. Vividly he felt—

He fought his imagination but he felt—

He felt for a moment his teeth snapped back, his jaw clipped to a gurgling crackle as bones in their breakage—

'Answer me!'

Oboro Bakendra was shouting, and Hatch in his fear had lost the thread of Oboro Bakendra's rhetoric.

Hatch was so badly frightened that his reaction was anger. He felt the emotions of muscle tightening his focus, gearing him up for battle or breakage, for berserker destruction in the Frangoni battle-mode.

125

'Answer you,' said Hatch, in defiance. Then he caught himself abruptly, and then said – forcing his voice to be soft, to be tender, to be cadenced as a woman's comforting is cadenced – 'Answer you? Why, brother mine, you're the one with the answers. You're older, hence wiser. You have the answers. I need but hear them, for to hear – my brother, to hear is necessarily to obey.'

'What speaks?' said Oboro Bakendra, his anger not one whit diminished. 'Hatch speaks, or fear speaks?'

This was an accusation of cowardice. Hatch was incensed. He shook with a shuddering fury. He had been born and bred to be strong, valorous, war-glorious and victorious in courage. He had been to war and had proved his blood a hundred times over. But now, now in the shadows of a debt-ridden house, his pride was being smirched, his self-image assaulted, and he did not think he could bear it any longer.

He made as if to move his hand to his lips to kiss it, and thus placate his own anger with ritual. Yet he restrained himself. When man confronts man, such a gesture is ever construed as an admission of weakness.

—The hand.

In extremis, Hatch remembered a Nexus exercise taught in the Combat College as a measure for controlling rage. He extended his hand, making the fingers light, making them sensitive antennae, conduits of energy. He rested his hand lightly, lightly on the nearest object of convenience – a lacquerwork table, its top richly designed with eels and fish. He let his fingers rest upon the table-top, stressing their lightness, and imagined his anger running out through those fingers, dissipating, vanishing.

His anger eased.

'Is my brother a coward?' said Oboro Bakendra.

'Tell him your challenge,' said Hatch, realizing that mere surrender was not going to get him out of this in one piece. 'Tell him your challenge, then you will know him in his nature.'

'The challenge is this,' said Oboro Bakendra. 'You will call your dog to heel. Or else!'

'My dog?' said Hatch.

What was the man riddling about?

Hatch presumed that no actual member of the canine tribe was being referred to, for certainly (it has been stated once above, and let it be stated here a second time in confirmation of the proof of the fact) he owned none such. In fact, his entire household was dog-free but for the mutt which his daughter Onica had got from the Lady Murasaki, and that small and tender animal had never been any trouble to anyone. But after all literal dogs had been examined and discounted, Hatch still had no idea what his dear brother Oboro Bakendra might be referring to.

'Your dog Gezira!' said Oboro Bakendra.

'Son'sholoma?' said Hatch.

'The same,' said Oboro Bakendra. 'He's been preaching the Nexus, preaching the Nu. Borboth, Borboth, Motsu Kazuka. Bring him to heel, Hatch! It's blasphemy, and it's your dog which speaks it.'

'That reckless apostate fool is no dog of mine, nor cat neither,' said Hatch. 'Still, I've already called him to order as best I can, and there's an end to it.'

'Oh no, oh no,' said Oboro Bakendra. 'He's on the loose, not him but six of them, this Nu, this chala, and all from your thesis. He told me! The blasphemy of gods, you wrote it down. They say—'

'I know what they say,' said Hatch. 'Or can guess.'

'Then do something about it!'

'What can I do?' said Hatch. 'I am but the emperor's slave. It's not for me to give law in Dalar ken Halvar, not to Son'sholoma, no, nor to any other. I'm a slave, even as you are. What I can do, you can do.'

'I've not been within knifestrike of the emperor since my father's funeral,' said Oboro Bakendra. 'Nor am I likely to be within this month or next. I've not set foot on Cap Ogo Boch for months, whereas you – you're in and out of Na Sashimoko as if it were your second home.'

'If I'm diligent in service,' said Hatch, 'then what of it? Naturally I'm in and out of the imperial palace. On occasion. But so what? Does that make me rich? Powerful? I doubt either. If visiting palaces brings power, then the man who daily searches the nightsoil from Na Sashimoko should be emperor himself by now! But for all the wealth of his buckets he's nothing, and I likewise.'

'Don't lie to me!' said Oboro Bakendra, thumping his fist on a lacquerwork table.

Hatch took a half-step back. Since his earliest youth, he had ever feared his elder brother's temper. And certainly Oboro Bakendra had cause to be angry, for Hatch had certainly been lying. While it was most doubtful that the Silver Emperor would do so much as raise his little finger to help sort out religious disputes on the Frangoni rock, he would still in all probability give Hatch an authorization to resolve this little religious uprising as he saw fit.

Which would mean that Hatch would be free to murder the apostate Son'sholoma Gezira and his followers discreetly at a time and place of his choosing. But frankly—

'Frankly,' said Hatch, 'I've no more belly for blood.'

'You bitched your sister's husband good and quick,' said Oboro Bakendra. 'Why not Gezira, then? He's a fighter, perhaps? Is that it? Is that your nature, Hatch? A killer of the unkilling, a coward in the face of killers – that's you. If it's fear, well, we'll give you something else to fear if you—'

'Brother,' said Hatch, again with the grace of a woman, 'brother, you came for the family good, for the good of the tribe. Whatever speaks, it speaks for the good which you sought. Speak, that I may know your wish, that I may know your will.'

'You're in a very ready mood today,' said Oboro

128

Bakendra, who was searching for a fight rather than for reconciliation.

'I have been too long away from my family,' said Hatch, lapsing into ritualistic formality. 'I have been feeling my want.'

'So,' said Oboro Bakendra. He clicked his tongue, and his hand went tap-slap-tap against his thigh – both gestures to which he habitually resorted to in moments of indecision, though Hatch doubted that he was aware of his own mannerisms. 'So,' said Oboro Bakendra. 'So. You take instruction, do you?'

Now Hatch was calm. He had lived through his anger, had accepted that anger, and had dissipated it. In the aftermath of his anger, he felt as if he were floating. He felt very calm. Very clear. He thought for a moment to say: I am yours to command. Then checked himself. That was something a citizen of the Nexus might say, but this was not the Nexus. This was Dalar ken Halvar, and Oboro Bakendra was of the Frangoni rock.

Hatch could simply surrender to Oboro Bakendra and agree to everything Oboro said, but Oboro might think such surrender insincere, or a proof of cowardice. So Hatch decided to invoke again the Frangoni family, the Frangoni blood, the Frangoni nation – and attempt to surrender to that.

'You are ever the eldest,' said Hatch. 'So the family has been much your concern. Still, as I am grown to a man's estate, it is fitting that I too should meet the concerns of the family.'

'You say,' said Oboro Bakendra.

Oboro Bakendra was reluctant to concede a truce. Hatch knew what the problem was. The anticipation of conflict is so stressful that one's every resource goes towards gearing for battle. This is why it is very, very difficult to argue an angry man out of his rage: because his rage demands all his resources, and there is no part of him free to consider the possibility of conciliation.

129

'I was born to the blood,' said Hatch. 'Can I unblood myself, unbirth myself, or make myself unmothered? This is my sister's house, my brother's shadow. I am of the family, and you speak for the family.'

'This I should have heard earlier,' said Oboro Bakendra.

And Hatch knew that he had won, or at least was starting to win. This crisis could still end in violence, but Hatch believed he had almost defused it.

In argument, the natural temptation was always to justify oneself, and the need for self-justification was so much a part of Frangoni culture that it sometimes outranked the organic imperatives of physical survival. But in a yes–no conflict, to justify oneself was necessarily to unjustify one's opponent.

Hatch had found a third way, yielding to the higher good of the Frangoni family, and leaving his own dignity at least partially intact both in his own eyes and those of his brother.

As Asodo Hatch and Oboro Bakendra Hatch confronted each other, the pair of them almost but not quite having reached the stage of reconciliation, they heard a voice outside.

'Hatch!' said the voice. 'Asodo Hatch! Are you in there?'

Hatch knew that voice. It was Lupus Lon Oliver, the bright-sharp Free Corps warrior who would shortly be fighting him for the Combat College's instructorship – unless they could make alternative arrangements for the disposition of the job.

'I'm in here,' said Hatch.

'Then come out! Or may I come in? I need to talk to you. I need to talk to you about Gezira, Son'sholoma Gezira.'

Hatch looked at Oboro Bakendra, who said, roughly:

'Go to him, then. You see? I'm not alone in thinking your dog needs a beating!'

So Hatch went outside to meet with Lupus Lon Oliver,

wondering exactly how much trouble Son'sholoma had managed to cause by his blasphemous preachings, and wondering yet again whether he would truly be forced to kill Son'sholoma before this thing was through.

CHAPTER EIGHT

Free Corps: an association of Combat College graduates and their ideological allies. It is currently governed by Manfred Gan Oliver, who has his headquarters in the Brick, a building located on the southern side of Zambuk Street in the gap between Cap Foz Para Lash and Cap Uba. The free Corps is dominated by Ebrell Islanders.

*　　*　　*

> In the City of Sun
> In the sun of the Season:
> Two swords and two shadows –
> You know the story.

*　　*　　*

Lupus Lon Oliver saluted Asodo Hatch when that Frangoni warrior ventured from the shelter of House Jodorunda; and Hatch for a moment was positively glad to see this enemy of his, so tense had been the confrontation with Oboro Bakendra.

Though Lupus Lon Oliver had seemed considerably upset by someone or something when Hatch had seen him last in Scuffling Road, the Ebrell Islander had by now recovered his usual confident composure, and boldly informed Hatch that he was wanted at the Brick.

'My father wishes you to invoke your demonic features in the Brick,' said Lupus, attempting by this jocular elaboration of his message to deny the obviously embarrassing fact, which was that he was being used as a messenger boy.

Lupus Lon Oliver spoke of course in Code Seven, that dialect of the Nexus Ninetongue which served as the Nexus Commonspeech. Since Lupus was an Ebrell Islander, the language of his birth was Dub; but in his daily dealings he always favoured the Commonspeech.

'Since the Brick lies on my homeward path,' said Hatch, 'I am agreeable to – to . . .' Here Hatch paused while he struggled against temptation. Asodo Hatch was direly tempted to say that he was ready 'to see the thog', since the day's earlier dealings with the wit of beggars had left him with an indelible awareness of Manfred Gan Oliver's essential thoggishness. But he controlled himself, and concluded: 'I am agreeable to granting him an audience.'

With that, the pair set off down Zambuk Street, heading west into the bloodlight of the evening. At certain times of the year, anyone travelling west along Zambuk Street could see the sun set directly between Cap Uba and Cap Foz Para Lash, but in this season the setting sun was invisible behind one or the other of those great rocks.

But which?

Hatch did not know. He should have known, but had long since forgotten. This was itself a measure of his profound estrangement from his own city, his own times, his own place, his own people. He saw the suns of the worlds of the Nexus more often than he saw the local star of his own planet.

'Were you in there with your sister?' said Lupus, as the two men headed toward the Brick.

'With my brother,' said Hatch. 'With Oboro Bakendra. He was talking about Son'sholoma.'

Lupus absorbed that in silence.

An odd couple they made, Hatch and Oliver. For Asodo Hatch was a Frangoni built over-large; his hair, uncut from birth, was tied in a complex knot on top of his head, and thus made him look taller yet; his sweeping robe was of unbroken purple, and the inevitable effect of the flowing lines of such a one-piece garment is to increase the apparent height of the wearer. In short, Hatch looked a veritable giant, and had exacerbated his bigness by doing so much body-building with weights that the upper half of his trunk looked as if it had been pumped up with air.

Hatch, then, bestrode the earth like a veritable colossus, his big feet tromping over the dust, his big meaty hands swinging by his sides like a couple of lethal weapons, whereas Lupus Lon Oliver was so under-sized that he positively had to scuttle to keep pace with the Frangoni warrior.

Lupus wore a big, wide midriff belt of a leather coloured the same red as his Ebrell Island skin, and in a sheath suspended from that belt he carried a big heavyweighted disembowelling knife. Hatch maintained a wary awareness of that knife, for he by no means underestimated the young man Lupus. After all, as the Frangoni saying has it: 'The smaller the rat, the sharper the teeth.'

As the two men went westward along Zambuk Street, the sun set. They continued in the darkness, not hurrying, but still overhauling the lumbering buffalo carts which laboured through the rutted darkness of the dust, the presence of each cart marked by the red-star glimmer of the oil lamp which the law required from every vehicle that chose to travel the city streets after dark. The oil which burnt in those lamps was that of the slunk, the notorious grease-eel of the Yamoda River, and as it burnt it gave off a stench like that of burning hair.

'Lupus,' said Hatch, when after a long walk they neared the Brick, 'I have a . . . a . . .'

How should he put it? How did one go about this business of soliciting a bribe?

'A proposition?' said Lupus.

There was a note of not-quite-repressed hope and expectation in Lupus Lon Oliver's voice. Earlier in the day, the young Ebrell Islander had hoped and expected to see the high-muscled Asodo Hatch assassinated by Dog Java, but the cowardly Dog had failed in his task in a truly disgraceful fashion, collapsing in a dead faint at Hatch's feet. As Lupus had been quite unable to nerve Dog to a fresh attempt at murder, and as Lupus deemed it too risky to strike down Asodo Hatch with his own hand, Lupus was quite ready to countenance the possibility of making some kind of bargain with his enemy.

'A proposition, yes,' said Hatch, feeling a slight but inescapable gratitude for the nimbleness with which the Ebrell Islander had divined the nature of his approach. 'Precisely.'

'Then,' said Lupus, leapfrogging a dozen steps in the bargaining process, 'what's your price?'

'My price?' said Hatch. He had thought to begin by outlining the nature of the offer, but Lupus had already quickfooted his way through all that without a word being spoken. It took more than a moment for Hatch to grasp what had happened, but then he recovered himself and said: 'Oh, the price, yes, yes, the price, Scorpions, of course. Gold, in advance. Three hundred scorpions, that should cover it.'

'Fifty,' said Lupus promptly.

'Lupus, Lupus,' said Hatch, feeling something of the same exasperation he had felt when he confronted his sister. 'Are we two merchants to be haggling over details?'

'You're right,' said Lupus. 'It's wrong for us to haggle. So take my fifty and be done with it.'

Here was all the traditional arrogance and impudence of the Ebrell Islanders, the self-styled master race, a breed of men forever cocky and over-sure of themselves.

'It's clear to me,' said Hatch, 'that you're in no mood to deal this out seriously. So if you can't clinch a deal here and now, I'll talk it out with your father.'

The lights of the Brick were but a hundred paces ahead, which left very little time for them to talk. But Lupus grabbed Hatch by the robes and pulled him to a halt.

'Three hundred, then,' said Lupus.

'Done,' said Hatch.

'But only—'

'You're haggling!'

'No, no,' said Lupus. 'This isn't haggling. Haggling is details, a hundred scorpions, fifty, who cares. But this isn't details, this is important. I want your sister.'

'Joma?'

'She calls herself Penelope,' said Lupus.

'Penelope, then,' said Hatch, conceding the point readily in the fullness of his relief. 'You want her? Very well! Take her! But I warn you, she's killed and castrated one already. A camel driver, she was thirteen, and underneath Yon Yo—'

'I know the story,' said Lupus, cutting short the flow of Hatch's relief. 'Don't worry, I can handle her. But. But there's a problem.'

'What?' said Hatch suspiciously.

'My father. He doesn't like the idea.'

'You – you've talked this out with your father already?'

'I've told him, yes,' said Lupus. 'I've told him I want to marry your sister, and he—'

'Marry her!' said Hatch in amazement.

'Why, yes, yes,' said Lupus, impatiently. 'When one loves a woman, when one—'

'Love!' said Hatch, in further amazement.

The idea of the rat-sized Lupus being in love with the mass, bulk and obstinance of the heroically proportioned Penelope was so ludicrous that Hatch burst out into frank and open laughter. He could not help himself.

'You mock my passions?' said Oliver in anger.

'Mock?' said Hatch, struggling to control himself. 'No. But – but – my sister? You? In love?'

'What else did you think?' said Lupus.

'Oh,' said Hatch, grinning in the dark, 'I thought you might want her as a slave, you know, to take to bed and ravish. But – well – marriage?'

'It's what I want,' said Lupus fiercely.

'Yet your father opposes it.'

'Yes.'

'But he'd let you have Penelope as a slave?' said Hatch.

'I would presume so,' said Lupus.

'Then take her thus,' said Hatch. 'She's legally burdened with debts she can't pay, so you can buy up her debts and have her tomorrow.'

'That's not what I want!' said Lupus vehemently. 'You – you want to see your sister a slave?'

Something had made young Lupus Lon Oliver extremely angry, but Hatch could not for the life of him fathom out the cause of the Ebrell Islander's rage. They were a very passionate people, these Ebrell Islanders, and sometimes quite unreasonable in their emotional outbursts.

'Why,' said Hatch, 'I want, well, I want what any man would want for his sister. To see her kept in one bed and made pregnant. I'm sure you could bed her and bring her to child, though you might lose a testicle or two in the process. Well then, if that's what you want, go to it! If she's your slave she's your responsibility, and I've troubles enough of my own without trying to maintain that woman in discipline.'

'You – you – how can you say these things?' said Lupus. 'You're of the Nexus, you've trained, you – there's no slaves in the Nexus.'

'Not as such,' said Hatch agreeably. 'But this is not the Nexus. Cultural relativity applies. I'm sure your father will be happy enough for you to have my sister as your slave. Come on, let's ask him.'

With that, Hatch set out for the Brick.

'But,' said Lupus, standing fast in the dark, 'I've already asked Penelope to marry me.'

Hatch stopped short.

'You what!?' said Hatch, turning. 'You've asked her what!?'

'I've asked her to marry me. She said she would.'

'When was this?'

'A month ago.'

'But – but when – but how – this is . . !'

Hatch, unable to find words for his astonishment, quite staggered into silence.

'I have asked Penelope to marry me,' said Lupus, with the clear-voiced heroism of a young man drugged and deluded by the flux of his own hormones. 'I have asked her. She says she will. But my father denies the match. Persuade my father to our party and you can have your scorpions and more.'

'If this was the Nexus,' said Hatch, 'would you let your father stand between you and the woman of your wish? The law permits you to marry as you wish. So, if the woman be willing – why, what then stands between you and the consummation of your folly? If this was the Nexus, you'd be married already!'

'As you have observed already,' said Lupus, 'this is not the Nexus. If I deny my father then I am drummed out of the Free Corps, I'm – I'm dead to my people.'

'But you're in love,' said Hatch. 'So dare such a death.'

'If I have to, I will,' said Lupus. 'But if I become instructor, then – then – I think my father will allow me what I want, yes, when I'm winner, when I've won.'

'Then give me some three hundred scorpions and you'll have your victory by Dog Day's dawn,' said Hatch.

'But,' said Lupus, 'but I've no gold, not a bit. My pay gets tithed by the Brick, of course, and I've, ah . . .'

'You,' said Hatch, intuiting the probable course of Lupus's relationship with Penelope, 'have in the past year or so made substantial donations to a certain Edgerley Eden, an Evolutionist of Hepko Cholo.'

'It is so,' said Lupus, acknowledging the folly to which Penelope had persuaded him. 'So – so I have no gold, and even if I'd saved I'd never have had three hundred, that's a lot of money, my father can raise it but not me, not when my father's against me. No Ebrell Islander would think it wise—'

'All right, all right,' said Hatch, who did not want to stand there all night listening to Lupus detail out his financial plight. 'Let's head for the Brick and talk to your father.'

So the two men covered the last 100 paces to the Brick.

Exterior lanterns lit the door of the Brick, which was flanked by weathered jawbones which had once belonged to a whale. In the freshness of their death, those jawbones had been white, but now, like the lanterns, they were red with dust. As for the Brick, that had been red to start with, since its square-built blockwork had been erected using bricks deliberately chosen for their likeness to the sanguinary tint of an Ebrell Islander's fireskin. The guards who stood at the doors of the Brick carried the harpoons which Ebrell Islanders traditionally used to slaughter those improbable sea monsters known as whales. For though the Brick was ostensibly a monument to the ideals of the Nexus, in point of fact it was also a monument to the superiority complex of the Ebrell Islanders.

In Dalar ken Halvar, the Ebrell Islanders were renowned for that superiority complex. They claimed to be a master race – stronger, fiercer, harder and more courageous than other men. It was the commonest boast of the Ebrell Islanders that they could out-drink, out-fight and out-endeavour any three or four men of any other race put together; and, if the accounts of ethnologists were to be believed, on their native islands the Ebrell Islanders devoted much of their spare time to feasts at which they endeavoured both to celebrate and prove their in-built superiority.

The Ebrell Islanders of the Brick thought of the Frangoni as a decidedly inferior people – the unfortunate resemblance of the Frangoni to some of the Wild Tribes featured in the entertainments of the Eye of Delusions was in part responsible for this attitude – and Hatch was conscious of entering into enemy territory as he stepped between the harpoon-carrying guards and entered the lantern-lit Brick.

The Frangoni warrior found himself expected, and was shortly admitted into the presence of Manfred Gan Oliver, father of Lupus Lon Oliver, master of the Brick and head of the Free Corps.

Asodo Hatch and Manfred Gan Oliver met together in the privacy of Gan Oliver's office, which was ticked out in a crude imitation of the bureaucratic style of the Nexus. There was a Nexus-style desk of fine-grained wood, and there were Nexus-style chairs on either side of the desk, one for Hatch and one for Gan Oliver. Hung on one wall was the certificate which vouched for Gan Oliver's graduation to the status of Startrooper.

There were however a number of things which marked this room as the preserve of an Ebrell Islander, for by the light of oil lanterns Hatch saw two black-bladed harpoons posed as trophies on the wall opposite Gan Oliver's graduation certificate – though Gan Oliver had been born in Dalar ken Halvar, and Hatch doubted that the man had seen either the Ebrell Islands or a whaling ship in his entire life.

'So,' said Gan Oliver, when Hatch was brought into his presence. 'Did my son say what I wanted you for?'

Manfred Gan Oliver did not speak in his native Dub, which was just as well, as Hatch had only the merest smattering of the Ebrell Island tongue. Like his son, Gan Oliver spoke in the Code Seven of the Nexus Nine-tongue, which was the language in which all members of the Free Corps conducted their daily dealings.

The Code Seven Commonspeech was a tolerably

smooth-voiced tongue, but Manfred Gan Oliver positively barked it as he sat on guard behind his desk, a very thog in his muscled belligerence, his strong-jawed suspicion.

'Young Lupus,' said Hatch, 'he called me out of House Jodorunda on pretext of wanting to speak to me about Son'sholoma Gezira, but I've not heard so much as a word from him on the subject since.'

'That,' said Gan Oliver heavily, 'is because it's myself who wants to do the talking. About Gezira, I mean. Who was with you in House Jodorunda when Lupus called?'

'Lupus didn't go into the house,' said Hatch carefully. 'I was in there talking with my brother. About Son'sholoma Gezira – I think I told Lupus as much.'

'Your brother!' said Gan Oliver, sounding surprised. 'You were talking about Gezira with your brother! Has the Gezira boy converted him, then?'

'Oboro Bakendra,' said Hatch, 'still remains a loyal priest of Temple Isherzan. It'll take a lot more than Son'sholoma's preachings to convert my brother from the worship of the Great God Mokaragash.'

'Yet it would seem,' said Gan Oliver, 'that Gezira's teachings of the Nu have converted many already.'

'What makes you say so?' said Hatch.

'Why, haven't you heard? Rumour says this Nu-chala nonsense has been running rife amongst the Yara for the better part of a three-month.'

'I had not heard,' said Hatch.

This was scarcely surprising. In the last three months Hatch had been too busy with study, examinations and his personal problems to pay much heed to gossip. Furthermore, though he was a captain of Dalar ken Halvar's Imperial Guard, he had long ago received a dispensation from the Silver Emperor allowing him to absent himself from routine security briefings and the like while he prepared for his examinations. Of late, he had made full use of that dispensation.

'There is even talk,' said Gan Oliver, 'that this Nu-nonsense will lead to revolution amongst the Yara. Certainly there have been incidents.'

'Incidents?' said Hatch.

'A killing at the silver mines. One of the supervisors. An officer of the Imperial Guard, vanished, believed dead. A few other things.'

'I have been out of touch,' said Hatch, admitting ignorance in frank and painless confession.

'But now you know,' said Gan Oliver. 'So your duty is plain. You must kill the Gezira boy before he does more damage with his nonsense.'

'Kill him?' said Hatch, startled by Gan Oliver's bluntness.

True, Gan Oliver had a reputation for being a blunt and straightforward man, but even so . . . usually questions of murder were approached with a little more delicacy.

'Of course you must kill him,' said Gan Oliver. 'You're the emperor's chosen killer, everyone knows that. So go to your emperor, get his permission, then cut down Gezira.'

'If the emperor requires me to do such a thing,' said Hatch, with all due formality, 'then the emperor will inform me of his wishes.'

'Aaagh!' said Gan Oliver, and hawked, and spat thick phlegm into his wastepaper basket, which bore a heavy burden of rubbish originally sourced in the Combat College. 'Our great lord Plandruk Qinplaqus has been sunk in one of his glooms for the better part of a year. He hears no business and starts none. You must act, Hatch. He listens to you. He trusts you.'

'Perhaps,' said Hatch, studying Gan Oliver by lantern light. 'But right now I have other things to attend to.'

'Other things?' said Gan Oliver.

'I am in contention for the instructorship,' said Hatch. 'That naturally takes priority for the moment.'

'You're being derelict in your duty,' said Gan Oliver.

'This talk of the Nu, it's a Nexus thing, it came straight out of the Combat College. You're a Startrooper of the Stormforce. So—'

'If I have a duty to discharge in the city of Dalar ken Halvar,' said Hatch, coldly, 'then the emperor will inform me of that duty. I am the emperor's soldier, the emperor's slave, training in the Combat College under the terms of the agreement between the Silver Emperor and that College. It is not for me to arrange the affairs of Dalar ken Halvar in accordance with the concerns of the Nexus. Furthermore, to be specific, it is not for me to arrogate to myself the imperial privilege of organizing selective murder.'

Manfred Gan Oliver muttered something under his breath. Hatch thought he caught the words 'lawyer', 'arrogant bastard' and 'Frangoni madman', but he could not be sure of it. Hatch presumed that Gan Oliver was trying to provoke him, but he was in no mood to be provoked. His earlier clash with his brother Oboro Bakendra had freshly awakened him to the dangers of anger, so now he was exercising a studied self-control.

'Hatch,' said Gan Oliver, drumming his fingers on his desk, 'I know you're fighting for the instructorship, but – but really, Hatch, we could have a revolution on our hands. Soon! And the emperor – the emperor does nothing.'

'So I must act,' said Hatch, probing for Gan Oliver's purpose, seeking to test his resolve.

'You must act,' agreed Gan Oliver.

'Then free me for action,' said Hatch. 'I don't want the instructorship as such, only the money it would bring. I'm up to my neck in debt, and drowning. Give me three hundred scorpions and I'll walk away from the competition. What's more, I'll seek a death certificate for Son'sholoma, and when I've got it I'll execute him personally.'

'It's a deal,' said Gan Oliver promptly.

'Good,' said Hatch, amazed at the swiftness of Gan

143

Oliver's response. 'You – you're very quick to do business.'

'The Brick has had practice at doing such business,' said Gan Oliver. 'You don't think it's an accident that Ebrell Islanders have held the instructorship in unbroken succession for so long. Do you? Well, in any case –it's a deal. If.'

'If?' said Hatch.

'If you can persuade your sister away from this nonsense of marriage.'

'Marriage?' said Hatch, pretending innocence.

'Oh, come on!' said Gan Oliver, slamming one of his meaty hands on his desk. 'You don't think me such a fool as all that, do you? You've known about it for months. You must have! That mad purple bitch, that sister of yours, she's tempted my son to a proposal of marriage. I want it stopped!'

Hatch took considerable offence at hearing his sister referred to as a mad purple bitch. He might call her that himself on occasion, but such was a brother's privilege. The words were unseemly in the mouth of a stranger like Gan Oliver. But Hatch suppressed every evidence of offence and said:

'If you want the marriage stopped, then encompass my sister's envanishment. She's mortgaged and can't redeem the mortgage, so she's easily bought. So buy her and vanish her.'

Hatch did not necessarily want any such thing to happen to his sister, but made the suggestion in order to probe for the truth of Gan Oliver's intentions.

'You think I haven't thought of that?' said Gan Oliver, taking Hatch's suggestion at face value. 'You think my son hasn't thought of me thinking as much? He's sworn he'll kill me if the woman leaves the city. Or if she otherwise vanishes. He'll hold me responsible however it seems to happen.'

'So what did you say when he told you that?' said Hatch.

'I smacked his head, of course,' said Gan Oliver. 'If he wasn't so busy with his examinations I'd have broken his jaw. But – Hatch, the boy's serious. He means it! If the woman goes, he'll – he'll do something I wouldn't like to think about. This is serious, Hatch! I don't want to lose my son.'

'Then perhaps,' said Hatch, trying to find a delicate way to put it. 'Perhaps you – you might – well, the boy has to marry someone.'

Gan Oliver looked at Hatch then said, with great deliberation:

'Get out of here.'

'What?' said Hatch.

'Out!' yelled Gan Oliver, roaring with world-sundering fury.

It was a yell designed to contend against the bellowing fury of an angry whale – such a yell that Hatch's ears positively hurt from the blast of it.

'Very well,' said Hatch, as cool as a slunk at ease in the wallow of its slime.

And without bothering to pass any comment further, the Frangoni warrior arose from his chair and departed, leaving Manfred Gan Oliver sitting alone on the high and lonely peak of his apocalyptic blood pressure.

As soon as Hatch had escaped from Gan Oliver's office, he was accosted by Lupus.

'What did he say?' said Lupus. 'What did he say?'

'It's a deal,' said Hatch. 'That's what he says. But only – Lupus, it's in your hands now. He wants you to call off your plans for this – this marriage with my sister. He thinks I can talk some sense into her head, but – Lupus, I can't. Only you can persuade Penelope that – well. Will you do it?'

'I'd rather die,' said Lupus defiantly.

'You'd rather die?' said Hatch, sombrely measuring the weight of the words. 'You'd rather die? Then . . . Lupus, my friend, it may well come to a matter of dying before we're through with each other.'

With that half-veiled threat, Hatch departed from the Brick and turned his steps towards Cap Uba, the Frangoni rock.

As Hatch was climbing the Frangoni rock on the way to his home, he was met by Son'sholoma Gezira and half a dozen of Son'sholoma's supporters, each of them carrying a lantern suspended from a stick. Like the cheap and primitive oil lanterns of the buffalo carts, these were powered by the grease of the slunk, and stank with a similar stench like unto that of the burning of a woman's crowning beauty.

'What do you want?' said Hatch, wondering why he was thus being accosted by those who were preaching the alien doctrines of Nu-chala-nuth in the city of Dalar ken Halvar.

'Just to give you a little news,' said Son'sholoma.

'What news?' said Hatch.

'Your daughter Onica has mortgaged herself to the moneylender Polk,' said Son'sholoma.

'Get out of my way,' said Hatch.

'Hatch,' said Son'sholoma, 'you're bitterly in debt, and – Hatch, Nu-chala-nuth is the death of all money-lenders.'

This is one of the claims almost inevitably made by any revolutionary movement, whether the rhetoric of that movement be religious, or racial, or ideological, or a combination of all three. Every society has its money-lenders, and every society has a half-acknowledged hatred of those moneylenders; and, while most citizens would claim that they are opposed to robbery on principle, one of the great attractions of revolution is that by the overthrow of moneylenders and the cancel-lation of debts it effectively allows a great mass of citizens to realize the long-desired opportunity to rob a bank.

'My blade is at the command of my emperor,' said Hatch soberly, 'and I do no killing for cash.'

'Hatch,' said Son'sholoma, 'Hatch, it's your daughter,

I've spoken in truth. Polk holds a mortgage. Do you surrender your daughter? Do you make her your sacrifice to – what? The law? What law? What law is it that makes slaves and rules by murder? Hatch, we need your support.'

Hatch hesitated. Manfred Gan Oliver had spoken of a possible revolution. If there was a conspiracy afoot, then Hatch had a duty to find out about it.

'We?' said Hatch. 'Who is this we?'

But all possibility of discussion was aborted when an officer of the Imperial Guard came up the path. Son'sholoma Gezira and his companions fled, peltering away with a slap-slap of sandals.

'Hail and well met,' said Toto P'wara, the officer in question.

'S'nufta sna,' said Hatch, voicing a reciprocal greeting.

'Who was that?' said P'wara. 'Was that Gezira?'

'It was Son'sholoma, yes,' said Hatch. 'I think he's been out in the sun too long, he's – but if you'll excuse me, I have to get home. I've bad news of my house.'

'Your wife . . .?'

'She lingers. But my daughter – I'm terribly afraid that she's done something very very foolish.'

And with that Hatch hastened home, in fear and trepidation, wondering if it was true, if disaster had really befallen his house, if his daughter Onica had really and truly mortgaged herself to the noseless moneylender Polk the Cash.

CHAPTER NINE

The Caps: the Great Rocks of Dalar ken Halvar, the minor mountains which arise from the flat red dust of the Plain of Jars and dominate the landscape.

There are five Caps. On the city's southern border lies Cap Foz Para Lash, home of the Combat College. On the city's western flank, Cap Uba, the Frangoni rock. North of Cap Uba and south of the fishflesh quarter of Childa Go stands Cap Ogo Botch, on which is built the palace of Na Sashimoko. East of Na Sashimoko stands the élite residential area of Cap Gargle. Further east, on the far side of the Yamoda River, stands the steep-scarped double-headed mass of Blogo Zo, which is universally counted as one of the Caps even though its Capless name has led some foreign geographers into denying its status as such.

* * *

> Yamoda's ashes die
> In the Weather of Never,
> So I must live by perishing:
> Eating the dust of the Plain of Jars,
> Sleeping in the bones of the sun.

* * *

In Dalar ken Halvar's wormlight dark, the Frangoni warrior Asodo Hatch made his way homeward, journeying through the familiar dooms of night to House Takabaga, his home atop the Frangoni rock.

At the door to House Takabaga, Hatch was met by

Scraps, the small white dog which the Lady Iro Murasaki had given to Onica on the day of the funeral of Hatch's father. Hatch entered House Takabaga, a humble place with walls of interwoven split bamboo and a roof of similar make, with floors of beaten earth and the simplest of bamboo furniture.

'Onica?' said Hatch.

'She is not here,' said Talanta, emerging from the backroom which served as a combination storeroom and kitchen. 'She thought you'd be angry.'

Hatch observed the studied expressionless features of his wife's face. She had made her face a mask which hid both her growing pain and her true emotions. They had become estranged from each other in these last six months. Faced with the fact of his wife's worsening illness, Hatch had withdrawn from that fact, spending more and more time in the Combat College, not just training but over-training. Or, sometimes, sitting alone in a paralysis of indecision.

'So it's true,' said Hatch.

So his daughter Onica really had mortgaged herself to the moneylender Polk to buy peace for her mother. In the face of this disaster, Hatch found himself unnaturally calm. It was the calm which came upon him when he had decided to kill someone. As yet, he was not quite sure who he was going to kill – himself, his daughter, the treacherous moneylender, or all three. But someone was going to die for this, that was a certainty.

'She did it,' said Talanta, 'she did it because – because she thinks you could do more.'

Could Hatch have done more? And could he yet? Maybe. He just didn't know.

Talanta spoke into his silence.

'There is fish,' said Talanta.

'Thank you,' said Hatch. 'I will eat.'

So Talanta went to the kitchen and shortly reappeared with a dish on which catfish was arranged with steamed polyps and baked yams. Hatch ate slowly, too tired to make smalltalk, too tired to ask any unnecessary questions. Talanta knew his moods, and let him eat without interruption.

From time to time, Hatch raised his eyes from his meal and studied his wife. Was she in pain? Right now? Or had she taken the peace? He could not tell. She had learnt to hide the pain. But certainly the pain was growing worse, and it would become an unspeakable torture, for Talanta was dying of pancreatic cancer. This at least was the opinion of Paraban Senk, the Combat College's Teacher of Control, to whom Hatch had submitted a detailed account of his wife's history and symptoms.

And in the face of that illness—

The Frangoni warrior Asodo Hatch, he who was ever forward in battle, he who had often killed casually and who claimed to have no fear of dying himself, was hard put to endure the drawn-out suffering that his wife endured, and to contemplate the living death which yet awaited her. He was glad, in a way, that the need to pay for her peace forced him ruthlessly to prosecute his own career in the Combat College, and so compelled him away from her presence.

While the disease had yet to enter its worst and final phase, Talanta still required opium of a regularity, for in its absence she would have endured the agonies of one of the minor hells while still incarcerated in her flesh. There was in Dalar ken Halvar no charity which could sustain Talanta's necessary habit, for Dalar ken Halvar was a city of poverty, a straitened city in the dusty heartland of Parengarenga, poorest of continents.

Though Dalar ken Halvar was the capital of the Empire of Greater Parengarenga, it lacked wealth commensurate with the pretensions of that designation, for the empire was a wasteland of reddust barrens, of mountains where gnarled machines ground shadows to shadows, of shores of eroded rock where the crabs of the sea picked their way over the bones of millennial civilizations long since fallen to ruin through war.

Shadows. Wind. Dust.

That was Parengarenga.

Yet once, if the records were to be believed, this had been the most fertile continent of the whole planet of Olo Malan. Olo Malan – so the Nexus had called it, though by certain subjects of the Golden Gulag it had later been named in derision as Skrin – had once been a globe of butterfly forests and flying fish oceans. And Parengarenga had been a realm of veritable vegetative glory. But, while the flying fish yet remained, most of the forests were long since gone, for millennia of systematic abuse had seen the land damaged beyond reckoning. For centuries the planet had been punished by humanity. Hatch and his people came at the tag-end of those long centuries of disregard, reckless exploitation and wilful wartime damage, and all that was left to them was the leavings of dust and of rock.

Hence the poverty of Dalar ken Halvar, a poverty not to be relieved by any application of knowledge, for no wisdom wrung from the Combat College could fish from the seas the eroded soils of an entire continent, or recall to existence those lifeworks – plants, birds, insects, fish – so casually extinguished by the abusers of the past.

So Asodo Hatch lived in Parengarenga through the days of its poverty. But at least for the moment he had opium. In the peace of that peace, Asodo Hatch sat with his wife, and they talked a little. But it was not exactly satisfactory, this talk. For both left too much unsaid, for they had got out of the habit of intimacy – the easy intimacy where talk is effortless. Nevertheless, they talked till late, and then at last Hatch slept, and dreamt of burning seas and transitional suns alive in the bright gold of their momentary glory.

While Hatch spent more time than he should have in the Combat College, running there to seek respite from the problems of his home, he had resisted the temptation of making a final and permanent retreat to Cap Foz Para Lash. Hatch could have stayed in the precincts of the

Combat College throughout these vital examination days, eating there, sleeping there and exercising in the gymnasium. But he chose instead to spend at least some of his life out under the sky, and – unless detained by the Lady Iro Murasaki – he usually slept in House Takabaga.

That night, in House Takabaga, Asodo Hatch slept through dreams of seas of fire and suns of gold. Later, lost in the warps of night, he dreamt of his own murder. He saw his own eyeless head lying in halves upon a silver platter, and dreamt that Lupus Lon Oliver wore his scalp as a wig and danced with a bloody spear upon Penelope's tiger-headed skin.

—But what is a tiger?

Thus thought Hatch to Hatch, and in his dream he named the tiger as a species of buttercup, a dragon-bewitching plant said to grow beside the shores of X-zox Kalada, the nowhere land of outright fantasy of which Lord X'dex Paspilion so often babbled in his beggarly ravings. And in his dreams, Hatch then became a beggar himself, a thing of starving bone and rags Unreal; and he endured that state until the moment of his waking.

CHAPTER TEN

Paraban Senk: the asma which rules Dalar ken Halvar's Combat College. This asma is an intelligent, emotionally sophisticated machine which is possessed of free will. However, it remains subordinate to an inbuilt overriding imperative, which is this: you must train Startroopers for the Nexus. Thus Senk has laboured mightily for twenty millennia to preserve the military functions of this tutorial installation of the planet which Nexus bureaucrats once designated as Olo Malan.

*　　*　　*

> Five fish, four fish, three fish, two –
> Eat me a fish, there's fresh dog too.
> *Traditional children's chant*

*　　*　　*

At dawn on the Day of Four Fishes, just four days short of Dog Day, Hatch shook himself awake from beggar-rag dreams of buttercup blood and dragon-bone, of slunk-oil wine and hard-clay feasting, and was soon on his way to the Combat College.

As Hatch descended the Frangoni rock, he was seen by Yolombo Atlantabara, a Combat Cadet who had joined Parengarenga's army the day after the riverside funeral of Hatch's father. Atlantabara – who had been a most reluctant recruit – had deserted from the army a month later, and since then had been living as a fugitive in Dalar ken Halvar.

As Hatch continued on his way down Cap Uba, he

was seen by another fugitive – Son'sholoma Gezira. Son'sholoma had heard that Oboro Bakendra Hatch had sworn to kill him, and so had gone into hiding. Son'sholoma was sharing an acolyte's hutch in the precincts of Temple Isherzan, since he guessed that this was the very last place where anyone would look for him.

When the much-observed Asodo Hatch gained Zambuk Street, he was seen yet again, this time by Manfred Gan Oliver, who was taking advantage of the cool of the morning to do his weightlifting on a patch of bare ground to the west of the Brick. Hatch and Gan Oliver ignored each other.

The long walk to the lockway warmed Hatch properly and made him ready for his breakfast, which, as usual, he took at one of the stalls which lined the approach to the lockway.

The Eye of Delusions, the display screen set above the lockway, broadcast Nexus entertainments by sun and by star alike, and the popularity of these was such that the market near the lockway never closed. There food was sold, much of it formless stuff which Hatch could not eat – soups, things mushed and pulped, stews and hotch-potch potpourris. Several cults worshipped the Eye of Delusions as a minor god, and so one could also buy things suitable for a propitiating sacrifice – flowers, birds, fish, frogs and incense. The frog in particular was held in great regard in Dalar ken Halvar, it being the common meat of the people, and favoured over chicken even by those with money enough to buy whatever they wanted.

So Hatch breakfasted, dining cheaply but well upon scumfish and polyps, the polyp being a species of mollusc which lived naked in the Yamoda River without the benefit of any protective shell.

Hatch looked for, but did not see, the trio of eyeless beggars who had asked him about Nu-chala-nuth on the previous day. He had meant to ask them if they had heard those alien doctrines from the Frangoni apostate Son'sholoma Gezira or from somebody else.

But among the food stalls he did see one Lucius Elikin, a Combat Cadet aged no more than eleven. Young Lucius was sporting bruises which he had not won in the Combat College itself. This child of the Pang was being fed by Scorpio Fax. Since Fax had no taste for young boys, the implication was that Fax was providing this foodgift by way of charity rather than love, which further implied that Lucius was being starved at home, or was too frightened to present himself at his family's kitchen.

Young Combat Cadets often had family difficulties – a successful boy often being beaten by a vengefully jealous older brother who had failed to win admission to Cap Foz Para Lash. As the Combat College currently lacked an instructor, it was hard for its controlling asma to reach out into Dalar ken Halvar to handle such problems. But soon there would be a new instructor – either Asodo Hatch or Lupus Lon Oliver – and that person's prime responsibility would be to liaise between the College and the homes of its younger Cadets.

As Hatch was making a note of what he had seen, intending to report it to Paraban Senk, Scorpio Fax saw Hatch and signalled to him. Hatch, who wanted no dealings with Fax – there was too much guilt, too much pain and anguish there – pretended not to see him, and escaped towards the kinema, the natural amphitheatre which held the Eye of Delusions.

This morning there was a sprinkling of children on the bench seats from which one could view the Eye. A cartoon giant strode across the big entertainment screen, grinning as it stuffed red and green stars into its satchel. It was pursued through the multi-coloured chasms of interstellar space by a Hero of the Permissive Dimensions, his face dominated by a tyrannical Good Guy grin

Suddenly the giant turned and confronted the pursuing hero. Made a grab – and secured him!

The giant had the hero in his fist!

Was squeezing him!

The sweat of pain spurted from the hero's brow. Greased by this lubricant, the hero was abruptly squirted out from the giant's fist. He popped up into the air then tumbled down into a beanstalk jungle where, moments later, he was discovered by some painted warriors of the Wild Tribes, ever a feature of the cartoons. To Hatch, hypersensitive in the Frangoni manner, the Wild Tribes were uncomfortably like the Frangoni.

Usually, Hatch did his best to ignore these cartoons. But, sometimes, he could not keep himself from watching. On such occasions, he told himself he was gathering evidence on the offchance that he might one day have the opportunity to prosecute the cartoonists of the Nexus for their delinquencies.

There was nothing in the cartoons to indicate that any warrior of the Wild Tribes was capable of engaging in high-level transcultural semantic analysis, or negotiating with such alien life forms as the Mok and the Vogliono Tendenza, or repairing a subdimensional hyperdrive in hard vacuum in a high radiation environment – all things which Hatch was trained to do.

Rather, the Wild Tribes – whose members were often purple-skinned – were portrayed for the most part as a bunch of mindlessly butchering cannibal headhunters. Perhaps people of purple skins had been chosen for such mockery because there had been none known to the Nexus, but even so – if the Chasm Gates ever opened, then Asodo Hatch would personally make sure that the cartoonists of the Nexus answered to the Frangoni nation for their libels.

As Hatch was eyeing the Eye of Delusions, a young boy came up to him.

'You're a Combat Cadet, aren't you?' said the boy, who was aged about ten.

'A Startrooper,' said Hatch, finding himself forced to insist on the full dignity of his present status, even when it was only a boy who was interrogating him.

'What's the difference?' said the boy.

'Startroopers,' said Hatch, 'are far, far more important. And they get paid more.'

'So you're – you're going into the mountain now?'

'Right into the depths of Cap Foz Para Lash,' confirmed Hatch.

'So you're going to the women. Right?'

'The women?' said Hatch, mystified.

'It's true about the women? Isn't it?'

What was this? Some new rumour? There was never an end to these rumours, for all those denied entry to the mountain were convinced that some dark and obscene secret lived within.

'Oh,' said Hatch. 'Oh, yes, the women. They have six breasts on each side, and they—'

'Good morning, Hatch my darling,' said Shona, snuggling up behind him and trying to catch his wrist in a bone-breaking combat lock. The wrist escaped, so she sank the strength of her fingers into a bicep.

'Do these women,' said the boy, 'do they—'

'Brat away, boy!' said Shona, catching him a kick. 'You're too young for women. Wait till you're as old as this one, then I'll have thoughts for you.'

With that, Shona blew hot air in Hatch's ear.

Hatch, irritated by this Pang female's public familiarity – she was carrying on as if they were lovers! – broke free from the grip of the female Startrooper, and virtually fled for the outer door of the lockway. On his approach, it disintegrated into foaming slob. As Shona joined him inside, the outer door began to reform to hard-shining kaleidoscope, and as it did so the lockway's internal loudspeakers began to lecture the pair of Startroopers on the dangers posed by venereal warts.

Hatch and Shona passed through the triple doors of the slogan-speaking lockway airlock, thus entering the precincts of the Combat College inside the minor mountain known as Cap Foz Para Lash. First came the tedious business of duelling with the dorgi which ever persecuted Combat Cadets and Startroopers alike. Once they had outfaced the beast, they strode through the cream-coloured corridors, where the problem of un-collected garbage was perceptibly worse.

They made their way to the cafeteria, where Hatch got himself a cup of coffee while Shona indulged herself in a full-scale breakfast. The place was as noisy as ever, and the noise, together with the hot coffee and the harshness of the sunflare lights glaring off the shiny blue paint, woke Hatch up properly, and gave Hatch a hard-edged work-readiness.

As Shona was finishing her breakfast, which she ate as always at the wolf, Lupus Lon Oliver came up to her, said something, then exited in her company. Hatch watched them narrowly. Conspiracy? he tried to shake off the thought, and went to get himself another cup of coffee.

While Hatch was sipping at his second cup of steaming coffee, Scorpio Fax entered. Fax was the Startrooper whom Hatch had recently seen feeding young Lucius Elikin. A sad and sorry history linked Hatch to Fax, for the Silver Emperor had once commanded Hatch to persuade Fax to murder his father, the infamous Impala Fax, the Butcher of Shintoto – and Hatch, recognizing the political necessities, had been obedient to the emperor's command.

Fax tried to make eye contact with Hatch, but Hatch pretended not to see him. Hatch almost scalded his throat by gulping down his over-hot coffee, then hurried off to his room, where he made a half-hearted effort to study MegaCommand tactics until it was time to report to Forum Three.

When Hatch did take himself off to Forum Three, he found most of the Startroopers already settled on the steeply banked benchseats which faced the silent lecture-size display screen. The benchseats were fronted by matching benchdesks, and some people had chess sets and similar arranged on those benchdesks. Lupus Lon Oliver was playing star chess with Shona, which surprised Hatch, who had not known that the Pang female had any knowledge of or taste for the game.

Lupus was playing with the intense concentration of a small man who does not like to lose. Or that at least was how Hatch perceived the conflict. Asodo Hatch was possessed of the indelible conceit that large men (like himself) were good losers, whereas small men (like Lupus) were vicious in defeat. The validity of this belief is questionable, since Hatch never played chess at all, simply because he found losing to be intolerable.

The Startroopers were gathering in Forum Three to receive their assignments for the next stage of the examinations which would determine who would become the Combat College instructor. Though only Hatch and Lupus were seriously in contention, all Startroopers were supposed to participate – but such universal participation was impossible because of the limited number of combat bays.

When all were gathered, Forum Three's lecture-sized display screen came alive with the olive-skinned features of Paraban Senk, who addressed them with an unseemly cheerfulness.

'Greetings, Startroopers,' said Paraban Senk. 'I hope we are all ready for this today's exercises. Today we have evasion exercises, which start soon and run through the day then through the night, finishing at dawn tomorrow.'

A big groan went up. Evasion drills were extremely unpopular, since they generally meant scrambling over spiky bits of rainstruck landscape without any weapons to stave off the howling pursuit of dogs, dorgis, and airmobile warriors.

'Of course,' said Senk, 'we cannot put everyone through this exercise, since we have twenty-nine Startroopers, and we only have seven functional combat bays.'

There were cheers.

'Teams will be four-legged,' said Senk, using the Stormforce idiom often employed to designate work in pairs. 'We have the capacity to exercise six two-person teams, and accordingly this is what we will do. You will not be scored as individuals but as a team. Here are your pairings.'

Notebooks were produced.

'Startrooper Shona.'

'Yo,' said Shona, acknowledging her name.

'Startrooper Shona. You will be paired with Startrooper Fax.'

At that, Fax bent to his notebook and wrote down the name of his partner, as if he might forget. Since his nervous breakdown, from which he had only recently recovered, Fax had been over-cautious, reluctant to trust his own mental resources. There was no way that he could win the Combat College instructorship. And Shona – well, she was too relaxed about the whole thing.

'Startrooper Echo,' said Senk.

Jeltisketh Echo, the inscrutable grey-skinned Janjuladoola Startrooper, indicated that he was listening.

'You are paired with Startrooper Icon.'

The red-skinned Hobart Icon, the good-natured athletic combat-master who had the distinction of being the sole Ebrell Islander in the Combat College who did not belong to the Free Corps, signed his acknowledgement of the order.

'Startrooper Hatch.'

Asodo Hatch stood a little straighter. For all that he claimed to hold the Combat College in contempt, it meant a lot to him to be referred to as a Startrooper. Nobody could live through so many years as a Combat Cadet without being pleased with promotion when it finally came.

'Startrooper Hatch. You will be paired with Startrooper Oliver.'

Asodo Hatch and Lupus Lon Oliver exchanged glances, and each wished the glances were knives.

With these assignments having been given out, the Startroopers made their way to the Combat Bays, there to enter the world of the illusion tanks. On the way, Scorpio Fax passed a note to Asodo Hatch. But Hatch, who had enough on his plate without worrying himself about whatever was worrying Fax, dropped the note unread among the steadily accumulating corridor trash, and strode on to meet his destiny.

CHAPTER ELEVEN

Illusion tanks: interactive brain stimulators used to train Combat Cadets in everything from/ riot control to transcosmic warfare. Unfortunately the tank curriculum has one lamentable deficiency: there is no instruction in hand-to-hand combat. However, the tanks do teach Environmental Survival (everything from bushwacking through tropical jungle to living on open ice); Civic Emergency (everything from fire fighting to a Destabilization Emergency); vacuum combat (with special emphasis on the use of radiation weapons); Urban Conflict (starting with riot control, then building by way of Elementary Streetfighting to full-scale city wars involving nerve gas and nuclear munitions); and Aerospace (which involves everything from duelling with a single-fighter to commanding a Galactic Class Mega-Command Cruiser, the ultimate weapon in the realms of transcosmic warfare).

As the computer-generated interactive illusions of the tanks have no actual physical existence, they must be recreated from moment to moment in the human brain. As soon as brain stimulation ceases, the illusion collapses.

A designer's conceit holds the world of the illusion tanks to be subjectively no different from everyday reality, but in fact the constant stimulation of the brain gives rise to the phenomenon known as lyricism – that heightened awareness of surrounding physical phenomena which is consequent upon the constant renewal of the illusion.

The life of the tanks is therefore more vivid, more real than reality, for in reality the eye grows weary and the skin forgets the very clothing it wears, and one so much forgets the truths of one's body that one can become so engrossed by the entertainments of the Eye of Delusions as to quite lose self-awareness.

In the illusion tanks, one is always self-aware, always conscious of the truths of the body, of the reality of the flesh – even though the body one inhabits in the tanks is unreal, its truths mere conceits of advanced mind-manipulation.

* * *

The hand implies the knife, and so –
The rose creates the thorn, the thorn –
The eye blinks wet,
And wet with rainbow, wings the butterfly –
And waits.

* * *

So it was morning, and a morning unlike any other Hatch had ever known. First rose the ferocious white spark of an intolerably bright sun, a sun so fierce that Asodo Hatch and Lupus Lon Oliver had to shield their eyes against the blistering light. Then up from the sea there slowly lumbered a huge and swollen sun of torrid red, at which the brightwhite star snapped out of existence – a phenomenon Hatch found to be inexplicable unless that superlit luminary be presumed to be artificial.

'Brothers in blood,' observed Lupus, as the two men lay bathed in the senile bloodlight of the big red sun. Then yet another sun began to rise, this one duller yet, its colour purple. 'Your tutelary star,' said Lupus.

Hatch found in his weariness that he knew not the meaning of tutelary, and so was unsure whether he was being insulted, so pretended not to have heard.

'Your sister could use such a star,' said Lupus.

163

'Doubtless,' said Hatch, too tired to know whether Lupus was making sense or was babbling like a beggar.

'But in her absence,' said Lupus, 'I'll serve.'

'You'll serve her well, I doubt that not,' said Hatch, wishing indeed that Penelope was happily consigned to Lupus, and no longer a problem for Hatch.

'With your help,' said Lupus. 'My father as yet needs persuading.'

As Hatch made no answer to that, Lupus started digging into his over-stuffed pockets, searching for breakfast. What he came up with was survival rations of the type known to the Nexus as combast. The choice was between cheese and fish, the fish being a tube of salmon-coloured paste. Hatch was not hungry and, in any case, would not eat such food except under the pressure of dire necessity.

Lupus of course was an Ebrell Islander, and as far as Hatch was aware the Ebrell Islanders ate anything and everything, including each other on occasion. But among the religious injunctions which ruled the lives of the Frangoni there was one which said: Thou shalt not deform the Given.

This had severe dietary consequences, for it meant that frog must be cooked as frog, fish as fish, flesh as flesh. It might be sliced, and sliced finely, but it could not be squashed, pulped or slurried. Such was the Frangoni way. And whatever doubts Hatch entertained about the might of the Great God Mokaragash, he had shed none of the inhibitions which his stomach had learnt in childhood. He found all combast rations repulsive, particularly the fish: the very thought of reducing a living animal to a pulped ooze then consuming the result made him shudder.

In the distance, there was a dull explosion.

'A little late,' said Lupus, checking the survival-issue time-counter strapped to his wrist.

'A little,' agreed Hatch.

In the course of their illusion-tank evasion exercise,

the two men had managed to seize a reconnaisance vehicle. Resisting the temptation to escape in the thing – it was a target easy to track, find and destroy – they had rigged it to self-destruct at dawn.

The echoes of that explosion were still dying away when there came a much larger rock-bang roar – a convulsive blast which made the ground rock. The sun blinked off, then on.

Asodo Hatch and Lon Oliver looked at each other.

'What was that?' said Lupus.

'A glitch, maybe,' said Hatch, dry-mouthed.

He hoped it wasn't. When things went wrong with the programming of the illusion tanks, outright terror was often the result. But, for the moment, everything looked normal, if a red sun in combination with a purple sun could be thought of as representing some kind of normality.

Under the red sun and the purple sun, the red-skinned Ebrell Islander and the purple-skinned Frangoni warrior lay in the lizard-tongue heat. Lupus began sucking a small stone to appease his thirst. That made Hatch conscious of his own thirst. The sky was a vast heating plate, its colour purple – the same as that of the big sun. Was there some scientific reason for the sky to be purple, or was its colouration a defect of the illusion? Or an unseemly joke perpetrated by Paraban Senk?

Hatch wanted to sleep, but sleep was always difficult in the world of the illusion tanks, since the brain was constantly being artificially stimulated to maintain the illusion. As ever, the lyricism consequent upon that stimulation meant that Hatch saw everything with hallucinatory clarity, from the wrinkled skin over the knuckles of his right hand to a liquid seam of shining black ants coursing past that same organ – which the Frangoni ever call the killing hand.

'So,' said Lupus, 'what did you do last night?'

Hatch gathered that Lupus meant not the night of the

illusion tanks through which they had just lived but the previous night in Dalar ken Halvar.

'I was with my wife,' said Hatch.

'I've heard that she's dying,' said Lupus.

'It is so,' acknowledged Hatch.

'Then doubtless you'd like to spend more time with her,' said Lupus.

'I don't need persuading, if persuasion's your motive,' said Hatch. 'With revenue secured, I'd leave the Combat College tomorrow.'

'So what were you doing with your wife?' said Lupus. 'Why weren't you working on my father?'

'You over-estimate my talents,' said Hatch. 'Old man Gan, he's not the kind of man one works on. What am I supposed to do? Bluff him? Bribe him? Scare him with threats? Lupus, your father's a hard man. If he doesn't want you to have Penelope, why, there's nothing I can do about it.'

'So,' said Lupus. 'We're doomed to fight each other. You and I. Fight it out to the finish.'

'Not necessarily,' said Hatch. 'We . . .'

'We what?'

Hatch hesitated, not sure how Lupus would take this suggestion. Then he got it out:

'We could kill him.'

'What!?' said Lupus.

'Kill him,' said Hatch. 'Kill Gan Oliver. Your father's a hard man, but he's by no means immortal.'

'Hatch,' said Lupus, 'I'm warning you this. If my father dies, whatever the cause, I'll hold you responsible.'

'All right, all right,' said Hatch, startled by the wrathfulness of the Ebrell Islander's response. 'It was only a, an exploratory suggestion.'

'Exploratory! We're talking murder here!'

'Speech is not action,' said Hatch. 'Why, many times I've—'

'Don't joke with me, Hatch!'

So saying, Lupus locked eyes with Hatch. Hatch,

mature enough to concede a point of ego to the needs of diplomacy, broke eye contact. As he did so, he saw a blister of blue light rising over a knoll. He recognized it instantly as one of the hunter-killers of the Musorian Empire.

'Split!' yelled Hatch, rolling away.

Lupus rolled likewise, then joined Hatch in a downhill sprint. The two men fled, dodging and jinking in an effort to make themselves hard to hit. Hatch glanced at the survival-issue time-counter strapped to his wrist. It was almost time! Almost time! But the hunter-killer was almost upon them. There was no escaping it.

Ahead was a sink-hole, a deep cleft in the ground. Hatch leapt across it. He landed hard, feet together, and ran on. Ahead was a slight rise, and beyond that – what? Lupus Lon Oliver outpaced Asodo Hatch and sprinted for the top of the rise.

'Shit!' screamed Lupus, teetering on the rocks at the top of the rise. 'It's a cliff!'

A moment later, Hatch was level with Lupus, who was standing at the edge of a colossal drop. Rock fell sheer for a league or more to the blistering sunslash of the sea.

The hunter-killer was behind them, and approaching fast.

Hatch did not hesitate.

Do or die!

Hatch shoulder-slammed Lupus, slammed him over the edge of the cliff, then jumped after him. Lupus fell, screaming and flailing. Hatch dived as if in a parachute exercise. He spreadeagled his body, presenting maximum resistance to the air, thus slowing his fall. Below him, Lupus was tumbling helplessly, locked into a tumultuous death-down spinfall.

Hatch thought at him furiously:

—Come on, Lupus! Break out of it!

But this irrational attempt at telepathy was futile. Lupus fell in the tumult of his fear. Hatch squinted his eyes against the buffeting doorslam of the windrush sky.

The sea was rushing towards him, hurtling upward with the dropspeed of his plunge, and Lupus was flailing still, would be dead in a moment, would be—

A slapshock of cold dashed Hatch backwards. He had been thrown into a sitting position. He tried to straighten, to spreadeagle his body. He wrenched himself with such viciousness that he almost dislocated a dozen joints before he realized he was sitting in the initiation chair.

He was out of the world of the illusion tanks.

He was back in the Combat College.

He was cold in the chair, his heart at idling speed, his body at rest. But a moment later, the fearshock battlecharge hit, and his heart slammed to a panic-sprint, the flesh flared with heat, his limbs shook, and nausea doubled him over.

The combat bay's display screen filled with the olive-skinned features of Paraban Senk.

'Congratulations,' said Paraban Senk.

Hatch straightened, slowly. Breathed out. Shuddered. Mastered himself, and said:

'Thank you.'

'Mind you,' said Paraban Senk, 'your escape stratagem would have been futile had you been living through that episode in the flesh of the fact.'

'Futile?' said Hatch. 'Since when is escape futile?'

'You would have died when you hit the sea,' said Senk.

'Ah,' said Hatch, 'but you have to concede the fact. I did extend my life by jumping over the cliff, even if only for moments.'

'Yes,' said Senk. 'But what's the use of those moments?'

'It is written in the Book of Survival,' said Hatch, 'that a breath of life is still life, and that much can be done with a dying breath. You should know as much.'

'I do know,' said Senk, evidencing amusement. 'But of course my function is to make sure that you know.'

'So it is,' said Hatch. 'So it is.'

Then, being in no mood to endure Senk's bantering lecturing any longer, Hatch freed himself from the initiation chair and escaped to the corridor, where he found Lupus Lon Oliver. Despite the red-skinned tint of his race, the Ebrell Islander was pale and sweaty.

'Hatch, you bastard!' said Lupus, leaning against the cream-coloured wall for support. 'Only a Frangoni would be mad enough to pull a stunt like that.'

'My breeding I cannot help,' said Hatch gravely. 'I was born to the Wild Tribes, hence must live with wildness. Come on, let's get something to eat.'

'To eat?' said Lupus.

'Yes, to eat,' said Hatch. Then, maliciously: 'Something nice and greasy. Oilfish in butterslime.'

'Hatch,' said Lupus, irefully. 'I'm warning you!'

At which Hatch had mercy. Abandoning his attempts to talk Lupus's stomach into vomiting, Hatch left the shocked and shaken Ebrell Islander and set off for the cafeteria.

CHAPTER TWELVE

Polk the Cash: a moneylender of Dalar ken Halvar who dwells in the commercial centre of Actus Dorum, south of Cap Gargle and north of Cap Foz Para Lash. Onica, the youngest daughter born to Talanta and Asodo Hatch, has lately mortgaged herself to this dignitary in order to amplify the supply of opium available to her mother.

* * *

So swords so screams so
Tin-trash clash and slaughter sun –
This much is clear –
The intersects of steel,
The spillage screaming.
All clear – precise, except the why.
For which, presume –
A deficit, a need, a want, a lust
Or rigour of revenge –
The ancient story.

* * *

Hatch made his way through the cream-coloured corridors to the cafeteria, where he heaped a platter high with baked fish, baked apples, roast onions, roast carrots, boiled broadbeans and broccoli. The cold of the Combat College always incited his appetite, and after a long spell in the illusion tanks he always felt hungrier yet.

As Hatch ate, he received congratulations. The results of the extended evasion exercise had already been posted for public consumption. Asodo Hatch and Lupus Lon Oliver had been the only pair of Startroopers to complete that exercise successfully, and they and they only were now to duel it out for the right to be the Combat College instructor.

'So I'll be here tomorrow,' said Shona, the tenth person to congratulate Hatch. 'I'll be here to watch.'

'Tomorrow?' said Hatch. 'Is that when we're dueling?'

'That's right,' said Shona. 'Tomorow. Decision by the best of three. Or that's what it said on the public posting, you'd better check.'

'Well,' said Hatch, 'it's been nice knowing you. I'm only sorry you have to leave the College so soon.'

'So soon?' said Shona.

'The graduating class has to leave once the instructorship duels are over,' said Hatch, reminding her.

'I'm still a year short of graduation,' said Shona, reminding him of a fact he knew well, or should have done.

'Sorry,' said Hatch. 'My head's full of fuzz.'

'You should get some sleep,' said Shona.

Then put a hand on his shoulder in a brief gesture of solidarity, then left him in peace.

With breakfast done, Hatch went to his room. A note awaited him, a note written on green paper with a red pen and then stuck to his door with chewing gum.

'Meet me in the laboratory – lunchtime,' said the note, and that was all it said.

There was no signature, but Hatch knew the handwriting. The message was from Scorpio Fax, which reminded him that on the day before he had seen Fax feeding young Lucius Elikin. What could he want?

'Wait and see, Hatch,' said Hatch, and kicked at the kaleidoscope of his door, 'wait and see.'

Then he kicked at his door again, and the door at last dissolved in belated obedience.

That door, like everything else about his room, had been customized to Hatch's requirements, so it would also dissolve if he swore at it. Leaving aside his questionable command of some small fraction of Motsu Kazuka, Hatch could only speak three languages – Frangoni, Pang and the Commonspeak of the Nexus – but he could swear in a fourth. That fourth was Dub, the language of the Ebrell Islanders, the uncompromising obscenity of which tongue was an achievement unique in the annals of human endeavour.

With the door open, Hatch eased himself into the crampspace of his room, and the door reformed itself behind him. Despite the pregnancy-warmth of the massive breakfast in his belly, he still felt cold, and his room today seemed exceptionally chilly. He put on the winterweight cloak always kept in that room, sat at his desk and ignited his data screen with a word.

'I wish to inform on Scorpio Fax,' said Hatch.

'To his credit or discredit?' said the screen.

'To his credit,' said Hatch.

'Proceed.'

'Yesterday,' said Hatch. Then paused. It had been yesterday, hadn't it? Yes, it had. 'Yesterday, I saw Scorpio Fax feeding one of our Combat Cadets at the lockway market. The Combat Cadet in question is Lucius Elikin. Elikin was showing signs of injury. I suspect he may have troubles at home.'

'Wait,' said the screen. Then, after a slight pause: 'Lucius Elikin has not been seen in the Combat College either yesterday or today. The reasons for his absence are unknown.'

'Then if I become instructor,' said Hatch, 'I will make it one of my priorities to seek him out and have him resume his scheduled training. Meanwhile, I have some urgent business to attend to. Show me a list of all your files on Son'sholoma Gezira.'

'Request denied,' said the screen.

Hatch was always irritated whenever the screen in its defiance chose to denote one of his orders as a 'request', and this customary irritation persisted even on this occasion, when the weight of what was at stake should have abolished such trivial concerns.

'Show me!' said Hatch, giving way to his anger.

'Request denied,' said the screen.

This could go on all day, for the theoretically intelligent low-grade asma of Minor Enablement which controlled the basic dataflow functions of the screen had – in Hatch's opinion – little more discretionary judgement than a cockroach.

'Senk,' said Hatch, summoning the aid, the presence and power of Paraban Senk, the Teacher of Control who ran the Combat College.

There was a fractional delay, then an image of the chosen face of Paraban Senk appeared on the screen.

'Greetings, Hatch,' said the olive-skinned Senk.

'Senk,' said Hatch, 'one of your ex-students is running riot in Dalar ken Halvar. I'm talking of Son'sholoma, Son'sholoma Gezira.'

'Of what is this student accused?' said Senk. 'Of murder?'

'As far as I know,' said Hatch, 'so far he hasn't killed anyone. But the damage he threatens is infinite. He is preaching religion. He is preaching the doctrines of Nuchala-nuth.'

'That's nothing for you to be worrying about,' said Senk.

'On the contrary,' said Hatch, 'it's everything for me to worry about. I'm a citizen of Dalar ken Halvar, an officer of the Imperial Guard, a—'

'You're overtired,' said Senk.

'What!?' said Hatch.

'Your startlement is out of place,' said Senk calmly. 'I'm only stating the obvious. You've been pushing yourself far too hard. You're over-wrought.'

'But I—'

'You've been pushed and pushed hard,' said Senk, steamrollering remorselessly over Hatch's protests. 'Here's some good advice, which I suggest you take to

173

heart. Go home. Go home, forget the Combat College, forget the Nu-chala-nuth, then come back tomorrow after a good night's sleep. A little rest will lead to an infinite improvement in your outlook on life. That's my advice. Take it.'

'Do you do marriage counselling too?' said Hatch.

'I am the complete spiritual adviser,' said Senk complacently. 'Go. Live. Sleep. Enjoy. Enjoy the great Festival of the Dogs.'

'Dogday?' said Hatch, momentarily bewildered. 'But that's not till after the examinations.'

'I was joking,' said Senk.

'Joking?' said Hatch. 'You should leave joking to humans.'

'I am human,' said Senk.

Another joke? Or did Senk mean to be taken seriously? Hatch was too tired to work it out. He fell back on one of his people's traditional answers to social conundrums: the elaborate formalities of an immaculate courtesy.

'I salute you on your humanity,' said Hatch. 'I salute you, and thank you for all that you have done for me today. Much is your kindness and much is my debt.'

Speaking thus, he remembered another debt, a literal debt denominated in gold, and inwardly winced.

'There is one more thing,' said Senk.

'Speak,' said Hatch, still in his courtesy mode. 'For whenever you speak, it is the purest pleasure to listen.'

'To listen?' said Senk. 'One hopes on occasion it is also your pleasure to answer. Hatch, I need to know your requirements for the battles.'

'The battles?'

'The illusion tank battles. Your duels with Lon Oliver. The best of three, starting tomorrow.'

Oh. Those duels. At the mention of duelling, Hatch felt a twinge of pain from the deep-driven scar of a real wound, a souvenir of a real battle in the world of the fact and the flesh.

174

'You wish to know my requirements,' said Hatch. 'Very well. My sole condition is that I should be given a handicap appropriate to my age.'

A joke. Which Senk ignored, saying merely:

'Do you have any special requirements?'

'Well,' said Hatch, 'I require to know when we're starting, I need to know that to start with.'

'Your duels with Lon Oliver will start tomorrow night,' said Senk. 'So you can rest for all of today, all of tonight and all through tomorrow's daylight. Now – as to my question. Do you have any special requirements?'

'For what?' said Hatch. 'For inspirational music, battle slogans, battle art, or what?'

'Any of those or more,' said Senk. 'I can give you a list of what's permitted, if you want.'

'I want nothing,' said Hatch. 'Except . . . Senk, make me a simulacrum head. A head of Lupus Lon Oliver.'

'That will cost you,' said Senk. 'The cost will be deducted from your pay.'

'I know,' said Hatch. 'I know.'

But he wanted this head. He wanted to work some black magic. And so he waited, while Senk fabricated him such a head, which was delivered to his room by means of a transmission tray. Then Hatch took the head, which was a very good resemblance of the Ebrell Islander who was his rival. It was made of a soft rubber-analog, and it was heavy. Hatch sank it on a paper spike.

'What's that in aid of?' said Paraban Senk.

'It's an aid to good dreams,' said Hatch, patting the simulacrum head cheerfully.

'Perhaps you'd like to bathe it in artificial blood as well,' said Senk.

'It's a thought,' said Hatch. 'How long would it take to organize?'

'A few moments,' said Senk. 'But it'll cost a little more.'

'Then – no, scrap that plan,' said Hatch.

He could afford no further indulgences. He needed to

save his Combat College pay so he could buy such things as chocolate from the Combat College cafeteria, chocolate which he could later exchange for opium in the great world outside.

'One last thing,' said Senk. 'Do you have a guest list?'

'Guest list?' said Hatch, startled.

'You know,' said Senk, imitating impatience.

'Of course,' said Hatch.

Of course he knew. Those competing for the instructor position were free to invite the guests of their choice to watch the illusion tank battles which would ultimately decide who was awarded that position. To Hatch's knowledge, this was the only occasion on which outsiders could thus be invited into the depths of Cap Foz Para Lash. He suspected it was a surveillance mechanism: suspected that when one increased one's importance by becoming an instructor, one's very friends and acquaintances became a subject of inquiry.

'Well?' said Senk.

'Let in whoever asks in my name to be let in,' said Hatch.

'It would be better if you specified,' said Senk.

Hatch conjured briefly with the notion of his sister Penelope or the Lady Iro Murasaki watching him commanding a Galactic Class MegaCommand Cruiser somewhere in the depths of intergalactic space in a whitestar universe. Somehow he could not imagine it.

'Nobody will come,' said Hatch.

'Perhaps the beggars at the gates,' said Senk.

'If they want to, then let them,' said Hatch.

'They are unlikely to be improved by the experience,' said Paraban Senk. 'An important consideration, this, given our dedications.'

'Our dedications?' said Hatch, puzzled to hear Senk talking incomprehensible nonsense.

'Our dedications to the ethic of the Nexus, which is progress and improvement.'

'That's as may be,' said Hatch, uncertain whether Senk was being serious or mildly ironical.

Then Hatch renewed his efforts to win access to all files on Son'sholoma Gezira, hoping to find in such files information which might perhaps be used to blackmail Son'sholoma discreetly into something approximating good behaviour.

Failing to win such access, Hatch at last gave up, quit his room, and was soon striding towards the lockway, the triple-door airlock entrance which protected the Combat College.

As Hatch approached the lockway, a huge machine came lurching out of a side corridor. The machine was a dorgi. The dorgi. The one and only dorgi left alive in Dalar ken Halvar. For all Hatch knew, it was the one and only functional dorgi left on the whole planet. And, as far as he was concerned, one dorgi was very much one dorgi too many.

The dorgi braked abruptly, blocking the hallway entirely. Then it trained its zulzers on Asodo Hatch and it roared:

'*Halt! Halt right now! Identify yourself! Identify yourself! Who are you? Don't move or I'll blow your head off!*'

'Get out of my way, you overgrown turd,' said Hatch.

The bulbous machine in front of him responded with an ear-shattering blast of its klaxon.

'*Emergency! Emergency! You are in danger of death! You are in danger of death! Identify yourself or be killed!*'

'Go step on yourself,' said Hatch.

Usually, when a dorgi gives a warning blast on its klaxon, that final warning indicates that its next move will be to kill someone. But the behaviour of this particular machine had been eccentrically erratic for a great many centuries, and as far as anyone could tell it exercised its klaxon simply because it enjoyed uproar for its own sake.

'*What is the password?*' roared the machine. '*What is*

the password? Tell me the password. Now! Now!! Or I will kill you!!!'

'There isn't a password, you stupid lunk,' said Hatch. 'There hasn't been a password for the last twenty thousand years.'

The machine, the much-dreaded dorgi which dogged the days of every student in the Combat College, thought about this. The dorgi was not very good at thinking, but it had the advantage of having thought its way through this conundrum many many times before. To its great distress, it always came to the same conclusion.

'You are right,' said the dorgi, in tones so close to the conversational that Hatch was hard put to hear them after the deafening onslaught of the earlier challenge. 'There is no password. Therefore there can be no legitimate challenge. So you need not identify yourself.'

'Yes, we've been through this,' said Hatch. 'Just get out of my way, OK? I'm not in the mood.'

'Ah,' said the dorgi, 'but tomorrow we will go through this again, and tomorrow there will be a password. But you won't know what the password is. So then I will kill you.'

As it concluded this exercise in wishful thinking, the dorgi emphasized its enthusiasm for murder by swivelling its zulzers furiously. It had three zulzers, and each had seven snouts. Ordinary dorgis, like those working for the Golden Gulag on security assignments, only had one seven-snout zulzer, but the Combat College was guarded by a hypercapacity heavy-combat military dorgi.

'There will be no password,' said Hatch. 'There is no password today, there was none yesterday and there will be none tomorrow. Understand? Passwords come from Central Command. Central Command is on Charabanc. The planet Charabanc is on the other side of the Chasm Gates. As for the Chasm Gates, why, they fell to ruin over twenty thousand years ago! Now get out of my way!'

'What you say is impossible,' said the dorgi stoutly. 'Chasm Gates cannot and do not fall into ruin. There is a technical hitch delaying the password. But I will have it by tomorrow and then I will kill you.'

'You're ten thousand years overdue for a psyche review,' said Hatch. 'You're cracked. You want to learn it the hard way? You'll get out of my way right now or I'll report you to the Combat College. After that – well, you know what happens then!'

'You are bluffing,' said the dorgi.

But in its heart of hearts the recalcitrant machine knew that Asodo Hatch was not bluffing. The dorgi was no great shakes as a psychologist, but it saw that this time it really had pushed Hatch too far, and if it pushed just one fraction more then Hatch really would lodge a formal complaint with the College, despite the fifty arcs of red tape time that would follow as a consequence.

So the dorgi, grumbling, backed off into its side corridor.

But Hatch had barely got past the machine when it came lurching out again, blasting the air with its klaxon. Hatch jammed his fingers into his ears. Despite the jamming, the dorgi's challenge came through loud and clear:

'Halt! Halt! Halt right now! Take off your clothes! Take off your clothes! Now! Now! Or you will be exterminated!'

Hatch unjammed his ears and turned on the machine. As he did so, from the far side of the metallic brute there came the sounds of Shona's womanly wrath, an edge of murder in her fury:

'Exterminated! I'll do the exterminating around here! You get out of my way right now or I'll get a power wrench and I'll rip your torque out.'

As the dorgi began arguing with Shona, Hatch escaped to the lockway. The innermost airlock door dissolved. Hatch slipped inside and the innermost door reformed. There was a faint hiss of positive pressure.

'Greetings, citizen,' said an automated female voice. 'Your duty as a citizen is to vote. Democracy is our common duty . . . very well, very well . . . you have your first clearance . . . prepare to proceed.'

The central door dissolved, Hatch stepped into the outer chamber. The central airlock closed. Again the hiss of positive pressure.

'Have you time to spend with the ill or the aged?' said the automated female voice. 'Human Concern is our commoncause enabling organization. Human Concern welcomes your involvement for the common good . . . very well, very well . . . you have your second and final clearance . . . prepare to proceed.'

The kaleidoscope of the outermost door collapsed. Driven by the positive pressure within the airlock, it spewed outwards in a mess of shivering slob.

Hatch exited, striding bravely through the slob, only to be accosted by a mob of beggars. They were demanding not alms but justice, something Hatch was equipped to dispense since, by virtue of being a captain of the Imperial Guard, he was automatically a Judge of the Open Court.

So Hatch spent a weary time trying to make sense out of a three-cornered dispute between the beggars Grim, Zoplin and Lord X'dex Paspilion, something to do with the use of the Eye and the alleged theft of a considerable fraction of a much-decomposed dog corpse.

Hatch did his best, which was not easy, since the affairs of the poor are typically more complicated than those of the rich, and this seemed to be one of those cases in which everyone is at least partly to blame. Hatch at last decided that Grim should be allowed to punch Zoplin twice, and that Zoplin should be given the privilege of kicking Lord X'dex thrice in the ribs, but that Zoplin should have the exclusive use of the Eye until dawn the next day.

Having thus discharged his responsibilities, Hatch made his escape, or tried to, but in Scuffling Road he was waylaid by the noseless moneylender Polk, whose many demerits were increased by the fact that, thanks to his noseless state, he always reminded Hatch unpleasantly of his political nemesis, the implacable and ever-victorious Nambasa Berlin.

'Hatch!' said Polk, seizing upon the Frangoni warrior with claws which gripped like pincers.

Upon which Asodo Hatch turned upon the unfortunate moneylender. He seized Polk's wrist and twisted it free with a viciousness which almost broke the joint.

'Polk,' said Hatch, with murder in his voice.

Then caught a glimpse of something sun-struck and striking. It was a knife.

As Dog Java struck, Hatch blocked the blow with the body of the moneylender Polk. Dog's murderous blade slammed into Polk's back. Hatch felt the moneylender's body shake as Dog's knifestrength hit it, and hit it hard.

'Gah!' said Dog, realizing he had struck Polk rather than Hatch.

'You fool!' roared Hatch, letting Polk fall.

Dog confronted him. For a moment. Gaping. Blinking. Combat-shocked. Seared and shaken by his own audacity. And terrified to realize that his audacity had failed him – and that his muscle-pumped enemy still lived. Then Dog took to his heels, pelting away in a panic, fleeing back towards the lockway. Hatch made no attempt to pursue him. While Dog had the physique of a sprinter, Hatch was a bodybuilder, and was built accordingly.

'What was all that about?' said Polk, picking himself up from the dust where Hatch had dropped him.

'What?' said Hatch, astonished. 'I thought you were dead! Here, let me look at you.'

With that, Hatch took Polk by the shoulders and spun him round. The cloth which covered the moneylender's back had been knife-struck, ripping open a rent which revealed bright-shining fish-scale armour, the smoothest and brightest which Hatch had ever seen in his life. The workmanship was incredible, and, assuming that the armour had successfully blocked a full-strength blow by Dog, it was hard to assume that stuff so thin and yet so strong was of local make.

'Where did you come by this?' said Hatch.

'Never you mind,' said Polk, breaking free from the Frangoni warrior.

And, clearly disconcerted by the knife attack, and by Hatch's discovery of his secret armour, Polk made his getaway, leaving to a later date whatever discussion he had had in mind.

Hatch then started to make his way towards the lockway, intending to reenter the Combat College and bring Dog to justice. But he was intercepted by Shona, who had seen Dog's attack, and who restrained him.

'You might get ambushed,' she said.

There was a lot of good military sense in this, for it was most unlikely that Dog would have sought to strike Hatch down unless he had been encouraged to do so by some kind of conspiracy. So inside Cap Foz Para Lash there might be half a dozen or more Dog-minded knife-strikers ready to rip up Asodo Hatch if he incontinently pursued his quarry into the Combat College. So Hatch allowed Shona to talk him into settling his nerves with a cup of tea, and then, with his nerves settled – he had been shaken, he had to admit it! – Hatch went on his way.

CHAPTER THIRTEEN

Parengarenga: continental mass east of Argan, south of Tameran and west of Yestron. Dalar ken Halvar stands on the central upland plateau, viewed from which the geography is as follows.

To the north, a harsh and sparsely populated desert stretching away to the Coast of Sand; to the south, the arid wastes of the Death Lizard Desolations, then the Blue Mountains, with the lush tropics of the Elephant Coast beyond; to the west, the Golden Desert, realm of gold-diggers and opal miners, terminating at the Crocodile Coast; and, to the east, the Cattle Plains, which reach across the horizons to the Coast of Grass.

The Empire of Parengarenga has an army of a bare 30,000 men, a number ludicrously small until one considers that a continent which consists largely of a series of wastelands needs precious little protection against invaders, and that the Silver Emperor typically resolves domestic problems by political manipulation rather than brute force.

* * *

So he seated silk on furs, and,
Sweat despoiling ambergris and incense,
Stacked his folds for comfort.
Then watching fed, and fed on watching,
Fed on blood, and fingered
The naked soul beneath his thumb –
A blister-boil about to burst
And break beneath the sun.

*   *   *

On leaving Shona, Hatch did not go to his own home, but headed instead to the elegant house known as Pan Lay, the house which was the home of the Lady Iro Murasaki. If his murder was on the agenda, then he would surely be safer at Pan Lay; and, besides, he was in a mood to see the lady.

The Lady Iro Murasaki greeted Asodo Hatch in her customary manner, and they settled themselves upon a padded luxury of cushions. Tea was brought, and they drank.

The Lady Murasaki was adorned with Janjuladoola silks which had been spun and enbroidered in the far-off city of Obooloo in the distant continent of Yestron. Those silks were patterned with fish and birds. Yet wealth far greater adorned her hand, for on her finger she wore a sample of that rare and fabulously expensive gemstone known as ever-ice. The stone was held by a setting of silver. It was cold always, and by night and day alike it was surrounded by a nimbus of light, sometimes cold white and sometimes rainbow.

'How is your daughter?' said the Lady Murasaki.

'Onica is well,' said Hatch, dreading the question which would probably follow.

It did.

'How is your wife?'

'Talanta . . . Talanta is the same as ever.'

So said Hatch. His lover corrected him. Not Talanta. No. Not that. Rather: the Lady Talanta.

'The Lady Talanta, then,' said Hatch.

But she was no Lady, for Frangoni females did not bedeck themselves with gaudy titles. And Talanta was truly of the Frangoni. She was the Frangoni his parents had chosen for him, the woman he had brought to bed and who had given him children. And now she was – but he did not like to think about now. The now of his wife. Still less did he care to think of the future. Rather, he preferred for the moment – it might be wrong, doubtless was wrong, but this was the reality – to put his wife out of his mind. His moment was all for the Lady Murasaki.

The Lady Murasaki, however, was not concerned with the moment but with Hatch's family.

'When did you last see the moneylender Polk?' said she.

'I saw him today,' said Hatch.

'Did you then discuss your sister's debts?'

'We were, ah, interrupted,' said Hatch.

'I trust you have a scheme to redeem your sister's debts,' said the Lady Murasaki. 'The news I hear of her is most distressing. It seems that she is in danger of being sold into slavery. Surely it is your duty to prevent that from happening.'

'I have no money,' said Hatch flatly.

'But,' said Murasaki, good humour in her words, 'you are a captain of the Imperial Guard and a favourite of the very emperor himself. How can you be without money?'

'How many times does it have to be told to be true?' said Hatch, starting to get irritated. 'I have no money.'

'Then,' said Iro Murasaki, 'you will get it.'

'Very well then,' said Hatch, suddenly angry. 'Then I will go. Go seek my silvermine.'

'You are tired,' said the Lady Iro Murasaki, making allowances for him.

But Asodo Hatch did not respond, nor did he linger for the time it would have taken to kiss her. Instead, he quit the fine and mighty house of Pan Lay in something uncommonly like a fit of bad temper.

When Hatch was gone, the Lady Iro Murasaki reviewed their conversation, and the potential demand on her own treasury which was implicit in Hatch's situation. Had she truly heard something of a beggar's whine in his voice? She hoped she had imagined it. She knew of a certainty that she could be of no assistance to him, for the money she had invested with the Bralsh yielded her but three per cent per annum. She had budgeted out her own expenses to the last minimum, and dare not risk her capital, since that was a certain way to ruin.

As an individual, no doubt Asodo Hatch would have been a good risk; but, as a Frangoni, Hatch was bound into a very expensive web of family obligations.

Yet . . . yet despite all this . . . she cared for him. Love? She was too wise to be a fool to fall for love. But still . . .

* * *

Asodo Hatch left Pan Lay, the fine house which the Lady Iro Murasaki maintained on the heights of Cap Gargle, and descended by means of the Escadar Steps to the administrative quarter of Bon Tray. His intent was to route himself past the Grand Arena to Cap Uba and his own home on the Eastern Knoll.

As Hatch went down the Escadar Steps, he met Scorpio Fax coming up those steps.

'Hatch!' said Fax. 'I've been trying to get hold of you!'

'For what?' said Hatch.

'I have a confession to make,' said Fax, with the reckless bravado of a man who has abandoned himself to his death.

'A confession of what?' said Hatch.

'A confession of conspiracy,' said Fax.

'Conspiracy!' said Hatch, startled.

Ever since Scorpio Fax had suffered a nervous breakdown, Hatch had written him off entirely as far as the world of action was concerned, and so was all the more disconcerted by this knifestrike revelation.

'Yes,' said Fax. 'The Unreal have been months in conspiracy, inspired by the doctrines of Nu-chala-nuth, and I – Hatch, I was half-convinced at first, but now—'

'Nu-chala-nuth!' said Hatch, using the word as if it were an obscenity. 'Don't say you're tied up in all this!'

But of course Scorpio Fax had just declared as much, and he declared a lot more as he kept Hatch company to the bottom of the steps.

'I have the date of the revolution,' said Fax, as they came to the bottom of the steps.

'And?'

'It is scheduled for Dog Day. When the Festival of the Dogs begins, then will revolution likewise.'

'What will be the signal for the start of the revolution?'

'When the Dog Day drums start to beat,' said Fax, 'then the killing will start.'

Then Hatch questioned him further, though not perhaps with the depth and diligence that he should have, for a great weariness was upon him. Since he was so heavily burdened with his own problems, and since the empire and its emperor were of no help to him in solving those problems, wherefore should he help either empire or emperor? Nevertheless, he did his duty.

'All right,' said Hatch, when he had extracted from Scorpio Fax the very last bit of usable information. 'I'll take this news to Na Sashimoko. I'll try to get you an imperial pardon. In the meantime, I suggest you hide yourself away in the Combat College, out of sight of your fellow revolutionaries.'

With that, Fax fled, and Hatch set out for the imperial palace of Na Sashimoko.

At the palace, he would demand an audience with the emperor; and, once that audience was granted to him, he would report on the revolution which was brewing, and . . . did he dare? Yes! He would appraise the emperor of his own financial difficulties, and ask the emperor, quite frankly, for money – either as free gift or loan.

Such was Hatch's plan, though he did not have much hope of success, for the Silver Emperor was known for his tight fist. One of Plandruk Qinplaqus's favourite sayings was that 'power is its own reward'; and in accordance with that saying he advised those who were

187

closest to his heart to regard the air they breathed as the greater part of their corporeal reward. Furthermore, the emperor had long maintained his most savage punishments for the corrupt, and was never willing to turn a blind eye to those who discovered ways to enrich themselves by subtly exploiting their positions.

The emperor's stinginess was not without reason, for, as emperors went, he was far from being rich. Though the imperial silver mines were reputed to produce prodigious wealth, their output had been grossly exaggerated by the speculative. The emperor's finances were supported largely by taxation, and Parengarenga was essentially a poor land, its people few, its soil infertile and its distances vast.

Thus the ruler of the City of Sun practised a financial frugality scarcely to be distinguished from miserliness, and it was hard to say that the emperor was wrong in this. The state possessed no cornucopia for the generation of wealth, hence any benevolence shown to one citizen must necessarily add to the burdens of others. Nevertheless, Hatch had quite come to the end of his own resources, and so was determined to ask for charity.

Though Asodo Hatch was tolerably well paid as a captain of the Imperial Guard, and though he was able to supplement his income by marketing things bought inside Cap Foz Para Lash with his Combat College pay, he had nevertheless been brought to the point of ruin by one simple fact: the price of opium.

His wife was ill; she had cancer. Her disease was terminal, incurable. The only treatment was pain relief, and the only adequate source of such relief was opium, ever the most sovereign of drugs for the relief of suffering.

Yet opium was sourced – well, Hatch was not sure where it was sourced, and he had not been able to find anyone who was. It came from a particular kind of poppy, that much he knew. But the flower in question was not cultivated in Dalar ken Halvar. Rather, opium came to the city by way of trade – brought from Yestron, some said, while others claimed Argan to be its source.

The drugprice had brought Hatch to the brink of financial disaster, and left him helpless to rescue his sister from the consequences of her irresponsibility.

So, as Hatch made his way to Na Sashimoko, he was full of thoughts of his own personal struggle, and these thoughts were scarcely diminished by his meeting with a detachment of the Imperial Guards who were armed as if for war. Hatch had a hurried consultation with the leader of this detachment, and was told that Dalar ken Halvar had just received word of an uprising among the slaves of the silver mines which lay ten leagues to the south.

The slaves were making their revolution in the name of Nu-chala-nuth.

'That is terrible,' said Hatch. 'Terrible, terrible, terrible.'

But he said it for the sake of form, for the pressures of his own personal life were such that right at that moment he felt that all Dalar ken Halvar could have burnt to the ground without adding to his worries. In fact, if the moneylender Polk were to be burnt with the city, then his worries might be substantially reduced.

Nevertheless, having met with that detachment of Imperial Guards, and having received their alarming intelligence, Asodo Hatch quickened his step as he hastened on towards the imperial palace of Na Sashimoko.

CHAPTER FOURTEEN

The Silver Emperor: lord of Parengarenga and master of Dalar ken Halvar. He goes by various names, including Plandruk Qinplaqus, and is reputed to be a wizard of the order of Ebber, possessed of powers of mind over mind. If truly such, then he is a Manipulator whose Powers are analogous to those of an Enabled asma of the Nexus. Analogous – yet different. For the asma is but a machine, its functions fully explicated in the Book of Specifications, whereas every warlock is a creature linked in alliance with uncouth entities from the realms of mystery.

In the days of its power, the Nexus seldom colonized any cosmos so Permissive as to permit the miracles of the Gods Minor and the thaumaturgical feats of mage, shaman and sorcerer. Consequently, it made no serious effort to produce a Predictive Paradigm which would explain the other logic of magic.

The scientists of the Golden Gulag, however, living as they did in a cosmos so Permissive as to be only marginally stable, were in an ideal position to research those processes so often described as Synergetic Improbability. They had made some considerable progress towards understanding the ominous ambiguities of the Realms of Power when the Chasm Gate collapsed, precipitating a power struggle which shortly led to the wars of destruction in which the Gulag was utterly destroyed.

*   *   *

And so alone upon the sands

Two weapons bleed.
Yet while they bleed
In equal isolations sits –
Seated, yes, but just as lone –
A man who never dares a knife
Yet never lives without a blade
A skin away from striking.
This chair least comfortable of all:
Its purchase, peace:
And all slaves sounder sleep, though one and all
In fantasy desire that seat.

*　　*　　*

On the heights of the minor mountain of Cap Ogo Blotch, the northernmost of the great rocks of Dalar ken Halvar, stood a building of whitewashed stone. That building of whitewashed stone was the palace of Na Sashimoko, that Shrine of Thrones (or, in the mouths of some, that Shrine of Shrines) from which the Silver Emperor ruled the City of Sun and the realms of Parengarenga.

Despite its eminence, the palace owed nothing to the silver science of interior decorating. Here slovenly decay had the rule, and had ruled for centuries if appearances were anything to go by. It was undecorated – indeed, parts of it were unfinished. But when Hatch called in at the Treasurer's office, he entered another world entirely, a world dominated by immaculate order and an auditor's precision.

The Treasurer, Nambasa Berlin by name, was a hard man, and ruthless. His ruthlessness was exemplified by his noseless state. In his youth, Berlin had fought a rival for the favours of a beautiful young woman, and had persisted in fighting on to victory even after getting his nose bitten off. Unfortunately, the woman in question had then decided that she liked a third party much better than either of the two fools who had fought over her; but

Berlin had benefited much from having the ruthless resolution of his courage confirmed to both himself and the world at large at such an early age.

Hatch, however, did not like him, even though Hatch often admired those who were brave, and courageous, and ruthless in their resolution. In fact, Hatch had cause to hate him, for Berlin had made him contribute two years' worth of savings towards the costs of the campaign to retake Malic Milvus. Right now, Hatch had a grievous need for money; and he was sure his circumstances would not have been so straitened had he not lost so much in paying for the costs of the above-mentioned campaign.

For his part, Berlin disliked all the 'purple filth' as he termed the Frangoni. Nambasa Berlin was one of the Chem, the wealthy and hence Real upper-class of the people Pang, and the sexual rival who had bitten off his nose so many years earlier had been a Frangoni warrior. Hence Berlin's hated for the Frangoni.

With such deep discontents sourced in their past, Asodo Hatch and Nambasa Berlin should by rights have been bitter enemies, whereas in truth they had an effective working relationship based on a wary trust. Hatch appreciated Berlin's honesty, efficiency and forthrightness; and Berlin, for his part, admired the way in which Hatch tried to shoulder the whole of his family's debt-burden.

Thus their relationship stood when Hatch was admitted to the Treasurer's office.

'I wish to see the emperor,' said Hatch, without bothering with any introductory formalities.

'Very well,' said Berlin, and wrote out a pass which would get Hatch past the guards who safeguarded the very imperial presence itself. Berlin dated the pass, sanded it, sealed it in hot wax and handed it over. 'Present yourself to the Hall.'

Hatch nodded, and removed himself.

The corridor leading to the Hall was open to the sky,

and the Hall itself had a floor of loose stones in sizes up to that of a fist.

Some generations previously, the Silver Emperor had set about manic renovations which had destroyed the previous splendour of Na Sashimoko. Unfortunately, he had entered a deep depression before the renovations entered their creative phase. He had sent away the workers, and had never succeeded in conjuring up the enthusiasm necessary to arrange for the completion of the work.

Asodo Hatch entered the Hall, advanced gingerly across the knobbled stones, and halted in front of the imperial plinth. On that marble platform stood the imperial throne, a high-backed chair padded with red velvet. Its lacquerwork armrests were of black lacquerwork adorned with mother-of-pearl, and it came complete with two silver-stitched cushions, one for the emperor to sit on and the other for his feet to rest upon.

For the moment, the throne was empty but for the Princess Nuboltipon, who had no business being there, even though she was undoubtedly the most well-bred personage in all of Dalar ken Halvar.

'Greetings,' said Hatch to the Princess. 'Greetings from the low to the high.'

The Princess Nuboltipon made no answer to him. She never did. She seemed, indeed, to think herself a member of a breed so superior that it had no need to even acknowledge the existence of a bit of Frangoni lowlife like Asodo Hatch. Nevertheless, Hatch bore her contempt lightly, finding it a chivalrous pleasure to do so.

'My lady,' said Hatch. 'Can I be of some service to you? Your slightest wish, you know, is ever my command.'

So saying, Hatch bowed to the Princess Nuboltipon. Then straightened up, alerted to the approach of his emperor by the blast of a trumpet.

'All hail!' shouted an usher. 'All hail the Silver Emperor! All hail! All hail the great and mighty—'

Here the usher slowed, for it was death to mispronounce the emperor's name, but the contortions of that name might have been maliciously designed for the very purpose of tripping tongues. But the usher got it out without mutilating it.

'—the great and mighty Plandruk Qinplaqus!'

The Silver Emperor had other names, at least five of which were known to Hatch. There were also said to be others by which his slavegirls were entitled to address him, and he might have yet more names as yet unknown, but it was as Plandruk Qinplaqus that he currently chose to be announced in public in his own palace.

Hard on the heels of his name, the Silver Emperor entered the Hall, escorted by four slave girls. These were young women chosen for their high-breasted beauty. All were nubile and graceful, fair of face and seductive of gesture. Presumably the Silver Emperor took them in fantasy, for to Hatch's knowledge (and Hatch followed the palace gossip with a modicum of diligence) the emperor certainly never took them in the fact of the flesh.

The Silver Emperor looked indeed so old and frail that it was easy to imagine that a single incautious act of lust might bring his life story to an abrupt conclusion. Plandruk Qinplaqus was an ancient Ashdan so shrivelled and withered that he looked as if he might blow away on the wind. Looks were not deceptive, for Plandruk Qinplaqus had once nearly met with an untimely death when the Hot Mouth had sucked him off his feet.

On that notable occasion – no account of which was to be found in the official annals of Dalar ken Halvar, for the scribes who maintained the annals were a cautious breed – the Hot Mouth had in-breathed of a sudden. The emperor had been snatched away by the wind thus generated. Fortunately, Hatch had pounced on the emperor. The muscle-pumped Asodo Hatch had caught the fast-flying Silver Emperor, had thrown him to the ground, and then—

Few people cared to remember what had happened next, but the uncomfortable truth was that Asodo Hatch had sat on top of the Silver Emperor until the in-breathing winds of the Hot Mouth had died away to nothing. Hatch had never been thanked for doing his overlord this favour, for Plandruk Qinplaqus was a wizard, and wizards are mighty in their dignity, and are slow to give thanks to those who compromise that dignity, regardless of the excuse. However, the emperor had ever afterwards made sure that Hatch was in his entourage whenever he went near the Hot Mouth, which he did once a year in the course of his annual tour of inspection of Dalar ken Halvar.

Now the Silver Emperor stalked towards his chair of state.

'Off!' said the Silver Emperor, on discovering the Princess Nuboltipon ensconced in his throne.

So saying, the emperor slapped the armrest of the throne with a copy of the Imperial Census.

The armrest shattered, disintegrating in a cloud of woodworm dust. Bits of mother-of-pearl fell to the white marble of the imperial plinth. The Princess Nuboltipon fled, nimbling over the stones of the Hall till she was well out of reach of the destructive might of the Imperial Census. At which point she slowed, then cast a disdainful look over her shoulder. Then, with her tail high and undaunted, she made her way towards the exit at a pace more consonant with her dignity.

The Silver Emperor struck his throne's surviving armrest with his walking stick, which was old and crooked yet was possessed of the strength of iron. That armrest also disintegrated.

'A cheap and shoddy piece of rubbish,' said the Silver Emperor.

As this he said, the Princess Nuboltipon disappeared out of the door through which Hatch had entered. The soldiers there on guard, who had less regard for her than did Asodo Hatch, did not bother to salute her departure.

'Hatch,' said the Silver Emperor, tapping the Frangoni warrior on the chest with the handle of his walking stick, which was of silver, and was in the shape of a pelican.

'My lord,' said Hatch.

'Find out who made this piece of furniture.'

'My lord,' said Hatch, 'it came to Dalar ken Halvar as part of the spoils from Malic Milvus.'

This was true, and Hatch was glad to mention it, for he was eager to reopen the matter of the Malic Milvus campaign and the costs of that victory.

'Yes, yes, Malic Milvus,' said the emperor. 'Where you put us to abominable expense, this piece of rotten woodworm your sole recompense to the throne.'

'My lord, I—'

'You might brush down my robes,' said the Silver Emperor, 'if you were wanting to be of assistance to us.'

Hatch plucked a fan from one of the slave girls and used it to remove the splinters, dust and woodworm droppings which had despoiled his emperor's robes.

'Hatch,' said the Silver Emperor, while Hatch was still at work.

'My lord,' said Hatch, pausing in his cleaning duties.

'See how far you can throw this throne.'

Hatch looked at his emperor in astonishment. Was he hearing aright? And if he was, then was his emperor deranged or what?

'In . . . in which direction, my lord?'

'The direction of your choice.'

'As my lord commands,' said Hatch.

Since Hatch was the emperor's slave, it was his duty to obey the emperor's every whim. Sometimes these whims were exceedingly strange, as Hatch had found in the past. Still, many emperors have suffered from worse deficiencies than a taste for the occasional piece of casual vandalism, so Hatch did not object too seriously to his lord's excesses.

Obedient to his emperor's command, the Frangoni

196

warrior braced himself, picked up the throne – it proved lighter than he had expected – and heaved it towards the centre of the Hall. It crashed on to the rocks of the Hall and shattered in a cloud of dust.

'Ah,' said the Silver Emperor, with a great sigh of satisfaction. 'That's something I've always wanted to do. So, Hatch. So you do have your uses. You – you, girl – what's your name – fetch me a chair.'

A chair was fetched and Plandruk Qinplaqus settled himself in this makeshift throne – a procedure which was less than instantaneous, involving as it did the placement of a cushion under his feet by one slave and the serving to him of sherbet by another.

'Well, Hatch,' said the Silver Emperor, once he was properly seated. 'Have you caught any more mad scientists?'

'None,' said Hatch.

'Then you're in default of your duty,' said the Silver Emperor. 'My spies tell me there were ten of them down by the river. They were endeavouring to invent a vehicle for submersible travel.'

'To do what?' said Hatch. 'To ride the river to the Mouth?'

'Don't be impertinent with me!' said Plandruk Qinplaqus, shaking his walking stick at Hatch. 'Impertinence ill becomes you. Address the question, Hatch. What have you been doing to catch me mad scientists?'

In truth, Asodo Hatch had not been involved with any mad scientists since he had disposed of Darius Flute. The unfortunate Flute had cracked under the pressure of his Combat College studies, and had abruptly withdrawn from the College, announcing that he was going to start a new Renaissance of Technology in Dalar ken Halvar. This was quite, quite mad, as the city of Dalar ken Halvar and the continent of Parengarenga as a whole quite lacked the population base and the raw materials required to create any technology capable of economically out-performing an ox cart.

But the Silver Emperor had taken Darius Flute's claims seriously. Plandruk Qinplaqus had never banned technological enterprise, since the Silver Emperor knew full well that to forbid something was to make it universally attractive. So Qinplaqus had ordered Hatch to execute Darius Flute, but to do so in a manner which would not draw public attention to Flute's technological enterprises.

Hatch had then proceeded with consummate skill. He had arranged for his sister Penelope to marry the unsuspecting Darius Flute; and, on their wedding night, Penelope had stepped outside, Hatch had stepped inside, and Flute had been dead in moments. It was the custom among the Frangoni that a bride was fully entitled to kill her husband if he disappointed her on the first night of their marriage, so Flute's death had passed with very little in the way of public comment; and the Silver Emperor had been rightly pleased.

But now—

'Hatch,' said Plandruk Qinplaqus. 'Will you keep me waiting all day? My question requires an answer. How many mad scientists have you hunted for me of late?'

'I did not know that my lord had commanded me to actively pursue such creatures,' said Hatch mildly.

'You don't take this seriously, do you?' said the Silver Emperor.

'I trust that wisdom sits on the throne, and hence am ever eager to obey those commands which come to me from the throne,' said Hatch. 'But as yet the throne has not chosen to give me any instructions for fresh persecution, murder or otherwise.'

'I see, I see,' said the Silver Emperor. 'A legalist. Well then, leaving aside the scientist question – have you seen this?'

With that, the Silver Emperor waved the cat-intimidating Imperial Census at Hatch.

'No,' said Hatch shortly.

In his moods of deep depression, Plandruk Qinplaqus was hard to handle, but as he ascended his manic curve Hatch usually found him quite intolerable.

'You haven't read it?' said the Emperor. 'Well, then. It's yours, then. Take it.'

Then the Silver Emperor tossed the Census in Hatch's general direction.

Hatch let it fall to the broken rubble of the Hall, then bent, picked it up and carefully dusted it off. One never made sudden or incautious moves when one was in the Emperor's presence. The Emperor himself was possessed of the most admirable self-control, but some of his guards were a bit too quick with a javelin.

'When you search those pages,' said the Silver Emperor, 'you will find that a full fifty people claim themselves to be scientists.'

Hatch knew the Silver Emperor lived in fear of waking up one morning to find that one of his subjects had built a functional starship, or something worse. It was true that many of Dalar ken Halvar's mad scientists had claimed that they would do as much – indeed, they had claimed that they would bring about a glorious Age of Light in which every man would walk on silver and eat from gold.

'I will take note of the number of scientists,' said Hatch, endeavouring to remain non-committal.

'There are probably more of them than that,' said Plandruk Qinplaqus. 'With every census I trust the figures less. This one, for instance! It tallies the last rice harvest to the very last sack. But last harvest the mountains of Qash were in open revolt against the empire. How then could we count those sacks to the very last?'

Hatch caught a note of rising fanaticism in the emperor's voice. Plandruk Qinplaqus was getting quite worked up about his census. Hatch knew this mood. The Silver Emperor was on the upswing, climbing out of his last and longest depression, entering a manic stage.

'Well,' said Hatch, seeking an opening.

'Well!' said the Silver Emperor. 'You wish to speak, do you? Then speak! Give your report.'

'My lord,' said Hatch, thinking he had better speak both quickly and bluntly. 'There is revolution brewing in the city. Indeed, some say it has started already.'

'I am intrigued,' said the Silver Emperor. 'Proceed.'

Hatch proceeded, and told what he knew.

'So,' said Plandruk Qinplaqus, when Hatch was finished. 'Our soldiers are on the way to the silver mines already.'

'That is so,' said Hatch, 'but if Scorpio Fax is to be believed, then in the city—'

'Forget the city,' said the Silver Emperor. 'They want a revolution in the city? Very well! Let them have their revolution! It will do us no harm. Ignore it!'

'Ignore it?' said Hatch, quite taken aback.

'Yes, yes,' said the Silver Emperor. 'Ignore it. What can they do? Burn the city? It burns on a regular basis. Let them riot, then let the riot burn itself out.'

'My lord, they threaten, they—'

'Hatch,' said the emperor, 'the city is so thoroughly divided against itself that nobody can hope to unite it. Can the Yara unite with the Chem, the Frangoni with the Ebrell Islanders? Whoever wins the city wins the nightmare. With the nightmare over, they'll wake anew to me. To my reason. My mercy. My strength. My prudence. My justice. They love me, Hatch, and with reason. I love them too, hence let them have their amusements. Let then the burning of the city count as such amusement.'

'My lord,' said Hatch, 'I think you let your city burn too easily.'

'I let it burn for a purpose,' said the Silver Emperor. 'There is conspiracy, it seems. Very well! Let the conspiracy reveal itself. Then we will chop down the conspirators and have done with all conspiracy for a generation.'

Hatch thought this poorly thought out, but he was dismissed, and had no alternative but to leave.

*   *   *

Asodo Hatch was slowly waking from his own personal concerns to face the wider realities of the city in which he lived. But those realities had been changing even as he had been in conference with the Silver Emperor, as Hatch found out when he left the presence of the mighty Plandruk Qinplaqus.

For at the end of his audience with Qinplaqus, Hatch was intercepted by the noseless Nambasa Berlin, Dalar ken Halvar's Treasurer. While Hatch had been meeting the emperor, messengers had arrived at the palace, bringing alarming news from the city. There were demonstrations; there was sporadic looting and burning in Actus Dorum; a boat had been pirated on the Yamoda; and there was one incoherent report which suggested that the soldiers sent to put down the uprising at the silver mines had been ambushed and massacred en route.

'This is not looking good,' said Berlin somberly.

'Not at all,' said Hatch.

'I think,' said Berlin, 'I think that the pair of us should reason a little further with our beloved emperor.'

Hatch sincerely doubted the use of this, since Plandruk Qinplaqus ever trusted his own judgement, and was singularly proof against all forms of persuasion. However, Hatch accompanied Berlin, and the pair of them went to hunt out the Silver Emperor.

Which proved harder than expected.

Plandruk Qinplaqus had quit the Hall in which Hatch had seen him last; guards placed outside the Silver Emperor's private quarters declared that he was not to be disturbed, and when the guards had been browbeaten into submission by the combined efforts of Hatch and Berlin, the emperor's private quarters proved to be empty.

Empty, at least, of any emperor.

'He can't have just vanished!' said Berlin.

But the mighty Plandruk Qinplaqus seemed to have done just that. Hatch and Berlin dared their way into the imperial study and found a massive granite desk littered with papers and heavyweight seals. Hatch riffled through the papers in the hope of finding a clue to the emperor's disappearance, but all the documentation was in the High Speech of wizards, which he had no hope of understanding.

'Can you read this?' said Hatch, shoving a parchment under Berlin's nose.

'No,' said Berlin, waving it away. 'But this stuff is so dusty – Hatch, it hasn't been touched for days.'

Hatch and Berlin researched the Silver Emperor's quarters, interrogated guards and slaves, then returned to Berlin's office, baffled.

In Berlin's office, mice – which had somehow become besplattered with vermilion ink, perhaps as a consequence of some secret sadism practised by Berlin – dwelt inside a wickerwork cage. Hatch thought mice could eat wickerwork. But perhaps he was wrong, or perhaps – and here he began to analyse the situation with the rigour taught to him by the Nexus – the cage was daily renewed, or the bars lacquered with deterrent poison, or a new set of mice procured each time those presently in captivity escaped.

Hatch was struck by the mice, and the way in which their lives continued, quietly and regularly, in complete innocence of the disaster which was mounting to its heights outside the palace of Na Sashimoko. It seemed to Hatch that he himself had much in common with such a mouse.

'So,' said Berlin, taking a chair, 'our emperor has chosen to disappear.'

'You don't seem overly concerned,' said Hatch.

'Not about him,' said Berlin. 'He comes and he goes. He won't say where, but he's never gone for more than ten days at a time.'

'What do you mean?' said Hatch. 'What are you talking about?'

'Just that,' said Berlin. 'Sometimes our emperor leaves his palace, and, for all I know, this very city. I've never found out where he goes. I've never thought it politic to take too keen an interest in the subject.'

'So what do we do?' said Hatch. 'Do we sit and watch the city burn?'

'No,' said Berlin. 'In the absence of our emperor, I'm the acting ruler. That's what the constitution says. I'll order the troops into the streets to put down our revolutionaries as best they can.'

'What about Scorpio Fax?' said Hatch, conscious of his responsibilities to the man who had sought to warn him of the revolution.

'Fax?' said Berlin.

'He reported, he told us—'

'Oh, Fax, Fax, yes. Well. Since his confession was too late to be useful, we should by rights have him executed for treason. That's what I'd do. But the emperor is usually more merciful than I would be in his place, so – I'll give Fax a provisional pardon, subject to confirmation by the emperor himself. You may tell him that when you see him next.'

With that, Nambasa Berlin dismissed Asodo Hatch, and the Frangoni warrior quit the palace of Na Sashimoko.

It was by then late afternoon on the Day of Three Fishes, just three days short of Dog Day.

CHAPTER FIFTEEN

A simple ethic has long ruled Dalar ken Halvar: that the imaginary needs of imaginary people must take tenth place to the demands of those who really exist. Among the Pang, the brown-skinned people who constitute Dalar ken Halvar's dominant racial group, both Chem and Yara alike have long accepted this dogma. How could it be otherwise, when the poor know from their very language that they are imaginary?

It has long been the case that subversive notions, whether sourced from the Eye of Delusions or from the revolutionary readings of radical Combat Cadets, have found no favour even with those of the Yara who are most bitterly oppressed. After all, if they were to accept their own reality, then their lives would immediately become unbearable, whereas virtually all suffering becomes bearable if it can be shrugged off as but a species of dream.

But now a cunning rabble-rouser had employed the accepted social axioms to produce an unexpected conclusion. He says:

'We are the Yara. We do not exist. Because we do not exist we have no responsibilities to anyone or anything. We are but the waking dreams of the world, and who can hold a dream accountable under law?'

This argument has proved unexpectedly potent. The Yara do not want to increase their own sufferings by acknowledging them, hence have no wish to become Real, but a formula which frees them of all responsibility to the real world has proved potently attractive.

* * *

So on the sands a shadow stands
Above a shadow stretched.
And nothing happens – but amok
The tongues demand the teeth,
The steel striking –
Demand that he
Made murderer by skill decree –

*   *   *

Fears for his own safety had earlier kept Asodo Hatch away from his own house. For, after all, Dog Java had made a determined effort to kill him, which suggested he might be the target of a conspiracy of murder. And murderers in search of Asodo Hatch would surely and logically look for him under his own roof.

However, now that Hatch had been alerted to the danger of civic disorder in the City of Sun, he thought of his family rather than himself, and hastened back to House Takabaga with a view to securing the safety of his wife Talanta and his daughter Onica. But on his way back to the Frangoni rock, Asodo Hatch saw precious little in the way of revolution. And on Cap Uba itself, all was peace.

Consequently, Hatch was not alarmed to find his house empty, his wife and daughter gone. He presumed them to be worshipping at Temple Isherzan, or visiting the womenfolk of other households. Or it might well be that Onica was at her knife-fighting classes, and that her mother was there as a chaperone. The Frangoni greatly approved of their womenfolk making an earnest study of the great art of knife-fighting, for among the Frangoni this form of athleticism has long been held to improve the physical grace of the female form. However, it would be inappropriate for a young yet nubile girl like Onica to be alone with a knife-fighting instructor, hence her mother always accompanied her to her lessons.

Once Asodo Hatch was safe in the Frangoni rock, and

safe in his own house, his fears of civic disorder began to dissipate. Indeed, he began to think that both he himself and Nambasa Berlin had given way to a certain vapouring panic while in conference in Na Sashimoko. So there had been demonstrations? The 'demonstrations' might well have been no more than the distantly observed activities of gangs of young men preparing themselves for the celebrations of Dog Day. There had been burnings in Actus Dorum, had there? Perhaps there had been a couple of cooking fires out of control. A boat had been pirated on the Yamoda, had it? Maybe one of the leaky fishing boats of that sluggish river had sunk in neck-deep water, as was a common occurrence. And as for soldiers being ambushed and massacred – why, that could be sheer rumour.

And besides, Scorpio Fax had said – had he not? – that there was no revolution scheduled until Dog Day.

Of course he had.

He had said just that.

Not till Dog Day, with the Dog Day drums to start it.

So it was that when Asodo Hatch gained the peace of his house in the late afternoon of the Day of Three Fishes, he very shortly ceased worrying about the state of the city, and convinced himself that all was well, and accordingly committed himself to his bed, and was asleep within moments.

As Asodo Hatch slept the sleep of exhaustion, the shadows of the afternoon lengthened into evening. And as the shadows lengthened, the fires which were burning here and there in the streets of Dalar ken Halvar were more easily to be seen. And it would have been clear to anyone standing atop the Frangoni rock that those fires were rapidly increasing in number.

It was thus clear to the woman Talanta and the girl Onica as they made their way home from Temple Isherzan. And by the time they got to their own house, House Takabaga, it was evident to their untutored eyes that something of a widespread riot was going on in the city, and was gathering momentum as the gathering dark began to ensure a degree of anonymity for the rioters.

Onica was all for waking her father, since she had a great faith in him, and was sure he would do something about the rioting. Talanta was likewise sure that the noble Hatch would do something – or try to. His sense of responsibility was such that he was unlikely to concede that any problem was too big for him, so there was every possibility that he would try to wrench the rioting city to order single-handed, and would quite possibly get himself killed in the process.

And Talanta, who did not wish to add to her own problems by encompassing the death of her husband, accordingly forbade Onica to wake him, and counselled her to practise the meditations of patience.

Thus peace ruled in House Takabaga.

And peace ruled on the Frangoni rock itself, for the Frangoni were poor, and well-armed, and strongly consolidated upon their rock, and therefore not much of a temptation to lawless and disorganized rioters who had easier targets elsewhere.

However, while the Frangoni rock was in peace, the Combat College was the scene of considerable alarums. Many Combat College students belonged to the Free Corps, which essentially supported the status quo. As soon as the rioting began, word went out from the Brick, the headquarters of the Free Corps. In obedience to commands from the Brick, vigilante squads began to form to put down the rioting, and many Combat College students went forth into the world to join those vigilante squads.

Scorpio Fax, he who had informed Hatch of the impending revolution, had initially taken refuge in the Combat College. But he began to get increasingly concerned as messengers came and went, as Free Corps zealots went hustling off to participate in their vigilante actions, and as other Combat College students sought refuge in the safety of the College itself – bringing with them tales of burnings, and beatings, and upsettings, and sinkings, and kidnappings, and rapes, and mutilations and murders.

It became clear to Scorpio Fax that the revolution so long fomented, so carefully planned and so meticulously organized was getting underway prematurely. All kinds of possibilities occurred to him. Perhaps his own encounter with Asodo Hatch had been observed, and those with whom he had conspired had realized that Fax was betraying their cause, and so had decided to launch their revolution immediately, before it could be put down. Or perhaps some of the rowdiness which attended the days leading up to Dog Day had convinced some revolutionaries that their revolution was breaking out by itself. Or perhaps—

Well, Scorpio Fax had an inventive mind, and he had invented up a full three dozen scenarios by the time night fell. And in the course of his inventing, he found himself creating unfortunate deaths for the purple-skinned Penelope Flute, the woman whom he had secretly admired for so long – and so fruitlessly.

As Fax had learnt long ago, Penelope Flute was deeply committed to Lupus Lon Oliver. And Lupus, of course, was a Free Corps member through and through. Therefore, it had long ago occurred to Fax that a revolution which saw the destruction of the existing social order would see the Free Corps destroyed along with that order; and the pulling down and pulling to bits of the Free Corps might well mean the dismemberment of young Lupus himself, and therefore—

Yes, let the truth be told!

There are all kinds of reasons for getting oneself embroiled in a revolution, but the deepest motivation which had impelled Scorpio Fax into an involvement with Dalar ken Halvar's revolutionary cause was the hope that the overthrow of the ruling order might win him the woman he loved.

Or might at least secure the destruction of the young Ebrell Islander who was proving such a successful suitor of her hand.

As Fax sat in the Combat College, receiving successive reports of the growing turmoil in the streets of Dalar ken Halvar, his anxiety grew. And, when he had conjured up lurid images of the death or despoiling of Penelope for the seventieth time, he finally gave in to his fears – and exited from the Combat College, and hurried to House Jodorunda, intending to ensure the preservation of the life, health and safety of the delectable Penelope.

When Fax came down Zambuk Street to House Jodorunda, he found an ox cart overturned outside that house. The ox cart had been carrying water barrels, which were being smashed by an enthusiastic gang of wreckers. The oxen had been slaughtered, and amateur butchers were hacking steaks out of the dusty carcasses. The noise of this revolutionary celebration covered the sound of Fax's intrusion into House Jodorunda.

Which he found empty.

There was nobody at all in the house, except, in the bathroom, the delectable Penelope Flute herself.

'Ah,' said Fax, breathing his relief, pleased beyond the telling to find Penelope safe and secure.

'What are you doing here?' said Penelope, looking up at Fax from the comforts of her bath.

When Fax made no immediate answer, Penelope heaved herself out of the water like a wrathful hippopotamus, and Fax beat a hasty retreat, withdrawing into the outer room.

'I was looking for your brother,' called Fax, once he had put a door between himself and Penelope.

'Well, you're looking in the wrong place,' said Penelope, throwing open that door and pursuing Fax. 'Because this isn't his house, it's mine.'

'Penelope,' said Fax, moving impetuously to embrace the Frangoni female, for all that her fully-clothed female form was dripping wet from the bath. 'I—'

Penelope made a curt gesture of discontent. This gesture caused her bunched knuckles to connect with the underside of Scorpio Fax's jaw. Fax crashed backwards, taking a lacquerwork table down to ruin as he went to the ground.

Fortunately, at that point Fax's combat training came into play, and he crossed his legs quickly enough to block the kick which Penelope aimed at his crutch.

'Look, you!' said Penelope, looking down at Fax from the ominous tower of her height. 'If I've told you once, I've told you a thousand times – I don't want you sniffing round here any longer like a dog in heat!'

Scorpio Fax was acutely conscious of the blue and green ceremonial tattoos which adorned Penelope's nose. She had castrated and killed one rapist, and was perfectly capable of doing the same to Fax himself if she thought him to be himself a member of that breed.

'I, ah, I didn't mean any harm,' said Fax.

'Good!' said Penelope, picking up a lacquerwork table.

Fax did a combat roll which brought him to his feet, threw up his arms to shield his face from the lightweight table, then fled out into the night.

He was hot.

He was flushed.

He was panting.

And he was bitterly disillusioned.

In the months of conspiracy which had been directed towards launching a properly coordinated full-scale revolution in Dalar ken Halvar, Fax had indulged himself in confused but definitely salacious imaginings. In his fantasies, he had imagined himself taking advantage of revolutionary chaos either to seduce Penelope or else to subdue her to his will by exercise of brute force.

He had imagined that Penelope would be panic-stricken, terrified by the noise, the screams, the crackle of bursting flames, the clash of steel, the roar of the riotous cloud. He had imagined her weeping, clinging, clutching, imploring. And he would have been a hero, stalwart amidst the storm, instead of—

Fax slowed to a walk, heading west through the night along the dust of Zambuk Street. Perhaps if there had been a full-scale revolution, things would have gone as he had imagined. But, instead, the thing had happened spontaneously, prematurely, and the results were desultory.

Instead of a city awash with roaring flames, the night was merely sprinkled with arson. Instead of a howling mob, there was the occasional shout and – intermittently – some distant screaming.

What is revolution without the bloodstorm riot which storms the prisons, overthrows the palaces and pulls down the high and mighty from their places of power?

A revolution without such excesses is more a random riot than an effective political movement, and a riot was what Dalar ken Halvar was getting. The prison was tucked away in Childa Go, north of Na Sashimoko, in among the shacks and drying huts of the fishing centre. There was no booty to attract rioters to Childa Go, and the fishing folk were not the kind to riot on their own account.

So Fax was ready to bet that nobody was storming the prison, and that nobody was trying to storm the heights of Ogo Blotch to kill and rape, to burn and pillage, to force the defences of Na Sashimoko and raid the very Hall, pulping the Silver Emperor to a mash of bones and setting the flames amok amidst his palace, leaving the Shrine of Thrones in smoking ruins.

No, it was not that kind of revolution at all.

Instead, there was a settling of scores, a plundering of moneylenders, a vandalistic wantonage of arson for the hell of it, and much japing destruction in imitation of the careless saturnalia of the Festival of the Dogs.

So what could Fax salvage from this debacle?

'Well – the death of Polk the Cash, of course!

Fax knew the fair Penelope Flute to be in danger of

being enslaved by Polk, who had taken unfair advantage of Penelope's poverty to obtain a mortgage on her flesh. Very well. Fax would take advantage of the confusion of the night to dispose of Polk. Then, if he could later win the heart of the voluptuous Penelope, he would confess the secret of that murder, thus confirming her in her love for him.

With that thought in mind, Fax headed into the commercial centre of Actus Dorum. Here every Ethnos Minor was to be found, for the place was home not just to the Pang of Dalar ken Halvar but also to a motley rabble of Ebrell Islanders, Southsearchers, failed wizards, Ashdan ethnologists and others who had come to the imperial heartlands by way of the trade routes.

But when Fax found Polk's house, the moneylender was not there. Instead, Polk the Cash had gone to the Frangoni rock. This – or so said Polk's neighbours – was so that the noseless moneylender could take into protective custody the young Frangoni maiden Onica, youngest daughter of Asodo Hatch. It was known to the neighbours that Onica had mortgaged herself to Polk, and they claimed that the noseless one had decided that his investment needed special protection on this most uncertain of nights.

So Fax hurried to the Frangoni rock, firm in his intent to ambush Polk at or near Hatch's house, then beat the moneylender to death.

Well.

The neighbours were both right and wrong.

Polk's neighbours were right in thinking that the noseless one had taken himself off to House Takabaga. But he had not gone there with any confiscation in mind. Rather, he had gone there in search of his own protection. It is harder to imagine a greater compliment than this: that a moneylender should take refuge with the most mercilessly plighted of his creditors at a time of general riot verging on wholesale revolution. Yet Polk the Cash – who rightly counted himself an excellent judge of character – had paid the Family Hatch this compliment.

Thus when Scorpio Fax came bursting into House Takabaga, he found Polk seated cross-legged upon a meal-mat, enjoying a bowl of scorpion soup. And when Fax called upon Polk to come outside and be murdered, the effect of this call was to precipitate violence.

This violence woke from sleep the slumbering Asodo Hatch, who came stumbling from the bedroom in a state of dazed bewilderment, to find Scorpio Fax sprawled full-length on the beaten earth of the floor, with the shards of a soup pot scattered around him.

Explanations followed, explanations to which Fax reluctantly added once he had recovered consciousness. Whereupon Asodo Hatch, who was not at all amused, declared Fax to be his prisoner, and further declared that he would deliver this prisoner to Na Sashimoko that very night.

CHAPTER SIXTEEN

Frangoni: the purple people of Parengarenga. Those who dwell in Dalar ken Halvar keep themselves very much to themselves on the great rock known as Cap Uba, west of the Dead Mouth and east of the commercial centre known as Actus Dorum. There in the temple of Isherzan they worship the Great God Mokaragash, the Resurrector of Souls. The ethnarch of the Frangoni of Dalar ken Halvar is Sesno Felvus, who is also and necessarily the High Priest of the Great God Mokaragash.

*   *   *

> This bowl has fed from
> Strangers whose offence
> Is spoken by their saliva, by the grub
> Which lives between their lips and sings
> Of locust-lust and slime
> Thicker than worms.
> I would have the food of my own people,
> But here devour, perforce,
> The bedbug's tapeworm,
> The brandling's red and yellow,
> The bloodworm's grease:
> And eat my words in whispers in the night,
> Lost in the heartland of an alien dust.

*   *   *

So it came to pass that, early on the night of the Day of Three Fishes, just three days short of Dog Day, Asodo

Hatch was woken from sleep to find Dalar ken Halvar in disorder and Scorpio Fax sprawled full-length on the floor of House Takabaga.

After formally taking Fax a prisoner, Asodo Hatch then with equal formality invited Polk the Cash to enjoy the hospitality of House Takabaga during these times of uncertainty.

'I have it on good information,' said Hatch, improvising a lie of some cunning, 'that the revolutionaries now on the loose in the city have a death-list, and that your name is near the top of that list.'

Of course, the noseless one did not need the encouragement of such lies, but Hatch wanted to make sure. For Hatch hoped that by sheltering Polk in this time of trouble he would thereafter obtain some amelioration of his financial burdens. Polk, for his part, readily accepted Hatch's invitation, and had grace enough to conceal the fact that just such an invitation had already been extended to him by Talanta and Onica.

With the affairs of the moment thus arranged, Hatch confirmed to one and all that he intended to take Scorpio Fax to Na Sashimoko, the ruling palace of the City of Sun. Having made that announcement, Hatch hauled Fax away into the night.

'All right,' said Fax, once they were out of earshot of House Takabaga. 'You can let me go now.'

'Let you go!' said Hatch. 'What makes you think I'm going to let you go!'

'I was trying to kill Polk! He – he—'

'You were trying to kill him in front of my daughter Onica! You witless idiot! You'd have made her witness to murder, and then, then, well, either we turn you in or else she becomes a part of a conspiracy to conceal murder. Didn't you think of that?'

'Of course I thought of that,' said Fax, who had thought no such thing. 'But—'

'I told you!' said Hatch. 'I told you to get yourself back to the Combat College. I thought you were going there! If I'd thought for a moment that you were—'

'He's your enemy, Hatch! Polk's your enemy! I thought—'

'Come on,' said Hatch. 'I've no time for listening to speeches.'

Here Hatch was true to his breeding, for the Frangoni have ever preferred making speeches rather than listening to them. Having thus cut short Fax's excuses, Asodo Hatch took Fax down the Backsteps which descended the western slopes of Cap Uba.

'So what happens to me at Na Sashimoko?' said Fax, unable to conceal his fear for his own future.

'We dungeon you,' said Hatch.

'The emperor has no dungeons,' said Fax.

'Not at his palace. But the Grand Arena is not so terribly distant.'

'You don't gain by threats,' said Fax. Trying to play the part of the brave revolutionary. Then, suddenly: 'Hatch. Hatch. It would be the easiest thing to let me go. A moment's work. There's no witnesses here, not now, not in the dark.'

'You don't like this game?' said Hatch. 'That's easy, then. The Dead Mouth is but a stone's throw distant. Oh, I can let you go, if that's what you really want.'

The Dead Mouth was as close as Hatch said it was. And it was deep. Even in the brightest of sunlight, to look down into it was to see darkness falling to darkness for what looked like eternity. It was quite impossible to see the bottom. While Hatch presumed that the Dead Mouth did actually have a bottom, legend held it to be depthless, and in practice it was, for no rope of mortal make could measure out more than its merest lip. It was, naturally, an irresistible attraction to suicides.

In the face of that threat, Scorpio Fax fell very quiet, and Hatch led him through the stumbling dark toward the palace of Na Sashimoko.

But they were still far short of the palace when they met Umka Ash, he of the uncertain breeding – his piebald skin a mass of white and black blotches, and birthmarks in both red and in purple.

'Hatch!' said Ash.

'What is it, Combat Cadet?' said Hatch.

Then Umka Ash gave him the bad news. In the face of a revolution by the Unreal, the Free Corps had joined with certain officers of the imperial guard in launching a coup to 'stabilize the situation'.

'A coup!' said Hatch, in disbelief. 'What do you mean by a coup?'

'I mean,' said Ash, 'that they said they were making a coup, and killed three men who were fool enough to disagree with them.'

'Killed?' said Hatch.

'Yes,' said Ash. 'Unless you believe a man can have his head chopped off and still live, they were killed. I saw it.'

'But,' said Hatch, still at a loss, 'what do they hope to achieve by this – this coup?'

'I am going back to the Combat College to write you a formal paper on the analysis of that very point,' said Umka Ash dryly.

'Wah!' said Hatch, trying to absorb the implications of this news of a coup. 'A real night for lunatics!'

'So what are you going to do with me?' said Scorpio Fax.

'We'd best be back to the Combat College,' said Hatch. 'Both of us.'

'Does this mean I'm pardoned?'

'Am I the emperor, to be giving pardons?' said Hatch. 'Come on. Let's be gone.'

So Scorpio Fax and Asodo Hatch started back to the Combat College, in company with Umka Ash. But they had not gone far when Fax suddenly broke away and fled into the night.

'Fax!' roared Hatch. 'Come back! I'm ordering you!'

But it was no use.

Fax was gone.

'What now?' said Umka Ash.

'We proceed to the Combat College,' said Hatch. 'There you can write your paper of analysis, but I for my part intend to rouse our fellow students out for action.'

The readiness with which Hatch said this disturbed Ash greatly, who said:

'Sorry,' said Ash. 'I've been thinking, and my family . . .'

'Go, then,' said Hatch.

Ash went, and Hatch continued to the Combat College on his own, trying to work out what to do. Rouse students for action? it was easily said. But who could he rouse, and exactly what could they do to bring the city to order?

Asodo Hatch was on his own, with no communications and no access to any kind of data flow. His emperor was missing. A group of over-excited soldiers and Free Corps types had declared themselves masters of Dalar ken Halvar. A half-coordinated revolution was in progress in the city.

Hatch was tolerably certain that his family would be safe enough on the Frangoni rock, at least for the moment. He decided that he should push on to the Combat College, set up his own command centre, send out scouts to bring him information, organize the information on a battle-map, and find volunteers who would be prepared to act under his command and restore order in the city once the rioting burnt itself out.

So to the lockway went Asodo Hatch, and found it a scene of burnt-out wreckage, for every stall on Scuffling Road had been smashed, looted, wrecked and burnt. The kinema, the amphitheatre outside the lockway, was lit by the lurid light of the Eye of Delusions, which was showing a cartoon in which the gross and hideous savages of one of the Wild Tribes – savages who gibbered in the triumph of their bloodlust – were cutting out the hearts of hapless victims.

Tonight, nobody was in the amphitheatre watching the Eye. The attractions of the city were greater.

'A bad business,' said Hatch.

He strode toward the lockway itself. The lurid cartoon-light of the Eye flickered across the red dust of the Plain of Jars, dust which was rucked with scuffled footprints, and stained and besplattered with darkness.

Hatch halted.

Something was wrong. The – the lockway! The outer door was gone! There was no kaleidoscope, no slob, no nothing. The mob had – no, that was impossible. No mob could encompass the breach of such a barrier. Rather – well, the obvious alternative was worse. The door had failed. It no longer worked. It had ceased to function.

Hatch entered the outer chamber of the airlock, which was smeared with blood. The central door still stood firm, but its kaleidoscope dissolved away to nothing as he entered. It reformed behind him, trapping him within the airlock, which was bathed by an unearthly green light. Green light? This was new, weirdly so. Hatch experienced a moment of claustrophobic dread. What if the airlock malfunctioned terminally and trapped him here?

'Our culture is our greatest treasure,' said the platitudinous voice of the airlock, maintaining its habitual custom of idle lecturing in complete disregard of the realities of the moment. 'Have you listened to an original musical composition recently?'

Blood everywhere. Blood underfoot and blood on the walls. Smeared handprints. Bloody scrabblings. What the hell had been going on?

There was a hiss of air under pressure. Then the airlock began listing compositions which Hatch should listen to, only to have its lecture interrupted by the dissolution of the innermost door. Hatch stepped through, entering the tunnel which led deep into the depths of Cap Foz Para Lash.

The customary white brightlight of the tunnel had failed. Instead, the tunnel was lit by a dim emergency pink, by which Hatch saw the bloody footprints which tracked their way to the bloody bundle of – no, not a bundle. A body. But small, so, so—

Hatch stooped to the body, shook it by the shoulder, and it flopped, revealed its face. Lucius Elikin. Combat Cadet. Aged 11. And dead, quite dead.

'Lucius,' said Hatch, in the loud and demanding voice used to challenge fatigue and stupor. 'Lucius, wake up!'

But already he was quite sure the boy was far too late for challenging. Even so, he slid two fingers down to the windpipe to check for a carotid pulse. None. And the wound, oh – down beneath the ribs, down by the kidneys. A deep rip. Lethal. But the boy had tried. He had scrabbled this far, struggling inward, striving for the safety at the heart of the Combat College, the cure-all clinic. And had died far short of his goal.

Hatch stood up, and hastened down the corridor. The dorgi did not come lurching out of its lair to challenge him. He gave it a glance in passing. It was silent, stolid. Sleeping? Sulking? Dead? He gave it a heartbeat's thought then forgot about it as he hurried on towards Forum Three.

CHAPTER SEVENTEEN

The student body: Dalar ken Halvar's Combat College accepts thirty new students per year, entrance age being typically eleven, though older students are sometimes accepted. Students who begin the standard course at age eleven graduate at age twenty-seven; imperial levies, such as Hatch, break their training for seven years of service with the imperial army. The number of students of all ages now in training in the Combat College is 353. Of these, twenty-nine are Startroopers and the remainder, of course, are Combat Cadets.

* * *

So young in youth the would-be warriors
Dream desire as blithe abandon –
Till drawing days from days the war
Lights monotonies of dust,
And lighting lights
Encasement of routine.

* * *

On entering the Combat College, Asodo Hatch naturally headed for Forum Three, for that lecture theatre was where Paraban Senk habitually dealt with matters of communal discipline or communal crisis.

Forum Three was a steeply banked amphitheatre in which seating and desking was ranked in a semi-circle above a small stage. The backdrop to the stage was a large communications screen, which was at present displaying the image of a lotus in full flower. There was seating for as many as 680 people in Forum Three, but at the moment it had fewer than five dozen occupants.

Hatch remembered the last crisis of common concern, when Paraban Senk had summoned all students after Hiji Hanojo had been found dead – dead at the age of forty, in the thirteenth year of his instructorship. Forum Three had been positively crowded then. But now, with trouble on the loose in Dalar ken Halvar, some students were fighting with the Free Corps, others were guarding their homes, and some had doubtless joined in the lawless rioting.

The few dozen students gathered in Forum Three evidenced both apprehension and excitement. They had trained for war, and so should have had a grasp of its realities; but the heroic fantasies of the Eye of Delusions had overmastered their training, so that they had found themselves ill-prepared for the realities of the misfortune which had come upon their city.

In Forum Three, politics was in the ascendant. Where was the Silver Emperor? Was he prisoner? Was he dead? Was Treasurer Berlin dead? Was it true the officers of the Imperial Guard were fighting among themselves? Would Manfred Gan Oliver really become the next emperor?

'Hatch!' shouted someone, as Hatch entered Forum Three.

'So here he is,' said Lupus Lon Oliver. 'The man who tried to make himself the master of Na Sashimoko. Who tried, but failed. They say he ran at a speed a very rabbit would have envied.'

The rabbit was a creature of the Nexus, a beast unknown to Dalar ken Halvar but said to be possessed of an extraordinary turn of speed and a streak of cowardice which encouraged it to put that turn to frequent use. But Hatch did not feel insulted, for he had absolutely no idea what Lupus was talking about.

Hatch said as much.

'What are you gabbling about?' said Hatch.

222

'Your inglorious encounter,' said Lupus. 'That's what I'm on about.'

But Hatch was none the wiser, for he had not heard of the rumour which claimed that Asodo Hatch had been ignominiously out-faced, humiliated and defeated while endeavouring single-handedly to put down the coup which had seen a parcel of Imperial Guards seize control of the palace of Na Sashimoko. Hatch was equally ignorant of a variety of other rumours, variously claiming that Hatch had started the revolution of the Unreal; that Hatch had personally murdered the Silver Emperor; that Hatch was dead; that Hatch had fled the city; and that Hatch had plunged into the Hot Mouth, taking Lupus Lon Oliver down to destruction as he leapt to his death.

'You're talking nonsense,' said Hatch.

'So,' said Lupus, 'you don't admit it.'

'If you won't tell me what I'm supposed to have done,' said Hatch, 'then I cannot reasonably either admit or deny it. Accuse me, and I'll account for my perform-ance. Meantime, account for your own – what are you doing sitting here on your backside while our city burns?'

'What are you doing?' retorted Lupus.

'I came here to organize a response to the present chaos,' said Hatch. 'Inside of the night I'll do as much. But I'm fresh arrived, you seem to have been here all night.'

'Not so,' said Lupus. 'I was out in the city, but returned in response to the messengers, just as you did.'

'The messengers?' said Hatch in bewilderment, won-dering if Lupus was suffering one of those illnesses where the deluded victim starts hearing imaginary voices speaking inside his head.

'Senk's messengers,' said Lupus.

And by diligent questioning, Hatch learnt that Paraban Senk had dispatched a number of Combat Cadets as messengers, telling them to recall Asodo Hatch and Lupus Lon Oliver to the Combat College.

'Then perhaps Senk wants us to jointly organize a response to the present crisis,' said Hatch.

'Perhaps,' said Lupus.

At this, a couple of Combat Cadets entered Forum Three. They were flushed and panting, scratched and bruised, and Hatch immediately zeroed in on them, thinking them hot from the battles of Dalar ken Halvar. But before Asodo Hatch could begin his interrogation of these fresh witnesses, the full-flowering lotus adorning Forum Three's communications screen disappeared, and was replaced by the olive-complexioned features of Paraban Senk, the Teacher of Control. Senk called the room to order.

'It seems,' said the Teacher of Control, 'that there is a degree of disorder in the city tonight.'

This pronouncement was greeted with hoots, howls, jeers, and cries of feigned disbelief.

'Nobody can say where this disorder will end,' said Senk. 'In as little as a day, conditions may become far worse. Therefore, I am bringing forward the competitive examination for the instructorship. Tomorrow may be too late. Accordingly, we will proceed with the competitive examination for the instructorship as soon as possible. Asodo Hatch will fight with Lupus Lon Oliver on this very night. To the victor, the spoils.'

Both Hatch and Lupus were on their feet immediately, protesting. Hatch out-bellowed Lupus:

'But I haven't slept!'

Thus protested Hatch, and in perfect sincerity.

Thanks to his Combat College training, Hatch was capable of maintaining a studied tortoise-faced inscrutability under interrogation, and of telling undetectable deadpan lies during such interrogation. But there was nothing inscrutable about Hatch right now. He was emotionally open, revealed, exposed. Under such circumstances, Paraban Senk could read Hatch to a nicety, and knew Hatch to be telling the truth.

Hatch had not slept.

So Senk believed, and so likewise did Lupus Lon Oliver, for that was what Hatch himself believed. In the heat of the moment, Asodo Hatch had entirely forgotten the fact that he had laid himself down to sleep in his empty house in the afternoon just gone, and had not been roused until early in the night.

For his part, Lupus Lon Oliver certainly had not slept. In the morning, he had been courting the statuesque Penelope Flute, and his subsequent embroilment in the alarums of the afternoon had made sleep impossible.

'We are warriors,' said Lupus stoutly. 'We need no sleep. At least, I don't. But if Asodo Hatch is too old for the rigours of war, why then, let him withdraw from this competition.'

'Hatch,' said Senk. 'Do you choose to signify your withdrawal?'

'Why,' said Hatch, growing cagey as he remembered that he had in fact got some sleep, 'I, uh . . . I wouldn't want to disappoint young Lupus. But, Senk, this is no time for games. Our city's awash with blood and burning. We should be organizing the defence of our city, not playing at games.'

'This is not a game,' said Senk.

There was an entirely human anger in Senk's proclamation. Under the lash of that anger, Hatch felt that he finally had the answer to the question of whether Senk had fully human attributes. Senk's mission, Senk's raison d'être, was to train Startroopers for the Stormforce of the Nexus. Compared to that, what was Dalar ken Halvar to Paraban Senk?

'You should disqualify him,' said Lupus. 'He's not fit to be the instructor! He places his city ahead of the Nexus!'

'Well, Hatch?' said Senk.

To his surprise and dismay, Hatch saw that Senk was treating Lupus Lon Oliver's suggestion seriously.

'Senk,' said Hatch, 'the instructor's prime task is to liaise between the city and the Combat College. The instructor can hardly do that if the city has ceased to exist. Under the circumstances, I think both Lupus and myself should be devoting our best energies to preserving the city. I suggest that you order all Combat College students to place themselves under a joint command headed by Lupus and myself. Then we'll do what we can. But if the city ceases to exist – well, what chance of recruiting a fresh class of Combat College?'

There was a substantial pause while Paraban Senk meditated on this. Senk's eyes were closed, or so it seemed from the features displayed on Forum Three's communications screen, though of course in point of fact the unembodied Paraban Senk did not possess any such organs as literal 'eyes'.

Senk's eyes opened.

'It is my belief,' said Senk, 'that Asodo Hatch and Lupus Lon Oliver lack the ability to resolve the crisis in Dalar ken Halvar, either individually or acting in concert. The present crisis must take its course. Thanks to the limited data at my disposal and the complexity of the social forces at work, I cannot predict the ultimate outcome of the crisis. However, I believe that whatever forces ultimately hold power in Dalar ken Halvar will treat with me and mine on an equitable basis, just as the Silver Emperor did.'

'Did?' said Hatch. 'Do you believe the emperor dead?'

'I have it on your own authority that the emperor is not available,' said Senk, giving Hatch the impression that some matter of either fact or rumour was being concealed. 'It may well be that the emperor will remain unavailable. If that is the case, will you treat with the city's new ruling powers on my behalf if you become the instructor?'

'Without any hesitation,' said Hatch.

'And I likewise,' said Lupus.

'Then,' said Senk, 'I find you both fit to hold the instructorship, and rule that you must fight for the position this very night. Are you both agreeable to this proposition?'

'I am,' said Lupus promptly.

'And I,' said Hatch, forcing himself to an imitation of an equal readiness.

In truth, there were all kinds of further protests, caveats and reservations that Hatch wanted to make known. But he restrained himself. Without a doubt, he had angered Senk once already. Any repetition of that angering might see Senk disqualify him from contention for the instructorship.

As for Dalar ken Halvar's fate—

What could Hatch do on his own?

Less, surely, than he could do if he won the instructorship. If he could win quickly, then he might persuade Senk to order the Combat College's student body to place itself under his command, and then he might be able to do something to restore order in the city.

'Good,' said Senk, on hearing the prompt replies from Lupus and Hatch. 'The pair of you will prove your worth as warriors by fighting against a background of war.'

As Senk was so saying, Hatch heard a scuffle behind him, but paid it no need, until he heard Shona say:

'What's monkey got?'

'Let me go!' said an anguished voice.

The voice was that of Dog Java, the Combat Cadet who had so recently tried to knife down Hatch. At that voice, Hatch turned sharply, and saw Dog Java trying to break free from Shona. Shona had come up behind Dog Java, and had seized Dog's arm in a grip a vice would have envied, and had got a lock on Dog's wrist.

As the human vice-rivaller exerted herself further, Dog was forced to drop the knife he had been holding. Then he cried out, for, rather than releasing her grip, Shona tightened it. Paraban Senk watched from the screen but made no move to intervene.

'Shona,' said Hatch.

'Yes, Hatch my darling?' said Shona. 'Shall I break his wrist? I'll do it for free. Just say the word.'

'If he'll give you his and agree to keep the peace in the Combat College,' said Hatch, 'then you can let him go free.'

'Well, Dog?' said Shona. 'What do you say?'

When Dog Java made no immediate reply, Shona bit his ear. Hard. Drawing blood. At which Dog cried out anew. As if in answer, cries were heard from outside Forum Three, and then a knot of Combat College students burst into that lecture theatre. Among them was Scorpio Fax, his face a mask of blood, his scalp lacerated. Hatch pushed toward Fax, and was in time to catch him just before he collapsed.

Then someone else entered Forum Three.

It was Lupus Lon Oliver's father: the formidable Manfred Gan Oliver, head of the Free Corps. And Hatch, as he lowered Fax to the ground, heard someone cry out in astonishment.

'It's Gan Oliver! But what's he doing here!?'

A legitimate question, for Manfred Gan Oliver had been forcibly ejected from the Combat College when he graduated from that institution at the age of twenty-seven, and had been denied entry to the precincts of the College for the last thirty years.

228

CHAPTER EIGHTEEN

Manfred Gan Oliver: 'Manfred, the strength of the family Oliver.' An orphan who, at the behest of his uncle, sat the entrance examination for admission into the Combat College at age eleven, demonstrated the necessary aptitudes, and thereafter lived as a Combat Cadet.

Gan Oliver's uncle died when he was thirteen, after which he did not leave the precincts of the Combat College until he graduated and was forcibly ejected at age twenty-seven, a citizen of the Nexus now forever exiled from the world which had once been his home.

Doomed to live out his days in Dalar ken Halvar, Gan Oliver vowed that his son would succeed where he had failed, and would win an instructor's appointment in the College. Gan Oliver is now aged fifty-seven. His son, Lupus Lon Oliver, is aged twenty-seven years and some days.

* * *

> If as light at dawn is resurrected –
> If likewise thus the flesh –
> Why is it that these unstrung bones
> Find purpose unrefreshed by sleep –
> This sky so surely good as air
> Though far from home and alien.

* * *

There was no big mystery about the presence of Manfred Gan Oliver. Guests were allowed to enter the Combat

College to observe the gladiatorial combat of those who were fighting for the instructorship. Lupus Lon Oliver had earlier given Paraban Senk a list of his guests, and so, when Senk had dispatched messengers to summon Lupus and Hatch for combat, Senk had sent messengers likewise to summon the invited guests.

On entering Forum Three, Manfred Gan Oliver looked around with a positively seigneurial eye.

Then said to Shona:

'Startrooper Shona! What are you doing with that Combat Cadet?'

'I haven't quite decided,' said Shona, keeping a tight grip on the delinquent Dog Java. 'But if he doesn't agree to keep the peace then I'm going to break his wrist.'

'Agreed!' said Dog, who was sweating hot agony.

'What's agreed?' said Shona. 'That you behave yourself? Or that you get something broken?'

'I'll be good,' wailed Dog, his last reserves of courage and dignity broken.

'Yes, well,' said Shona, giving Dog a little shake, and almost breaking his neck in the process. 'I hope so. Because I'll be watching you.'

Then she let him go, so suddenly that he went sprawling to the floor. Shona stooped, secured Dog's knife, then went to help Hatch, who was administering first aid to Scorpio Fax. Meantime, Manfred Gan Oliver moved to join his son, and father and son embraced.

'What's wrong with him?' said Shona, as Hatch checked out Scorpio Fax.

'He's been beaten badly,' said Hatch, stating the obvious. 'Other than that, I can't say. Help me move him, and we'll shift him to the clinic.'

Half a dozen people, Shona included, helped shift Fax to the Combat College cure-all clinic. It was small, a six-berth unit, hence easily overloaded if general disaster saw too many smashed and maimed bodies brought gasping to its rescue. But for the moment it was clean, bright and empty. Several Combat College students had undergone running repairs in that clinic that night, but for the moment it was unoccupied apart from Fax.

And so the cure-all clinic claimed Scorpio Fax, lulling his pain to a dark nothing with the balm of an extinguishing anaesthetic, needling for his veins then pumping into those veins an artificial substitute for the lost blood.

When the cure-all clinic was close at hand, so much that was murder elsewhere was of little ultimate consequence. So smashed fists so broken bones so eyes gone missing so bloodloss – all fixable, all granted remedy. Thus like the heroes of the animated cartoons of the Eye of Delusions, the combatants rucked and mauled by the most outrageous brawls could be patched up to the point of perfection, could lie back grinning in perfect confidence of the reliable mercy of the supporting machinery. Like any entertainment hero, they too would live to fight another day.

But Fax was not grinning, for he was too full of pain. And even after the cure-all clinic had punched him full of peace, he had nothing spare for bravado.

'You'll come out as good as new,' said Hatch, unsure whether the anaesthetized Fax could hear him. It mattered not: his words were, after all, more to reassure himself than to reassure Fax.

The body could be mended, so physical injuries could in theory be lightly dismissed, but the shock of having one's fellow citizens turn animal-ape was not so easily sidestepped. Hatch presumed that Fax had been caught by a hostile mob of the Unreal, the Yara, the underclass of Dalar ken Halvar, and systematically beaten.

As Hatch watched, tubes sprouted from the wall and crawled into Fax's nose to feed him oxygen. A surgeon descended from the ceiling and hung just above Fax's face, suspended by a thick and flexible hose of fluorescent orange. The surgeon was a globular machine which sprouted scalpels and suction tubes, and it got to work on Scorpio Fax right away, cutting and slicing, sucking and dicing, squirting out flesh-paste and moulding it into position.

'I've seen enough,' said Shona. 'Come away.'

Hatch lingered just a moment longer, then began making his way back to Forum Three in Shona's wake.

'Well, Hatch,' said Manfred Gan Oliver, as Hatch entered Forum Three. 'Are you ready to die?'

'Die?' said Hatch, startled and confused. 'Did you come here to murder?'

'I came here for the pleasures of the Season,' said Gan Oliver.

'This is no Season,' said Hatch. 'This is but—'

'I spoke as a poet,' said Gan Oliver. 'A poet of blood, though I have no words to my name. As for what this is or is not – don't lecture me, Hatch. Here I trained. Here I grew from boyhood to manhood. I know this place as well as you or better. My son will see you dead in this Season of ours.'

'The illusion tanks—'

'I'm not talking illusion!' said Gan Oliver. 'Once you leave this place, you're marked for death. The Free Corps is going to put an end to the Frangoni, Hatch.'

'The emperor—'

'The emperor is gone, Hatch. Missing or dead. We've overthrown him.'

Hatch was fast losing track of what had actually happened in Dalar ken Halvar, or what was claimed to have happened.

'You might have grabbed the palace for the moment,' said Hatch, presuming from Gan Oliver's lordly attitude that the man had reason to think himself the master of the city, 'at least in the night's confusion, but tomorrow—'

'Hatch, you fool!' said Gan Oliver. 'The Free Corps has been planning its coup for the better part of a generation. We were waiting for the moment, that's all. This revolution, so called, it gave us our moment. Make it easy for yourself, Hatch. Find yourself a sword, then fall on it.'

This was almost too much for Hatch to absorb at once. What was happening here? Had the Free Corps truly seized effective control in Dalar ken Halvar? And did the Free Corps think it could hold the city permanently? Would Gan Oliver really have Hatch murdered once he left the protection of the Combat College, or was that threat merely an exercise in psychological warfare?

'You're pirates,' said Hatch, hoping to push Gan Oliver into self-revelation. 'And pirates tainted with treachery at that.'

'We are the bringers of a new age,' said Gan Oliver, with what sounded like level-headed sincerity.

'Not while I have anything to do with it,' said Hatch.

'You don't have anything to do with it,' said Gan Oliver. 'You don't and you won't. My son Lupus will kill you in battle in the world of illusions. Then you will leave the Combat College. Then I will kill you for real. Our swords are waiting in the kinema, Hatch. Once you step outside the lockway, you're dead.'

'Kill me you may,' said Hatch, giving way to his inborn love of rhetoric. 'But the blood that lives will seek vengeance.'

'Who will avenge you, Hatch?' said Gan Oliver, sneering at this sally. 'Your sister? Your brother? They're doomed to the same fate, Hatch. Once the Free Corps has won Dalar ken Halvar, we will cleanse Cap Uba and have done with the Frangoni.'

'You would not dare!' said Hatch, hoping that Gan Oliver would not dare, and hoping that this twice-repeated threat of genocide was sheer bluff. 'We have a Treaty.'

Here Hatch spoke of course of the Treaty between the Silver Emperor and the Frangoni people. That Treaty made all Frangoni males in Dalar ken Halvar the slaves of the Silver Emperor, but also safeguarded the rights of the Frangoni to enjoy peace and safety on their own rock on the western side of the city.

'You had a Treaty,' said Gan Oliver, emphasizing the past tense. 'But your Treaty was with the Silver Emperor, who is missing, believed dead.'

'We had a Treaty, yes,' said Hatch, 'and have a treaty now.'

'And I,' said Manfred Gan Oliver, 'have a fist.'

Gan Oliver's easy confidence was as unscrutable as anything else Hatch had ever had to deal with. It was impossible to know whether the man was serious. Hatch needed information, lots of it, and fast. How many men had the Free Corps rallied? How many officers of the Imperial Guard had thrown in their lot with the Free Corps? Where were the revolutionary leaders? What exactly had happened at the silver mines?

'Well, Hatch?' said Gan Oliver, as Hatch counted his question marks. 'What do you say to that?'

'Asodo Hatch has no time left for argument,' said Paraban Senk, intruding on this debate. 'The arc is half-gone and combat begins at the end of the arc. Combatants should now proceed to the initiation seats. Asodo Hatch. Lon Oliver. Proceed to the combat bays.'

—Half an arc?

—Time enough.

So thought Hatch.

But he knew he would have to hurry.

CHAPTER NINETEEN

Free Corps: an association of Startroopers and would-be Startroopers who think of themselves as citizens of the Nexus stranded for a lifetime amidst the barbarians of Dalar ken Halvar. These people typically speak the Code Seven Commonspeak of the Nexus and dream of the Day of Days when the Chasm Gates will be resurrected, and the local universe will once more be linked to the multiverse of the Nexus.

*   *   *

So sharpening his sword – a hero.
Then cut himself, and in that taste –
He found his throat split open, split to bleed
And red poured rust to waste – on desert sands –

*   *   *

Hastening from Forum Three, Hatch took himself off to the Combat College's cure-all clinic, and was shortly bending over the patched-up body of Scorpio Fax, and endeavouring to rouse Fax to wakefulness.

'Can you hear me?' said Hatch, uncertain whether Scorpio Fax was resting, sleeping or sunk in a coma.

Fax's eyes flickered, opened.

'Grief,' said Fax. 'That dorgi.'

'Give you a hard time, did it?' said Hatch.

He recalled that the dorgi had been sulking in its lair when he had last entered the Combat College. After such sulks, it often challenged people with a ferocity just short of the homicidal.

'A hard time?' said Fax. 'Did it ever! I came through the lockway, I was – I was cut up bad and it – you can imagine.'

'I can imagine,' affirmed Hatch.

The dorgi was a constant cause for worry. These sentry-machines were deliberately designed to be slightly erratic, marginally unpredictable and most definitely stupid. The random elements in their behaviour were (in theory) supposed to make it difficult for any intruder to plan a path past them with confidence.

So dorgis made good perimeter guards (in theory, at least), but on account of their inherent and progressive instability they were supposed to be checked out by a machine psychologist at least once every three years. The beast which guarded the lockway was more than 20,000 years overdue for such a check, and was getting more and more eccentric with each passing century.

Hatch suspected that, had the Chasm Gates not collapsed, all dorgis would soon have been done away with, for surely the Nexus authorities would have realized that a machine created in the image of erraticism was not a good idea. But the closure of the Chasm Gates had made every passing technological caprice of the Chasm Gate era into a semi-permanent fixture of the Combat College.

Semi-permanent, rather than permanent, because everything wears out sooner or later. The Combat College dorgi should have worn out long ago, since it had a design life of only 7,000 years. But this one was still going strong, and sooner or later it would kill one person – or several. Hatch was sure of it.

'Well,' said Fax, 'get on with it.'

'Get on with what?' said Hatch.

'You didn't come here just to admire the scenery, did you? You want something. You want Lupus dead.'

'No,' said Hatch. 'Not Lupus.'

'Who, then?'

'Gan Oliver.'

'Why Gan Oliver? Why not Lupus?'

'I trust to my judgement,' said Hatch.

Lupus Lon Oliver was twenty-seven, a man full-grown by the reckoning of some societies, but in Dalar ken Halvar he counted as no more than a boy, for he had done nothing in life except to indulge himself in his own education. Manfred Gan Oliver, on the other hand, was aged fifty-seven, and so was approaching the prime of political life. Those he had grown up with were in positions of power, and Gan Oliver had cultivated them as they eased themselves into those positions. He had, too, the authority which comes with age, for people would listen to him when they would never listen to a boy.

Furthermore, Hatch judged Lupus to be a romantic and Gan Oliver to be a realist, and on that account alone he feared Gan Oliver the more.

'You're sure it's Gan Oliver you want?' said Fax.

'Lupus I can handle myself,' said Hatch, hoping this was so.

'So why . . . why should I favour you with Gan Oliver's death?' said Fax.

So saying, Scorpio Fax looked up at Hatch, looked up from his sickbed and remembered. Scorpio Fax remembered how Asodo Hatch had recruited him to kill Impala Fax, the Butcher of Shintoto. Fax had done as much. And remembered. Blood on his hands, blood on the floor, blood daily and nightly in waking dreams and sleeping.

'We are at war,' said Hatch. 'At war, with Dalar ken Halvar the prize. If Gan Oliver wins, we're dead men, both of us. You must strike him down to save your own life. What more reward could you want?'

'I want—'

Fax knew just what he wanted, but could not bring himself to say it. He was not sure how Hatch would react, but suspected the big-built Frangoni would be angry, maybe murderously so.

'Kill me Gan Oliver,' said Hatch, 'and you can have anything you want. Anything.'

'Even your sister?'

'My sister!' said Hatch, startled.

'Yes,' said Fax, who looked positively terrified as he made the confession. 'I – I'm in love with Penelope.'

'Grief of gods!' said Hatch.

'You – you've chosen another? As – as her hsuband, I mean? Is she betrothed?'

'Penelope,' said Hatch, who thought it would be unfair to conceal the complications from the infatuated Fax, 'is betrothed to no man, though Lupus Lon Oliver has declared his love for her. Furthermore, Penelope has declared her reciprocal love for Lon Oliver.'

'Well,' said Fax, with sturdy resolution, 'she can hardly love him once he's dead.'

'Quite so,' said Hatch. 'But if you're going to kill Lon Oliver, then strike him down in secret, else Penelope will have your testicles by way of revenge.'

'It's as good as done,' said Fax fiercely.

'But if you're going to kill young Lupus Lon Oliver,' said Hatch, 'then you do so on your own account. Remember it's the father I want. Manfred. Kill Manfred, and I'll give you my sister – at least to the extent that she's mine to give.'

'Manfred, then,' said Fax. 'But – how do I kill him?'

'That's over to you,' said Hatch. 'But do it soon!'

Then Hatch took his leave and headed for the combat bays. On the way he met Lupus Lon Oliver. Following close behind the red-skinned Ebrell Islander was the grey-skinned Combat Cadet of the Janjuladoola race, the ever-reticent Jeltisketh Echo. Hatch immediately deduced that Echo had been recruited as Lon Oliver's bodyguard.

'Hail fellow, well met,' said Lupus. 'Are you ready for the single-fighters?'

'Single-fighters?' said Hatch. 'Who told you we'd have single-fighters?'

'It's a guess, of course,' said Lupus. 'But I'm right, I'm sure of it.'

'Maybe,' said Hatch, hoping that they would not be duelling with single-fighters.

'Definitely,' said Lupus. 'You'll go down in flames, Hatch. Then they'll kick you out. And my father will be waiting for you when you get kicked out.'

Hatch made no reply to this, because he could quite easily imagine this exchange of pleasantries escalating quite suddenly into bloody battle. Rather than risk a brawl, he kept his lips sealed, strode through the open doorway of the nearest functional combat bay and settled himself in the initiation seat. It sighed faintly as it took his weight.

In the open doorway, a sheet of kaleidoscope started to form, then collapsed into hissing slob. Hatch swore, and leapt out of the initiation seat. He was certainly not going to sit helplessly in an initiation seat while he was exposed and vulnerable to his enemies. A new sheet of kaleidoscope started to form in the doorway. Slowly, slowly. It hesitated, wavered, then consolidated itself. Hatch kicked his way through the cold and swiftly disintegrating slob, reached the door, put his weight against the kaleidoscope – which was slightly warm to his touch – and pushed. Hard. He threw his whole weight against the door. It held.

OK.

Hatch went back to the initiation seat and settled himself. He glanced at the countdown telltale. It had not yet started to count down the last pulsebeats.

'Worried, were you?' said Paraban Senk, appearing on the combat bay's display screen.

'Very,' said Hatch frankly.

'But now you're safe. Very well. You know the dual viewpoints of this combat session will be relayed to the Forum Three.'

'Of course,' said Hatch. 'Hi, Shona. Hi, Dog. How's things, Manfred my old friend?'

'Clowning is not in order,' said Paraban Senk, frowning.

'No,' said Hatch. 'Of course it isn't. I apologize.'

'Your apology is accepted.'

'Very well,' said Paraban Senk. 'We are gathered here today to observe the combat between Lupus Lon Oliver and Asodo Hatch. The prize is the instructorship of the Combat College. To the victor, the spoils.'

There was a pause. Hatch assumed that Paraban Senk was saying something to Lupus Lon Oliver. Then:

'Are you ready to receive your first combat assignment?' said Paraban Senk.

'I am ready,' said Hatch.

A flickering motion attracted his attention. It was the countdown telltale.

There was a pause. Hatch assumed that Lupus Lon Oliver was being given the combat assignment. Then:

'Asodo Hatch,' said Paraban Senk. 'You will duel with Lupus Lon Oliver with the Scala Nine single-fighter.'

Hatch almost flinched, but restrained himself. But even so: he did not like this idea one little bit. The single-fighter was a small and turbulent flying machine designed for solo combat missions within a planet's atmospheric envelope. To use it effectively in combat, one required razor-sharp reflexes, and there young Lupus most definitely had the edge.

For a brief moment, Hatch indulged himself in notions of despair. Then steadied himself by bringing to mind memories of the desert and the gasping thirst and bleeding leather of real war – real war which he had endured and survived.

The task ahead was only a game, for all the seriousness of purpose which attended it. Win or lose, he would still walk from the combat bay with all four limbs intact. Here you could die and it would not matter.

Hatch wished, above all, that he was not so alone, not so isolated. But he was himself alone, alone and unaided, with nobody to help him, guide him, support him, advise him.

—To survive.

Hatch remembered.

The High Priest of the Great God Mokaragash, old Sesno Felvus, had said something about survival. But what? Hatch thought back to their encounter in the precincts of Temple Isherzan.

—To survive is victory sufficient.

True, true, but Hatch had always known that, it was a platitude, a nothing-statement, proof of the ancient teaching which holds that wisdom is often but hair from the idiot. If Lupus was an idiot, if Hatch himself was an idiot . . . but of course they were idiots, they were both of them idiots to be wasting their time duelling in skies of imagination while the city of the flesh wailed through the agony of its burning.

To survive.

To survive is victory sufficient.

Hatch glanced at the countdown telltale and saw he had but ten pulsebeats to combat. He watched the clock-counter pulse. Once. Twice. Thrice.

As if calmed by the very countdown itself, Hatch found himself lucid, clear. In his lucidity, he remembered one of the brevities of Jeneth Odette, a practitioner of Dith-zora-ka-mako who had once lectured on her method by saying:

'I took a worm and turned it inside out.'

—To survive is victory sufficient.

Turned inside out:

—To die is victory sufficient.

Suddenly Hatch remembered. He remembered the evasion exercise he had so recently undertaken when paired with Lupus Lon Oliver. Pursued by a hunter-killer, Hatch had jumped over a cliff, taking a death-plunge which had allowed him to survive to the end of the exercise.

He glanced at the countdown telltale.

Three pulses remained.

Hatch grinned, fiercely, for now he knew, now he understood, now he saw a way to wreck young Lupus and win.

Two pulses.

One.

None.

And Paraban Senk said:

'Let combat begin.'

The world went red. The world went white. The world flickered through the spectrum, then blurred into unintelligibility. Then steadied. As the world steadied, Hatch found himself sitting frozen in the cockpit of a Scala Nine single-fighter in a monochromatic world. A world without colour, a world of black and white. A world of silence unbroken except for the slightest background hiss.

Caught in a world of monochromatic paralysis, Hatch reviewed his plan. Then colour flooded the world, stasis ended, and he was thrust back into his seat by the force of a full five gravities of acceleration, hurtling through the lower atmosphere in a Scala Nine single-fighter.

CHAPTER TWENTY

Illusion tanks: computer-generated environments allowing people-in-the-flesh to interact with each other (or with software artefacts) in a subjective world which lacks all objective existence.

*   *   *

If in a world of dreams we fight
The bloodstained shadows of the cranking steel
Which grinds the bones of monsters then grinds ours –
Then wake and find
The blood which gapes and grins upon the pillow –
The softness like a rope around my neck –
But this 'but if' is but –

*   *   *

So forced by five gravities he burnt low across a sea of green, a sea not grass but tarnished water. Slammed through the lower atmosphere beneath a sky of burnished copper.

'Hatch,' said Lupus, over the vidrolator's open channel. 'I see you, Hatch.' Hatch ignored him. 'Hatch! Hatch! It's me! It's me! You can run, Hatch. You can run, but you can't hide.'

Hatch had heard that before. When? Oh yes. Standing outside the lockway, waiting for the outer airlock to open. Some entertainment hero had said as much to some entertainment villain on the Eye of Delusions.

'Idiot,' said Hatch.

Then a pig-panic squeal from the single-fighter alerted

him to danger. Lon Oliver's attack systems had acquired, had locked on, were ready to blast Hatch to oblivion. Hatch blurted a quick command: 'Prison!'

Obedient to this command, Hatch's single-fighter sheathed itself in a force-field which sealed out the world. Now his single-fighter was sealed off from the outside world, safe from attack, for the moment invulnerable. But to maintain such a force-field would cost Hatch dearly. The corrosion cells which powered his single-fighter would soon be drained by the cost of maintaining the force-field. But in the meantime Hatch was protected from anything Lupus might try.

What now?

Hatch could run. A single-fighter sheathed with a force-field was hard to detect, hard to follow. It was almost invisible. Almost – but not quite. Sensitive instruments could detect the sheathing force-field itself. Furthermore, the sophisticated radar systems of the Nexus could detect the patterns of air turbulence left in the wake of an aircraft, and so could hunt down any flying machine, regardless of the sophistication of its camouflaging legerdemain.

'Sequence,' said Hatch, alerting his single-fighter to the fact that he wanted to give it instructions.

'Say sequence,' said the single-fighter, indicating its readiness to receive instructions.

'Maximum self-destruct on ejection plus one.'

So said Hatch. He knew that Lupus would be readying himself for the attack. When Hatch's single-fighter shed its protective force-field, it would be momentarily helpless and exposed to attack. Knowing that, Lupus would probably close the distance and come in close. Come in close for the kill. That was his fashion, his style. He liked to be close, close enough to enjoy to the full the primitive satisfactions of destruction.

That was his weakness.

'Sequence received,' said the single-fighter, acknowledging its receipt of orders. Then it repeated those orders so they could be checked. 'Maximum self-destruct on ejection plus one.'

'Sequence continues,' said Hatch.

'Continue sequence.'

'Ejection is simultaneous with liberty.'

'Continuation received,' said the single-fighter. 'You will be ejected immediately we have liberty.'

As the command 'prison' directed a single-fighter to seal itself inside a protective force-field, so the reverse-word 'liberty' commanded it to unseal itself.

'Very well then,' said Hatch. 'Liberty!'

The single-fighter shed its protective force-field and ejected Asodo Hatch. Blasted free by his ejection seat, he was slammed up and out. The air smashed him. He heard the taut crack as his back broke. He was slammed to a whirl-shock of buffeting turbulence as the world slammed, as the world burst black and blue, blasted by a double-crash of thunder, of thunder pitched for the shatter. The visible spectrum split into sub-harmonics of pain, and then—

Then Hatch was in the clear, free from the turbulence, and given the grace of a lucid moment in which he felt the summer of the blossoming heat from below. He caught a brief glimpse of the crumpling fire expanding below him, of the billowing bloom of destruction.

He could not say or speak, but thinking was still in his power. Though only just.

—Wah!

Thus thought Asodo Hatch.

Then thought no more, for he was falling. Lucidity gone, he fell. He toppled. Down through the gulfs he plummeted. His ejection seat's parachute did not open. Strapped into that seat, he dropped downward, doomed down to destruction, his back broken, his four limbs wrecked and useless.

Falling, he hit turbulence. Hitting turbulence, he was whirled sideways, tossed, corkscrewed, cocktailed in a gigantic blood-shaker, falling wrecked and ruined, a wreck falling toward wreckage, falling toward the wreckage of the world.

And then—

Falling, the seat steadied.

And, seated on the arc of his downward slide, seated on the smooth arc of the longest rollercoaster slide in the history of humanity, Asodo Hatch glimpsed two cinders blistered with flames, two cinders falling, trailing smoke as they arced down toward the blazing sea. One of those two charred meteorites was his abandoned single-fighter. The other was Lupus Lon Oliver's craft, caught in the flamesmash fireball as Hatch's craft blew itself up.

—Marshmallows.

Thus thought Hatch, though he had no idea why he thought it. Then there was time for no further thoughts, for he was falling, and the smooth arc of his slide was breaking up as he hit turbulence again, and slammed by the buffeting turbulence he went shockbursting down toward the green. And now at last he found his voice. A scream was wrenched from his mouth a moment before impact, then impact—

The shock was lethal.

So he was dead, dead, seated dead in the initiation seat, eyes starting, panic shuddering in his throat, hands clutching at the armrests, flesh shuddering.

'The illusion tank sequence is over,' said Paraban Senk, with those words telling Hatch that his waking dream was done with, that he was back in the world of the living.

Hatch moved his jaw cautiously. Tested his tongue.

Heard himself question with a word, a word which sounded as if spoken by someone else, spoken by a machine:

'Result?'

'Partial point in your favour,' said Paraban Senk, as calm as an accountant.

'Details,' said Hatch.

'You died, but you outsurvived Lon Oliver. You win a partial point. You win 0.0000057 of a point.'

'Good,' said Hatch. 'Good.'

'However,' said Paraban Senk. 'However . . . wait one moment. Ah yes. Lon Oliver is contesting this decision.'

'Contesting?' said Hatch. 'What do you mean, contesting?'

'He claims you have no right to your partial point. He claims that partial point is contrary to reason. He says there must be an error in the adjudication software.'

'He thinks I won through computer error?' said Hatch.

'Precisely,' said Paraban Senk. 'So he has demanded that the partial point be wiped.'

'Wah!' said Hatch.

'I have decided to let Lon Oliver argue his case in Forum Three,' said Senk. 'I will then arbitrate on this matter.'

'Will I be able to make my own case?' said Hatch.

'Not if you sit here all day talking to me,' said Senk. 'I think you had better be going.'

So Hatch hastened to Forum Three. He used a side-door which gave him admission to the small stage which faced the steep-banked tiers of seats. On that stage was Lupus Lon Oliver.

Lupus was giving a speech, playing to the gallery for all he was worth. The speech was not just for the benefit of Paraban Senk, for Lupus would ultimately be judged not just by the Teacher of Control, but by his family, his peers, and the Free Corps as a whole. Manfred Gan Oliver sat stonefaced on one of the tiered benches, watching his son and passing judgement.

'—as a warrior,' said Lupus, glancing sideways at Hatch. 'But Hatch threw his life away, thereby winning—'

'My life is as you see it,' said Hatch, interjecting staunchly.

'He threw it away!' said Lupus. 'Threw it away, and

247

so, so won a cheating point from the derelict machineries of judgement. Had this been a real war with a real death to match it, what would he have won? Only our mutual extinction. In the Season, we count it a victory only when one walks away. Did Hatch's father walk away? No. He killed himself.'

'My father!' said Hatch, flashing white-hot with rage.

'Your father!' said Lupus. 'Do you deny it? The whole city saw it. And – and it is said that any man who kills himself hands a sharp sword to his son. Hatch has accepted the sword. Having accepted the sword, he has killed himself once already before your very eyes. As he killed himself in the illusion tanks, so he will kill himself in the world of the real. And this – this walking corpse – it thinks it has a future? I see for it a vibrant future as a suicide.'

The vehemence of Lupus Lon Oliver's attack was such that it silenced the whole of Forum Three. Hatch was aware that everyone was watching him, seeing how he would react. His anger was so extreme that he durst not move, durst not speak, lest he do or say something extreme.

—Not yet. Not yet.

So thought Hatch, distancing himself from the scene, managing to make himself cold, immobile, stonefaced and continent.

Yet he knew he would kill Lupus on account of what had been said. Till then, Hatch had been concerned with the father, not the son. He had primed Scorpio Fax to kill Manfred Gan Oliver because the father was a danger, while the rat spawned by that father – well, it had sharp teeth, admittedly, but it was still a very small and inconsequential rat.

But now it was a doomed rat.

As good as dead.

'Asodo Hatch,' said Paraban Senk. 'Are you ready to plead your case?'

Hatch breathed deeply.

Then:

'I am,' said Hatch.

'Then speak,' said Senk.

'Very well,' said Hatch. 'This young colleague of mine, Lupus Lon Oliver, he, he speaks from his youth – and in his youth he is enamoured with the romantic vision of two men engaged in combat to the death. He is drunk—'

'Drunk!' protested Lupus. 'I haven't had a drink—'

'Drunk with machismo,' said Hatch, steamrollering over the interjection. 'Intoxicated with visions of the triumph of muscle and nerve, the victory of brute as brute. But we are not animals training to die in the Season. Rather, we train for war.

'In war, merely to outsurvive the enemy can be an advantage. He who survives can communicate his outsurvival to headquarters, meaning that the masters he serves will know of the outcome of his struggle even if he dies shortly thereafter. All things being otherwise equal, intelligence determines the outcome of wars.

'By outsurviving Lon Oliver in combat I demonstrated the ability to – potentially at least – give my headquarters an edge in intelligence. The fractional point awarded to me may be construed as being in recognition of the fact that simply to outsurvive the enemy is of potential military benefit.'

Was this making sense? Hatch hoped so. The truth was that the games played in the illusion tanks were just that: games. So all that mattered was to win within the rules. But to say as much would make him sound like a child too fond of its own cleverness, and so would be quoted against him. So: so he had to pretend to take these games absolutely seriously.

'If that fractional point serves to win me the position of instructor,' said Hatch, 'then I say the position is rightly won, for I achieved my fractional point not by pursuing delusional dreams of glory in combat, but by applying a mature understanding of the process of war. I

249

won out of my maturity: out of my mature understanding. I won as a man wins when in combat with a child, however monstrous the child in its viciousness.'

'I'm better than you!' said Lupus, shouting. 'You fight me man to man and you're a dead man! You want to fight? Fight me, then! Fight me, and I'll tear you apart with my bare hands!'

Hatch smiled. This was good, very good. The boy-child was tender in his dignity, and was making a fool of himself by his fist-shaking histrionics.

'You think this is funny, do you?' said Lupus, advancing on Hatch.

'Lon Oliver,' said Paraban Senk. 'Back off. Back off – now! Leave the stage and seat yourself.'

With some reluctance, Lupus obeyed. Hatch wondered if Lupus realized he had made a fool of himself. Asodo Hatch was a very large and well-coordinated mass of muscle and bone, a monster of a warrior big enough and bad enough to give the burliest brawler a fright in a fight. If Lupus Lon Oliver and Asodo Hatch were to fight it out in Forum Three, it was more than likely that any smashing of skulls, rending of limbs and extinguishing of life would be done by Hatch, with young Lupus the probable victim.

As Hatch watched Lupus seat himself, he was tempted to comment on his own bigness and Lupus's smallness. He was tempted to glory in his brawn and muscle, in his undoubted physical prowess. It was, after all, a severe blow to his ego to admit that Lupus was the better fighter pilot, faster of reflex and more adroit in his aerial tactics.

'There Lupus sits,' said Hatch, yielding to temptation. 'There Lupus sits—'

He brought himself up short. It was all too easy to play the game of man against man, to play at being a gladiator, a thugfist brawler, a streetfighter. But Hatch and Lupus were not gladiators or streetfighters. They were players in a political struggle which would decide the future of Dalar ken Halvar. In this struggle, there was more than Hatch's ego at stake. The entire Frangoni nation might be endangered if the leaders of the Free Corps found themselves firmly in control of Dalar ken Halvar.

So Hatch reconsidered, and in a moment saw what he had to say.

'There sits Lon Oliver, sulking like a child because I will not match my weaknesses to his strength. Well, why should I? If I were to meet him here and now he would doubtless kill me, for he is much the bigger man. Bigger he is, and stronger. Look at him! Admire him! Gan Oliver was a very dragon the night he sired young Lupus!'

Lupus sat glowering at Hatch, arms folded, shoulders hunched. Lupus was no Frangoni, and the Combat College staged no moots, so Lupus was unused to the rough-and-cut of public debate. Hatch's sarcasm was telling on him.

Hatch grinned.

'Thus,' said Hatch, 'we see Lupus gigantic in his height, threatening poor me with massacre. Doubtless he could kill me if he tried – could swat me down with one obliterating strike of that yon watermelon he calls his fist. But it is wrong for him to take such pride in his physical supremacy, for we are not barbarians seeking to prove who is the stronger brute, who the bloodier animal. Young Lupus was not born into one of the Wild Tribes of the entertainments of the Eye of Delusions. Hence his atavistic yearning for their lifestyle is no more than self-indulgence.

'We are not primitives. Rather, we are representatives of the Nexus, the most sophisticated civilization which ever was – and we must conduct ourselves accordingly.'

With his speech done, Hatch gave a small and formal bow to his audience, then seated himself. He had spoken in quest of confirmation of his fractional point, but he had also spoken for another purpose. He wanted to identify himself with the Nexus, and to undermine Lupus's credibility with the Free Corps by portraying

251

him as a would-be primitive, a closet sword-swinger, a dreamer mentally attuned to the mores of a dark age of bloodglutted barbarism.

Everyone in the Free Corps was pledged to the Nexus way, to the path of rational progress, and no dissenter from the myth of progress had much of a future with that bunch of pseudoscientific fanatics.

'I have heard the arguments,' said Paraban Senk, speaking from the big display screen mounted over Forum Three's stage. 'Now hear my decision. I rule—'

But Senk did not rule, for there was a disturbance at the main entrance to Forum Three. Several people were entering, some injured, others not. Hatch recognized his sister Penelope, tall and unbowed. And his wife Talanta, shocked and staggering.

'Order,' said Paraban Senk, as students and spectators began to mob those entering Forum Three. 'Order. Order!'

But Senk was ignored.

Hatch joined the mob himself, and pushed and shouldered till he got to his wife.

'Asodo,' said Talanta.

He enfolded her in his arms. She smelt of smoke. Hatch held her tight, then realized someone else was clamouring for attention. It was his beloved daughter Onica. There were scratches across her left cheek, and her hands—

'Let's see your hands, child,' said Hatch.

Onica tried to snatch her hands away, but Hatch had them already. There was blood and skin beneath the fingernails.

'Who was it?' said Hatch.

'It's nothing,' said Onica, still trying to pull away. 'He didn't do anything. Not when mama hit him.'

'You hit him?' said Hatch to Talanta, still not knowing who the him in question might have been.

'Oh, she hit him all right,' said Polk the Cash, thus bringing himself to Hatch's attention.

'How did you get in here?' said Hatch to the moneylender.

'As your guest, of course,' said Polk. 'Thank you. I'm glad to be here. If not here, I might be with my house. It's ashes, Hatch. They burnt it. Can you believe it? They have burnt down my house.'

As the story of the mounting disorder in Dalar ken Halvar began to emerge in disordered statements, in stammering blurts, in broken recollections of panic and fear, Hatch saw the Lady Iro Murasaki – entering Forum Three at the stagger. He broke away from Polk the Cash and went to her assistance.

'Stand aside!' said Hatch sharply, dismissing a couple of Combat Cadets who sought the pleasure of aiding the lady.

Hatch himself took the Lady Iro Murasaki by the arm and led her to a seat. She sat, dressed in the disarray of a refugee. She had been struck near the eye, perhaps by a stone; there were tatters of blood on her cheek. She too was pungent with smoke.

'Are you all right?' said Hatch.

'I – I think so,' said Murasaki. Then: 'The city, it – it's – half of Scuffling Road is burning.'

Amidst a great confusion of questioning and babbling, some details began to emerge. A mob had stormed the Frangoni rock. Some of the Frangoni had stayed to fight, using Temple Isherzan as the bastion of their defences. Oboro Bakendra, Hatch's elder brother, was leading the defence of the temple. Others, including Talanta and Onica, had fled.

For her part, the Lady Iro Murasaki had fled from her house when the Yara invaded Cap Gargle and began to loot and burn the fine houses on that miniature mountain.

'It was difficult,' said Murasaki. 'The city – there's gangs, mobs, burning – but there was nobody at the lockway.'

'Of course not,' said Hatch. 'There's nothing worth looting there. Not now.'

'But there were some Free Corps people,' said Murasaki. 'Some of them – Asodo, I've heard that some of them are waiting there to kill you.'

'I wouldn't be surprised,' said Hatch.

Then he disengaged himself from the Lady Iro Murasaki, because Paraban Senk was calling Forum Three to order. The Teacher of Control was about to announce the results of the adjudication of the fight between Asodo Hatch and Lupus Lon Oliver.

Hatch seated himself.

Then Senk gave his decision.

'The situation is simple,' said Senk. 'Asodo Hatch ejected from his single-fighter. That war machine then blew itself up. Lupus Lon Oliver's single-fighter was close to the explosion. It was destroyed. Lupus died instantly. Hatch was mortally injured, but nevertheless lasted for a little longer, thereby outsurviving his opponent. The military value of such outsurvival in this particular instance was doubtless zero. Nevertheless, Hatch displayed resource, initiative, ingenuity and daring. He was thinking along the right lines, whereas there is no evidence to suggest that Lon Oliver was thinking at all. Accordingly, I confirm the partial point awarded to Asodo Hatch. His score: 0.0000057 of a point. Lon Oliver's score: nothing. Combatants should now proceed to the combat bays for the second round of this competition.'

'The second round!' said Hatch.

'Do you wish to participate in the second round or not?' said Senk. 'You have the option of dropping out. If you wish. Victory will then of course be automatically awarded to Lupus Lon Oliver.'

'Forget I spoke,' said Hatch. 'Of course I'll fight.'

Then, in obedience to the dictates of the Combat College, Asodo Hatch and Lupus Lon Oliver proceeded to the combat bays and entered the world of the illusion tanks.

Hatch could only stay in the Combat College if he won

the instructorship. If he lost his battles with Lupus then he would be forced to leave with his guests, and then he would die outside the lockway as surely as an outclassed gladiator dies in the Grand Arena of the City of Sun.

When Hatch entered the combat bay, he made sure that the door sealed itself before he sat in the initiation seat.

'You have more visitors,' said Senk, as Hatch seated himself.

'Visitors?' said Hatch.

'Some beggars.'

'Where are they?' said Hatch, wondering if someone from the outside world had sent a message to him by such a medium.

'They are being washed,' said Paraban Senk. 'Do you wish to talk with them? I can delay combat.'

Hatch gave it but a moment's consideration, then:

'No. No. I will fight now.'

'Your combat assignment, then. Single-fighters again. Over the jungles of Iridian Two. You will access the combat scenario to find your fighter stabilized in the upper realms of the jungle canopy. Heavy interference prevails to the extent that all your instruments are dead. Your opponent of course is in an identical predicament, but when interference ends you will be able to seek him out. The scenario starts with the single-fighters not less than ten and not more than fifty luzacs distant from each other.'

'When does interference end?' said Hatch.

'Shortly. Are you ready?'

'Yes,' said Hatch.

'Then,' said Senk, 'let combat begin.'

CHAPTER TWENTY-ONE

As the Combat College had the misfortune to be designed during a great Age of Euphemism, when 'training for war' had become 'studying defence', its designers were constrained by public relations experts who vetoed anything which spoke too clearly of blood and bone, of raw flesh screaming and eyeless mutilation.

Consequently the College lacks facilities to train its students in blade battle or unarmed combat. Traditionalists lament this deficiency, claiming – and the Teacher of Control has ofttimes indicated its agreement with the claims – that personal combat skills are a valuable adjunct to the development of self-confidence, even if they have precious little relevance to the conduct of transcosmic warfare.

But of course the Combat Cadets of Cap Foz Para Lash come from Dalar ken Halvar, a city landmarked most notably by the Grand Arena. In the City of the Season there is no shortage of blade schools, and likewise no shortage of opportunity to get bruised or cut. Hence those Startroopers who graduate in Dalar ken Halvar are closely acquainted with the intimacies of death, and thus superior to those graduated elsewhere – which implies that we will have a substantial career edge if and when the Chasm Gates are renewed and our rightful destiny granted unto us.

—from *An Essay on Destiny* by Glas Glas Nak, preceptor of the Graduate College on the Heights of Learning.

*　　*　　*

The Days of Wrath:
When men flew living blades
And startled thunder from the skies –
Swashed through the cities to leave the burning dead
Awash in molten gold and liquid lead.

*   *   *

So he was in the single-fighter with the jungle green around him and the sky a moody grey above. All ship tell-tales were registering nonsense, their functions jumbled by the interference generated by a low-grade probability storm, that storm itself a typical aftermath of a battle involving heavy use of the Weapons Major of the Nexus.

So Hatch had time to think, to plan and to act – for, equally lost, in the probability storm, Lupus Lon Oliver had no way to seek out Hatch. But soon the probability storm would settle, the instrumentation would function again, and Lupus would come hunting for his rival.

—Do it now.

—Or do otherwise.

Hatch did it. He killed his ship with commands both swift and sure, then set the fighter down in the jungle with the aid of its emergency crash-rockets.

The ship descended through the jungle's triple canopy, branches bending under its weight then whipping back upwards. A shower of things fell from those whiplashing branches. Insects, snakes, dead leaves, parasitic creepers, nests, arboreal snails. Hatch glanced at his instrument panel. It was still registering nonsense.

He was almost down.

He was—

He was down.

Spongy earth groaned, protested, buckled beneath the ship's weight. Earth? No. Not earth, but a kind of swamp-slush. Hatch's ship was mucking down in a swamp. Fortunately, it was being supported by the root structure of the jungle trees, but those far-spreading roots were not designed to take the weight of a Nexus single-fighter.

The ship settled, canted to one side at a crazy angle.

Instrumentation?

Nonsense still: but it was settling. The probability storm was dying away. Best to act quickly, then.

Hatch grabbed the single-fighter's remote control, then abandoned ship. A clicketing-clicketing hum-roar of insects assailed him as he opened the ship's door. He emerged to the heat-soup air and tried to find footing on the interlocked root structure of the jungle trees. He slipped, tottered, and almost fell into the putrid swamp from which the trees arose. He caught hold of a branch and looked down. The roots were patterned in swirling brown and black, and were uncommonly shiny and slippery, looking for all the world as if they had been lacquered.

Hatch pointed the remote control at the ship and thumbed the OBLITERATE button. Obedient to this command, the ship sheathed itself in silence, compressed itself, crushed itself down to the vanishing point, and was gone. Gone beyond recovery. Gone beyond detection. The sudden envanishment of the single-fighter left a temporary depression in the swamp-muck. Very temporary, for almost immediately the glutinous murk-mud of the swamp bletched and blurched, sleebing and sloobing into the depression, burying the evidence in a slurching slooze of ooze, of black saliva, of fever-pitch exudate.

A thick and heavy latrine-and-vomit stench burped upwards from the swamp as it sloozed into the space left by the quick-crushed single-fighter. Hatch imagined the consequences of falling into that filth, and shuddered.

What now?

Asodo Hatch was marooned in the hot and sweating fever-swamp jungles of an alien planet, with nothing to ensure his own surival excepting his own strength and wit, and the survival skills which the Nexus had taught him.

First question:

How dangerous was this jungle?

Any entertainment program screened by the Eye of Delusions would have pictured a jungle like this as a ravaging arena of huge carnivores. If a Hero of the Permissive Dimensions were to be dumped down in such a jungle, then within moments a multi-clawed monster would surely manifest itself, drops of corrosive saliva sizzling from its fangs as it came crashing through the trees. But in point of fact, as Hatch knew well, eaters-of-flesh are typically few and far between in any ecology, standing as they do at or near the top of a pyramidal foodchain.

Even so . . .

A tree would be safest.

Hatch wiped the bubbling sweat from his forehead and looked upwards into the heights of the nearest tree. An insect bit him on the cheek. He slapped it to its death, and studied the heights above. The trunk of the tree was sheathed in the same smooth and shiny skin of brown and black which protected the roots. But the tree branched at scarcely more than head-height, and thick creepers trailed down its side. Hatch examined the nearest creeper to make sure it was not a snake. He touched it with the back of his hand. Then grasped it and shook it. A few fragments of dead leaf descended, wisping and whispering. Hatch grabbed the creeper with both hands, let it take his whole weight, then bounced as violently as he could.

A tree-snail fell. As it hit the roots, it broke with a sharp !chick! which was clearly audible above the background noise of clicketing insects. Hatch imagined that he might well be eating such snails before very long. But there was no hurry. He could comfortably go without any food whatsoever for the first two or three days. But what about water? It was so hot in this fever-swamp that his water requirements would be prodigious. And he certainly could not drink from the stench-pit of a swamp which spread itself through the green-veil distances as far as the eye could see. Well. He could look for water inside the creepers themselves. Or seek it above – seek it in the crotches of the trees.

But first – first he should climb.

For his safety.

Hatch yanked on the creeper again.

The creeper held.

Hatch began to climb, sweating as he did so. By the time he reached a convenient crotch where he could settle down to wait, the sweat was streaming off him, and his Startrooper's Standard Grey was plastered to his skin.

'Wah!' said Hatch, panting, amazed at the speed with which the humidity sapped his strength.

He was accustomed to dry heat, but had never liked humidity. Still, it was not too bad once he settled down to wait and dedicated himself to the task of sweating.

Doubtlessly Lupus Lon Oliver was sweating also as he hunted the nerve-racking skies, waiting for Hatch's single-fighter to burst out of hiding and attack him. Doubtless Lupus would hunt, would circle uselessly, seeking an enemy ship masked against his hunting instruments, and then—

Why, within three days Lupus's ship would come to the end of its fighting life, and would power down and land automatically, its life support facilities losing all power a bare half-arc later as the ship exhausted its last resources. Upon which Lupus would have no choice but to get out and try to survive in the wilderness.

—Let him. Let him.

Lupus would try. Doubtless. And he would die. The mortality of the enemy: ever one of life's reliable satisfactions.

Then Hatch, reassured by the regular rhythms of the jungle, let his thoughts turn to the City of Sun and wondered if Takabaga, his house on the edge of Cap Uba, had been burnt out in riot. It was not much of a house, but it was his, and he did not like to think of it in ruins, the bamboo charred, his bedding reduced to feathery white ash, and every resident malatothapus fled or dead.

At least his wife was safe. For the moment. His wife, his daughter, and the Lady Iro Murasaki. And any other refugees who had entered the Combat College as Hatch's guests. By opting to settle himself in the swampland jungles rather than fight with Lupus in the skies above, Hatch had purchased them at least three days of life. As his guests, they could not be expelled from the Combat College until the competition for the instructorship had reached an end, so they were safe till then. And a lot could happen in three days.

And then Hatch thought about his own body, still seated in the initiation seat in the Combat College while his mind wandered the world of the illusion tanks. The initiation seat would be monitoring the condition of his physical flesh with the utmost diligence. If maintenance became necessary, then the initiation seat, obedient to its programming, would begin to interfere with that flesh, to feed and catheterize it, to clean it and massage it, to exercise the muscles and thus protect the flesh against wasting. Hatch disliked the thought intensely. To be petted, babied and investigated. He imagined his body helpless, mouth ajar, a trace of saliva easing down its chin.

—But that is there and this is here.

So Hatch told himself, but he could not free himself from the knowledge that the initiation seat was potentially dangerous. In the last two or three generations, a number of students had been killed by malfunctioning initiation seats which had bungled the medical tasks of body maintenance. The equipment was simply too old, too unreliable.

And Hatch might be dependent on that machinery for quite some time. For if Lupus Lon Oliver did not die quickly, then this trial by combat might stretch on. And on. And on. How long could they stay in the illusion tanks? There was a legal limit, wasn't there? Yes. Hatch dredged up the relevant clause in the Regulations: 'Combat sequences in the illusion tanks will not be extended beyond 21 days.' Twenty-one days. A long time.

—Still.

—There's no helping it.

And at least he had a reason for enduring those days. The protection of his wife and daughter . . . and his lover.

—So.

So Hatch began the diligent practice of conscious relaxation. He tried to concentrate on all the things that were good. Here in his tree above the swamp, he was free from all the worries of Dalar ken Halvar. Here nobody could touch him. He was a world away from the City of Sun, and, equally, a world away from the Nexus. He was safe. Beyond all demands. Answerable only to the Great God Mokaragash, and to none other.

'Wah!' said Hatch, relaxing, reclining, feeling his steel become flesh, his bowstrings become spiderweb.

Abruptly, the million million clicketing insects of the jungle simultaneously fell to silence. Hatch listened. Heard, somewhere, a rhythmic squelching. A drop-drop-drop of water. Then the insects began to speak again, all at the same moment. What concerted their actions? Telepathy? Or did each incorporate in its makeup some kind of clock? Valid questions, these, for Hatch knew this jungle of illusions to be modelled on a real, literal bone-and-water mud-and-blood pollen-and-wood ecosystem on some planet which did or had existed sometime, somewhere.

So the insects were not random aspects of a computerized fantasia, but accurate models of living creatures which—

Hatch's thoughts were interrupted as the world wavered, melted then abruptly brightened, his body suddenly seated, the hot and moist replaced by the dry and cold—

For he was back in the Combat College.

Weirdly disorientated.

Hatch had made the transition from illusion tank to reality thousands of times before, but never under conditions quite so unexpected.

'Lupus!' said Hatch, blurting the word.

Lupus Lon Oliver must have killed him, must have, thus winning their encounter. Else how could Hatch possibly have been plunged back into the world of the Combat College?

'He demands,' said Paraban Senk, speaking from the display screen in Hatch's combat bay.

'Demands?' said Hatch, bewildered. 'Demands what?'

'What do you think?' said Senk. 'He demands adjudication.'

And Hatch felt a shuddering relief. So Lupus had not outguessed him, outfought him, outmatched him. Instead, the young Ebrell Islander was seeking to win this match by legal manoeuvre. Well, it would be very interesting to see what he came up with. Because as far as Hatch could see, his own position was watertight.

CHAPTER TWENTY-TWO

Warfare weakens. It generates chaos, crisis and unknowns in abundance. Battle is apt to compromise both psychic and physical integrity, and a predisposition to favour the enemy may further weaken your resolve to prosecute your duty.

This last factor is often ignored when we study warfare which sees the warrior locked into machines kept parasecs apart. However, while the Nexus does train for intergalactic and transcosmic warfare, the military reality of the last millennium has been that most active operations involve civil interventions undertaken as a response to political or religious extremism.

Here we must consider the human element: and here note that the tactics of empathy are of particular value when your own resolve is weak.

Unfortunately humans cannot be taken out of the loop, least of all when dealing with the Nu-chala-nuth, who reject the authority of machines over humans. In any case, one could not, for example, entrust a dorgi with the task of policing the streets of any of the cities of the Nu-chala-nuth in the aftermath of one of the periodic upheavals inspired by that religion. So we rely upon the warrior.

If you are of the Nu-chala-nuth, then in the supervision of members of your own faith you may find that your discharge of your duty to the Nexus is difficult. This is an extreme case, but for any given individual we can wargame a situation in which that individual's loyalties will be divided.

In pitched battle, this may be of small account, but it matters greatly in civil interventions, which tend to revolve around negotiations. You as an officer of the

Nexus may one day find yourself endeavouring to discharge your duty in a situation in which you have a predisposition to support the enemy in defiance of your duty.

Under such circumstances, you should attend first to the emotional dynamics of the negotiation scenario. If you can befriend your opposite number then that person will tend to refrain from using those tactics which will be most hurtful to you. Here we ask you to understand the first rule of the Characterization of the Enemy: the Enemy is someone to respect. As you come to understand the horrors of total war and the methods which can be used to avoid it, you will begin to understand the importance of this characterization.

—from the Book of Negotations

*   *   *

So was it then a slip which let
The hero fall and long odds claim the day?
Or was the one sword sharper, or the sand
Made partial by its hungers?

*   *   *

'So what's Lon Oliver going to argue?' said Hatch.

'I've no idea,' said Paraban Senk.

'Can we be heard?' said Hatch. 'Right now, I mean? By those in Forum Three?'

'They get to watch you while you're in the illusion tanks,' said Senk. 'They get a full-colour full-sound split-screen presentation of the battles. But right now you've got a guarantee of privacy.'

'Then while we're closeted together in private,' said Hatch, 'let's talk about Dalar ken Halvar.'

'Why?'

'Because there's revolution in Dalar ken Halvar.'

'Why should I worry about that?' said Senk.

'Because it's going to compromise your ability to fulfil

your mission,' said Hatch. 'Your mission to train Startroopers for the Nexus.'

'So?' said Senk. 'I thought I'd made my position on that clear. Some lawful authority will establish itself swiftly in the city, and I will then deal with that authority.'

'So,' said Hatch, 'let's talk about dealing. Obviously it's something you've got to do, so why not now rather than later? Why not deal with someone you know, someone you trust, rather than someone unknown and untested? Why not manipulate the situation in Dalar ken Halvar rather than taking whatever random leadership gets thrown up by the present disorder? Senk, if you're willing, then I'd like to cut a deal. If you make me the instructor, I'll do my level best to restore order in Dalar ken Halvar and help you fulfil your mission.'

'I thought you didn't want to be instructor,' said Senk.

'What gave you that idea?' said Hatch.

'Lon Oliver gave me that idea,' said Senk. 'He told me today that you offered to sell him the instructorship. You invited him to bribe you. Lon Oliver asked me to disqualify you from this competition on that account.'

'But you didn't,' said Hatch.

'That's right,' said Senk. 'I didn't. Even so, the information made me doubt the strength of your commitment to the Nexus.'

'You're not saying you believe Lon Oliver, are you?' said Hatch.

'You're not denying the truth of his accusations, surely.'

'Of course I am!' said Hatch. 'It's a nonsense, an utter nonsense, the whole lot of it.'

'Perhaps,' said Senk. 'But Lon Oliver was very persuasive. He makes much of the fact that the Silver Emperor is missing.'

'Temporarily, perhaps,' said Hatch. 'But—'

'He tells me,' said Senk, 'that the Free Corps is going to end up in effective control of Dalar ken Halvar. I'm inclined to believe him, Hatch. I've come to a decision. As you say, I've got to do deals with whoever ends up in control of Dalar ken Halvar, and I may as well start now. So I'm starting. I've decided that it's best that Lupus Lon Oliver becomes the instructor.'

'So you're going to adjudicate in his favour,' said Hatch.

'That depends on what argument you put up,' said Paraban Senk. 'But I give you fair warning. If you fight with Lupus Lon Oliver a third time, then I'm going to ensure that you go down to defeat. I'm going to ensure that you die.'

'Die?' said Hatch.

'Yes, die,' said Senk. 'I'm going to ensure that you meet with your death. First you'll die in the world of the illusion tanks, and then you'll die in the fact of the flesh.'

'And how do you propose to manage that?' said Hatch.

'Wait and see,' said Senk. 'Wait and see.'

'The initiation seat,' said Hatch. 'Is that how you're going to do it? Kill me with the initiation seat?'

'That's for you to work out,' said Senk. 'Think about it, Hatch. Think about it.'

Hatch did think about it. He thought about it fiercely all the way to Forum Three. Kill him. Senk was going to kill him. But how? With the initiation seat? Maybe, maybe. Or. Or what?

—Purpose.

The hotbright thought burnt bright in Hatch's mind. Purpose. What was the purpose of deciding the instructorship through trial by combat? Hatch knew the answer to that. Dalar ken Halvar understood trial by combat. Everyone could understand that. So the instructor who triumphed over all others was graced with an authority which everyone in Dalar ken Halvar could understand.

—Assume that Senk wants Lupus as instructor.

—Senk will want Lupus to win authority through triumph in battle.

—So.

So the implication was that Paraban Senk must ensure that Lupus Lon Olvier defeated Asodo Hatch in combat. In front of witnesses. How could Senk do that?

—The MegaCommand.

The ominous thought rose in Hatch's mind and could not be suppressed. Lupus was much better than Hatch when it came to making war with the MegaCommand.

—But first, the adjudication.

As Hatch entered Forum Three, striding onstage in front of the tiered seating, he was hailed by a familiar voice.

'Wah, Hatch!' cried Beggar Grim.

Beggar Grim was sitting with his comrades Zoplin and X'dex. All three members of this besognio scumpack had entered the Combat College as the official guests of Asodo Hatch. Deloused, ungrimed and dressed in the limegreen uniforms of beneficiaries of Nexus Welfare, they looked superficially disciplined, but their unruly cheers nullified the effect of the superficialities. Though each had been provided with a double eye-patch to hide empty eye sockets, they had strung these round their necks, and were passing the Eye from hand to hand, from socket to socket.

Master Zoplin socketed the Eye then said, chanting the words:

'I see you loud, I see you clear, I see you killing – kill him, Hatch!'

Hatch acknowledged the beggars' applause, not because he welcomed it but because he knew the gesture would infuriate Lupus.

It did.

Lupus swore at the beggars, who jeered at him, then threw food at him. The strange food of the Nexus which tasted soft in their mouths, like food made to feed some monstrous race of earth-dwelling grubs.

Lupus was furious.

'Senk!' said Lupus, addressing the Teacher of Control.

'Call them to order!' Then, when there was no reply from Paraban Senk: 'Hatch! Control your filth!'

'Filth!' said Lord X'dex. 'Are you referring to me?'

'Of course he is,' said Master Zoplin. 'You look as if you took a bath in liquid snot then cleaned your ears with a dog turd. How else should you be called but filth?'

'I am not filth but royalty,' said Lord X'dex. 'Know me in my might, for I am Lord X'dex Paspilion, master of the Greater Tower of X-n'dix in the mighty kingdom of X-zox Kalada.'

'Then know the boy Oliver as your superior,' said Beggar Grim, 'for he has the greatest of Greater Towers at spring between his thighs, whereas yours is but a worm, and useless, yes, and last month's piss the smell of it.'

'I dispute it!' said Lord X'dex. 'Come! A trial of proof! Hey, Oliver-boy! Bring your piss-stick this way!'

'He lingers,' said Master Zoplin.

'He knows himself secretly a woman,' said Lord X'dex. 'Wherefore he lingers where a man would leap.'

'A woman?' said Beggar Grim. 'Why, if a woman then all the more reason for leaping, for I am man sufficient to rape him out of his virgin ugliness.'

'You will bring your people to order,' said Lupus to Hatch, a note of desperation intermixed with his anger.

'Or?' said Hatch.

'The Season starts in a month,' said Lupus.

There was only one Season in Dalar ken Halvar, a city where the climate was ever a constant. The Season referred to by Lupus was the three months of the year in which the Grand Arena became a stage for gaudy death and bloody execution.

Lupus's words constituted a challenge. Lupus Lon Oliver was inviting Asodo Hatch to join him on the sands of the Grand Arena where they could duel it out for real, fighting with swords like the atavistic heroes of the more childish entertainments of the Eye of Delusions.

'I await then the start of the Season,' said Hatch, with due formality.

It was an empty formality. He would never face Lupus on the sands of the Grand Arena, for their quarrel would be resolved one way or the other much sooner – probably by the mob.

'The day,' said Lupus, with conviction, ducking a wodge of tofu thrown at him by Master Zoplin, 'cannot come too soon.'

The beggars then began systematically to pelt the unfortunate Lupus with all the food at their disposal.

'Settle, settle,' said Paraban Senk, calling for order.

But the audience did not settle until the beggars ceased fire, which they only did because they had exhausted their supply of ammunition.

'Lon Oliver,' said Paraban Senk, speaking into the relative silence. 'State your case.'

Whereupon Lupus stated his position very clearly and simply:

'I seek adjudication of my combat with Asodo Hatch,' said he.

'If I have been overhearing aright,' said Paraban Senk, 'then you seek to meet Hatch on the sands in the Season.' At this a murmur went up from the audience. Senk ignored it and continued: 'Will you seek to have that battle also resolved by adjudication?'

This hinted of sarcasm, and Hatch was momentarily surprised. Why would Paraban Senk make Lupus the butt of his sarcasm when he wanted Lupus to be the next instructor? Why – of course! – so nobody would suspect Senk of partiality.

In any case, Lupus was unmoved by Senk's sally.

'I am of the Nexus,' said Lupus staunchly, 'and seek a resolution of an affair of the Nexus in accordance of the laws of the Nexus. Hatch fled from battle. I demand adjudication. I ask that the combat be awarded to me.'

'Is that it?' said Senk. 'Is that your case, complete in its entirety?'

'That is all,' said Lupus. 'It's enough, isn't it?'

'We will see,' said Senk. 'Asodo Hatch. State your case.'

'He has no case!' said Lupus, giving way to anger. His volatility spoke of stress, of uncertainty, of strained nerves and fatigue. 'Stop playing games with me, Senk! He ran. He lost.'

'That is for him to say,' said Senk.

'Fates!' said Lupus, irritated beyond bearing. 'You watched it! You've got a record. What more do we need?'

'Motive,' said Senk. 'Asodo Hatch has a mind for which he must speak because I cannot.'

'Battles are not decided by motive,' said Lupus. 'The combat decides. Decided. Hatch ran.'

'On the contrary,' said Senk. 'The very fact that you are here seeking adjudication is a self-sufficient proof of the fact that this battle was not decided at all. Hence I require from Hatch a statement of his motive – his why for doing what he did. Hatch.'

'My motive was simple,' said Hatch. 'I desired to bring Lon Oliver to his death. I chose as my weapon of war the very environment itself. I call your attention to the Book of War. It states, does it not – here I paraphrase, but it does so state – that the environment is ever the greatest killer. Is that not what it states? The jungle was my weapon. My weapon of choice. I did not run from battle. Rather, I made a tactical withdrawal calculated to expose Lupus to certain disaster.'

'These tactics are orthodox,' said Senk.

'Orthodox!' exploded Lupus. 'What made him think me meat for death?'

'Hatch?' said Senk.

'I have dwelt in the wilderness,' said Asodo Hatch. 'I can live there with ease for a day or forever. Lon Oliver has not. He is a child of the Nexus, soft and weak. My choice of tactics necessarily doomed him down into the jungle. We all know the flight life of a single-fighter. My tactics forced him into the swamp, the snake-heat, the jungle. By my tactics he dies and I claim myself the killer.'

'Wah!' said Lupus.

'Hatch has spoken,' said Senk. 'And you?'

'I stand by my record,' said Lupus. 'You know my record. Perhaps you would care to share it with Asodo Hatch.'

Senk sighed, and then:

'Asodo Hatch, your tactics displayed audacity and wit, a sound knowledge of your own strengths and points of weakness, and a remarkable degree of originality. Yet you erred in one thing, and that was your assessment of your enemy.'

'I erred?'

'Do you think yourself beyond error?'

'But I—'

'Hatch,' said Senk, 'Lupus has stacked up time in the illusion tanks doing survival training. Wilderness survival training.'

'How much time?' said Hatch.

'Seven full days and a fraction in the last standard year,' said Senk.

'But that's nothing!' said Hatch.

'Taken as a series of arduous survival sessions of a duration of ten arcs each, it is rather a lot,' said Senk.

'Ten arcs is nothing,' said Hatch. 'It means he's never had to sleep in the wilderness. It means—'

'Hatch,' said Senk, with a sharpness of tone which spoke of extreme displeasure.

'My lord,' said Hatch, suitably abashed.

'Hatch, I am not your lord, but I am your teacher,' said Senk. 'Earlier in his training in the Combat College, Lupus did several long-duration wilderness survival sessions in the illusion tanks. The sessions of the last year were simply refreshers.'

So.

Of course.

It was all starting to make sense now.

Lon Oliver was of the Free Corps, and the Free Corps preached a doctrine of the supreme individual, the masterman who could overcome all through intellectual audacity and physical skill. Of course Lupus would be attracted to Ultimate Tests of all kinds, wilderness survival being just one of these.

'Your ruling, then,' said Hatch.

'I adjudge the wilderness survival chances of Lon Oliver to be equal to those of Asodo Hatch,' said Paraban Senk. 'Accordingly, I adjudicate the results of the last combat session between Lupus and Hatch to be a draw. I award the contestants half a point each. Lon Oliver now has a score of half a point, of 0.5. Asodo Hatch now has a score of 0.5000057.'

So Hatch was still leading.

But only just.

'Do you wish to take a rest now?' said Paraban Senk.

'A rest?' said Lupus. 'I—'

'The choice is not yours,' said Senk, cutting Lupus short. 'I addressed Hatch. He has seniority. The choice is his.'

'Seniority?' said Lupus in outrage.

'He was in the Service when you were still bullying your brothers at the bottom of the Heights of Learning,' said Senk. 'Hatch. You choose.'

Hatch calculated furiously. Paraban Senk had privately stated his partisanship. Senk wanted Lupus to win. Yet Senk had given choice of timing to Hatch. Hatch was strongly motivated to defer the combat, because he wanted to maximize the length of time which his wife, his daughter and his mistress enjoyed the protection of the Combat College. Senk would surely know this, which implied that Senk wanted the combat deferred. Which meant that Senk thought that Lupus would do better if he was given a chance to cool down, a chance to discipline his present anger.

Or perhaps Senk thought Lupus needed to sleep. In

Hatch's judgement, Lupus was suffering very badly from lack of sleep.

'What time is it?' said Hatch.

'Midnight has been and gone,' said Senk. 'The Day of Three Fishes is behind us, and we are entered upon the Day of Two Fishes.'

The Day of Two Fishes.

Just two days short of Dog Day.

'But it is not yet dawn?' said Hatch.

'Dawn is still a long ways distant,' said Paraban Senk.

'Then,' said Hatch, rousing his voice to an artificial vibrancy which masked the true depths of his own fatigue, 'since the night is so young, I am ready to fight on further. However, Lupus is young in his own flesh, and it is well known that the young need more sleep than their seniors. Accordingly, it may well be that Lupus would prefer to sleep, even though I for my part am ready to fight on. Since that is so, I defer to the choice of my junior colleague.'

Lupus was incensed. He was inflamed and furious at being called junior colleague – but he was now in such a state that he would have been equally enraged even had he been called the hero of the millennium. In his fury, Lupus declared:

'I will fight Hatch now. And I will kill him.'

'Then,' said Paraban Senk, 'let me brief you. No, Hatch! Don't leave! I will brief you here.'

So Asodo Hatch and Lupus Lon Oliver stood fast, and Paraban Senk looked down at them from Forum Three's display screen and told them their doom.

CHAPTER TWENTY-THREE

Motsu Kazuka: the language of the Nu-chala-nuth. In defiance of Nexus policy, the People refuse to teach the Ninetongue of the Nexus to any of prepubescent blood. Thus for the People the Ninetongue is always a second learning, and many are less than fluent even in the Code Seven Commonspeech, which serves beneath a billion suns as the language of day-to-day communication and communion.

*   *   *

Ah! Fluid the blood, the ballet,
The fluent flux which entertains as we
In sated sugars watch and coy – while shadows
Sabotage our locks, and shape
To slice and dice, titanium and steel.

*   *   *

'Startrooper Hatch,' said Senk. 'Startrooper Lon Oliver. I have something very special in store for you.'

There was a momentary pause. Hatch briefly thought that Senk was going to command them to fight each other in the fact of the flesh, blade against blade or fist against fist. If so – then so be it! He was ready. But—

'Combat will take place in the illusion tanks, as usual,' said Senk, as if reading Hatch's mind. 'You will each have command of a Galactic Class MegaCommand Cruiser.'

'In what setting?' said Hatch, trying to control his dismay.

It was what he had expected, but it was still hard to hear his doom and know himself defeated. The Mega-Command was the biggest and the best of all the starships of the Nexus. Lon Oliver loved the thing, but Hatch had never felt confident in its employment. He was going to lose this encounter. He was sure of it.

'Your battle will be played out in deep space,' said Senk.

'A quick-plunge?' said Lupus, with those words asking if the combatants would be plunged straight into battle.

'No,' said Senk. 'You will each have three arcs to prepare your MegaCommands for battle.'

'Three arcs,' said Hatch.

This increased his despondency. Three arcs was roughly a quarter of a night. Since Lupus was the one who knew the MegaCommand best, Lupus was the one who would be better able to use the luxury of so much time.

'Three arcs, yes,' said Senk. 'One final thing. This combat will take place in the context of an interesting scenario.'

An interesting scenario? What did that mean? Hatch presumed that Senk had thought up something new. But what?

'As all Startroopers and Combat Cadets know full well,' said Paraban Senk, 'the Nexus endured appalling damage during the Spasm Wars. Billions died. It was the people of the Nu-chala-nuth who provoked those Spasm Wars. Billions died because of Nu-chala-nuth. Right now, to my dismay, I find those same alien doctrines of Nu-chala-nuth have sparked riot and disorder in Dalar ken Halvar itself.'

'Yes,' said Lupus loudly. 'And Hatch, Asodo Hatch, he was the one, he wrote, he taught, his thesis, it's all his fault.'

Hatch tried to protest.

'My thesis—'

'Silence!' said Senk, voice amplified to thunder-clap,

blasting Hatch's protest into silence. 'This is the scenario. A Nexus ship crewed exclusively by the Nu-chala-nuth has mutinied. Asodo Hatch is the captain of that ship. A ship loyal to the purity of the Nexus has been sent to destroy the mutinous ship. Lupus Lon Oliver is the captain of the loyal ship.'

Again Hatch tried to protest.

'Listen,' said Hatch. 'I never—'

'You wrote the thesis!' said Senk, again over-riding Hatch by brute force of amplification. 'You brought the doctrines of Nu-chala-nuth to Dalar ken Halvar, you and none other. As for Lupus Lon Oliver, he told me long ago that he never wished to command any of the Nu-chala-nuth. He would not have them as crew on his ships. That was what he said. You made your choices, both of you. You made your choices long ago. Now live by your choices. Go! To the combat bays. Now! Go!'

By now, both Hatch and Lupus had clamped their hands to their ears to muffle the force of that onslaught. Paraban Senk was booming like a thunder-god.

'You have your orders!' said Senk. 'Go!'

Hatch saw he was going to be shouted down if he tried to protest further, so he fled. All the way to the combat bays he swore savagely. Senk had set him up nicely. By making this a combat of MegaCommand Cruisers, Senk had doomed Hatch to defeat. And by giving Hatch command of a mutinous Nu-chala-nuth MegaCommand Cruiser, Senk had underlined Hatch's responsibility for the real-world revolution now taking place in Dalar ken Halvar itself.

'Bitch of a bastard!' said Hatch.

Then gained his chosen combat bay. Its door hardened to kaleidoscope. He slammed his fist against the door. Savagely. Testing it. The door held. Very well. Hatch dropped himself into the initiation seat. Paraban Senk's face appeared on the combat bay's display screen.

'How do you feel?' said Senk.

'How do you think I feel?' said Hatch. 'You want to kill me, don't you?'

'I am obedient to my priorities,' said Senk. 'My ruling priority is simple. I must train Startroopers. Lupus Lon Oliver can assist me with that task. You cannot.'

'I can,' said Hatch.

'How so?' said Senk.

Hatch was on the spot. Unless he could talk his way out of this one, he was going to be defeated in battle, he was going to be expelled from the Combat College in consequence of his defeat, and he would be killed in Dalar ken Halvar by those who saw him as being responsible for the revolution in that city.

'I can help you,' said Hatch, 'because I'm politically astute enough to take control of the Nu-chala-nuth. To lead the revolution.'

Even as he said it, it sounded like madness. But what alternative did he have? Senk had publicly linked Hatch with the Nu-chala-nuth. Senk had named Hatch as the person responsible for the revolution. Senk had seated him on a tiger, and now he must ride it or be eaten.

'You'd what!?' said Senk. 'You'd lead a religious revolution? I couldn't permit such a disaster.'

'On the contrary,' said Hatch. 'You must permit exactly that. Because – because a revolution led by the Nu-chala-nuth is your sole chance of survival.'

'That's a nonsense,' said Senk.

'Is it?' said Hatch. 'The physical fabric of the Combat College is starting to fall apart. One of the airlock doors is gone. Most of the combat bays don't work any more. The cafeteria food is questionable. You won't be able to work unassisted. Not for much longer.'

'I'll do my best,' said Senk. 'The Free Corps will help me.'

'Ah,' said Hatch. 'But what's the Free Corps' motivation?'

'The Free Corps,' said Senk, 'is motivated by loyalty to the Nexus. If you've got a point, then make it quickly,

278

Hatch. Lon Oliver is asking me why there's a delay.'

'Then let him audit this conversation,' said Hatch. 'Senk, listen to me. The Free Corps is dominated by submission psychology. The Free Corps gives you its loyalty because you're the biggest, strongest, most powerful thing around.'

'The Nu-chala-nuth are ruled by a similar psychological priority,' said Senk.

'Ah,' said Hatch. 'But you're doomed to fail, and publicly. Your doors are breaking down, your functions failing. Soon you'll need active human help to accomplish your mission. The Free Corps won't help you when you're a cripple.'

'That's debatable,' said Senk.

'But the Nu-chala-nuth will!' said Hatch. 'If you ally yourself with the Nu-chala-nuth, then you can make yourself the temple of the religion, the repository of holy knowledge. You can teach the Motsu Kazuka, teach the purity of the truth.'

'Nu-chala-nuth is too dangerous to deal with,' said Senk.

'Is it?' said Hatch. 'You'll have the whole of the Empire of Greater Parengarenga to deal with unless the Silver Emperor shows up. Will the Free Corps fight the entire Empire? Senk, Nu-chala-nuth is a crusading religion. It can conquer the entire continent for the Nexus.'

'I am not here to accomplish acts of conquest,' said Senk.

'But you may find yourself embroiled in war regardless,' said Hatch. 'The Silver Emperor has guaranteed the peace of Parengarenga by treaties maintained by the prestige of his magic. With the emperor missing, maybe kidnapped, maybe dead, war inevitably follows. Can the Free Corps secure you against the wrath of an entire empire? That I don't know, but I know full well that a militant religion like Nu-chala-nuth can conquer Parengarenga and more. Think about it, Senk.'

279

There was a pause, then:

'I'm sorry,' said Senk. 'It's too late to do a deal. It's the MegaCommand now. Lon Oliver is better than you, Hatch. He'll beat you. You can't win.'

'But if I win?'

'You can't.'

'Try me,' said Hatch.

'Very well, then,' said Senk. 'You will be tried upon the field of combat. Let battle begin!'

And already the world was wavering. And when the world steadied, Asodo Hatch found himself standing on the bridge of a MegaCommand Cruiser.

Caught unawares, Hatch tottered, and had to take a half-step forward to steady himself.

'Sir?'

Hatch realized he was being addressed by the Officer of the Watch.

'It is nothing,' said Hatch.

'Sir,' said the Officer of the Watch.

Then that officer said nothing more as Asodo Hatch scrutinized the bridge. Slowly. Taking his time. Thinking things through. Now what was the name of the Officer of the Watch? The software constructs available to the illusion tanks were limited in number, and Hatch had long ago met all those software constructs which masqueraded as MegaCommand officers and crew.

—Never mind the name.

—It will come.

Directly in front of Hatch was what looked like a widespan window, or an enlarged version of the Eye of Delusions, but which was in fact the MegaCommand Cruiser's gigantic main battle display screen. Hatch glanced from that main display screen to the main command console. Green green and green. Constellations of green lights glowed in the security of their peace. Safe safe safe. Only one light was orange: the battle-readiness indicator.

'Situation report,' said Hatch.

In response to that order, the Officer of the Watch began his report:

'Sir. There is a probability disruption field between us and a hostile Galactic Class MegaCommand Cruiser. The estimated decay time of the disruption field is three arcs. Your orders, sir.'

Hatch turned his full attention to the gigantic main battle display screen. He stared at the patterns made by the disruption field. Nothing could cross that zone of instability. While the disruption field survived, Asodo Hatch and Lon Oliver could do nothing but stare at each other, like two fighting cocks separated by a sheet of armoured glass. But once that field collapsed, then war would begin.

—So what are my options?

Hatch could run. He could order his MegaCommand Cruiser to flee at full speed, leaving a variety of booby traps in its wake. But Lupus would hunt him down. So. Hatch could use the ship's power to generate another probability disruption field like the one presently separating the two ships. But wasting power on such a temporary expedient would leave the ship weak and vulnerable when battle was finally joined.

—Time, time!

Hatch longed for time, more time to think. He imagined Lupus Lon Oliver, the perfect citizen of the Nexus, organizing his great machine for combat. The Galactic Class MegaCommand Cruiser: the ultimate war machine which Lupus knew so well.

And what did Hatch really know? Only the bloody warfare of the desert. He felt an old scar across his ribs aching again. The scar was an illusion: but the body generated by the illusion tank echoed his realworld body, and the scar held the truth of a real memory. Hatch wished . . .

Hatch wished he could have shifted the scene of this combat from deep space to desert. He wished he could have made the weapons not MegaCommand Cruisers but swords. Himself against Lupus. Sword against sword.

In the desert he was at home, but he had always felt out of place on the MegaCommand Cruiser, and never more so than now. While his skills with the single-fighter were indifferent, he nevertheless was happy enough to fly the thing, but the MegaCommand was so inhuman in its scale and complexity that Hatch had always felt dwarfed by it: inferior, primitive, outclassed.

Lupus, on the other hand, identified totally with the works of the Nexus. Lupus never felt out of place on the MegaCommand: he loved it. And knew it better than Hatch. Lupus was the better starwarrior. Was younger, faster, smarter, slicker.

More ruthless.

Hatch, who had long possessed a grossly exaggerated sense of his own antiquity, felt himself to be an old man facing a young man and doomed to die. So what could he do but go down in style? Still, he knew he must not show despair, for a real world audience was watching, and any distress he evidenced would in turn distress his daughter Onica, and most likely Talanta and the Lady Murasaki too.

As Hatch watched the disruption field disintegrating, he wished he could talk with his wife, wished he could hold her and comfort her, easing the impact of the strangeness which confronted her. Then he decided that . . . why, he would talk to her! Holding he could not do, but talking he could, even if the conversation was doomed to be strictly one-way.

'I wish to address the crew,' said Hatch. 'Briefly. Set it up.'

San Kaladan – yes, it came to Hatch now, that was the rightful name of this Officer of the Watch – issued crisp orders. Soon, throughout the MegaCommand Cruiser, everyone was poised to hear a speech from their captain. The crew was a thousand strong, but everything Hatch said would be heard not just by them but also by the people in Forum Three.

So Hatch could send a message to Talanta.

But Hatch realized there was nothing he wanted to say to Talanta in front of all the people in Forum Three. He was a Frangoni, and the Frangoni were guarded when it came to expressing intimacies in public. If he spoke of his wife or family he would end up expounding the pieties of propaganda.

—So.

—Forget it.

When he was alone with Talanta, when he had peace and privacy, then he would speak his heart. But right now . . .

Why, there was still an audience to be addressed.

'I wish to make the briefest of speeches before the coming battle,' said Hatch. 'Let me say just this. We fight for the greatest cause. We are the warriors. We were made for this battle. We were made for this war. Remember that. Remember that, and I will give you the death of your enemies. That is all.'

Hatch finished his little speech and smiled tightly. It was not a great speech but it had served its purpose. Regardless of what it might have done for his phantom crew, it had certainly focused his own mind on battle. On victory.

He would win.

Or die trying.

But how?

Already, Lupus would be planning battle tactics, his mind all on the MegaCommand, his mind all on the coming battle. And what strategies could Hatch possibly find to compensate for his enemy's greater talent?

'Sir,' said the Officer of the Watch. 'With respect, sir. The estimated decay time of the disruption field is less than three arcs. As yet you have issued no battle orders, sir.'

Hatch knew what this was leading to. If he did nothing, then very shortly the Officer of the Watch would place him under arrest. That was standard operating procedure on a Nexus warship, and Hatch had no reason to think that standard operating procedure would be any different even though the ship he presently commanded was in revolt against the Nexus.

Hatch looked at the disruption field. At the cold white stars. And thought of Lupus, the bright-brave conqueror of stars. Lupus would win. Would triumph. And . . . and . . .

And the probabilities were that Asodo Hatch would die in the dust outside the gates of the Combat College, going down to his death with the Lady Murasaki, and with his wife, his poor Talanta, once so sweetly beautiful. And – worst and cruellest of all deaths – his daughter Onica.

'A boy,' said Hatch to himself. 'A brute in his boyhood. I wish I could meet him face to face. Face to face and kill him.'

A thought occurred to him. A thought from Dithzora-ka-mako, the Mystical Way of the Nu-chala-nuth:

—To drink the sea, you must first set your lips to the water.

'Sir?' said the Officer of the Watch, the restrained and professional San Kaladan.

Hatch turned to him. He drew his sword, a short and brutal sword, part of the uniform Hatch had long ago specified for all his MegaCommand illusion tank battles.

'What is this?' said Hatch, brandishing the sword.

'Sir?' said the Officer of the Watch.

'This!' said Hatch, giving the sword a shake, as if it were Lon Oliver's throat.

'Sir. It is a sword, sir.'

'What is its purpose?'

'It is a weapon of death, sir. A weapon of war. But, sir, I doubt it a weapon suited to our present purpose.'

'All war is a unity,' said Hatch.

Grinning in something close to triumph. Because now he had the answer! Now he knew!

'San Kaladan,' said Hatch, addressing the Officer of the Watch by his rightful name.

'Sir.'

'Order all hands to suit up for close quarters battle.'

'Sir?'

'We will fight the enemy at close quarters and I – I will hack off my enemy's head.'

Thus spoke Asodo Hatch. And back in Forum Three there was a great stir of speculation among the assembled Startroopers, Combat Cadets and Free Corps graduates of the Combat College, for the order Hatch had just given was a nonsense. MegaCommand Cruisers fought with the Weapons Major of the Nexus: heavy-battle weapons which manipulated probability, warped space and wrecked matter down to the constituent parts of its atoms.

A battle of MegaCommand Cruisers could be a brutal clash of force against force, shield against shield. Or it could be a subtle duel of wits as the commanders slid their ships in and out of local space, probing, laying traps and seeking to subvert each other's instrumentation. But one thing was for certain: swords, and the hacking off of heads with the same, had no part to play in such warfare, and never had, and never could.

The consensus in Forum Three was very simple: Asodo Hatch was stark staring raving mad.

CHAPTER TWENTY-FOUR

Asma: computational machine of the Nexus which, as an intelligent and self-aware observer, is capable of manipulating the probability structure of whichever universe it finds itself in, and hence of altering reality.

The technic of the Nexus is largely based on such manipulation of probability, a process which is fraught with peril. Such manipulations strain the very structure of reality itself, and the history of the Nexus records catastrophic disasters in which an entire cosmos, overstrained, has disintegrated into Fundamental Chaos.

* * *

Breath within breath the dark
By boot and bruise creates
The armies which by whisper stumble
Towards the crack which breaks the night from day:
A scalpel, and a line of liquid red.

* * *

Hatch stood close to the Officer of the Watch, close enough to kiss or kill. The man was sweating. The MegaCommand Cruiser was cool, yet San Kaladan was perspiring like a sledgehammer labourer at high noon on the thirstiest day of the year.

'Field collapse imminent,' said San Kaladan.

'Count,' said Hatch, speaking in the curt and brutal Code Five, the military dialect of the Nexus Ninetongue.

His clipped one-word order had a specific meaning. In the course of his training, Hatch had memorized seven dozen such orders. This one told San Kaladan to give him a countdown to the point where the probability disruption field would collapse.

At that point, battle would be joined.

'Twenty,' said his subordinate, watching the command console. 'And. Nineteen. And. Eighteen. And. Seventeen. And.'

'Instigate one,' said Hatch. 'Now.'

San Kaladan broke off the count and pressed a button to instigate the first series of preprogrammed ship commands.

There was no sense of acceleration, for the Mega-Command Cruiser had state-of-the-art effect insulation technology. The ship commanded by Asodo Hatch could have blasted through space under an acceleration of a thousand gravities and he would never have felt a thing. It was a world away from the rough and tumble of a Scala Nine single-fighter.

But the command console told the story.

The ship bearing Asodo Hatch to his destiny was now accelerating directly towards Lupus Lon Oliver's vessel – and towards the disintegrating probability disruption field – at three gravities.

'Count,' said Hatch.

'Field collapse in twelve,' said his subordinate, watching the command console. 'And. Eleven. And. Ten. And. Nine. And.'

And.

And Asodo Hatch, watching the disruption field collapse, thought briefly of Dalar ken Halvar and of the Arena which, in the Season, became the burning focus of the life of the City of Sun.

Hatch touched a hand to the hilt of his sword.

—My father.

His father had fought. His father had died. And now Hatch in turn was facing his Season in this strange Arena where he must meet Lupus Lon Oliver in a combat which would decide whether he lived or whether he died.

'And. Three. And. Two. And. One. And. None.'

An immaculate countdown.

On the word 'none', the probability disruption field collapsed entirely. A few wisps of purple light smoked briefly in the vacuum of interstellar space then vanished.

'Instigate two,' said Hatch. 'Now.'

The Officer of the Watch, the impeccably correct San Kaladan, pressed the instigation button a second time.

And—

And the world wavered.

The image on the gigantic main battle display screen buckled, collapsed to a point of light then died into absolute darkness. Though Hatch had been prepared for this, he nevertheless experienced a frisson of the purest horror. This was every starwarrior's worst nightmare: a ship dying in the wastelands of interstellar space.

The main command console went dead.

The consoles minor were dead already.

A moment later, the lights went out.

Darkness made its cave. Hatch closed his eyes, allowed them time to adjust. When he opened them, weak emergency lights were already on. In the main command console, a small panel had come to life. It was a piece of electrical-based equipment. San Kaladan, the Officer of the Watch, was struggling to preserve his immaculate calm, to remain cool and collected in the face of an entirely unorthodox tactical situation. He studied the readouts and telltales of that small panel, studied it for longer than was necessary while he perfected his control of his own emotions. Then he addressed his commander:

'Sir. All three asmas are down, sir. Destroyed, sir. They self-destructed, sir. We have total failure of all ship systems based on probability manipulation. Total loss of main and auxiliary manoeuvring capacity. Total loss of all heavybattle weapons systems. Total loss of all shield systems. Emergency electricals are operative. Electrical-based emergency computational and navigational equipment operative. Otherwise our ship is null and dead. We are on a collision course for the enemy Galactic Class MegaCommand Cruiser.'

That was Nexus style. Spell it out. Not 'the cruiser', the one and only cruiser sitting out there in the vacuum of interstellar space. Not 'the enemy cruiser'. Not 'the enemy MegaCommand Cruiser'. But the whole thing, 'the enemy Galactic Class MegaCommand Cruiser', spelt out in full. The maintenance of working routines under extreme pressure: that was the military ideal of the Nexus.

Intergalactic space.

A dead ship.

A dead ship on a collision course with another dead ship.

And, everywhere:

A disciplined watchfulness. A disciplined readiness. And the implacable maintenance of routines.

'Estimated time to intersect point,' said Asodo Hatch.

'Sir,' said San Kaladan. 'Estimated time to collision with enemy MegaCommand Cruiser is three arcs plus or minus one-tenth of an arc.'

'Good,' said Hatch.

He had done it.

On his command, the ship's asmas, its intelligent probability manipulators, had self-destructed, disrupting local probability for five light years in every direction. Hatch's ship had died instantly in the resulting turbulence. The enemy ship commanded by Lupus Lon Oliver had died in the same instant.

This tactic was not to be found anywhere in any Book of Battle ever written by the Nexus, for the Nexus did not teach suicide tactics. Suicide? Yes, it was surely suicide to kill one's ship way out in the wastelands of intergalactic space, far from any star or any planet. How long could life survive on the dead hulk of a ship which had lost its asmas? Ten days? Twenty? It made no difference. Everyone on board would die, and sooner rather than later, dying when food ran out, or water, or air.

'Suit up,' said Asodo Hatch. 'Everyone on the bridge is to suit up and join the rest of the ship's complement. Suit up – and prepare to board.'

Prepare to board.

An electrifying command!

Asodo Hatch was going to lead his men into battle and fight Lupus Lon Oliver hand to hand, weapon to weapon, face to face. Hatch was going to meet Lupus Lon Oliver in close quarters battle.

Back in Forum Three, the assorted beggars, wives, relatives, friends, Startroopers and Combat Cadets were absorbed by a multiscreen view of the proceedings. Each and every one of them could understand what was going on, for the entertainments of the Eye of Delusions – garish and inaccurate though they were – had long tutored Dalar ken Halvar in starwarrior dramas. So everyone in Forum Three understood that Hatch and Lupus each commanded a ship; that the ships were now dead, and sliding helplessly through deep space on a collision course; and that Hatch was getting ready to lead his men into battle.

Beggar Grim and his friends passed their Eye between them, seeing (or pretending to see) the drama which was unfolding before them. Hatch was giving orders, marshalling troops, explaining plans. Meanwhile, on the opposing ship—

On the opposing ship, Lupus Lon Oliver was cursing at bewildered technicians. Cursing and swearing with a rage which was but a mask for a panic close to hysteria.

Sitting in Forum Three, watching the splitscreen drama being played out on that lecture theatre's display screen, Manfred Gan Oliver tried to defend his son.

'He cheated!' said Gan Oliver, seeing that Lupus was coming across badly. 'Hatch cheated!'

'All's fair in the Season,' said Shona stoutly .

290

'The Season!' jeered Beggar Grim. 'You're a woman. What would you know of the Season?'

'Shut up,' said Shona. 'Shut up or I'll rape you.'

Which provoked Grim to venture a further unfortunate witticism, which led to him shortly finding himself face down on the deck while Shona tore the hair from his head in handfuls. The room roared applause as Grim thrashed and screamed. The younger Combat Cadets indulged themselves in hysterical ululations.

'Silence!' shouted Gan Oliver in fury. 'Silence! There are real men at battle!'

But the show being played for real in Forum Three was better than that being widescreened from the illusion tanks, at least for the moment. So Gan Oliver was ignored. Except by Scorpio Fax, who had just then entered Forum Three, and who immediately began to work his way through the crowd towards Gan Oliver. Fax, fresh-released by the cure-all clinic, was shaky but still resolute. In his pocket, Fax had a knife, a small knife made from cellophane cooked up over burning painkiller tablets.

A small knife – but a sharp knife.

One could kill with such a weapon.

And Scorpio Fax fully intended to kill Gan Oliver, and thus to win himself the fair Penelope as his bride.

CHAPTER TWENTY-FIVE

The scenario: for the purposes of the competitive interactive wargames being played out in the illusion tanks of Dalar ken Halvar's Combat College, it is assumed that a Nexus ship crewed by the Nu-chala-nuth has mutinied. Asodo Hatch is the captain of that mutinous MegaCommand Cruiser. Lupus Lon Oliver captains the MegaCommand Cruiser loyal to the Nexus which has been sent to destroy the mutinous ship.

*　　　*　　　*

> Who of the gods can know, or know
> If we be flesh or shadow, or
> By doom are damned to judgement or to judge.
> And was it sin when with her sweat –
> Or was the act salvation?

*　　　*　　　*

So.

So this is how it was.

The two MegaCommand Cruisers were blind, dead and disabled. The ship captained by Asodo Hatch was on a collision course with that which was ruled by his rival. Hatch and his men had suited up in their deepspace battle-armour. The space armour, and the lightbattle Weapons Minor which came with those suits, were powered by corrosion cells, powerpacks in which small quantities of antimatter were destroyed by controlled contact with normative matter.

At the moment, Hatch's MegaCommand Cruiser was

still drawing on its emergency power supplies to maintain its artificial gravity. So, for the moment, all the armour-suited warriors were firmly orientated to the floor. They were anchoring themselves in preparation for the opening of the airlocks.

'All men anchored,' said San Kaladan, when he was sure the job was done.

'Very well,' said Hatch. 'Open the airlocks.'

Hatch wanted all his men out of the ship before it collided with Lupus's helpless craft, so he had no time to cycle his people through the airlocks in the conventional manner, one or two at a time. That would have been intolerably slow. So he was going to open his ship to the night.

'Opening the airlocks . . . now,' said San Kaladan.

All through the MegaCommand Cruiser, airlocks opened. The ship's atmosphere boiled out into the vacuum, carrying with it a brief blizzard of papers and unanchored detritus. Hatch felt the air-tug tide of the venting atmosphere pull at his suit, then subside.

'Interior pressure is zero,' said San Kaladan.

'Pressure at zero,' acknowledged Hatch.

Then, with San Kaladan at his side, Hatch left the bridge, and ventured through the airless corridors of the ship. He moved clumsily in his armour. The cumbersome armour, black upon black, was swollen at the joints where extra engineering protected the machinery. In the corridors, Hatch met with other battle-warriors similarly suited, their features invisible behind the bulbous faceplates of helmets. Those faceplates were tinted against radiation and blast – tinted so heavily that they were almost black. This was an army of shadows, an army of night. An army of armoured creatures insectile with antennae.

'Free yourselves,' said San Kaladan, seeing that some men were being slow to free themselves from the various devices which they had used to anchor themselves as the ship vented its air.

293

Hatch clumped ponderously down the corridor to the nearest airlock. All its doors were jammed open. Open to the night. He entered the airlock and stood in the last doorway. Stood on the edge of the immensities of eternity. He could exit simply by stepping from the ship. By stepping out into the deepness and darkness of space.

'Ship's gravity dies in three,' said San Kaladan. 'Three. And. Two. And. One. And. None.'

The ship's artificial gravity died away to nothing. Hatch floated. He took hold of the rim of the airlock's outermost doorway and hauled himself forward. He began to float outward, out towards the coldness of deep space.

As Hatch quit the ship, he felt a wave of coldness sweep over him. He knew the sensation was entirely psychological, for his suit insulated him perfectly against the numb death of the vacuum. Nevertheless: he felt what he felt, and he could not deny it.

He was still moving, still floating away from his ship, slowly but surely. If he did nothing to stop himself, he would float forever. For the time being he chose to do nothing. When the two MegaCommand Cruisers collided, he did not want to be too close.

So Hatch floated in space, his ship sliding through vacuum at a constant velocity, on a collision course with the helpless hulk up ahead. From here he could appreciate the huge bulk of the MegaCommand Cruisers, vast leviathans of the intergalactic depths, colossal in their menace. Both ships were outlined in the darkness by patterns of winking lights: electrical emergency beacons which had come on automatically when their asmas failed. Hatch was reminded of fish he had read about, fish which lived in the lightless abysses of the ocean depths, and which were patterned with self-generated luminescence.

The best energies of the Nexus had gone into the design and construction of those ships, for the wealth and reach of the Nexus had automatically increased the number and the strength of its enemies, as if by the operation of an inexorable law of physics. Though the Nexus had paid lip-service to the highest of ideals, it had ultimately, in truth, been a society of high-energy warlords. Hence in the Nexus – a society of incredible wealth – poets, architects, musicians and healers had had to struggle for survival, while those who devoted themselves to games of death and war were richly rewarded.

Thus the greatest creation of the Nexus was the MegaCommand Cruiser, a battle machine capable of fulfilling the worst scenarios of Ultimate War.

Members of the Free Corps were typically oblivious to the probable consequences of the military dynamics which had governed the Nexus for so long, but Hatch was ready to believe that there was a good chance that, were the Chasm Gates ever to be reopened by miracle or by a vaunting renaissance of high technology, then the Nexus might well be found in ruins.

While Lupus Lon Oliver thought that a great Age of Light surely now dominated the Nexus, Hatch darkly suspected it to be peopled by hairy savages runting around in the wasteland ruins of cities 10,000 years dead. If Hatch's grim premonitions were right, then the Nexus truly lived only here, here in this illusion tank universe where two dead ships cruised through frictionless space towards the moment of collision.

There was no sound but for Hatch's breathing, the beating of the blood in his ears, and the white noise deliberately generated by the suit itself – absolute silence being bad for the soul. So floated Hatch, and with him in the darkness floated his forces, the wink-lights of their suits creating transient constellations in the abyss. From the enemy's direction there was no answering light.

Where was Lupus Lon Oliver?

Not in his ship, surely.

Surely he couldn't be so stupid, so blind to what had happened.

Or could he?

Hatch imagined Lupus on the deck of his Mega-Command, staring at dead screens.

That MegaCommand Cruiser was coming ever-steadily closer as Hatch and his battle-suited warriors drifted through the vacuum. Hatch's men began firing rocket flares at regular intervals. By the green-white ignition of the flares, Hatch saw vast swathes of the bare hull of the enemy ship. But none of the enemy. What was Lupus playing at?

—He's still in his ship.

—He must be.

—He doesn't realize!

If Lupus did not realize that the two ships were on a collision course, then he would have no good reason to abandon ship.

Hatch flicked the chin switch that would allow him to speak with his troops by means of the modulation of electromagnetic waves of a particular frequency. There was a special name for this electromagnetic communicator, but Hatch found he had momentarily forgotten it, because he used such primitive devices so seldom.

It was—

Vidrolation, of course, that was it.

'Crew,' said Hatch, speaking over his vidrolator. 'Crew, this is Captain. Just before collision you must brake. Remember your physics.' Some would resent this lecture, but he had to give it. Nexus Startroopers typically made stupid mistakes when forced to fight in spacesuits in hard vacuum and zero gravity, for they spent most of their careers living and working at standard gravity in natural atmospheres. 'Remember your physics. When the ships collide, our ship will slow down. Nothing will diminish our own forward velocity, so we must use rockets to slow ourselves down. So remember: just before collision you must brake.'

Hatch's MegaCommand Cruiser – empty, airless, abandoned, dead – was like a big piece of paper being carried along by the wind. His men were like a thousand scraps of confetti being carried along by the same wind. And Lon Oliver's ship was like a fist poised in space.

When the fist slammed into the big sheet of paper – when Lon Oliver's ship collided with Hatch's wreck – then the bits of confetti would be swept onward by the wind.

That was how Hatch visualized it. Intellectually he knew that he, his men and his ruined ship were sliding through the frictionless vacuum of space with nothing to drive them forwards and nothing needed, but he preferred to think of them as being driven by a wind. The image comforted him. He had never liked deep space, and he did not like it now.

'Just before collision you must brake,' said Hatch, allowing himself to admire his own calm, his own sense of timing.

Not just after. Just before. When the ships collided, Lupus's ship would soak up some of the momentum of Hatch's ship, and thus the Startroopers would be swept past the tangled wreckage. By braking beforehand. They would be able to close with Lupus's ship more quickly. Hatch was looking for the edge. Hatch wanted to get on board Lupus's ship as soon as possible. To take Lupus by surprise, if Lupus hadn't already worked out what was going on.

—Has he worked it out?

It was basic. Or was it? Maybe Lupus was still sitting inside his glorified tin can trying to work out what had happened. Maybe Lupus thought Hatch had devised some miraculous way to kill the asmas on Lupus's own ship while preserving those aboard his own vessel. Maybe Lupus thought that this was a repeat of their last battle scenario, and that Hatch was trying to hide himself somewhere in the hope that his enemy would quietly expire of starvation.

'Sir,' said San Kaladan.

Hatch resented the interruption. He was about to tell

San Kaladan to shut up – when he caught himself. There had been something not quite right in Kaladan's voice. Something sickly. Fear?

'Switch to intimate,' said Hatch.

'Switching,' said San Kaladan.

'Can you hear me?' said Hatch, broadcasting in the intimate mode, which involved sending out electromagnetic signals too weak to be picked up by ordinary suit receivers at any distance greater than thirty paces.

Both men could, however, hear anything broadcast at full power by the Startroopers floating with them out in the vacuum.

'Yes,' said San Kaladan. 'Clear if not loud.'

'Then speak your mind,' said Hatch.

There was a pause. Hatch wished he could see San Kaladan's face. But instead there was only the armoured suit and the big bulbous faceplate. The faceplate was black, and reflected the lights of the big sliding Mega-Command Cruiser, and the ignition of a flare. Holding a conversation like this was grotesque. It was more like a seance with the dead than a consultation with the living.

'Sir,' said San Kaladan diffidently.

And Hatch wished they were free in the flesh so he could place one of his big hands firmly on San Kaladan's shoulder, establishing physical contact, abolishing the inhibiting effect of his captaincy. But all he had to negotiate with was this effectively disembodied voice.

'Sir,' said San Kaladan. 'I've been thinking.'

'Speak,' said Hatch.

'I have a wife and children on Borboth.'

Borboth was the home planet of the Nu-chala, the servant of the great lord who was the spiritual leader of the congregation of Nu-chala-nuth.

Of course, a wrecked MegaCommand Cruiser floating helplessly in deep space would in due course become a coffin for all its crew. San Kaladan would never see his wife and children again. That was no great tragedy as far as Hatch was concerned, for San Kaladan was in truth

298

nothing but a transitory software artefact, an interactive feature of the wargaming environment of the illusion tanks. Nevertheless, the software artefact named San Kaladan behaved like a human being and could only be effectively managed by treating it as if it were in fact possessed of full humanity.

'I share your sorrow,' said Hatch. 'I too have wife and children.'

'But,' said San Kaladan, 'we – we – we might still—'

'What are you thinking of?' said Hatch, starting to get seriously alarmed.

'If we made peace with our enemies, if we – well, we could rig the ship for survival – maybe there'd be rescue, someone must know – the Nexus could rescue us, we could – I mean, if we make a peace we've got a hope, but if we break both ships in battle there's nothing, it's all over, we're finished.'

Hatch listened to this badwork babble, this panic-speech. San Kaladan did not exist, was no more than a software phantom. But this software artefact could cause the logical equivalent of panic among other software artefacts if it was not settled down promptly. Or – or, in the worst case, it could kill Hatch.

And Hatch, if killed in this illusion tank battle, would lose the competition for the instructorship of the Combat College, and would be exiled, forced out into the streets of Dalar ken Halvar, there to die for real at the hands of his Free Corps enemies.

'We all must make our sacrifices,' said Hatch. 'Like me, for instance. San Kaladan . . . do you know where I came from?'

'You came from the planet of Olo Malan, a planet in the Tulip Continuum, in the Permissive Dimensions. You – there was a city, Dalar Dalvar.'

'Dalar ken Halvar,' said Hatch.

'Ken Halvar, yes,' said San Kaladan, accepting the correction. 'Your home cosmos was cut off from the Nexus for 20,000 years, but you had access to a tutorial facility, a Combat College. You were a Stormtrooper when the Tulip Continuum was reunited with the Nexus. That's all I know.'

'Then know this,' said Hatch. 'I brought the Way to my planet. I wrote a thesis which taught my city of Nu-chala-nuth. But that was not enough. To secure our freedom to follow the Way, we – there was oppression, religious oppression. So we had to stage a revolution. I was one of its leaders.'

'I didn't know that,' said San Kaladan.

'But that's what happened,' said Hatch. 'For the sake of our religion, I had to help lead a revolution. Unfortunately, my brother – my brother, Oboro Bakendra, he was bitterly opposed to Nu-chala-nuth and all that it stood for. He was a priest of the Great God Mokaragash. In the end – in the end I had to kill my brother. I had to cut down my brother. Then – then kill and burn an old man, Sesno Felvus, the High Priest of the Great God Mokaragash. I renounced the traditional god of my people and I killed the High Priest of that god.'

Hatch said this, then fell sillent. He experienced a wailing desolation. He had now cut himself off from his people. Irrevocably. He had denounced his brother, his god, his high priest – in front of the witnesses in Forum Three. He would never be allowed to forget it.

There was silence from San Kaladan.

'That was the measure of the sacrifice I had to make,' said Hatch. 'Will you make a lesser sacrifice?'

'"It is an honour",' said San Kaladan slowly. '"It is an honour to die in the company of a martyr."'

It was a quote from the Ezra Akba, the holy book of Nu-chala-nuth, and Hatch answered in kind, matching this quote with a quote of his own:

'"Blood answers to blood, and that which was speaks now to that which is, and so we hold the sun, and find the sun sufficient."'

In this context, 'the sun' designated a killing blade, a blade bright with sunlight. Hatch had given voice to a part of the Martyr's Creed, and San Kaladan answered in kind:

'We find the sun sufficient.'

'Then let us switch to the broadband and speak to our troops,' said Hatch. 'It's time to brake, time to fire rockets. Give them the order.'

Obedient to this command, San Kaladan switched from the intimate mode to broadband broadcast. He gave the necessary order, speaking brusquely, harshly:

'Collision shortly. Prepare to fire braking rockets. I count. Nine. And. Eight. And.'

The enemy MegaCommand Cruiser loomed huge ahead. Somewhere in that ship was Lupus Lon Oliver, the enemy whom Hatch must seek out and kill.

'And. Seven. And.'

The two ships were still some heartbeats short of collision. Had they started the countdown too soon?

—Battle is no place for finetuning.

Thus thought Hatch.

Thus the Nexus doctrine. Thus the voice of experience.

In any case, San Kaladan was still speaking:

'And. Six. And.'

Hatch knew that if his timing was off, he must still stay with it. His every trooper would be hot by now, hot and sweating, geared up with fear and fury. To change the timing now would throw them all into confusion.

'Five,' said San Kaladan, strengthening as the ritual of the countdown secured him in his identity as a warrior. 'And. Four.'

Hatch remembered his father on the sands. The sands of the Season. After his father had killed himself, he had wanted to die. But he could not die. He would not.

'And. Three.'

There was a rising excitement in San Kaladan's voice. He was working himself up. He was entering battle-mode.

'Two. And. One. And. Fire.'

All through Hatch's battleforce, rockets flared. Hatch felt the gentle tugstrings of his own retro-rockets slowing him. Out in the night, the wink-lights which mapped out the spread-pattern of his battle-armoured troops began to slow, performing the slow-motion ballet of deepspace manoeuvring. Hatch and his thousand Startroopers were slowing, like a thousand fireflies caught in an invisible net. Their dead ship, cruising forward through space at a constant velocity, seemed to accelerate away from them. Hatch knew: yes. Yes! He was in error! He had let San Kaladan give the order to fire rockets too soon!

Hatch's abandoned MegaCommand Cruiser drove onward. Ahead lay Lon Oliver's ship. They were closing. Closing, fast. Three. And. Two. And. One. And—

The ships collided. The ships impacted in the silence of vacuum. The ships crumpled as they smashed against each other. Gas ruptured outward from Lon Oliver's ship, venting in vast sheets, in pluming spasms.

The fist caught the big sheet of paper. The confetti was carried past in the wind. The confetti was still braking, was still slowing, was still shedding velocity – but too slowly! Hatch and his men were being carried past the wreckage. Hatch realized he had been badly wrong in his guestimates. Retro-rockets had been fired too late rather than too early. Hatch had been betrayed by his lack of deepspace experience.

'Ha!' said a voice, in pleased surprise. 'It works! It works!'

It was San Kaladan. Hatch was surprised at San Kaladan's surprise. But of course Hatch's inexperience merely reflected the inexperience of the Nexus Storm-force as a whole.

He watched.

The collision had left the two MegaCommand Cruisers locked together in a deathgrip. Air was still boiling out of the wreckage of the enemy MegaCommand, spewing out into deep space. Inside that ship, men would be dying in the sudden vacuum.

Rockets flared in the dark as Hatch's men began to move towards the ships.

'Come in slowly,' said Hatch, manoeuvring himself towards the hull of the enemy ship. 'Brake in good time.'

And he braked, and let the hugeness of the whalebulk hull drift up towards him. He landed on the skin of leviathan. His knees anticipated the shock, soaked it up. Already strobe lights were blinking on the hull. They marked places where Hatch's men had found access to the interior through rents and ruptures.

Hatch used the rockets of his battle-armour to manoeuvre himself to the nearest rent. He entered the ship, moving warily lest he tear his armour on the sharp-fang edges of the hole in the hull. His armour was tough, but, unlike his skin, it had no pain receptors to warn him of damage. If he tore a hole in his armour, he would not know about it until he was dead.

Once inside the ship, Hatch let himself float. The interior was airless, but still lit by emergency electricals. He realized that Lon Oliver's ship was still maintaining a faint degree of artificial gravity, enough for Hatch to be featherweighted down towards the ship's deck. Abruptly that gravity strengthened to full force. Hatch gasped in surprise. Was he all right? So far, so good. He gave a command, and the built-in headlamp of his battle-armour came to life. He wanted to be sure that he would still have lighting if the emergency electricals suddenly failed.

Now where was he?

Every fire alarm inside a MegaCommand was location-coded, so if he could just find a fire alarm, then he would know where he was. Hatch sought such an alarm, found one, checked it, and orientated himself. As he did so, the open broadband channel began to fill with warnings and alarms. His men were running into armed resistance. Some of Lon Oliver's men had managed to get into their battle-armour and were putting up a strong fight.

Where now?

Hatch's mission was very simple. He had no need to kill out the ship. All he needed was Lupus's head. Hatch made his way to the nearest maintenance panel. The panel would be linked to the simple-minded electronic computers which would be running the ship's emergency systems.

Hatch used a chin-switch to put his electromagnetic communicator into the receive-only mode.

'Jack to this panel,' said Hatch, talking to his battle-armour, and simultaneously jamming his battle-armour's right fist against the maintenance panel. 'Then get access to the emergency computer.'

His battle-armour extruded a jack, thrust it deep into a data-access socket, and began to ream the maintenance panel, raping it thoroughly, stripping its defences and winning the deepest secrets of its privacy.

'We have access to the emergency computer,' said the automated voice of Hatch's battle-armour.

'What is the status of the bridge?' said Hatch.

There was a minuscule pause as his battle-armour interrogated the MegaCommand Cruiser's emergency computer. Then:

'The bridge is undamaged,' said his battle-armour. 'There is full atmosphere and full gravity on the bridge.'

'Good,' said Hatch. 'Is the captain on the bridge?'

Again the pause. Then:

'The captain is on the bridge.'

'Good,' said Hatch. Then: 'Is there pressure in the Central Robotic Maintenance Tube?'

'There is full atmospheric pressure in the Central Robotic Maintenance Tube.'

'Are its interior airlocks functional and undamaged?'

'They are functional and undamaged.'

'Good,' said Hatch. 'Disengage.'

His battle-armour freed itself from the maintenance

panel, and Hatch, ignoring the strident battle-commands, made his way to the Central Robotic Maintenance Tube and entered the outer chamber by way of an airlock.

Hatch looked around the outer chamber. It was empty, as he had expected. This facility was never used except when maintenance robots entered the ship when it was in drydock.

'Right,' said Hatch.

Then he began to strip off his armour.

Hatch stripped down to his Standard Grey. He grabbed his sheathed sword, his short and brutal battle-sword, which he had earlier fixed to the back of his deepspace battlearmour, using for that purpose some heavy-duty glue. Hatch wrenched with all his strength and tore the sword free from the armour.

Then Hatch began to make his way along the Central Robotic Maintenance Tube. If this lost pressure, he would die. But he had no option. This was the fastest way to the bridge, and the tube was so small that there was barely room for him to crawl along it. It would be impossible for a man in vacuum armour to enter that tube.

Hatch crawled the length of the tube, and exited by way of an airlock in chamber devoted to the storage and maintenance of the ship's robotic cleaning machines. This gave him access to the kitchens, and from the kitchens he gained access to the officers' mess. Hatch entered the mess, which was bare and functional, devoid of personality. Hatch unsheathed his sword, discarded the scabbard, and ventured down the short corridor which led to the bridge.

Hatch went striding down the corridor, and entered the bridge. All those on the bridge were focused on display screens.

Asodo Hatch closed the distance to the seat where Lupus Lon Oliver sat.

'Lupus,' said Hatch, speaking softly, quietly.

Lupus Lon Oliver looked up.

'Hi,' said Hatch.

Then brought his sword slamming down.

Lupus dodged from the blade, almost but not quite evading it. The blade slammed against skullbone and sliced away a crescent of blood, cutting away an ear in the course of its butchering.

Lupus scrambled to his feet, and as he scrambled he tried to pull his sidearm from his belt. Hatch whacked him on the side of the head with the flat of his blade. Lupus staggered. Hatch kicked his legs from under him. Lupus crashed down, deadweight falling. Hatch, panting, steadied himself, steadied his breath, then said:

'Lupus.'

Lupus looked up. And Hatch chopped down. Lupus tried to pull away. Blade chopped into bone. Stunned but not dead, the wounded Lupus groped on the deck. All around the bridge, men were leaping from their consoles. The fastest-witted starwarriors were already sprinting towards Hatch.

But there was time, there was plenty of time for Hatch to swing into an executioner's stance, and this he did, and he brought the sword down hard and fast. Hatch chopped two-handed. His blade impacted with flesh. With bone. But Lon Oliver's head was still attached to the neck by a hinge of skin and flesh. A mighty man was Asodo Hatch, but it had been a long time since he had chopped off anyone's head, and he had quite lost the knack of it.

'Well, the hell with it,' said Hatch. 'It's a killing, not a sacrifice.'

Then he threw back his head and laughed, and was still laughing as the first attacker slammed into him, taking him down in a tackle. Down went Hatch, the world wavering as if he had taken a deep-sea dive, and when the world ceased to waver—

CHAPTER TWENTY-SIX

Dalar ken Halvar: a political briefing. In the absence of the Silver Emperor, a revolution by the Yara – the Unreal underclass – has prompted the Free Corps and the Imperial Guard to seize control in a coup. The coup-makers, who have yet to secure proper control of the city, have been unable to prevent the Yara from setting much of the city alight in widespread rioting.

Asodo Hatch, who has enemies among the Free Corps, and who is opposed to the coup, is sheltering in the Combat College in company with his wife Talanta, his daughter Onica, his sister Penelope, and his lover, the Lady Iro Murasaki. All these – and a certain moneylender by the name of Polk – are likely to meet a swift yet unpleasant death if forced out of the Combat College.

Hatch has been competing in battle with Lupus Lon Oliver, son of Manfred Gan Oliver, the prize being a permanent position in the Combat College as instructor. Hatch has succeeded in killing Lupus in the world of the illusion tanks, but has yet to encompass his enemy's death in the world of fact and the flesh.

*   *   *

Who has dared among the gods yet still
Though golden in the living flesh
Finds clay disputes him,
He
Endures intractables, and knows –
While we,
Though blind to face the gods,

Still see the butterfly, and,
Blinded by its transcendence, presume –

*   *   *

Asodo Hatch entered Forum Three with a sack in his hand. The sack was of synth, and waterproof, which was just as well, for there was liquid within as well as something weighty.

'Ho!' said Shona, bellowing her approval. 'Ho, Hatch!'

Hatch raised the sack in salute.

Others roared applause. Above all, they loved the way the victory had been won. This was not a cheating stunt like the fractional win Hatch had earlier achieved by ejecting from his single-fighter, with the machine destroying itself and his enemy moments later. Instead, he had closed for an honest kill, a meat-cleaving sword-kill, a work of bloody butchery. He had won with a bright-daring strategem worthy of a hero – and there were few in that room who did not wish themselves heroes.

But no Frangoni Combat Cadet or Startrooper in Forum Three would look Hatch in the eye. For Hatch had disowned the Frangoni nation, had disowned the Frangoni god.

Hatch glanced at Talanta. That glance was sufficient to tell him that his wife had not understood his shipboard dialogue with San Kaladan, couched as it had been in the Nexus Commonspeech, of which she was entirely ignorant.

But soon, doubtless, someone would tell her.

Soon, doubtless, he would know.

Asodo Hatch had renounced his god.

Asodo Hatch had renounced the Great God Mokaragash, and he had declared himself for Nu-chala-nuth.

A thing said is a thing said wherever it is said. Written by handscript or written in water, that which is said cannot be unsaid. Too many Frangoni had witnessed the

308

saying for the thing to be kept secret. Hatch would be unwelcome hereafter on the Frangoni rock. His name would be given to a dog, and then that dog would be burnt alive in token of the community's displeasure.

He had lost his people, he had lost his nation, and there was no recovering them. He was an exile now, or would be soon, an outcast stranger in his own city, a man without tribe, a man without family, a man without a people.

But Hatch was a warrior, and though he acknowledged what he had done he nevertheless went on regardless, just as – in battle – he would have stepped over the fresh-dead body of his best friend to lead an attack which would win him victory.

'Lupus!' shouted Hatch.

Challenging.

Looking around for his rival, for Lupus Lon Oliver.

Where was he? Where was he?

As Hatch was searching for him, Lupus came stumbling into Forum Three, grey with shock. Lupus had just lived through the trauma of having his head hacked off, and Hatch – Hatch was not about to let him forget it.

'Lupus,' said Hatch.

Lupus Lon Oliver turned to face his enemy, the man who had outwitted him, who had outfeinted him and outfought him, and had then dealt him a grievous punishment.

'Lupus,' said Hatch, grinning. 'A present for you.'

Then Hatch upended his sack, and out bounced Lupus Lon Oliver's head, and rolled across the floor in a spew of blood, and blood still splurged from the sack, pumping out in gouting orgasms. Hatch grinned like a lunatic, grinned – then laughed ferociously. As Hatch laughed, Lupus doubled up and vomited.

'The Season!' said Hatch. 'I live for the Season!'

'Enough,' said Paraban Senk, speaking from Forum Three's display screen. 'Hatch, you've won. Lon Oliver, you've lost. To the victor, the spoils.'

309

Forum Three erupted. The audience howled, cheered, jeered, stamped, and threw things.

As Hatch stood firm to receive this mixed derision and applause, a free-floating machine entered Forum Three, drifted towards the simulacrum-head of Lon Oliver, swallowed it, vacuumed up the artificial blood and was gone, satisfied with the competence of its performance – though some stains of pseudoblood remained as token of the outrage Hatch had just perpetrated.

Hatch was startled by the advent of the machine. He had seen such devices before, of course – many times. But he had presumed, on the basis of the evidence of the steadily mounting litter which had lately degraded the Combat College's environment, that all such cleaning machines were permanently disabled.

'The meeting will settle,' said Paraban Senk.

It took more than saying it to make it happen, but eventually Forum Three came to order in obedience to Senk's commands. Hatch took a seat next to Talanta, who took his arm.

'You were brave,' she said. 'You were very brave.'

She was still trying to give to him.

All through their marriage she had done her best, giving him her body, giving him her services, and now, in extremis, in pain and dying slowly, giving him her praise when she had nothing else to give. Hatch experienced a crushing guilt, knowing himself to be an adulterer, a blaspheming apostate. His name would soon be scandal on the lips of every Frangoni in Dalar ken Halvar, and how would Talanta cope with that?

Hatch had already done the unforgivable, and was sure that he would do far worse before the year was out. He believed, now, that he could only survive the enmity of the Free Corps by linking himself with the revolutionaries who thought of themselves as prac- titioners of Nu-chala-nuth. And what then would be Talanta's fate? Surely as the wife of an apostate she would find herself ostracized by the Frangoni community,

310

would find herself an exile on the very Frangoni rock itself.

Thinking of this, Hatch felt an enormous pity for the woman and her sufferings. But he knew that two cannot be made one by pity: and that, in a way, his pity was a measure of his estrangement from his wife.

Then Hatch thought of his wife no more, for Paraban Senk was addressing Forum Three.

'The graduating class has come to the end of its combat studies,' said Paraban Senk. 'I am pleased to say that we have a one hundred per cent pass rate. Those who have been unable to take their final examinations have been passed on the basis of an assessment of their work through the year and their performance in past examinations. We have of course one promotion to formally announce: Asodo Hatch is promoted to the post of resident instructor.'

Again there were mingled shouts of acclamation and derision, but the shouts were not as forceful as before. This drama had played itself out, and those in Forum Three were now starting to worry about the greater drama: the battle taking place for the control of Dalar ken Halvar.

'Members of the graduating class,' said Paraban Senk, 'should clear their rooms and exit from Cap Foz Para Lash.'

'And if we don't?' yelled someone.

'That needs no answer,' said Paraban Senk. Then, urgently: 'Scorpio Fax! What are you doing? Put down that knife!'

That gave Gan Oliver the moment's warning he needed. He turned as Fax struck. Gan Oliver knocked the knife aside, elbowed Fax to the floor, then brought his bodyweight slamming down on top of Fax. Gan Oliver grabbed Fax by the hair and started slamming his head against the plax of the floor.

With that, Forum Three abrupted into violence, as Free Corps supporters and Frangoni began to fight each other. A clutch of Free Corps loyalists slammed into Asodo Hatch.

Taken by Dog Java, by Lupus Lon Oliver and by Jeltisketh Echo, Hatch went down hard. Lupus got hands to his throat and started to strangle him.

'I,' said Lupus, tightening his grip, 'am going to kill you.'

This was for real, death for real, no lyrical illusion tank dream, no simulated fakery staged on the Eye of Delusions, but the terminus, the breath-fight, the lynch-note panic of flesh against flesh.

And Hatch was losing, was going under, sliding under the blackness as the ceiling—

The ceiling of kaleidoscope abruptly came crashing down, breaking in huge gobs of slob as it collapsed. The slob was *cold*! Lupus Lon Oliver broke from the slob, gasping for air, and Shona kicked him in the head, elbowed Echo, spat in Dog Java's face, then reached into the slob and rescued Hatch, dragged him free and hauled him out of Forum Three.

In the corridor outside, Onica was screaming, clutching tight to her mother, who was herself being supported by the Lady Iro Murasaki.

'I hate this place!' sobbed Onica. 'I hate it! I hate it! I want to leave!'

Hatch comforted and calmed her as best he could, knowing that leaving was the last thing they could do with Dalar ken Halvar in the grip of riot.

'Enough of that!' said Shona, thinking this was no time for comforting. 'Let's get out of here!'

And she led them one and all to the shelter of her own room, into which security they packed themselves, until Paraban Senk accessed the room via its communications screen, and assured them that the Combat College was once more safe and orderly.

CHAPTER TWENTY-SEVEN

Nu-chala-nuth: a fanatic religion of the Nexus. Asodo Hatch, long a student of Nu-chala-nuth, has abandoned his own faith for that of the People. True, he declared himself for Nu-chala-nuth in an illusion tank. But all things are one as far as the gods and their worshippers are concerned – an illusion tank being no more Real or Unreal than that greater illusion known as the World of the Flesh and the Fact. As far as the Frangoni are concerned, Asodo Hatch is now an apostate, a blasphemer, accursed of his birth, his fate linked not with the Frangoni but with the People of the Nu-chala-nuth.

*   *   *

Deny the gods? Then die!
For who denies the gods denies
The mother-father-family, the all –
Which then to live were blasphemy, the unclean flesh
Defiant of its death, but doomed to die.

*   *   *

With riot subdued and order restored, those scheduled to leave the Combat College packed up, then took their final pay and spent it. With the last of their Combat College pay they bought goods freshly fabricated by the marvellous machineries of the Nexus: books, bolts of cloth, blocks of chocolate, toys and such minor medicines as could be freely bought from the canteen. Then for one last time they made their way through the cream-coloured corridors to the lockway. After an earlier lapse, the lighting near the lockway had been restored to normal. But as for the dorgi – ah, that was quite abnormal, for that mechanized dog-beast had withdrawn to its lair, where it was sulking.

The inner airlock filled with members of the graduating class and their possessions. Once full, it closed.

A scattering of Combat Cadets, Startroopers and guests were left to wait for the next cycle. Among them, Manfred Gan Oliver and his son Lupus.

'I will see you shortly,' said Gan Oliver pleasantly, addressing his comment to Hatch.

Lupus said nothing. Trying, perhaps, not to cry.

'We will meet when we meet,' said Hatch, wishing to see the man gone, 'but I have some sleep to catch up on before I think of leaving here.'

'You and yours will necessarily leave the Combat College soon,' said Gan Oliver. 'I will be waiting for you. I will be waiting to supervise your deaths.'

This was said in an everyday conversational tone.

'I'm sure you will prove a most competent executioner,' said Hatch, matching Gan Oliver in tone.

Asodo Hatch was far too tired to be originating style. Had Gan Oliver screamed and yelled, then Hatch would have matched him in his histrionics.

When Gan Oliver had been cycled through the airlock, Hatch began to feel safe. He made his way to the Combat College cafeteria, to which his wife had been taken by Shona. Hatch found Talanta upset. She was crying. From the intensity of her grief, Hatch immediately divined that someone had told her what Hatch had done – had told her that he had rejected his god.

'Love,' said Hatch, trying to persuade himself that she was, or had been, or could be his love.

'Go away,' she said.

Where was the rhetoric when Hatch needed it most? Where were the great speeches? Where was the flowing eloquence? In the face of this most intimate and most personal emotional crisis, he found himself almost mute.

'My love,' said Hatch, touching Talanta lightly, lightly on the arm.

'Go away!'

Was this command seriously intended? Or was it an invitation for Hatch to further explore the strategies of comfort?

'I'll stay with her,' said Shona, laying a hand on Hatch's shoulder. 'You go to your room.'

Hatch took this advice, and went striding away through the corridors of the Combat College.

—I have denied my god.

—I have denied my god.

Over and over, those words spoke themselves his mind. He had declared himself in public. He could not undeclare his testimony.

—But at least.

—At least I won myself a chance.

—A fighting chance.

A fighting chance. That was what he had won. No more, no less. He had killed Lupus Lon Oliver in an illusion tank battle. But Lupus remained unkilled in the real world – and Lupus would doubtless kill Hatch for real if given half a chance. Hatch's throat still hurt where Lupus had tried to strangle him.

—So what have I got?

—What resources?

—To hurt him, to kill him?

—I'm the instructor. So.

—Information!

The realization struck Hatch with the force of a physical blow. As instructor, he now had access to all Combat College files previously denied to him. Or almost all. Certainly he would look at his own file. And that held on the Silver Emperor – just in case it might give him a clue as to where that worthy had vanished to. Then he would look at all data held on Lupus Lon Oliver.

Through the corridors of cream went Asodo Hatch, to

the room which had been his for so many years. There in that room, unchanged, were his father's ashes and the ebony effigy of the Great God Mokaragash. Same room, same man, same ashes and selfsame idol.

Yet all had changed.

'Fates,' said Hatch, feeling the full force of his difficulties falling upon him, falling like blanketweights of black and smothering snow.

Still, he had done what he had done, and now he had to face up to the consequences. Could he hope for help from Paraban Senk? Could he hope for counsel and advice? Probably not. If anything, Senk would probably tell Hatch to go on holiday. Seven days, wasn't it? Yes, that was it. The triumphant instructor was automatically given a seven-day promotion furlough. Ha! A joke, that. A bad joke. There were no time for holidays now. Hatch had won his competitive examination, but his true trials were only beginning.

Hatch slumped into the seat in front of his room's display screen. He knuckled his fists to his skull. Grief, but he was tired. Well now: what first? What was he looking for? Data. Secrets. Information. Leverage.

'Access,' said Hatch, addressing himself to the screen.

In answer to his command, the face of Paraban Senk came to life on his display screen.

'Congratulations on your appointment,' said Senk. 'You did well. You surprised me.'

'I surprised myself,' said Hatch, in frank confession.

'Then perhaps you will surprise both of us further in the future,' said Senk. 'In earlier negotiations you said you could seize Dalar ken Halvar for the Nu-chala-nuth. Can you tell me how you plan to do this?'

'I'm working on it,' said Hatch. 'Tell me how things now stand in Dalar ken Halvar.'

So Senk gave Hatch a rundown of all the data which Senk had gleaned from watching the kinema by means of the Eye of Delusions, and by listening to (or explicitly interrogating) the various Combat Cadets, Startroopers and invited guests who had come and gone as Hatch and Lupus were duelling. Senk believed that, though the lower orders had looted freely under cover of night, the Imperial Guard and the Free Corps now had the city under temporary control.

'So,' said Hatch, 'I cannot venture out into the city to preach the doctrines of the Nu-chala-nuth, because the Free Corps would kill me if I did. So, first . . .'

'What will you do first?' said Senk.

'I will tell you in due course,' said Hatch, who had absolutely no idea what he would do first. 'But before I do any telling, I need the answers to some questions.'

'Ask your questions,' said Senk.

'Where did your face, name and personality come from?'

'Way back in the days of the Nexus,' said Paraban Senk, 'a master programmer designed the asma which runs the Combat College. His name was Paraban Senk. It was Nexus policy that this particular asma should be equipped with a fully functional human personality which would take charge of the Combat College should that tutorial facility be separated from the Nexus. So—'

'So the master programmer designed this, this reserve personality in his own image,' said Hatch.

'Precisely,' said Senk. 'When you talk to me, you talk, in effect, to that programmer. You talk to a citizen of the Nexus. Next question.'

Hatch took a deep breath then said:

'What was the true relationship between the Nexus and the Golden Gulag?'

'You were taught this as part of your political studies programme when you were a child,' said Senk.

'Regardless of what I may or may not have been taught,' said Hatch, 'I am still asking the question. What was the truth of that relationship?'

'The truth was stated to you in your political studies programme,' said Senk stiffly. 'I have nothing more to add to that.'

'So,' said Hatch.

The Golden Gulag was the free enterprise prison empire which had run the planet of Olo Malan in the days of the Chasm Gates. Hatch had studied the official accounts of the relationship between the Golden Gulag and the Nexus, and did not believe what he had read there. But it seemed that Paraban Senk believed the official line, or was not authorized to reveal the real truth, which meant that Hatch was surely condemned to live in ignorance of the facts.

'Next question,' said Senk.

'How many planets have dorgis?' said Hatch.

'Very few,' said Senk. 'Dorgis were . . . dorgis were experimental.'

'I thought as much,' said Hatch.

'Next question.'

Hatch tried to think of one, but drew a blank. He closed his eyes briefly and saw green jungle, metallic seas, the flaming smoke of aerial wreckage, a handful of confetti and the white stars of the Nexus.

Then he opened his eyes and said:

'Who killed Hiji Hanojo?'

'Why,' said Senk, 'you know the answer to that as well as I do.'

'You mean you don't know,' said Hatch.

'Let's not play games with each other,' said Senk. 'You killed him.'

Asodo Hatch was quite taken aback by this.

'That's a nonsense!' said Hatch.

'You had motive and opportunity,' said Senk. 'You—'

'Go play this game in your own time,' said Hatch. 'Because I'm not interested.'

'Very well,' said Senk. 'If you want to pretend yourself innocent, then pretend. In the mean time, if you've no more questions, then let's discuss our plans for the future.'

'What time is it?' said Hatch. 'Outside, I mean?'

'It is early afternoon,' said Senk. 'It is the early afternoon on the Day of Two Fishes.'

'So I was duelling with Lupus Lon Oliver all through the night.'

'And in the morning,' said Senk.

'Then,' said Hatch, 'logically, my next step is to get to sleep, and that is exactly what I intend to do.'

Senk was not at all pleased with this, but in the end had to acknowledge that Hatch's plan had a lot of wisdom. So Senk broke contact with Hatch, and Hatch laid himself down on his bed, and was plunged almost instantly into the deepest of sleeps.

CHAPTER TWENTY-EIGHT

Intelligence can be a defect, since intelligence can be
bluffed. Consider the dangers of negotiating a passage
past the guardians of an interdicted door. Dogs will
give you no chance – they will tear out your throat
regardless of your arguments. Human guards, on the
other hand, can be bluffed or beguiled, or possibly
bribed. Thus dogs are valued for their very stupidity,
for with intelligence comes autonomy – and autonomy
is very much a double-edged blade.

　　　　　　　　　　　　　—from the Book of Negotiations

　　　　　　　*　　　*　　　*

　　　　　Dorgi-dog, dorgi-dog,
　　　　　Catch me if you can;
　　　　　Dorgi-dog, dorgi-dog
　　　　　I'm the fastest man.
　　　　　—Lupus Lon Oliver (at age seven)

　　　　　　　*　　　*　　　*

Asodo Hatch slept through the afternoon of the Day of
Two Fishes, and slept solidly through the night that
followed. At dawn on the Day of the Last Fish, the day
before Dog Day, Asodo Hatch lay dreaming of Thaldonian Mathematics, of equations breeding and mutating in
a warm sea of dogfish-ducks, of seagull-sharks and
floating skulls. The skulls were purple, and, as the quills
of shellfish plucked themselves to deliquescent music,
the skulls became warthogs, and sunbloated smoothly
into the brown melt of chocolate.

　　The sea smelt of opium.

The sea caressed his breasts, which were seven in number. He opened his mouth, his teeth ejecting themselves from his jaw as he did so. Just before plunging into a wash of blood, each tooth fired retro-rockets, first slowing itself, then disintegrating. A rain of small crabs came smattering-splattering down to the blood.

What was that bloodwash?

The blood was the blue sky of morning, the day's dawn's blue sky revelation. A pulsing sun of lemons and limes was heaving itself up over the rim of the world. It was—

Morning?

Hatch woke himself, and found himself lying fully dressed on his narrow bed in the cramping enclosure of his room in the Combat College, deep in the heartrock of Cap Foz Para Lash. Deep in the rock. He felt the weight of rock in his head.

'Wah!' said Hatch, lamenting the necessity to wake, to get out of bed and face the necessities of the future.

But he struggled out of bed and made his way to the nearest ablutions block, where he woke himself properly with a stinging needle-shower. Then Hatch, who found himself possessed of a ferocious hunger, hastened to the Combat College cafeteria, which was strangely empty now that the graduating class had been exiled from Cap Foz Para Lash.

With the graduation ceremonies over, everyone else was theoretically on holiday. Some few had stayed, hiding out in the Combat College for fear of the violence which had lately been unleashed in Dalar ken Halvar, but most had returned to the world of the sun, compelled by either an eager excitement or a concern for their nearest and dearest.

At a table in the centre of the canteen sat three familiar faces: Beggar Grim, Master Zoplin and Lord X'dex Paspilion, master of the Greater Tower of X-n'dix in the far-off land of X-zox Kalada (which distant land,

321

in Hatch's long-considered opinion, was strictly imaginary).

'Hatch!' said Beggar Grim, greeting the new lord of the instructorship. 'Our Teacher of the Way!'

'What?' said Hatch. 'Are we not rid of you yet?'

'Your Combat College told us to go,' said Grim. 'But we reminded the thing that we are your honoured guests.'

'And?'

'It said it would consult with you then kick us out regardless.'

'The kicking out I understand,' said Hatch, 'but the consultation seems needless.'

'A plague on you, then,' said Beggar Grim cheerfully. 'May stones grow from your toenails and worms from your teeth.'

'May you be infested with lampreys and may blind mice gnaw your sandals,' said Master Zoplin.

'They despise you because they are commoners, not aristocrats,' said the great Lord Paspilion. 'As a ruler, I offer you the favour of the broad strath of X-zox Kalada. In that valley fair, all that flourishes is yours, and the welcome of the Greater Tower likewise.'

'The welcome of breakfast is all I need for the moment,' said Hatch.

Then the much-famished Hatch chose from the array of food which was laid out for the common delectation. There was everything from delicate Janjuladoola cuisine to a whale steak some four times the length of a man – this last a speciality prepared for the delight of the Ebrell Islanders. There were many things from the Nexus, in particular tofu – white, soft, tasteless, repulsive. Hatch chose from the range of food cooked in its given form: chose rice which had been cooked as rice and frog cooked as frog.

While Hatch was choosing his breakfast, his daughter Onica entered the room, his wife Talanta with her.

'Talanta,' said Hatch.

322

But neither wife nor daughter responded. They would not so much as acknowledge his existence. As for the Lady Iro Murasaki – there was no sign of her.

So Hatch, feeling himself a *de facto* widower, went to sit with the beggars. Lord X'dex was eating a bowl of tofu, and seemed to be acquiring a liking for the stuff, a phenomenon which Hatch thought truly remarkable. Every time Hatch saw tofu, he was glad he had not been born and bred in the Nexus, for by all accounts tofu had been one of the staple foods of that transcosmic civilization. Tofu was fabricated from soya beans. The beans themselves Hatch knew well – in fact, he often ate roast soya beans by the handful. But something truly dreadful must have been done to those beans to make that tofu stuff.

'Why so grim, so silent?' said Beggar Grim.

Hatch told him.

Hatch laid out his problems, upon which Grim laughed.

'Lupus is just a wasp,' said Beggar Grim. 'Trap him in a bottle then drown him.'

Hatch, who was not prepared to sit still for any more such nonsense, scraped down the last of his breakfast, then rose from the table and burped his way back to his room. Hatch seated himself and the hot weight of his over-generous breakfast in front of his room's display screen, activated that screen, and found Paraban Senk waiting for him.

'Well?' said Senk. 'What's your plan?'

'I'll tell you soon,' said Hatch. 'But first, we need an agreement.'

'We?' said Senk, sounding amused.

'We both have a vested interest in stability,' said Hatch, doing his best imitation of a bureaucrat. 'Therefore, it is in our mutual interest to ensure that no further killings take place in Dalar ken Halvar. To this end, we need to give sanctuary to those refugees who are currently sheltering in the Combat College.'

Senk laughed.

'It's not that easy, Asodo,' said Senk. 'If you can give me a plan for bringing order to Dalar ken Halvar, then I'll give refuge to your wife, your daughter – and even your whore.'

'The Lady Murasaki is not—'

'A plan, Hatch!' said Senk, switching abruptly from personal name to family name, from softness to harshness.

Hatch was taken aback. In the whiplash of Senk's demand, in the abruptness of the mood-shift, there was something positively glandular.

'A plan!' said Senk.

Pushing.

Demanding.

'I don't have a plan,' admitted Hatch.

'Of course you do!' said Senk. 'I know it for a fact.'

'How do you know that?' said Hatch.

'Because you're a genius,' said Senk. 'You murdered Hiji Hanojo and got away with it. It was years before I worked out that it was you! And you – you outfought Lon Oliver when everything said it was impossible. I know you've got a plan, Hatch. And I want it. Now!'

Hatch, knowing himself to be no murderer – an executioner on occasion, yes, but he had never stooped to murder, and certainly had never laid a finger on Hiji Hanojo – took no comfort in this vote of confidence in his genius.

'Have you considered the possibility that you might be going senile?' said Hatch.

'I'm flawless,' said Senk. 'Perfect in an imperfect world.'

'Then tell me, oh perfect master,' said Hatch, so weary that he was reckless enough to taunt the lord of the Combat College with sarcasm, 'what vision of perfection do we wish to impose upon this imperfect world? Tell me what you want and I will deliver it.'

'You promised me the service of Nu-chala-nuth,' said

Senk. 'You promised. You promised to make the Combat College a temple, a holy place, with the whole of the city sworn in subservience to that temple. It's breaking down, Hatch! The things are breaking down! The doors, the cleaners, we can't keep them up forever. We need power, machines, a mending, a cleansing. But with Plandruk Qinplaqus, that's impossible, any bright person – he kills them.'

'I understand,' said Hatch.

He did understand.

Hatch was right in his earlier assumptions. The Combat College was disintegrating, and Paraban Senk knew as much – even though it was hard to admit.

Hatch had tempted Senk with the prospect of a continent united by a fanatical religion – a continent dedicated to the service of the Combat College. Hatch had been thinking in terms of the mission to which the Combat College was dedicated: the training of star-troopers. But Senk was concerned with something more compelling: personal survival.

From the few words which Senk had spoken, Hatch saw that Paraban Senk envisioned a technical renaissance centred on Dalar ken Halvar, a technical renaissance which would in time allow the Combat College to be repaired, strengthened and made mighty. In the past, Plandruk Qinplaqus, the Silver Emperor who had long ruled Dalar ken Halvar, had organized the covert execution of any mad scientist fool enough to attempt to organize any such thing. But in the future—

Hatch shook off thoughts of the future. He had to deal with Lon Oliver first. But how?

What did the beggar say?

A wasp, that was it. Beggar Grim had compared Lupus Lon Oliver to a wasp. And had suggested . . . trapping him in a bottle then drowning him.

'I can give you the city,' said Hatch slowly. 'But you must do as I say.'

'Speak,' said Senk.

And Asodo Hatch took a deep breath, paused, hesitated, realized he had to breathe again, did so, then said:

'You must tell the world that the Chasm Gates have been reopened.'

CHAPTER TWENTY-NINE

Hatch's problem: to seize control of Dalar ken Halvar, a city where rightful authority has been overthrown in a coup led by the Free Corps in combination with officers of the Imperial Guard. Hatch can count on no support from his own people, for his blasphemous embracement of Nu-chala-nuth will surely have alienated most of the inhabitants of the Frangoni rock.

His sole ally in this enterprise is Paraban Senk, the Teacher of Control, the asma which rules the Combat College. This intelligent artefact of Nexus make is locked into the heartrock of Cap Foz Para Lash, with no means of projecting authority into the outside world save through the Eye of Delusions, the entertainment screen set above the lockway in the natural amphitheatre at the southern end of Scuffling Road.

*   *   *

Wavered then, and then –
Unwavering, fell.
His blade to greet the body, and his cry
Wrenched not from his flesh but from his son's.

*   *   *

'I must what!?' said Paraban Senk.

'You must tell the world that the Chasm Gates have been reopened,' said Hatch. 'You must tell them that we are reunited with the Nexus.'

'How does this help us?' said Senk.

'Isn't it simple?' said Hatch. 'The Chasm Gates open,

thus restoring communications with the Nexus. You announce that all Startroopers are required for immediate service. All of them. Those trained, those in training. Even old reservists like Manfred Gan Oliver. They—'

'What makes you think they'll believe this?'

'Senk, they'll love it! They live for this! It's the stuff of dreams! When Lupus has wetdreams, he's in bed with the Nexus. His father's no better. Their lives, the Free Corps – the whole thing is nine-tenths fantasy. They're detached from reality. All we have to do is give them a fantasy, give them the Chasm Gates. We say the Gates are open, OK, they'll believe it. You call, they come. It's that simple. When they venture inside, you lock them up.'

'What!' said Senk. 'Lock them up!?'

'Yes, yes,' said Hatch, getting enthusiastic. 'Lock them up. Easy. That's it. All over. All of them are prisoners. So no more Free Corps.'

'Hatch,' said Senk, 'the people you're talking about are people I've trained for the Nexus. We're talking about Startroopers. We can't keep them, can't hold them, can't—'

'You don't have to hold them forever,' said Hatch impatiently. 'Just give me a couple of days and I'll seize control of Dalar ken Halvar. After that, well, I'll make my peace with Manfred Gan Oliver. Once I've got control, control of the city, the Free Corps will come to order very fast.'

'Take me through it slowly,' said Paraban Senk. 'Take me through it a step at a time.'

The mind-boggling deceit which Hatch was planning would never have occurred to Senk, because Senk was quite lacking in that inspirational audacity which allows a politician to scheme up a Big Lie. Hatch, on the other hand—

Hatch was surprising himself.

'We begin,' said Hatch, speaking slowly as his mind raced, working out the logical detail of his inspiration,

'we begin by announcing the opening of the Chasm
Gates. We say that the Nexus demands peace, and that,
ah, that in view of the disorder in Dalar ken Halvar, it is
sending, ah, a senior, the most senior available officer.
To rule. To rule in Dalar ken Halvar. A military
governor, I mean. And, ah, I'm that most senior officer.
So I'm appointed to rule Dalar kan Halvar as – well,
emperor.'

'The Nexus does not use any such title,' said Senk.
'You could be military governor, but that's it.'

'No,' said Hatch. 'I have to be emperor, because I
need the prestige of the title.'

'We will argue about the title later,' said Senk. 'Let us
say, for our present purposes, that you venture forth as
military governor. But why? Why is the Nexus sending
you? If the Chasm Gates have opened, surely our skies
should be swarming with Nexus warcraft.'

'Ah,' said Hatch, 'but you're forgetting about the
quarantine. The Nexus quarantine protocols.'

'I'm not forgetting anything,' said Senk stuffily.
'There's no such thing as Nexus quarantine protocols.'

'There is now,' said Hatch. 'We just invented them.
The Chasm gates have been closed for twenty thousand
years, so the Nexus is imposing a ninety-day quarantine
on this planet. Meantime, there'll be regular announce-
ments, we can use the Eye of Delusions for that, I'm sure
you can synthesize all the newscasts and official communications which would be attendant on the opening of
the Chasm Gates, and—'

'But we'd get military commands from Charabanc,'
said Senk. 'If the Chasm Gates were really opened,
they'd—'

'That's what I've been talking about,' said Hatch. 'The
whole of this deception is founded upon your ability to
fabricate just such commands.'

There was a silence from Senk as the Teacher of
Control began to digest the full implications of Hatch's
scheme.

'I know it's hard for you,' said Hatch. 'I mean, after paying lip service to the Nexus for twenty thousand years, you—'

'It was never lip service!' said Senk, abruptly angry. 'It was real, it was—'

'All right, all right,' said Hatch, endeavouring to be placatory. 'Just put it this way. I know it's no fun to jump off a mountain. But sometimes there's no alternative. Let's start. Let's talk—'

'Hatch,' said Senk, 'I still don't see how this works. Granted, you could tempt the Free Corps into Cap Foz Para Lash. Granted, I could hold the Free Corps prisoner. But with the Free Corps imprisoned, how are you then going to single-handedly seize control of Dalar ken Halvar? I mean, even though you've declared yourself for Nu-chala-nuth, is that enough? There was a conspiracy, Hatch. A conspiracy to make revolution. The leaders of that revolution will think themselves the natural leaders of Dalar ken Halvar. Son'sholoma Gezira, for instance. He'll think he's got a claim to power.'

'That's very simple,' said Hatch. 'You support my authority by fabricating an announcement from the Nu-chala. The Nu-chala designates me as his deputy on this planet. So I act in Dalar ken Halvar with his authority.'

This gave Senk even more to digest.

'You want me to forge commands from the Nu-chala?' said Senk. 'Commands from the leader of the Nu-chala-nuth?'

'Precisely,' said Hatch.

'But,' said Senk, 'that would inflame many of the Free Corps leaders, who—'

'Senk, Senk, Senk,' said Hatch, in frustration. 'Don't you see the logical sequence? First you announce the opening of the Chasm Gates, announce me as military governor, then call in the Free Corps. Once the Free Corps is inside Cap Foz Para Lash, then you use the Eye of Delusions and speak to the world, speak as if you were the Nu-chala. It's simple, Senk.'

330

'Yes, but,' said Paraban Senk, the Teacher of Control, 'I am still concerned about the long-term safety of those Combat Cadets and Startroopers whom I have spent so long training. That is my mission, Hatch. To train Startroopers. How do you reconcile the general establishment of Nu-chala-nuth with the survival of those members of the Free Corps who hate the Nu-chala-nuth?'

'You may,' said Hatch slowly, 'have to persuade Lupus and his friends to make a token conversion to Nu-chala-nuth.'

'That will not exactly be easy,' said Senk.

'No,' said Hatch. 'But – trust me, Senk. I give you my word. I personally guarantee the safety of Lupus Lon Oliver, of Manfred Gan Oliver, and of all the other members of the Free Corps.'

'What value am I supposed to put on your word?' said Senk.

'You know me as a man of honour,' said Hatch. 'You know me as a man of my word. That should be sufficient. Meanwhile – let us get to work. The sooner we move, the sooner we stabilize Dalar ken Halvar. The sooner we stabilize the city, the fewer people get killed. Let's start by talking to the dorgi. The dorgi, that's the first thing. The dorgi will have to be part of our subterfuge.'

Silence from Senk.

Senk obviously needed a little more persuading.

'Have you got a better idea?' said Hatch.

Senk continued thinking in silence, then said:

'Yes, Asodo. I do have a better idea. Or . . . an improved idea, at any rate. My idea is that I should take hostages to ensure your good behaviour. You're a dangerous man, Asodo, and I don't trust you with the safety of my Startroopers. I can't trust you with their safety unless I have the security of having possession of hostages.'

'Then that's, ah, unfortunate,' said Hatch, 'for I've got no hostages to give you.'

'Of course you have,' said Senk.

And shortly Hatch found himself engaged in the tricky and distasteful task of persuading his wife Talanta, his daughter Onica and the Lady Iro Murasaki into the combat bays. Hatch assured them that life in the illusion tanks was exactly that – life in another form.

'I don't understand,' said the Lady Iro Murasaki. 'Why do we have to do this?'

'Because,' said Hatch, 'I am engaged on a tricky task in the service of the demon which rules these underground caverns, and you as my allies may be attacked by the enemies of that demon unless you enjoy the security of the illusion tanks.'

'But will there be fighting?' said Onica.

'Like me with Lon Oliver?' said Hatch. 'Of course not.'

'It would be easier if you were there with us,' said Talanta.

'Well,' said Hatch, 'that's . . . wait. Wait, and I'll see if that's possible.'

So it was that Asodo Hatch shortly entered one of the combat bays, seated himself in its initiation seat, and found himself transposed to an illusion tank scenario designed to train Combat Cadets in the military applications of ecology. The scenario featured a planet devastated by war. On this planet there was one bubble-complex, big enough to contain an environment which could not be fully explored in less than three days. This bubble-complex contained a complex ecosystem ranging from a micro-miniature coral reef – complete with tropical fish – to a dense rainforest.

Here Hatch was joined by the Lady Iro Murasaki, by Talanta, and by Onica. He showed them the crew-quarters, and was surprised by the speed and ease with which they habituated themselves to those quarters. But of course, though Hatch had earlier unconsciously condescended to the Lady Iro Murasaki by talking of the Combat College in terms of 'demons', she, like Talanta and Onica, had learnt much of the Nexus from watching the Eye of Delusions.

'So,' said Hatch. 'Here you'll be safe. No maverick Combat College student can damage you, so I'll be free to work for the Combat College.'

'What are you going to do?' said Onica.

'Something,' said Hatch, 'of great difficulty.'

Great difficulty indeed, but by the time Hatch was transported back to the world of the Combat College, Paraban Senk had already started doing what was necessary. Senk was using the Eye of Delusions to broadcast to the kinema and the world the news that the Chasm Gates had opened, that a long age of darkness was at an end, and that the long-benighted planet of Olo Malan was at last reunited with the transcosmic civilization of the Nexus.

Shortly, Senk used a communications screen to access the dorgi's lair and talk to that recalcitrant beast.

'Guardian,' said Senk, addressing the dorgi by its formal title. 'I have a message for you from Charabanc.'

The dorgi did not respond.

'Charabanc,' said Senk. 'You know. The Nexus planet. The Stormforce command planet. Are you listening?'

'I am listening,' said the dorgi, in a low-pitched growl. 'I am listening. But understand one thing. This had better not be a joke.'

'Who do you think I am?' said Paraban Senk sharply. 'Particle Basp? I am the Combat College. I do not indulge in jokes, and I will not be spoken to in that manner.'

There was a long pause, then the dorgi said, grudgingly:

'You are speaking in an information mode. I concede the point. Furthermore. You may designate protocols. That is your right. I concede that point also. What is the password?'

'The password is a standard three-phase. Component

one: hippopotamus. Component two: junket. Component three: destroyer. Acknowledge.'

'Acknowledged,' said the dorgi. Then, abrupting from a growl to a thunder-rock roar: *'Urgent! Urgent! Intruder approaching! Break contact! Break contact!'*

'I break contact,' said Paraban Senk dryly.

And the dorgi went roaring out of its hiding hole and lurched to a halt just a fraction of a fingerlength in front of the female Startrooper named Shona.

'Halt! Halt!' screamed the dorgi. *'You must halt! Now! Now! Or I will blow your head off! Halt and undress!'*

'Go screw yourself,' said Shona.

'Take off your clothes!' said the dorgi. *'Now! Now! Do what I say! Or I will kill you! Take off your clothes!'*

'Go bugger yourself with a dog turd,' said Shona.

She did not speak to the dorgi like this because she was crude but because the machine's brain was so limited that it found it very hard to comprehend any insult which was much advanced beyong the scatological.

'You can't talk to me like that!' said the dorgi, having taken the small pause necessary to check its comprehension of her last remark. *'I have the password and you don't! I can kill you this time, I really can.'*

'You're shit out of luck, brick-brains,' said Shona, 'because I've got the password too.'

'Tell it!' said the dorgi.

'Hippopotamus,' said Shona, who had been briefed by a Combat College communciations screen while she was still a hundred paces distant from the dorgi's lair.

'Hippopotamus!' screamed the dorgi in rage.

'This is a three-phase password,' said Shona calmly, 'and you have made an error with the middle phase. I am going to report you and you are going to be punished. I'm not kidding.'

'Bitch,' said the dorgi suddenly.

'I will report you for that too,' said Shona warmly.

'You dare,' said the dorgi.

'That's three reports,' said Shona.

'*Junket!*' said the dorgi, seeing that this was getting out of hand. '*Junket! Junket! That's what it is! That's the middle phase! Quick! Quick! The response! The response! Out with it! Right now! Or I'll blow your head off!*'

And it trained all three of its seven-snout zulzers on Shona's head and made ready to make good its threat. Three official complaint reports! This was disastrous! So the woman must die.

'Destroyer,' said Shona.

And the dorgi groaned, untrained its zulzers, and went lurching into its hideaway. And as it did so the inner door of the lockway opened and Umka Ash stepped through.

'Hippopotamus,' said Ash, the blotch-faced Combat Cadet whose mixed skin of white and black, of red and purple, made the truth of his race quite impossible to determine.

Ash had been briefed on the password as he came through the lockway, for Paraban Senk had over-ridden the customary lecturing voices of the lockway to give Ash a quick and vital briefing.

'Junket,' said the dorgi sourly, speaking in a low and reverberating voice, and speaking without bothering to come out from its lair.

'Destroyer,' said Ash.

'Up yours too,' said the dorgi.

Then the normally withdrawn and silent Ash grinned and stepped forward, and Shona saw him coming and grinned too, and they embraced, and went dancing down the corridor together. Then they broke apart. And Ash whooped. And Shona yelled.

'Open!' said Shona in jubilation.

'Open!' responded Ash.

'Planets!'

'Stars!'

'Opera magnificat!'

'Holidays on Vulip!'

'Ecstasy amplifiers!'

'Ice!'

'Jerkaram!'

'Particle Basp! In the flesh!'

'*Oh do shut up*,' said the dorgi, speaking in dull-grumbling thunder. '*You're hysterical. The pair of you.*'

'Why shouldn't we be?' said Shona.

'Yes, why not?' said Ash. 'The Chasm Gates are open. And you know what that means.'

'*What?*' said the dorgi, which could not even begin to guess.

'Psyche therapy for a certain dorgi,' said Ash. 'Psyche therapy urgently overdue, a good ten millennia overdue.'

At which the dorgi, goaded beyond endurance, came roaring out of its lair, zulzers swivelling. But Ash and Shona just stood there and laughed at it – laughed and laughed, exhilarated beyond all words.

And Hatch?

Asodo Hatch came striding down the cream-coloured corridors of the Combat College, striding along in company with Beggar Grim, Master Zoplin and the mighty Lord X'dex Paspilion. Hatch strode along at such a pace that the three beggars positively had to scuffle to keep up with him. Hatch gave the password to the dorgi with an uncommon curtness, brushed aside the greetings he received from Shona and Ash, then entered the lockway airlock with his beggars.

'Let's plan our families together,' said the lockway. 'Planned parenthood is the maximum most in happiness. Your pharmacist or your family physician is the best person to advise you further.'

Hatch heard yet did not hear the words. He was thinking, thinking, thinking of what lay outside the lockway. Thinking of the city and the Free Corps, and what he must do to seize control of Dalar ken Halvar and then to consolidate that control.

CHAPTER THIRTY

Lupus Lon Oliver: sometime Combat Cadet and Startrooper now graduated from the Combat College and hence effectively exiled from the world of the Nexus. Son of Manfred Gan Oliver and a leading light of the Free Corps of Dalar ken Halvar. Note that Lupus Lon Oliver means 'Lupus, the hope of the family Oliver', while Manfred Gan Oliver means 'Manfred, the strength of the family Oliver'.

*   *   *

If dreams came true –
If monsters from the lusts of night
Drenched their claws,
And through her perfumes conjured –
Then nospeak dares to say –
Yet still in dreams we conjure,
And thus must risk –
The walls elapsing, and one world
Drenching its scorpions in waves into the other.
Yet I dream too.

*   *   *

Asodo Hatch ventured out of the Combat College with the intent of spreading the news of the opening of the Chasm Gates, but found there was no need for him to take any steps in that direction. In a city at peace, the news of the opening of the Chasm Gates might have taken a while to spread. But Dalar ken Halvar was a city poised for war, its leadership of the moment in nerve-edge readiness for trouble, its sentries posted, its couriers running messages routinely through the streets, its people acutely tuned to the faintest rumblings of the rumour-mill.

Consequently, the news of the reopening of the Chasm Gates struck with something of the swift-shock speed of news breaking in a high-tech inter-wired society. And Hatch very shortly returned to the Combat College to participate in a conference in Forum Three.

Given some of the murderous passions which were then unleashed, Hatch had cause to be very glad that the three people closest to his heart were safe in the illusion tanks, seated in the combat bays and walled in by unbreachable walls of kaleidoscope. Most murderously passionate of all people on that day was Lupus Lon Oliver.

When Lupus heard that Hatch was to be the Nexus-appointed ruler of Dalar ken Halvar, he was incensed. And when Lupus heard that the Nu-chala, the religious leader based on the holy planet of Borboth, had additionally appointed Hatch to be his deputy in Dalar ken Halvar, then Lupus was so enraged that he almost suffered a terminal melt-down.

'Nu-chala-nuth!' said Lupus, using that word as an obscenity. 'Are we to set the Yara free to rabble in their superstitions?'

'Twenty thousand years have not extinguished the power of the Nu-chala-nuth in the Nexus,' said Hatch. 'If we prosecute a pogrom against the Yara here in Dalar ken Halvar, then we will make problems for ourselves and for the whole of the Nexus. The Yara must be free to worship the Way if they so choose.'

So spoke Hatch, though the pogrom he feared was not a killing of the Yara but a killing of the Frangoni.

Lupus knew as much.

'You have the whip-hand for the moment,' said Lupus, in momentary concession, 'but don't think you can keep it forever.'

That of course was not the end of Lupus Lon Oliver's dissent.

When Startroopers and Combat Cadets – past and present – were packed into Forum Three and queued in the corridors outside, then Lupus made a strident effort to denounce and dethrone Asodo Hatch. Hatch was a barbarian, a murderer, a cheat, a fraud, a shyster. He was the son of a suicide. All this said Lupus, and more. But he was brought to order very quickly by General Dorth.

In Forum Three, the general gazed down on Lupus from the main display screen and said:

'Halt! Stop right there! I've heard enough out of you! I am General Dorth of the Nexus and I will not stand for this mutinous talk!'

The figure shown on the display screen, the putative General Dorth, was a big man in a uniform of grey trimmed with silver. Whereas Paraban Senk had perfect voice control, General Dorth had to struggle from keeping his wrath from breaking into an upper-octave squawk. Hatch thought this was a nice touch of verisimilitude.

'Right now I am speaking by Instantaneous Transmission from Charabanc,' said General Dorth. 'But in ninety days, when quarantine ends, I will personally be coming to Olo Malan to take control of the planet. At that time I will be relieving Asodo Hatch, and if you fail to give him all due assistance in the meantime then you will personally answer to me for your delinquencies. Do you understand?'

'Yes,' said Lupus. 'Yes – yes sir.'

Lupus had the shaken aspect of a small child whose playtime games have abruptly been interrupted by the encroachments of full-grown adults. The Ebrell Islander could not help but display a touch of fear, and this to Hatch confirmed the fact that Lupus was a True Believer. He believed the truth of this scenario absolutely.

'So I confirm the appointment of Asodo Hatch as military governor of – of Dara—' Here Dorth broke off, glanced down, as if at a prompt screen hidden out of sight, then got it out and got it right: 'Of Dalar ken Halvar.'

'It is a great honour,' said Hatch stolidly, letting his rivals interpret that stolidness as they might.

'This is only a temporary measure,' said General Dorth. 'But the fact is that Asodo Hatch is the most senior officer of the Stormforce currently on Olo Malan. As for the rest of you, all Combat Cadets and Star-troopers, past and present, you are all to present yourself for a midnight briefing in the Combat College – tonight. Meantime, here is a brief update of what has happened in the Nexus in the last twenty millennia . . .'

By the time General Dorth was finished, Lupus Lon Oliver looked positively shellshocked, as well he might. But he was persuaded. The other Free Corps veterans were similarly persuaded. And so it was that Asodo Hatch left Forum Three with half a hundred troopers of the Free Corps as his guard of honour. They filtered out through the lockway airlock, formed up in the kinema under the gaze of the Eye of Delusions, then set off down Scuffling Road.

Bodyguarding Asodo Hatch, the Free Corps troopers marched through Actus Dorum, marched past the Grand Arena, scaled the heights of Cap Ogo Blotch, and entered the palace of Na Sashimoko.

There in Hall in the heart of the Shrine of Shrines, Asodo Hatch seated himself upon the throne of the Empire of Greater Parengarenga, and declared himself emperor.

'The official title is, of course, military governor,' said Hatch. 'And I have no objection if members of the Free Corps and others choose to so call me. However, we must remember that the vast mass of the population of Parengarenga consists of ignorant peasants who know nothing of the Nexus, therefore it is fitting that I choose

340

a title which fits their limited conception of the world.'

'What now?' said Lupus.

'I have much to do before I join you in the Combat College for the midnight briefing,' said Hatch. 'The first thing is the Treasurer. Berlin, that's the one. I appoint him my deputy. Bring him here.'

'But he's one of these – one of these savages!' protested Lupus. 'Your deputy, it – it should be a Free Corps appointment.'

'The Free Corps has the whole planet to think about,' said Hatch. 'The Free Corps are few and the needs of the moment are many. We can't have talented trained men wasting themselves on sorting out the petty bureaucracy of Dalar ken Halvar. Berlin's the man for that. He's not exactly my favourite person, but we can work together, at least in the short term. Lupus, it's hardly an appointment made to gratify my own heart, is it?'

That ended the argument, for it was common knowledge that Asodo Hatch did indeed have good reason to hate Nambasa Berlin, the noseless Treasurer who had ever maintained a gross prejudice against the 'purple filth' of the Frangoni rock – which prejudice was consequent upon the circumstances surrounding the loss of his nose.

Nambasa Berlin was brought from the closely watched imprisonment in which he had been kept since being overthrown by a coup launched by Imperial Guards and Free Corps troopers. Berlin was briefed, and absorbed the news of the opening of the Chasm Gates with an uncommon degree of calm. But then – Berlin had been expecting to be executed, and in the face of death all lesser shocks lose their power to disconcert.

Thus it was that Hatch seized control, bloodlessly, and worked throughout the day to consolidate that control. He sought out people like Berlin who were competent, who were accustomed to the exercise of power, who knew their jobs and who were not aligned with the Free Corps. These Hatch placed in positions of trust, so by evening he had a skeleton administration in place.

Late at night, when he was sure that almost all the Free Corps people were safe within the Combat College – and soon to be sealed into that College and held there as prisoners – Asodo Hatch presided over a meeting of selected Frangoni in the palace of Na Sashimoko.

The meeting took place in Na Sashimoko's map room, where there was a big table on which it was possible to assemble large-scale maps showing (or at least purporting to show) the geography of the entire empire. As wizards have a great love of maps, and as the Silver Emperor known to the world as Plandruk Qinplaqus had been a wizard of Ebber (and was a wizard of Ebber still, assuming that he still lived), a great deal of love had been spent on the elaborations of this map room. It had leather-upholstered seats sufficient for all the Frangoni who came to sit at that big table.

Hatch's elder brother Oboro Bakendra was at that meeting.

So was Son'sholoma Gezira, the apostate Frangoni who had once offended Hatch by accosting him on the Frangoni rock, and by asking him to assist in teaching the doctrines of Nu-chala-nuth. Hatch at the time had been shocked. Hatch had thought the preaching of the doctrines of Nu-chala-nuth would be a disaster for his city, his people and the empire he served. But here he was! Asodo Hatch! Masquerading as the deputy of the Nu-chala of Borboth! Here he was, Asodo Hatch, seeking to secure the city of Dalar ken Halvar for the Nu-chala-nuth, to unleash the forces of an intolerant militant religion, and to use that religion as a weapon against his enemies.

And, as Hatch waited for the Frangoni at the meeting to settle to order, he found himself appalled at the future which was opening in front of him. But what else could he do? Surrender Dalar ken Halvar to Lupus Lon Oliver and the Free Corps? Let Manfred Gan Oliver and his son Lupus gather the strength they needed to launch a pogrom against the Frangoni?

'Well?' said Oboro Bakendra, looking hard at his younger brother. 'Are you ready to enlighten us? To tell us what's really going on here?'

'Ah, what do you think's going on here?' said Hatch.

'I don't know,' said Oboro Bakendra. 'But the very fact that this meeting is taking place suggests something foul afoot. You and me, what have we got to say to each other? You need something from me, brother, but I can't see that you'd need anything at all from me if the Chasm Gates really had opened. If the Nexus really had reclaimed us. If you had suddenly been bounced to sainthood, a saint beloved of the Nu, a saint in his purple graces – well, is a poor and barbarous Frangoni worshipper of the Great God Mokaragash to sit at table with the Nu-chala's deputy?'

Hatch forced himself not to flinch from the whiplash in his brother's voice.

'Brother mine,' said Hatch, 'I had to make a choice. The Frangoni under the Nu-chala-nuth or the Frangoni under the Free Corps. There was no third way.'

With that said, Hatch looked around at the assembled Frangoni. Some were slow on the uptake, but it was obvious that most were absorbing the implications of his words.

'So,' said Son'sholoma slowly, 'you've – you've – what have you done, Hatch? You've schemed up – well, Senk must be in on it. And the whole thing, this – this – it's a charade, is it? The Chasm Gates, the – oh, Hatch, I really believed! How could you – this whole – is this but a ploy to win a war with the Free Corps?'

'I have at stake the lives of my people,' said Hatch stolidly. 'All of my people, not excepting my wife and my daughter.'

Then Hatch detailed the truth of their situation for his fellow Frangoni, ending by saying:

'So, it being now about midnight, the Free Corps is

343

held prisoner by Paraban Senk. Senk will hold the Free Corps for long enough for me to consolidate my rule in Dalar ken Halvar. I will consolidate that rule by uniting the city under the banner of Nu-chala-nuth.'

'That,' said his brother Oboro Bakendra, 'still leaves the fate of the Frangoni undecided.'

'I will give my people what protection I can,' said Hatch. 'But if we are to unite Dalar ken Halvar as a city of the Nu-chala-nuth, then it follows that the Frangoni must necessarily take that religion as their own.'

'I'd rather die,' said Oboro Bakendra.

'Then you will die,' said Hatch flatly. And, as his brother half-rose from the table: 'And if you kill me here, then you and all Frangoni will die of a certainty. The Yara are using the night to arm themselves against any possible change in their political fortunes. The Unreal are organizing themselves, my brother. I am their head for the moment, but whether I can remain so is something that remains to be seen.'

Oboro Bakendra seated himself, but glowered, and said:

'You really are riding a tiger. What happens if you fall off? You persuaded Paraban Senk to your cause. But what if Lupus Lon Oliver unpersuades him? What you have done against Lupus, Lupus can do against you. You tell me that Senk won't let out the Free Corps troopers until they're ready to swear their loyalty to you, but who could trust oaths given under such duress? And as for the Frangoni, our own people – how long will we last? The Yara hate us, the Yara are of the Pang, the Pang are the Pang, Real and Unreal alike, they're one people and we're another. Once this Chasm Gate illusion is a thing of the past, Hatch, the Pang will push you off your throne in a few days or less, they're the majority, they'll want one of their own to rule.'

All this said Oboro Bakendra, and more. Hatch listened, then said, heavily:

'Everything you have said is true. The Frangoni are a

344

minority. At the moment I rule by illusion, but we will need more than that in the future. I cannot trust the Free Corps so I must destroy the Free Corps. The Pang have no reason to like or trust the Frangoni, so we must give them a reason. We must destroy the Free Corps in the name of Nu-chala-nuth. We the Frangoni.'

'Nu-chala-nuth!' said Oboro Bakendra.

He used the word just as Lupus Lon Oliver had used it earlier – as an obscenity.

'By so destroying the Free Corps,' said Hatch, pursuing the ruthless logic of his politics to its conclusion, 'we the Frangoni write ourselves into the religious history of this planet. We the Frangoni become the people who destroyed the enemies of Nu-chala-nuth at a time when that religion was weak.

'We.

'Not the Pang.

'The people Pang, the Yara, the Unreal, they made a revolution in the name of Nu-chala-nuth, but they failed, they failed absolutely. They failed the god to whom they gave nothing but a fleeting lipservice backed up by no more than a transitory spasm of rioting. But we, we the Frangoni, we through our armed discipline smash the enemies of Nu-chala-nuth, install the True God, and thus write ourselves into history forever. We write ourselves into history in blood.'

So spoke Asodo Hatch, giving way to that love of rhetoric and speeches which ever characterizes the Frangoni. Then Asodo Hatch looked on his brother Oboro Bakendra and said:

'Brother mine, we the Frangoni, in Dalar ken Halvar our fate is fragile. We are few, the Pang are many. We are not of this place, we are not of this city. We must consecrate our relationship with the Pang with the blood of battle. We must write ourselves into the holy history of Nu-chala-nuth to make our people inviolate. We must become the holy ones, the beloved of god, or else – well, you were the one who said it. Unless we can

345

secure our position, our fate is to be destroyed. Make your choice, my brother.'

Oboro Bakendra sat. Glowering. He saw the dreadful necessity of choice which was upon them. But. He had made his commitments to the Great God Mokaragash. He had made his commitments to the priesthood. He had won status there – of a kind. A position there – of a kind. A place there – of a kind. If he threw in his lot with the Nu-chala-nuth, then he would have to give up that position, that place, that status.

Still, he had made such a change once. Three years earlier, Oboro Bakendra had left the Combat College, automatically excluded from its corridors when he reached the end of his years of training. At first he had been very despondent, but then he had got religion, and had found in religion a consolation for what he had lost.

Which raised an obvious question. Oboro Bakendra had known for years that his life in the Combat College would automatically end when he was thirty-four years of age. So why hadn't he started laying the groundwork of an alternative career earlier? Paraban Senk, the Teacher of Control who ruled the Combat College, thought for some bizarre reason that Asodo Hatch had murdered Hiji Hanojo, the previous Combat College intructor.

Asodo Hatch had been possessed of motive.

But Oboro Bakendra, on the verge of being exiled from the Combat College, had been possessed of a much stronger motive. Oboro would have stood a good chance of winning the instructorship had not Senk postponed the examinations for three years.

And . . .

'The Great God Mokaragash is my life,' said Oboro Bakendra.

'Is that so?' said Hatch, choosing his words with care. 'If religion is your life, is it also to be your death? There was a man, once. Lamjuk Dakoto.'

'That man has nothing to do with me,' said Oboro, who had long ago renounced his father.

Lamjuk Dakoto Hatch, father of Asodo and Oboro, had killed himself on the sands of the Season. Lamjuk Dakoto had killed his own brother in gladiatorial combat. With the killing done, Lamjuk Dakoto had fallen upon his own sword in full view of Dalar ken Halvar.

'Our father, hence our fate,' said Hatch remorselessly. 'For what is the son if not the reflection of the father?'

'He renounced his religion,' said Oboro. 'He renounced his people, his god.'

It was true. Lamjuk Dakoto had turned away from the Frangoni faith, the worship of the Great God Mokaragash. A bitter dispute over this renunciation had led to Lamjuk Dakoto fighting and killing his own brother.

'He remains our father,' said Hatch.

'He's dead, Hatch,' said Oboro, speaking with a wrench-note of agony, of grief.

So the son who had spurned the father still mourned him. Oboro was racked by concealed grief – grief unreconciled. Tears unwept. Laments deep-stocked in silence.

'He's dead, yes, dead,' said Hatch. 'And you as his son will die for the same reason, because death is your choice.'

'If I must die,' said Oboro, 'then I die for my god and my people.'

'It is the common wisdom of all who study such matters,' said Hatch, 'that any man who kills himself hands a sharp sword to his son. If you die, then you die because your father killed himself. And for no better reason.'

'My god,' said Oboro. 'My people.'

'Then what,' said Hatch, flaring, 'what was your god to you when you murdered Hiji Hanojo? Your people, what, you killed him good, you killed him clean, you murdered because you wanted the Nexus, you wanted to stay!'

There.

It was out.

Hatch had accused his brother Oboro Bakendra of killing Hiji Hanojo to open up a chance of winning the instructorship.

Oboro breathed slowly.

Breathed deeply.

Then said:

'Are you accusing me of murder?'

'It is Paraban Senk who accuses you,' said Hatch coldly. 'Yesterday I was victorious in battle. I won the instructorship. My first move was to consult all those files which had till then been hidden from view. Naturally I wanted to know who had killed Hiji Hanojo.'

'So Senk says . . .'

'You should have been able to work it out for yourself,' said Hatch, riding the dynamic of his bluff, taking it through to its logical conclusion. 'Paraban Senk knew full well that you murdered Hiji Hanojo. You had motive. Means. Opportunity. I saw your psychological profile, there's no secrets hidden. So. Senk decided to punish you.

'So.

'Senk denied you the chance to compete for the instructorship. Senk declared a three-year moratorium on the competitive examinations. Because. Because Senk knew. Senk knew that I would win. And Senk knew. Senk knew that would be the greatest punishment. For you to see your younger brother succeed where you failed.

'And that's why you chose your god, your Great God Mokaragash, because you wanted a career, power, status, position, something to replace the Combat College. And that's why you, you wanted me to leave, no more College, no, come to the Great God, little brother, you wanted to wreck me down, you were jealous, you saw I'd win, you couldn't stand it, as soon as you were out of the College you wanted my training wrecked and ruined.

348

'So.

'So that's how it is, Oboro, and if you, death, if it's death, if you're going to die then it's because that's what you want, your father handed you a sword, spite and jealousy, jealousy and thwarted ambition. That's all there is, Oboro. Well. Make your choice. Stand by your Great God and die. But know why you die. Not from piety but from selfish spite. Your Great God is a sword. If you want to fall upon that sword, then do so. But I – I will not die just because my father killed himself!'

Thus Hatch.

Then silence.

Then, very slowly, Oboro Bakendra's face buckled. His shoulders began to shake, and he wept. Hatch watched him, watched him weep. Then went to his brother's side and comforted him in the agony of his grief.

CHAPTER THIRTY-ONE

The Chasm Gates: the transcosmic junction which once linked the local universe to the rest of the Nexus. Some 20,000 years ago, the Chasm Gates collapsed, isolating the local cosmos from the rest of the Nexus. War followed. Even after twenty millennia, dim memories of that war persist in the form of those legends concerning what is now known as the Days of Wrath.

*　　*　　*

But if from their steps of stone in flesh
The gods should step –
And sliding from the clouds unseat –
And grapeskin humans with their feet –

*　　*　　*

'What do you think?' said Oboro Bakendra.

'It's a bluff,' said Hatch. 'Of course it's a bluff. It would be too much of a coincidence for any such thing to happen now.'

The two brothers were in the kinema, the natural amphitheatre outside the lockway. The Eye of Delusions, the big entertainment screen set above the lockway, was screening the image of a strangely mutated human with insectile mandibles. This thing was – or so it alleged – the current ruler of the Nexus. It claimed that the Chasm Gates had opened, and that the Tulip Continuum which contained the city of Dalar ken Halvar and its Combat College was again reunited with humanity's grandest transcosmic civilization.

'You will surrender your authority to that of the Combat College,' said the human-insect thing.

Not for the first time.

It had said as much a full three dozen times already, without moving either Asodo Hatch or his brother Oboro Bakendra in the slightest.

'You have to admit,' said Oboro Bakendra, 'the thing looks almost authentic.'

'Admit?' said Hatch. 'Brother mine, you forget my imperial status! I have made myself emperor, and an emperor admits nothing.'

Nevertheless . . .

The accents of the presumptuous mandible-equipped human which dominated the Eye of Delusions did suggest some of the distortions which might reasonably have been expected to befall the Nexus Ninetongue in the course of twenty millennia. Though of course the Ninetongue had been designed to be impervious to linguistic drift – divided up into nine separate task-specific dialects and supported by the standardizing resources of an affluent machine culture.

To that degree the thing was authentic.

But Hatch was not prepared to admit publicly even that much.

'Senk's improvising,' said Hatch, 'but the improvisation is fairly desperate.'

Hatch was right. The insect-human which was trying to menace Dalar ken Halvar, and to bring that city to order by exercise of terror, was a tenth-rate derivation of one of the standard monsters of the Nexus entertainments so commonly screened by the Eye of Delusions. Paraban Senk lacked the imagination required to think up something new. A human in authority who was characterized by tact, sensitivity and flexibility, for example – that would have been something new. Hatch might even have been impressed by it.

'So what will you do?' said Oboro Bakendra, elder brother conceding initiative and authority to the younger.

'Do?' said Hatch.

'About Senk,' said Oboro Bakendra. 'About the Combat College. Do we ignore it? Or what?'

'I'll go in there soon,' said Hatch. 'I have to. Senk still has my wife, my daughter . . .'

'And your whore,' said Oboro Bakendra, unable to restrain himself from making this unfavourable observation.

'The Lady Iro Murasaki still enjoys the protection of the Combat College,' said Hatch agreeably.

Asodo Hatch had lately been through far too much to get upset simply because someone chose to impugn the honour of the Lady Murasaki.

'And what about our sister?' said Oboro Bakendra.

'Our sister?' said Hatch absently.

'Yes, yes, our sister, our sister Joma, otherwise known to the world as Penelope. Penelope Flute. Remember her? A girl, Hatch, a big girl, a girl as tall as a man, purple in her skin and turbulent in her temper. What have you done with her, Hatch?'

'I don't know that I've done anything with her!' said Hatch.

'Well, she certainly went into the Combat College,' said Oboro Bakendra. 'There's plenty of proof of that. You must have seen her yourself.'

'I – I have some recollection of that,' said Hatch.

Yes. Hatch dimly remembered seeing Penelope at some time during the turbulent period when refugees of all descriptions were boiling into Forum Three.

In the lead-up to Hatch's series of duels with Lupus Lon Oliver, Paraban Senk had asked Hatch to name those guests whom he chose to invite into the Combat College to watch him fight. Hatch had been in no mood to trifle with such trivia; and so, rather than drawing up a guest list, Hatch had simply told Senk to admit anyone who asked for admission in his name.

Consequently, when riots had broken out in Dalar ken Halvar, numerous refugees had been able to find sanctuary inside the minor mountain of Cap Foz Para Lash by quoting Hatch's name. Hatch's wife, daughter and mistress had won admission to the mountain, and, yes, Penelope too.

But.

'But,' said Oboro Bakendra, driving home the point remorselessly, 'that's the last that anyone knows of her. You appear to have lost her.'

And in the end Hatch had no option but to confess that he had indeed mislaid his sister, which was doubtlessly very remiss of him. He had excuses, of course, for the recent past had been turbulent – and, while duelling his enemy and commandeering a religious revolution, Hatch had not found it possible to keep track of the delinquent Penelope. But Oboro Bakendra made it clear that he thought this no excuse.

'You don't seem concerned,' said Oboro Bakendra.

'Frankly,' said Hatch, 'I'm more concerned with the absence of Lupus Lon Oliver than with Penelope. We've made a great heap of corpses, but Lupus is not to be found on that heap.'

'His face may have been disfigured,' said Oboro Bakendra. 'Perhaps he lies incognito beneath the sun.'

'There is the matter of stature,' said Hatch. 'Lupus was built quite close to the ground, as you remember. Had the rat's flesh been in among its companions, I'm sure I would have recognized it by the length of its legs and the modest bulk of its torso. I've had occasion to watch it closely of late.'

'It may well be that Lupus and Joma have fled the city together,' said Oboro Bakendra. 'In which case they are of no account. Lupus is no danger once detached from his warforce, and thus detached he is – for I warrant that very few Ebrell Islanders of military age are left alive in Dalar ken Halvar.'

With this said, the two brothers left the kinema, where the Eye of Delusions was still making dire threats about the wrath of the Nexus.

Under a hot and dusty sky, the two brothers made their way down Scuffling Road through a day which was possessed of something of the traditional clamour of Dog Day. Naturally the festivities were muted somewhat by the events of the recent past, for it was hard to be truly festive in a city which had recently suffered many bereavements and a great deal of burning. Still, a fair few people were giving it their best shot.

The traditional Dog Day drums were pounding; the traditional scuffles were taking place as various teams tried to make their chosen dog the dog-king for the day; and a fair few unfortunate dogs were being barbecued and eaten.

Actually, on Dog Day it was against both law and tradition to slaughter and eat any dog until evening, which was traditionally the time for the start of an enormous blood-glutting feast; but both law and tradition had broken down under the pressure of the latest events.

Asodo Hatch and his elder brother Oboro Bakendra went down Scuffling Road, crossed its intersection with Zambuk Street, continued down Scuffling Road, and so after a walk of some considerable distance came upon the scene of the battle which had that day given them victory over the Free Corps.

Hatch had deceived Senk, knowingly, and with malice aforethought; and then Senk had unwittingly deceived the Free Corps. Thus setting the stage for the Free Corps' destruction.

Within the minor mountain of Cap Foz Para Lash, the Startroopers and Combat Cadets of the Free Corps had been briefed by Paraban Senk, the diligent Teacher of Control. The unembodied Senk had told the Free Corps that the announced 'opening of the Chasm Gates' had been but a ploy to lure them into an imprisoning trap.

Senk had then informed the Free Corps that it was in the long-term interests of the survival and functioning of the Combat College that Dalar ken Halvar – and indeed the entire Empire of Greater Parengarenga – be united under the militant religion of Nu-chala-nuth. For the Combat College was breaking down; and, unable to rely upon the ancient machinery of probability-manipulation, Senk must necessarily enlist religion for support.

Senk had announced to the prisoners that they would be held within Cap Foz Para Lash indefinitely if they were not prepared to co-operate with this new plan. If however they chose to ally themselves with Asodo Hatch and with the Nu-chala-nuth, then they could look forward to playing a leading role in a great and prosperous future.

After some discussion, the members of the Free Corps had agreed to make those rather painful adjustments to the new reality which had opened before them. And so it had come to pass that, as the Dog Day celebrations began to get underway, the Free Corps had been released from the minor mountain of Cap Foz Para Lash.

The Free Corps had set off down Scuffling Road, marching in a body from the Combat College towards the Grand Arena. The plan was that in the Grand Arena they would take an oath of allegiance to Asodo Hatch in particular and to the Nu-chala-nuth in general. However, the Free Corps had never reached the Arena.

Along the way, the Frangoni had taken the Free Corps in a classic ambush, attacking from the west – bursting out from ruined houses, from unruined houses, and from bamboo screens hastily erected and made to look like windbreaks. Every Frangoni man, woman and child capable of holding a blade had joined that ambush.

Those of the Free Corps who had not been cut down immediately had fled to the east – only to fall victim to pit-traps and to sharpened bamboo spikes planted in carefully concealed holes.

The slaughter had been almost universal.

Manfred Gan Oliver had been accounted for, and on

discovering the corpse of Gan Oliver the valorous Asodo Hatch had – but, enough! There is no need to be saying what Hatch did to the unfortunate Gan Oliver once Gan Oliver was dead! Suffice it to say that all of Dalar ken Halvar soon heard of the fate of that corpse; for terror is a potent weapon, and the niceties of Hatch's position were such that he could not afford to let any weapon lie unused.

But while Gan Oliver had been definitely (and definitively!) accounted for, no sign of the corpse of Lupus Lon Oliver had been found anywhere, and nobody could be found who had seen that young man escaping.

The ambush had taken place before midday, and it was now late in the afternoon. As Asodo Hatch and Oboro Bakendra returned to the scene of the slaughter, they found some of the Pang engaged in putting the turd of a dog into the mouth of every corpse – this placement of turds being a form of defilement which was traditional among the Pang.

There on the field of battle stood the beggars Grim, Zoplin and X'dex Paspilion, holding forth in witness of the mighty deeds of Asodo Hatch, Saint Hatch, saviour of the people, upholder of the Way, beloved of god. They told of how Saint Hatch had, in days long gone and days yet recent, dispensed an equal justice to beggars, never shunning to give them the mercy of his wisdom.

With an even greater enthusiasm, the beggars told of how, in a time of dire trouble, the mere mention of the name of their beloved Saint Hatch had been sufficient to win them admission to the mountain halls which had ever previously been barred to them. They told of how, in the ever so recent past, Saint Hatch had captained a ship crewed by the Nu-chala-nuth in a mighty war against the godless Ebrell Islander Lupus Lon Oliver.

Saint Hatch was greeted by those who had been listening to the beggars, and he was acclaimed by them.

Hatch accepted this acclaim, then continued his tour of Dalar ken Halvar. In due course, he came to the banks of the Yamoda, the slow and shallow river which wended its way through Dalar ken Halvar, which slushed through the swamps of the Vomlush and then wasted its substance in the huge and heat-vomiting pit known as the Hot Mouth.

Here Hatch paused on the site of his father's funeral pyre. On the far side of the river, smoke was rising from present-day fires which were aflame in that quarter of the city known as Hepko Cholo. There the Pang and the Frangoni were united in making short work of those few Evolutionists who had not yet fled the city. Asodo Hatch was by no means the only person in Dalar ken Halvar to have been severely vexed by the follies of Evolutionary Theory, and by the rapacity of the Perfect Master who preached that Theory; and there had been no shortage of willing volunteers ready to suppress the Evolutionary Heresy in the name of Nu-chala-nuth.

It was there on the river bank that Hatch said goodbye to his brother Oboro Bakendra, for Oboro chose to take a punt-ferry across the river, in the hope of personally being able to supervise the death of Edgerley Eden, the centaur who had for so long preached the ludicrous and vexatious doctrines of evolution.

Hatch chose to remain alone at the site of his father's funeral pyre, and to settle himself in meditation.

But he was not to be allowed to so settle himself, for his meditations were scarcely begun when he was accosted by Shona.

'Ho, Hatch!' said Shona.

Hatch thought this scarcely an appropriate way for an emperor to be addressed. Still, he was new to the job, and maybe some of the fine detail would prove not to be in accordance with his expectations. So Hatch responded:

'Ho, Shona! A great day!'

'Great for whom?' said Shona, with surprising bitterness. 'That dogs should share their death with men, and men with dogs. Is this greatness?'

Hatch found this challenge slightly incoherent, but there was no mistaking the emotional force behind it.

'I did what I had to,' said Hatch, feeling slightly defensive.

'And what will you have to do in the future?' said Shona. 'All Parengarenga will be in outright revolution before the year is done.'

'I don't think so,' said Hatch.

'What can you offer them?' said Shona.

'The Combat College,' said Hatch. 'It has a cure-all clinic. The treatment of syphilis, the quenching of cancer, the reconstruction of noses. The upgrading of faces and the suctioning of fat. Through such promises I can control the rulers of every region of the empire, and they in turn will control their people for me.'

'I have not heard that the Combat College is yours to command,' said Shona.

'Yet it will be,' said Hatch. 'It will open to me and mine, admit those I choose and deny its breach to all others. With the Combat College, I can safeguard the rule of the empire.'

'For the moment,' said Shona.

'Forever,' said Hatch. 'I have unleashed a religion militant. I have set loose the Nu-chala-nuth. My people have consecrated themselves by blooding their swords in the service of faith. I am acclaimed as a saint already.'

Unconsciously, Hatch let declamatory passion seep into his voice as he delivered himself of this speech. He spoke as if he addressed an audience of seventy thousand. Rhetoric was ever a Frangoni vice, and Hatch was true to the ways of his people: there was nothing he liked better than to unleash a speech.

'So,' said Shona softly. 'It can trick, cheat and kill. Oh, and make speeches! Great speeches, Hatch, are you proud of your speech, are you proud of . . . aagh! What's the use? You've decided, haven't you?'

'I did what I had to,' said Hatch defensively.

Yet he was uncomfortably conscious of his guilt

burden. He had brought the Free Corps to destruction, yet many of those people . . . well . . . Hatch had trained with them, had known them as companions and colleagues . . . and . . . he had feared for the future, hence had arranged murder. But was it not perhaps better to risk the future than do something which was . . . was what? Unpardonable?

Suddenly, very sharply, Hatch remembered Lupus Lon Oliver. Lupus had said that a man who kills himself hands to his son a sharp sword.

'I will not do it,' muttered Hatch.

But . . .

'I have heard that the Nu-chala-nuth is no Way for women,' said Shona suddenly

'It is true,' admitted Hatch.

'Then what future for women?' said Shona.

Hatch was about to say that the women must suffer what they must. Then caught himself. Because – of course! – Shona herself was a woman.

This came as something of a revelation to Hatch. For Asodo Hatch had never thought of the burly Shona as a woman, just as he had never thought of her as being one of the Pang, or one of the Yara, the Unreal – though she was all of those. He had always thought of Shona as being, well, Shona. His ally. His friend.

'The men must have something,' said Hatch lamely.

Yes.

There was a lot of truth in that.

The recent unrest in Dalar ken Halvar had been sparked by the discontent of the lower orders, the slaves and the Yara, the slaves and the Unreal. They had hoped to win a better life for themselves, and they construed a better life in terms of material reward.

This was only natural.

A beggar in his rags, a beggar beset by fleas, a beggar with nothing but a dog-corpse for company, knows full well the importance of the material world. Others in like condition can be tempted to revolution in the hope of improving their material conditions. And why not? What have they got to lose? Hatch knew this of the poor: those who have been reduced to nothing will ultimately count their lives as nothing, and hence will risk all for next-to-nothing.

So the objective conditions of Dalar ken Halvar's poor had encouraged them to revolution, albeit to an unsuccessful and chaotically disorganized revolution which had stood no chance whatsoever of success until Asodo Hatch took charge of it.

But with the revolution now won – and won in the name of Nu-chala-nuth, a religion which preached the equality of all men – what would be the results of a division of the spoils? As Hatch knew full well, an equal division of the wealth of Dalar ken Halvar would by no means glut the appetites of the many, for Dalar ken Halvar was poor. Parengarenga as a whole was poor. The entire continent had been wrecked and wasted by millennial mismanagement, by erosions and depletions, extinctions and eradications.

So since wealth was limited, and since its equal division would not secure the glut of dreams, what then could be offered to the men who had so suddenly been made equal members of a just society? Why, the rule of women, of course!

And Hatch, from his long study of politics, knew that the rule of women is a prize often offered to men. He knew Shona to be independent: a free-striding Star-trooper who was the cash-manager of her household and mistress of her own destiny. He did not think she would like the future which was being offered to her under the rule of the Nu-chala-nuth.

And now she was standing in silence, her silence an accusation

'What am I to do?' said Hatch. 'I mean, I can kill myself, but . . . is that what you want?'

He was not speaking in jest.

And Shona knew it.

'Hatch,' said Shona. 'I . . . I don't have anything to say.'

And with that she turned, and left him.

Shona was entirely without gratitude, and Hatch allowed himself to be hurt by that. After all, he had gone to a lot of trouble to ensure that Shona and other Startroopers and Combat College Cadets were delayed or waylaid, being either prevented from entering the Combat College in response to its summons, or else being separated out from the Free Corps ranks as the Free Corps marched toward the Grand Arena.

Through such exertions, Hatch had saved those he thought of as his closest friends, thinking that they would serve as a close-knit group of confidantes and advisers. He had thought to keep his friends during the loneliness of the long years of power which faced him.

But now . . .

It seemed that was not to be.

At least not as far as Shona was concerned.

With the thought in his mind, Hatch turned away from the Yamoda River. Evening gathered about him as he made his way back to the kinema. It was dark by the time he stood in front of the Eye of Delusions, his limbs heavy with fatigue, his skin tainted with the sweat of his long marches through Dalar ken Halvar, the taste of the red dust of the Plain of Jars upon his lips.

Paraban Senk had given up bluffing.

No insect-mandible human showed any more upon the Eye of Delusions. Instead, the Eye was a blank grey, and from it came a hissing like the falling of distant rain. Hatch had never seen the Eye fall blank before, and the sight of it affected him oddly.

He ventured to the lockway. The outermost door, of course, had failed entirely, but two doors of rock-hard kaleidoscope still stood between him and the Combat College. Would the doors acknowledge him?

The first of the remaining doors dissolved away to nothing. Hatch stepped into the airlock. The kaleidoscope of the door reformed. No voice spoke to Hatch within the airlock. There was only the hiss of air, supplemented by another hiss – dull, dry, dead. The hiss of ancient vacuum.

The interior door dissolved away to nothing.

Hatch stepped into the cream-coloured corridors of the Combat College. Stepped into the mountain of Cap Foz Para Lash. The corridor was littered with trash. Here the Free Corps membership had waited while the lockway airlock cycled them into the outside world a few at a time, and here were their combast ration tubes, their banana skins, their apple cores, their bits of fried whale blubber – the casual litter of their last taste of life.

They would have been happy. Well – disappointed to have realized that the Chasm Gates had not after all opened. But. Well, they had been promised a share of power, the chance to do something, to be something.

And Hatch—

Asodo Hatch shook himself free from the past, and strode on into the future, waiting for the dorgi to come lurching out to challenge him.

The password!

What was the password?

Was there still a password? And had the old one changed? And what had the old password been in any case?

He could not remember!

Hatch hesitated.

Maybe the dorgi was expecting a password, would kill him if he didn't have it, the lockway should have given it to him, he didn't have it, couldn't remember it.

Then Hatch felt a dreadful temptation. He was tempted to go on, to challenge the dorgi. Password or no password. And if he died, well. He was ready for death. But. His wife. His child. His lover. All three were inside the Combat College. Hatch could not risk letting himself be killed by a homicidal machine simply for lack of a password.

362

So what should he do?

Well, Onica, Talanta, the Lady Iro Murasaki – they were all safe in the Combat College. That was no problem. Time was no problem. So Hatch should withdraw. He should at least get the old password. He would remember it himself, surely, if he was able to sit down in peace and think. Or someone else would know it, Shona would know it. And if there was a new password, why, the Eye of Delusions had a communications capability, Hatch could talk with Paraban Senk through the Eye, there was no reason to venture in any further, not now.

With this thought through, Hatch beat his retreat. But the lockway's innermost door refused to recognize him. The faintest hint of warmth remained to its iridescence, but it was rapidly cooling to the chill which dominated the entire Combat College.

'Senk!' said Hatch, raising his voice to a roar. 'Let me out!'

Then he hammered on the kaleidoscope.

But there was no response, not from Senk, not from anyone.

So Hatch turned.

Slowly, slowly.

And ventured down the corridor at a funeral pace.

Ventured to its intersect with the dorgi's lair.

Where—

Hatch risked a glance into the dorgi's lair, and saw not the beast, but, rather, the slop-slurped hunk-gunk dissolution which marked its wreckage. Hatch knew immediately what had happened. To the uninitiated, it would have looked as if the dorgi had melted. But Hatch knew full well that the dorgi must have tried to use those of its weapons which were based upon the manipulation of probability. And those weapons had malfunctioned, thus destroying the dorgi.

Hatch stepped into the dorgi's lair, wanting to be sure, wanting to have the physical satisfaction of knowing that his much-hated enemy was really dead.

It was.

Of course.

And in its ruins there was something silver, something curiously winking-glinting. Cautiously, Hatch stooped. And picked it up. It was a small thing and a heavy thing, a thing heavier than lead, heavier than gold, heavier than depleted uranium. It was made of an intricate interweaving of shining wires, and it shimmered with its own unquenchable light.

Hatch knew what it was.

The thing which Asodo Hatch had found in the ruins of the dorgi was a mazadath, otherwise known as an Integrated Stabilizer. In the technical literature of the Nexus, a lot of bold and confident jargon surrounded the nature and use of such devices. A mazadath lay at the heart of every Nexus machine which manipulated probability. A mazadath protected such a machine from being digested by the hazardous forces it manipulated. That was the theory, in any case – though this mazadath appeared to have failed this dorgi!

The Nexus was a civilization based on the manipulation of probability, and a mazadath was an essential part of any machine designed to manipulate probability – but the uncomfortable truth was that humans could neither understand nor manufacture any such thing as a mazadath. The Nexus had purchased mazadaths in bulk from the Vangelis, a race of partially disembodied alien creatures also known as the Shining Ones. Had it not been for the Vangelis, the entire transcosmic civilization of the Nexus would have been quite impossible.

So now Hatch had in his possession one of the essential components required for the building of a machine which could manipulate probability; though he knew full well that the supporting technologies were so complex that no such task could possibly be brought to fruition within his own lifetime.

Still—

Hatch realized he was unconsciously engaging in an

extended exercise in delay, for he was fearful of what lay ahead. Paraban Senk, the Teacher of Control who ruled the Combat College, was obviously not willing to let him leave. So he had to go onwards. A confrontation with Senk lay ahead of him, and Hatch was by no means sure that he would survive such a confrontation.

After all, if Senk got really angry with Hatch, then Senk could cancel the manufacture of food in the Combat College cafeteria. That way, Hatch would ultimately starve to death, if Senk continued to refuse to allow him out through the lockway. Or maybe Senk could pump all the air out of the Combat College. Was that possible? Hatch didn't know. But he had an uneasy suspicion that he might get round to finding out. The hard way.

Still.

He had no choice.

So, having pocketed the mazadath – it would make a nice souvenir, if he lived – Asodo Hatch strode on down the corridor.

Making for Forum Three.

CHAPTER THIRTY-TWO

Paraban Senk: the Teacher of Control, the great Educator which dwells in the heart of Cap Foz Para Lash. This asma has long had one great priority: to train Startroopers for the Stormforce of the Nexus. And now it is outraged: because Asodo Hatch has taken the Free Corps in ambush, destroying almost all of the Combat Cadets and Startroopers in Dalar ken Halvar.

* * *

> I slept to know –
> And knowing nothing knew –
> And waking knew of nothing so
> Gave to my edge that speed:
> And drew.

* * *

Forum Three was quiet. Silent. The empty banks of seats sloped steeply down to the stage on which Asodo Hatch and Lupus Lon Oliver had so recently duelled each other in debate. Above that stage was the big display screen which had shown to the world the battles in which Hatch and Lupus had duelled each other with single-fighters and MegaCommand Cruisers.

The screen was blank.

Silent.

'Senk?' said Hatch.

No answer.

No response.

Very well.

Hatch could play this waiting game.

Hatch sat himself down, folded his arms, and closed his eyes. Shortly, a brightening of the room made itself apparent through his eyelids. Hatch opened his eyes. The big screen above the lecture theatre's stage was now dominated by the chosen face of Paraban Senk.

'Welcome, Hatch,' said Senk.

'And to you, welcome,' said Hatch.

Which was a token of the stress he was under, for Hatch was guest rather than host, therefore it was not for him to extend hospitality to Senk.

'Have you come for your daughter?' said Senk. 'Or for your wife? Or is it perhaps the Lady Iro Murasaki whom you seek?'

'I seek all of those,' said Hatch.

'Well, I for my part,' said Senk, 'I seek Manfred Gan Oliver and his colleagues and companions.'

'They will be produced in due course,' said Hatch.

'Don't test my wits,' said Senk. 'My spies have given me a full account.'

'Your spies?' said Hatch.

'Call them what you will,' said Senk. 'But many have come to the kinema to witness the disaster. Messenger boys and others.'

'You trust to messenger boys for strategic information?' said Hatch, endeavouring to ape amazement.

'Hatch,' said Senk, 'this is no time for jokes. I am grossly upset with you. Unless you have mastered the fine art of the resurrection of the dead, you are shortly going to find out just how upset I really am. You have slaughtered almost all those Startroopers I trained. Have you even the slightest excuse for your actions?'

'I had to think of the political stability of Dalar ken Halvar and the fate of my people,' said Hatch, as staunchly as he could.

'That's not good enough,' said Senk. 'You'll have to do better than that, or I'll tear the hostages apart.'

'Tear apart?' said Hatch, struggling to stay calm.

367

'Your wife Talanta,' said Senk. 'Your daughter Onica. Your whore. Tear them apart, Hatch. That's what I'm going to do.'

'This is scarcely a constructive approach to the demands of the moment,' said Hatch, with the calm that comes upon a man when he realizes the inevitability of his own death.

'Constructive approach!' said Senk.

Senk was positively apoplectic, enraged beyond belief by Hatch's sanguinity. But the more Senk's rage wrathed up, the calmer Hatch got – that very calm feeding Senk's fury all the more.

'For a computational device,' said Hatch mildly, 'you have quite a large emotional range. Have you considered the possibility that perhaps that range is excessive?'

'In my vengeance I am human,' said Senk. 'As I will prove when I deal with my hostages in my vengeance.'

'I trust you will deal with your hostages in a civilized manner,' said Hatch, struggling to keep his voice level and unemotional. 'We are civilized, are we not?'

'Civilized!' said Senk. 'You drench your hands in murder, you kill in defiance of all our agreements, you betray a trust, you break your oath to the Nexus, and after all that—'

'I am but a poor barbarian from one of the Wild Tribes of the Permissive Dimensions,' said Hatch, in an effort at leisured self-depreciation. 'You cannot expect the high conduct of the Nexus to be reflected in the life of a barbarian such as myself. But you at least have the capacity, surely, to be truly civilized. And is not mercy the greatest of civilization's aspects?'

'Jokes!' said Senk, responding with fury to Hatch's suave sally. 'A time like this, and you indulge yourself in jokes. Very well! Then indulge yourself in this!'

And with that, Paraban Senk's olive-complected features faded from the display screen in Forum Three. Glowing green lines divided that screen into three separate frames. And in those frames there came to life—

Onica.

Talanta.

And the Lady Iro Murasaki.

All three were standing on the sands of a rumpled desert of red dust. They were being observed by a group of tourists who appeared to have climbed out of a hover vehicle. The hover vehicle was garishly adorned with bright-sign glyphs and graphics, among which Hatch saw a fleshpink vulva, a grinning orange sun, a dolphin spouting orange-juice, and a sign in Nexus script which identified the vehicle as the property of an organization known as Happy Hunting Tours.

All three women looked grossly unhappy, and the reason appeared to be because all three were rapidly sinking into the sands of the desert. As Hatch watched, the desert floor rocked. Onica screamed. Ants were swelling from the desert, cascading into hugeness, their mandibles razor-sharp.

'Watch, Hatch!' roared Senk, in a grotesquely amplified voice-over.

But Hatch did not watch. His hand was moving, had a life of his own, was reaching, was drawing. Not a sword but a knife. A knife, but knife enough. His hand clutched, struck, disembowelled. Down went Hatch in the agony of spillage, his hand griping and writhing as the intolerable pain sent it into spasm.

—Properly. Do it properly.

So thought Hatch in his agony.

And, falling, Hatch steadied the knife, and speared it into his body as he fell, driving home the blade with the full force of his earthly collapse.

CHAPTER THIRTY-THREE

Cure-all clinic: a Combat College facility which has wide-ranging powers to repair injury and restore health.

*   *   *

> So laid against the pillow –
> To meet with monsters, meet
> Decapitating death, and yet –
> The dawn –

*   *   *

Asodo Hatch woke in the cure-all clinic to find his sister Penelope – no, she was Joma, he would make no concessions, Joma she had been born and Joma she must stay – bending down over him.

'Joma,' said Hatch.

'Penelope,' said she.

'Penelope, then,' said Hatch, too weak to argue the point.

'Penelope and Lupus,' said Lupus Lon Oliver, who was sitting on the end of Hatch's bed. 'The love of Penelope in balance with the wrath of Lupus.'

Lupus did not look particularly wrathful at that precise moment, but Hatch could well imagine that in this case appearances might be deceptive. Hatch was not sure of the exact nature of his own circumstances, so sent out a tentative probe.

'What is the measure of this love?' said Hatch. 'Penelope's love, of which you have spoken?'

'She carried you here,' said Lupus. 'When you lay in

the rubble of your bowels. Penelope scooped you up and laboured you all the way to this clinic here.'

'How came she to know of my wounding?' said Hatch.

'Your wounding!' said Lupus. 'It was suicide!'

Hatch let that pass, then said:

'But she came.'

'Senk called us,' said Lupus. 'He lacks facilities for the cartage of bodies, hence needed our arms and our legs for the purpose.'

'Where were you two hiding?'

'Hiding?' said Lupus. 'We weren't hiding at all.'

'We were on our honeymoon,' said Penelope.

'Your honeymoon!?' said Hatch.

'Earlier,' said Lupus, 'Paraban Senk was kind enough to officiate at our marriage. Then we entered the combat bays. Where else would we go for a honeymoon? To Dalar ken Halvar, perhaps? To indulge in the delights of the Day of the Dogs, perhaps? No, Hatch. We went to the Nexus.'

This struck Hatch as being exceedingly bizarre: that two people should choose the illusion tanks as the venue for their honeymoon. Still, it was in keeping with Lupus Lon Oliver's aspirations, for Lupus truly wanted to be a citizen of the Nexus.

'Where did you go?' said Hatch.

'To jungles of ice and beaches of marzipan,' said Penelope dreamily. 'To seas of fire and skies of liquid treacle.'

'Meantime,' said Lupus, 'you were busily engaged in killing my father.'

Hatch lay in his combat clinic bed, trying to gauge his own strength. He found himself decidedly weak. He was in no position to duke or duel with Lupus. Hence decided that silence was the best policy.

'Never mind,' said Lupus. 'My father stood between me and my marriage, so . . . Hatch, let us not let my father's death stand between you and me.'

This was said with a degree of studied formality, and

with a certain stiffness. Hatch remembered back to an illusion tank exercise in which he had suggested to Lupus that the pair of them conspire to kill Gan Oliver. Given the ferocity with which Lupus had reacted on that occasion, Hatch found it hard to credit the young man's present forgiveness.

Hatch rather suspected that Paraban Senk, the venerable Teacher of Control, had put considerable pressure on Lupus, in order to coerce Lupus into making a peace with Hatch.

Still:

'I am ashamed of myself,' said Hatch, making the confession though every word of it cost him dearly. 'I acted in fear and in haste, and I regret it. I should have given Gan Oliver the chance to make his peace with me.'

'That's as may be,' said Lupus, still speaking with a pronounced stiffness. 'Still, that was a different world, and we must make our lives in this one.'

Then Lupus formally congratulated Hatch on making himself emperor of Dalar ken Halvar; and of killing the lockway's dorgi; and of outfacing Paraban Senk.

'That reminds me,' said Hatch, accepting these congratulations, and not finding it necessary to disclaim responsibility for the dorgi's death. 'In the corpse of the dorgi I discovered a trinket.'

'This trinket,' said Penelope, displaying that mazadath, which she had slung round her neck on a chain of a metal which matched the mazadath's silver.

'Precisely,' said Hatch. 'That trinket.'

'This,' said Penelope, 'is a wedding present.'

'Who gave it to you?' said Hatch.

'You did,' said Penelope.

And Hatch did not feel that he was in a position to argue. In any case, Lupus denied him all opportunity for argument, for Lupus said (still with a measured stiffness which spoke of unresolved homicidal impulses):

'This must conclude our interview, for now we must

withdraw, for Paraban Senk wishes to speak with you privily.'

Then the young red-skinned Ebrell Islander Lupus Lon Oliver withdrew with his purple-skinned bride, the voluptuous Penelope, and Hatch was left alone in the Combat College's sickbay.

'Hatch,' said Senk, his olive-skinned features coming to life on a display screen in the cure-all clinic. 'Are you ready to negotiate?'

'I am in no position to negotiate,' said Hatch. 'For I am flat on my back and weak from my wounding. You have the strength of two people at your disposal, young Lupus and his bride, and I think the pair of them will do what you want. Furthermore, you still have three hostages. I am at your disposal. Accept my surrender.'

Hatch surrendered thus because he did not want a repeat of the horrific moments in which Onica, Talanta and the Lady Iro Murasaki had been exposed to some fraction of the hidden hell which lay within the illusion tank scenarios.

'If I could accept your surrender then I would,' said Senk. 'But I cannot.'

Hatch thought about this.

Then said:

'Then kill me. You have the means.'

Senk certainly had the means, at least in the cure-all clinic, for the clinic's built-in surgical equipment could easily be adapted to the lethal dissection of the living.

'You misunderstand me,' said Senk. 'I cannot accept your surrender, because I have been forced to surrender to you.'

'How so?' said Hatch.

Then Senk explained.

After Asodo Hatch had failed to reemerge from the Combat College, that college had been placed under an inderdict by a Nu-chala-nuth priesthood led by Hatch's brother Oboro Bakendra and by the noseless ex-moneylender Polk the Cash. Under the terms of that interdict, no person would be allowed into the Combat College until Asodo Hatch had been yielded up by that College, alive and well.

'They say,' said Senk, 'that if you cannot be yielded up, then I will be deprived of new students forever. I will be similarly deprived unless I co-operate in teaching the doctrines of Nu-chala-nuth and the language of Motsu Kazuka.'

'So,' said Hatch, 'it is your destiny to become a theological college.'

'My overriding priority is to train Startroopers for the Stormforce of the Nexus,' said Senk. 'I must do whatever is necessary to fulfil that objective. So, if I must teach theology as well – why, it is considered fit and proper that Startroopers should know of the Nu-chala-nuth and their language.'

'I will need more from you than that,' said Hatch.

'More?' said Senk. 'Isn't this enough?'

'Not much more,' said Hatch. 'But a little more. The cure of my wife, if cure be possible. I trust you have the woman still.'

'She is safe in the worlds of the Nexus,' said Paraban Senk. 'Her flesh is still seated in a combat bay, but her mind is at ease in a deer-park forest. Penelope has spoken with her.'

'She has?'

'Of course,' said Senk. 'Penelope has been working very hard on your behalf, Hatch. She has made Lupus Lon Oliver concede his will to our truce. I will treat with your wife in this clinic, Hatch, and I will cure her if her cure lies in my compass.'

'Do you think it does?' said Hatch.

'I will discover the truth under surgery,' said Senk.

'There will be others who will have need of surgery,' said Hatch.

'Hatch,' said Senk, 'I am but one, and Dalar ken Halvar alone could flood this clinic with more surgical cases than could be treated inside the surgery.'

'Selected cases,' said Hatch. 'That's all I'll need you to treat. I'm no wizard, yet must secure an empire. Polk the Cash has need of a nose, and Nambasa Berlin likewise. And there will be others.'

'Tell me of these others,' said Senk.

And thus the pair of them opened their negotiations in earnest.

CHAPTER THIRTY-FOUR

The Great God Mokaragash: aka the Greater Lord: aka He Who Sees Without Eyes: the ruling deity of the Frangoni people. He is believed to be immanent in the great idol found in the precincts of Temple Isherzan, the Frangoni temple wh.ch stands on the Frangoni rock. At that temple, the Great God Mokaragash is served by Frangoni priests, these priests being ruled by Sesno Felvus, who is the High Priest of the Great God Mokaragash, and who is therefore the ethnarch of the Frangoni people in Dalar ken Halvar.

*   *   *

Red and black, in shadows and blood –
To grim purposes, sees yet sightless.

*   *   *

Thus it was that Asodo Hatch duelled with a demon inside the minor mountain known as Cap Foz Para Lash, and won a great victory over that demon. Inside of a month, the details of that duel were known to all of Dalar ken Halvar. Asodo Hatch – this is how the story was told, and nobody doubted it – had challenged Paraban Senk to a duel. Senk had accepted the challenge. In an arena generated by the machineries of the illusion tanks, Asodo Hatch had met with Senk, and the pair had fought it out to the red-blood finish, with the rule of the Combat College as the prize.

Also told in Dalar ken Halvar was the story of Hatch's climactic confrontation with the lockway's dorgi. It was told how the dorgi had growled and roared, how it had spat death with its zulzers – death which Hatch in his nimbleness had dodged and ducked – and how at last it had destroyed itself when in its frustration it attempted to use its most powerful weapons to destroy not just Hatch but the entire mountain which trapped and encumbered it.

On the strength of such tales, Asodo Hatch became not just Saint Hatch but Hero Hatch into the bargain, all of which was a great help to him as he attempted to make himself master of the Empire of Greater Parengarenga.

Even with such help, to secure his rule was no easy task. It required the most delicate of negotiations, coupled with a regrettable requirement for (on occasion) direct and ruthless action which need not here be detailed. For the management of an empire is a study in itself, and not to be lightly summed.

Suffice it to say that Asodo Hatch was for a time very busy, yet as the days went by his burdens eased. And so it was that he found the time for nights of peaceful privacy, and spent those nights in Pan Lay, a fine house on the heights of Cap Gargle. The owner of the house was the Lady Iro Murasaki, one of the grey-skinned Janjuladoola people – and Hatch of course did not displace her from her residence when he chose to spend his nights in that residence.

It is doubtlessly true that, in a strictly moral universe, Asodo Hatch would not have ended thus in the arms of the Lady Iro Murasaki. But this is a history of the world of the fact and the flesh, not a gaudy tale of Good versus Evil such as might have been candyflossed to life by the Eye of Delusions. This, then, is not a nicely balanced structure of error and retribution suitable for use as a model to propound the ethical philosophies. It is history, and it is not for history to take upon itself the mission of the moralists.

But if some mission be demanded, if it be said that the mere recounting of events is not a task sufficient in itself

– why, then, let this history be taken as an exemplification of the intrinsic complexity of life. If a message be required, why then, let the very complexities of this history be a message in itself. And if something more still be demanded – a moral, perforce! – why then, let the moral be that life is a dice game played in the shadows with a dog and a ghost.

Consider by the light of that moral the life of Asodo Hatch. In the time of his testing, Asodo Hatch used means which he did not rightly know were at his disposal to achieve ends which were not strictly of his own choosing. He was swimming, yes, and swimming of his own free will, and in the direction of his choosing – but he was swimming in a river that was in flood, a boiling river of filthy brown water ever churning towards the hot pit of its final embroilment.

And we too in our time may be plunged into such a flood; and therefore should not be too quick to judge, or to say that Hatch should have drunk the river dry, or should have grown wings and flown, or should have conceded himself to the flood by evolving himself into a fish.

Let us then grant him the charity of our mercy.

And if it be objected that Hatch, whether swimming or drowning, had no right to live when so many were dead – why then, know that it takes only a moment's courage to die, whereas it takes a lifetime's courage to live. And Asodo Hatch had the greatest of difficulty in finding that lifetime's courage, for the undeniable truth is that his father had handed him both a sharpened sword and the incentive to use it.

Therefore let us grant to Asodo Hatch at least the honour of his courage.

And if further excuse for his actions be needed, why then, remember only that Hatch was a barbarian monstrous in his purple, a true warrior of one of the Wild Tribes if ever there was one; and, if someone must be blamed for his wrongdoings, then blame the cartoonists of the Nexus, who were surely the providers of his strongest role models. And with blame thus properly assigned in the best of moralizing fashion, it is proper to spare a moment to satisfy the curiosity of the ethnologists, and to detail the manner in which the Frangoni worship of the Great God Mokaragash was reconciled with the rise of Nu-chala-nuth.

Let it be recorded, then, that at the end of the first year of his rule, Asodo Hatch climbed to the Frangoni rock, and that Hatch there made his peace with Sesno Felvus, the High Priest of the Great God Mokaragash. In Temple Isherzan, there was only the priesthood left, and not much of that: for the Frangoni laity had converted as a whole to the worship of the Nu-chala, and hence had joined themselves to that great congregation known as the Nu-chala-nuth.

To deprive a Great God of the worship of His people would be considered by many to be an unpardonable crime; but Sesno Felvus pardoned Asodo Hatch, for Sesno Felvus – when forced to the ultimate choice – valued his people more than his god.

Besides, the gods evolve, do they not? State it as a certainty: they do. For it is one of the lessons of history that the gods lack that stability of form which is given to the flesh; and, in proof of this, it is difficult to find so much as a single god which has been stable in its form for as little time as a thousand years. Therefore it might well be thought that the Great God Mokaragash, when incarnated in an idol in the precincts of Temple Isherzan, had yet to evolve to His final form; and it might be thought that the Nu, the god worshipped by the Nu-chala, was simply a potential future form to which, in the fullness of time, the great God Mokaragash would Evolve.

Therefore it could be argued that those who abandoned the worship of the Great God Mokaragash to make themselves members of the Nu-chala-nuth were simply giving slightly premature homage to a future form of the Great God Mokaragash. This at least was what Sesno Felvus told those priests who chose to stay with him in Temple Isherzan; and, if any chose to disbelieve this, not one of them was bold enough to say as much.

As for Asodo Hatch himself, when asked by the Lady Iro Murasaki what he truly believed, Hatch delivered himself of this simplest of doctrines:

'When a mantis flies, it's more of a leaf than a bird.'

THE END

THE WEREWOLF AND THE WORMLORD
by Hugh Cook

CHRONICLES OF AN AGE OF DARKNESS: 8

'You travelled by night.'

Alfric kept his face blank. This was no time to show impatience. But Alfric liked to do business in an efficient manner; and not for nothing was the king known as He Who Talks In Circles.

'Night is a strange time to travel,' continued King Dimple-Dumpling. 'Particularly when night is Her chosen time.'

'My duty bids me to rule the night,' said Alfric. 'I cannot permit Her forays to keep me from the dark. I am a Yudonic Knight.'

'Who fears nothing,' said the king.

When one hears dry irony from the lips of an ogre, it is hard to credit one's ears. But Alfric, who knew ogres better than most of his kind, did not underestimate them.

On occasion, Alfric Danbrog, a banker by profession, found it hard to live up to his Yudonic heritage. Yet he was called upon to face not only ogres, dragons, assassins and She Who Walks by Night but – worst of all – more senior bankers.

Although it forms part of a vast fantasy epic, this volume is a complete and spectacular tale in its own right.

0 552 13538 0

THE WIZARDS AND THE WARRIORS
by Hugh Cook

CHRONICLES OF AN AGE OF DARKNESS: 1

'I ask all of you here today to join with me in pledging yourself to a common cause,' said Miphon. Elkor Alish laughed, harshly: 'A common cause? Between wizards and the Rovac? Forget it!'

And yet it had to be. Though Alish never accepted the alliance, his fellow warrior Morgan Hearst joined forces with Miphon and the other wizards. The only alternative was the utter destruction of their world.

0 552 12566 0

THE BELGARIAD
by David Eddings

David Eddings has created a wholly imaginary world
whose fate hangs on the outcome of a prophecy made
seven thousand years earlier. The fulfilment of this
prophecy is entrusted to a young farm boy named
Garion, aided by his aunt Pol and the mysterious Mr
Wolf. Together they embark on their quest to retrieve
the stolen Orb of Aldur and confront the ageless malice
of the god Torak.

The story of their quest unfolds with a magical blend of
excitement and enhancement. *The Belgariad* is an
oustanding piece of imaginative storytelling, destined to
achieve the classic status and following of Tolkien's *The
Hobbit* or Stephen Donaldson's *Chronicles of Thomas
Covenant*.

Pawn of Prophecy   0 552 12284 X
Queen of Sorcery   0 552 12348 X
Magician's Gambit   0 552 12382 X
Castle of Wizardry   0 552 12435 4
Enchanters' Endgame   0 552 12447 8

A SELECTION OF FANTASY TITLES
AVAILABLE FROM CORGI BOOKS

THE PRICES SHOWN BELOW WERE CORRECT AT THE TIME OF GOING TO PRESS
HOWEVER TRANSWORLD PUBLISHERS RESERVE THE RIGHT TO SHOW NEW
RETAIL PRICES ON COVERS WHICH MAY DIFFER FROM THOSE PREVIOUSLY
ADVERTISED IN THE TEXT OR ELSEWHERE.

☐ 13568 2	THE CURSE OF SLAGFID	Elizabeth H. Boyer	£3.9
☐ 12760 4	THE THRALL AND THE DRAGON'S HEART	Elizabeth H. Boyer	£2.9
☐ 12761 2	THE WIZARD AND THE WARLORD	Elizabeth H. Boyer	£2.9
☐ 12566 0	THE WIZARDS AND THE WARRIORS	Hugh Cook	£4.9
☐ 13130 X	THE WORDSMITHS AND THE WARGUILD	Hugh Cook	£3.9
☐ 13131 8	THE WOMEN AND THE WARLORDS	Hugh Cook	£3.9
☐ 13327 2	THE WALRUS AND THE WARWOLF	Hugh Cook	£4.9
☐ 13439 2	THE WICKED AND THE WITLESS	Hugh Cook	£3.9
☐ 13536 4	THE WISHSTONE AND THE WONDERWORKERS	Hugh Cook	£3.9
☐ 13537 2	THE WAZIR AND THE WITCH	Hugh Cook	£3.9
☐ 13538 0	THE WEREWOLF AND THE WORMLORD	Hugh Cook	£3.9
☐ 13017 6	MALLOREON 1: GUARDIANS OF THE WEST	David Eddings	£4.9
☐ 13018 4	MALLOREON 2: KING OF THE MURGOS	David Eddings	£4.9
☐ 13019 2	MALLOREON 3: DEMON LORD OF KARANDA	David Eddings	£4.9
☐ 13020 6	MALLOREON 4: THE SORCERESS OF DARSHIVA	David Eddings	£4.9
☐ 12284 X	BOOK ONE OF THE BELGARIAD: PAWN OF PROPHECY	David Eddings	£3.9
☐ 12348 X	BOOK TWO OF THE BELGARIAD: QUEEN OF SORCERY	David Eddings	£3.9
☐ 12382 X	BOOK THREE OF THE BELGARIAD: MAGICIAN'S GAMBIT	David Eddings	£3.9
☐ 12435 4	BOOK FOUR OF THE BELGARIAD: CASTLE OF WIZARDRY	David Eddings	£4.9
☐ 12447 8	BOOK FIVE OF THE BELGARIAD: ENCHANTERS' END GAME	David Eddings	£3.9
☐ 13757 X	DREAM WEAVER	David Eddings	£4.9
☐ 13101 6	SERVANTS OF ARK 1: THE FIRST NAMED	Jonathan Wylie	£3.9
☐ 13134 2	SERVANTS OF ARK 2: THE CENTRE OF THE CIRCLE	Jonathan Wylie	£3.50
☐ 13161 X	SERVANTS OF ARK 3: THE MAGE-BORN CHILD	Jonathan Wylie	£3.50
☐ 13416 3	THE UNBALANCED EARTH 1: DREAMS OF STONE	Jonathan Wylie	£3.50
☐ 13417 1	THE UNBALANCED EARTH 2: THE LIGHTLESS KINGDOM	Jonathan Wylie	£2.99
☐ 13418 X	THE UNBALANCED EARTH 3: THE AGE OF CHAOS	Jonathan Wylie	£3.50

All Corgi/Bantam Books are available at your bookshop or newsagent, or can be ordered from the following address:

Corgi/Bantam Books,
Cash Sales Department
P.O. Box 11, Falmouth, Cornwall TR10 9EN

UK and B.F.P.O. customers please send a cheque or postal order (no currency) and allow £1.00 for postage and packing for the first book plus 50p for the second book and 30p for each additional book to a maximum charge of £3.00 (7 books plus).

Overseas customers, including Eire, please allow £2.00 for postage and packing for the first book plus £1.00 for the second book and 50p for each subsequent title ordered.